PRAISE FOR W.E.B. GRIFFIN
AND HIS BESTSELLING SERIES

BADGE OF HONOR

"Not since Joseph Wambaugh have we been treated to a police story of the caliber that Griffin gives us . . . as real as today's headlines."
—Harold Coyle, bestselling author of *Team Yankee* and *Sword Point*

"Readers will feel as if they're part of the investigations, and the true-to-life characters will soon feel like old friends. Excellent reading."
—Dale Brown, bestselling author of *Flight of the Old Dog* and *Night of the Hawk*

"Fans of Ed McBain's 87th Precinct novels better make room on their shelves . . . BADGE OF HONOR is first and foremost the story of the people who solve the crimes. The characters come alive."
—*Gainesville Times* (GA)

"Griffin has captured Philadelphia's tribal cop culture."
—*Philadelphia Inquirer*

"Griffin writes with authority about how an urban police department works—from the cop on the beat to the detectives to the chief of police . . ."
—*Amarillo Sunday News-Globe*

"Gritty, fast-paced . . . authentic."
—Richard Herman, Jr., author of *The Warbirds*

Turn the page for reviews of W.E.B. Griffin's
other acclaimed series . . .

THE CORPS

The New York Times bestselling saga—a stunningly authentic portrait of the Marine Corps, the brave men and women who fought, and loved, in the sweeping turmoil of World War II . . .

"THE CORPS combines the best elements of military history and the war story—the telling detail and political tangle of one mated to the energy and sweep of another."
—*Publishers Weekly*

"W.E.B. Griffin has done it again. This is one writer who can spin and weave some of the most fascinating military characters in today's market."
—*Rave Reviews*

"This man has really done his homework . . . I confess to impatiently awaiting the appearance of succeeding books in the series."
—*The Washington Post*

"Packed with all the love, action, and excitement Griffin fans have come to expect."
—*Forecast*

BROTHERHOOD OF WAR

The magnificent *New York Times* bestselling saga that made Griffin a superstar of military fiction—the epic story of the U.S. Army, from the privates to the generals, in the world's most harrowing wars . . .

"Griffin is a storyteller in the grand tradition, probably the best man around for describing the military community. BROTHERHOOD OF WAR . . . is an American epic."
—Tom Clancy, bestselling author of *Debt of Honor*

"Extremely well-done . . . First-rate."
—*The Washington Post*

"Absorbing . . . fascinating descriptions of weapons, tactics, Army life and battle."
—*The New York Times*

"A major work . . . magnificent . . . powerful."
—William Bradford Huie, author of *The Execution of Private Slovik*

"A crackling good story. It gets into the hearts and minds of those who . . . fight our nation's wars."
—William R. Corson, Lt. Col. (Ret.) U.S.M.C., author of *The Betrayal and The Armies of Ignorance*

THE MURDERERS

The sixth in the Badge of Honor Series

W. E. B. Griffin

SEVERN SH HOUSE

This title first published in Great Britain 1998 by
SEVERN HOUSE PUBLISHERS LTD of
9–15 High Street, Sutton, Surrey SM1 1DF.
by arrangement with the Putnam Berkley Group, Inc.

British Library Cataloguing in Publication Data

Griffin, W. E .B.
    The murderers - (Badge of honor series; 6)
    1. Organised crime - Pennsylvania - Philadelphia - Fiction
    2. Police - Pennsylvania - Philadelphia - Fiction
    3. Detective and mystery stories
    I. Title
    813.5'4 [F]

    ISBN 0-7278-5395-3

Printed and bound in Great Britain by
MPG Books Ltd, Bodmin, Cornwall.

For Sergeant Zebulon V. Casey
Internal Affairs Division
Police Department, Retired, the City of Philadelphia.
He knows why.

THE Murderers

ONE

Officer Jerry Kellog, who was on the Five Squad of the Narcotics Unit of the Philadelphia Police Department, had heard somewhere that if something went wrong, and you found yourself looking down the barrel of a gun, the best thing to do was smile. Smiling was supposed to make the guy holding the gun on you less nervous, less likely to use the gun just because he was scared.

He had never had the chance to put the theory to the test before—the last goddamned place in the world he expected to find some scumbag holding a gun on him was in his own kitchen—but he raised his hands to shoulder level, palms out, and smiled.

"No problem," Jerry said. "Whatever you want, you got it."

"You got a ankle holster, motherfucker?" the man with the gun demanded.

1

Jerry's brain went on automatic, and filed away, *White male, 25–30, 165 pounds, five feet eight, medium build, light brown hair, no significant scars or distinguishing marks, blue .38 Special, five-inch barrel, Smith & Wesson, dark blue turtleneck, dark blue zipper jacket, blue jeans, high-topped work shoes.*

"No. I mean, I got one. But I don't wear it. It rubs my ankle."

That was true.

Christ, that's my gun! I hung it on the hall rack when I came in. This scumbag grabbed it. And that's why he wants to know if I have another one!

"Pull your pants up," the scumbag said.

"Right. You got it," Jerry said, and reached down and pulled up his left trousers leg, and then the right.

Jerry remembered to smile, and said, "Look, we got what could be a bad situation here. So far, it's not as bad as it could—"

"Shut your fucking mouth!"

"Right."

"Who else is here?"

"Nobody," Jerry answered, and when he thought he saw suspicion or disbelief in the scumbag's eyes, quickly added, "No shit. My wife moved out on me. I live here alone."

"I seen the dishes in the sink," the scumbag said, accepting the three or four days' accumulation of unwashed dishes as proof.

"Ran off with another cop, would you believe it?"

The scumbag looked at him, shrugged, and then said, "Turn around."

He's going to hit me in the back of the head. Jesus Christ, that's dangerous. It's not like in the fucking movies. You hit somebody in the head, you're liable to fracture his skull, kill him.

Jerry turned around, his hands still held at shoulder level.

Maybe I should have tried to kick the gun out of his hands. But if I had done that, he'd have tried to kill me.

Jerry felt his shoulders tense in anticipation of the blow.

The scumbag raised the Smith & Wesson to arm's length and fired it into the back of Jerry's head, and then, when Jerry had slumped to the floor, fired it again, leaning slightly over to make sure the second bullet would also enter the brain.

Then he lowered the Smith & Wesson and let it slip from his fingers onto the linoleum of Jerry Kellog's kitchen floor.

"Where the hell," Sergeant Patrick J. Dolan of the Narcotics Unit demanded in a loud voice, paused long enough to make sure he had the attention of the seven men in the crowded squad room of Five Squad, and then finished the question, "is Kellog?"

There was no reply beyond a couple of shrugs.

"I told that sonofabitch I wanted to see him at quarter after eight," Sergeant Dolan announced. "I'll have his ass!"

He glowered indignantly around the squad room, turned around, and left the room.

Sergeant Patrick J. Dolan was not regarded by the officers of the Five Squad of the Narcotics Unit—or, for that matter, by anyone else in the entire Narcotics Unit, with the possible exception of Lieutenant Michael J. "Mick" Mikkles—as an all-around splendid fellow and fine police officer with whom it was a pleasure to serve. The reverse was true. If a poll of the officers in Narcotics were to be conducted, asking each officer to come up with one word to describe Sergeant Dolan, the most common choice would be "prick," with "sonofabitch" running a close second.

This is not to say that he was not a good police officer. He had been on the job more than twenty years, a sergeant for ten, and in Narcotics for seven. He was a skilled investigator, reasonably intelligent, and a hard worker. He seldom made mistakes or errors of judgment. Dolan's problem, Officer Tom Coogan had once proclaimed, to general agreement, in the Allgood Bar, across the street from Five Squad's office at Twenty-second and Hunting Park Avenue, where Narcotics officers frequently went after they had finished for the day, was that Dolan devoutly believed that not only did he never make mistakes or errors of judgment but that he was incapable of doing so.

Tom Coogan had been on the job eight years, five of them in plain clothes in Narcotics. For reasons neither he nor his peers understood, he had been unable to make a high enough grade on either of the two detective's examinations he had taken to make a promotion list. Sometimes this bothered him, as he was convinced that he was at least as smart and just as good an investigator as, say, half the detectives he knew. On the other hand, he consoled himself, he would much rather be doing what he was doing than, for example, investigating burglaries in Northeast Detectives, and with the overtime he had in Narcotics he was making as much money as a sergeant or a lieutenant in one of the districts, so what the hell difference did it make?

Coogan had absolutely no idea why Dolan had summoned Jerry Kellog to an early-morning meeting, or why Kellog hadn't shown up when he was supposed to, but a number of possibilities occurred to him, the most likely of which being that Kellog had simply forgotten about it. Another, slightly less likely possibility was that Kellog had overslept. Since his wife had moved out on him, he had been at the sauce more heavily and more often than was good for him.

It wasn't just that his wife had moved out on him—broken marriages are not uncommon in the police community—but that she had moved in with another cop. A police officer whose wife leaves the nuptial couch because she has decided that the life of a cop's wife is not for her can expect the understanding commiseration of his peers. Kellog's wife, however, had moved out of a plainclothes narc's bed into the bed of a Homicide detective. That was different. There was an unspoken suggestion that maybe she had reasons—ranging from bad behavior on Kellog's part to the possibility that the Homicide detective was giving her something in the sack that Kellog hadn't been able to deliver.

The one thing Jerry Kellog didn't need right now was trouble from Sergeant Patrick J. Dolan, which could range from a simple ass-chewing to telling the Lieutenant he wasn't where he was supposed to be when he was supposed to be, to something official, bringing him up on charges.

Tom Coogan wasn't a special pal of Jerry Kellog, but they worked together, and Kellog had covered Coogan's ass more than once, so he owed him. He picked up his telephone, pulled out the little shelf with the celluloid-covered list of phone numbers on it, found Kellog's, and dialed it.

The line was busy.

Two minutes later, Coogan tried it again. Still busy.

Who the hell is he talking to? His wife, maybe? Some other broad? His mother? Something connected with the job?

Fuck it! The important thing is to get him over here and get Dolan off his back.

He tried it one more time, and when he got the busy signal broke the connection with his finger and dialed the operator.

"This is Police Officer Thomas Coogan, badge number 3621. I have been trying to reach 555-2330. This is an emergency. Will you break in, please?"

"There's no one on the line, sir," the operator reported thirty seconds later. "The phone is probably off the hook."

"Thank you," Coogan said.

The fact that the phone is off the hook doesn't mean he's not there. He could have come home shitfaced, knocked it off falling into bed, or on purpose so that he wouldn't be disturbed. He's probably lying there in bed, sleeping it off.

That posed the problem of what to do next. He realized he didn't want to drive all the way over to Kellog's house to wake him up, for a number of reasons, including the big one, that Sergeant Dolan was liable to ask him where the fuck he was going.

He thought a moment, then reached for his telephone.

"Twenty-fifth District, Officer Greene."

"Tom Coogan, Narcotics. Who's the supervisor?"

"Corporal Young."

"Let me talk to him, will you?"

He knew Corporal Eddie Young.

"Tom Coogan, Eddie. How are you?"

"Can't complain, Tom. What's up?"

"Need a favor."

"Try me. All I can say is 'no.'"

"One of our guys, Jerry Kellog, you know him?"

"No, I don't think so."

"He lives at 300 West Luray Street. He's supposed to be here. Our Sergeant is shitting a brick. Could you send somebody over to his house and see if he's there and wake him up and tell him to get his ass over here? I've been trying to call him. His phone is off the hook. I think he's probably sleeping one off."

"Give me the address again and it's done, and you owe me one."

A nearly new Buick turned off Seventh Street and into the parking lot at the rear of the Police Administration Building of the City of Philadelphia. The driver, Mr. Michael J. O'Hara, a wiry, curly-haired man in his late thirties, made a quick sweep through the parking lot, found no parking spot he considered convenient enough, pulled to the curb directly in front of the rear entrance to the building, and got out.

A young police officer who had been on the job just over a year, and assigned to duty at the PAB three days before, intercepted Mr. O'Hara as he headed toward the door.

"Excuse me, sir," he said. "You can't leave your car there."

Mr. O'Hara smiled at what he considered the young officer's rather charming naivete.

"It's OK, son," he said. "I'm Commissioner Czernich's bookie."

"Excuse me?" the young officer said, not quite believing what he heard.

"The Commissioner," Mr. O'Hara went on, now enjoying himself, "put two bucks on a long shot. It paid a hundred ninety-eight eighty. When I come here to pay him off, he says I can park anywhere I want."

The young officer's uneasiness was made worse by the appearance of Chief Inspector Heinrich "Heine" Matdorf, Chief of Training for the Philadelphia Police Department, whom the young officer remembered very clearly from his days at the Police Academy. It was the first time the young officer had ever seen him smile.

"What did you tell him?" Chief Matdorf asked.

"I told him I was Czernich's bookie."

"Jesus Christ, Mickey!" Matdorf laughed, patting him on the back as he did so.

As the young police officer had begun to suspect, the driver of the Buick was not a bookmaker. Mr. Michael J. "Mickey" O'Hara was in fact a Pulitzer Prize–winning reporter employed by the *Philadelphia Bulletin*. There was little question in the minds of his peers—and absolutely none in his own mind—that he was the best police reporter between Boston and Washington, and possibly in an even larger geographical area.

Mickey O'Hara extended his hand to Matdorf's driver, a sergeant.

"How are you, Mr. O'Hara?" the Sergeant asked, a respectful tone in his voice.

"Heine," O'Hara asked, "have you got enough pull around here to tell this fine young officer I can park here?"

"The minute he goes inside," Chief Matdorf instructed the young officer, "let the air out of his tires."

"Thanks a lot, Heine."

"What's going on, Mickey?"

"I hoped maybe you could tell me," O'Hara said.

"So far as I know, not much. There was nothing on the radio."

"I know," O'Hara said.

"Going in, Mickey?" Matdorf asked.

"I got to pay off the Commissioner," O'Hara said. "And I thought I might take a look at the Overnights."

The Overnights were reports from the various districts and other bureaucratic divisions of the Philadelphia Police Department of out-of-the-ordinary police activity overnight furnished to senior police officials for their general information.

They were internal Police Department correspondence not made available to the public or the press. Mr. Michael J. O'Hara, as a civilian, and especially as a journalist, was not entitled to be privy to them.

But Mickey O'Hara enjoyed a special relationship with the Police Department. He was not in their pocket, devoting his journalistic skills to puff pieces, but on the other hand, neither did he spend all of his time looking for stories that made the Department or its officers look bad. Most important, he could be trusted. If he was told something off the record, it stayed off the record.

"Come on in, then," Chief Matdorf said. "I'll even buy you a cup of coffee."

He touched O'Hara's arm and they started toward the rear door of the building. There is a front entrance, overlooking Metropolitan Hospital, but it is normally locked. The rear door opens onto a small foyer. Just inside is a uniformed police officer sitting behind a heavy plate-glass window controlling access to the building's lobby with a solenoid switch.

To the right is a corridor leading past the Bail Clerk's Office and the Arraignment Room to the Holding Room. The Municipal Judge's Court is a small, somewhat narrow room separated from the corridor by heavy glass. There are seats for spectators in the corridor. Farther to the right is the entrance to the Holding Room, in effect a holding prison, to which prisoners brought from the various police districts and initially locked up in cells in the basement are brought to be booked and to face a Municipal Court Judge, who sets bail. Those prisoners for whom bail is denied, or who can't make it, are moved, males to the Detention Center, females to the House of Correction.

When the corporal on duty behind the plate-glass window saw Chief Matdorf, he activated the solenoid, the lock buzzed, and Matdorf pushed the door open and waved O'Hara through it ahead of him into the lobby of the PAB, where the general civilian populace is not allowed.

They walked toward the elevators, past the wall display of photographs of police officers who have been killed in the line of duty. As they approached the elevator, the door opened and discharged a half-dozen people, among them Chief Inspector Dennis V. Coughlin and Inspector Peter Wohl.

"Hey, whaddaya say, Mickey?" Chief Coughlin greeted him with a smile, and offered his hand.

"Hello, Mick," Wohl said, as he offered his hand first to O'Hara and then to Chief Matdorf.

Mickey O'Hara had not earned the admiration of his peers, or the Pulitzer Prize, by being wholly immune to the significance of body language.

Despite that warm greeting, neither of these two is at all happy to see me. That means that something is going on that they would rather not tell me about just now. And what are the two of them doing together this early in the morning?

"What's up, Mickey?" Chief Coughlin asked.

"I hoped maybe you would tell me."

Chief Coughlin shrugged, indicating nothing.

Bullshit, Denny.

"I thought I'd take a look at the Overnights," O'Hara said.

"They're on my desk, Mick. Tell Veronica I said you could have a look," Coughlin said.

Veronica Casey was Coughlin's secretary.

"Thanks, Denny," O'Hara said. "Good to see you. And you too, Peter."

They shook hands again. Chief Coughlin and Inspector

Wohl walked out the rear entrance. Mickey got on the elevator with Chief Matdorf and his driver.

"Jesus, I forgot something in the car," O'Hara said, and got off the elevator.

He went through the rear door in time to see Coughlin and Wohl walking with what he judged to be unusual speed toward their cars. He stayed just inside the door until they were both in their cars and moving, then went out and quickly got behind the wheel of his Buick and followed them out of the parking lot.

Those two are going somewhere interesting together, somewhere they hope I won't show up.

He turned on all three of the shortwave receivers mounted under the dashboard. The receivers in Mickey O'Hara's car were the best the *Bulletin's* money could buy. They were each capable of being switched to receive any of the ten different frequencies utilized by the Police Department.

One of these was the universal band (called the J-Band) to which every police vehicle had access. Each of Philadelphia's seven police divisions had its own radio frequency. An eighth frequency (the H-Band) was assigned for the exclusive use of investigative units (detectives' cars, and those assigned to Narcotics, Intelligence, Organized Crime, etcetera). And since Mayor Jerry Carlucci had gotten all that lovely ACT Grant money from Congress, there was a new special band (the W-Band) for the exclusive use of Special Operations (including the Highway Patrol).

Ordinary police cars were limited to the use of two bands, the Universal J Band, and either one of the division frequencies, or the H (Detective) Band.

Mickey switched one of his radios to the J (Universal) Band, the second to the H (Detective) Band, and the third to the W (Special Operations) Band, a little smugly deciding that if anything interesting was happening, or if Wohl and Coughlin wanted to talk to each other, the odds were that it would come over one of the three.

It quickly became clear that wherever the two of them

were going, they were going together and in a hurry. Wohl stayed on Coughlin's bumper as they drove through Center City and then out the Parkway and along the Schuylkill.

Nothing of interest came over the radio, however, as they left Center City behind them, and an interesting thought destroyed some of Mickey's good feeling that he had outwitted Denny Coughlin and Peter Wohl.

It is entirely possible that those two bastards have decided to pull my chain. They saw me watch them leave the Roundhouse, and before I got into my car one or the other of them got on his radio and said, "If Mickey follows us, let's take him on a tour of Greater Philadelphia." They're probably headed nowhere special at all, and after I follow them to hell and gone, they will pull into a diner someplace for a cup of coffee, and wait for me with a broad smile.

He had just about decided this was a very good possibility when there was activity on the radio.

"William One."

"William One," Peter Wohl's voice responded.

"William Two requests a location."

Mickey knew that William Two was the call sign of Captain Mike Sabara, Wohl's second-in-command.

"Inform William Two I'm on my way to Chestnut Hill and I'll phone him from there."

Damn, they got me! The two of them are headed for Dave Pekach's girlfriend's house. She's having an engagement party the day after tomorrow. It has to be that. Why else would the two of them be going to Chestnut Hill at this time of the morning?

Mickey turned off the Schuylkill Expressway onto the Roosevelt Boulevard extension.

I'll go get some breakfast at the Franklin Diner and then I'll go home.

He reached down and moved the switch on the third of his radio receivers from the Special Operations frequency so that it would receive the police communications of the East Division. He did this without thinking, in what was really a

Pavlovian reflex, whenever he drove out of one police division into another.

And there was something going on in the Twenty-fifth District.

"Twenty-five Seventeen," a voice said.

"Twenty-five Seventeen," a male police-radio operator responded immediately.

"Give me a supervisor at this location. This is a Five Two Nine Two, an off-duty Three Six Nine."

Mickey knew police-radio shorthand as well as any police officer. A Five Two Nine Two, an off-duty Three Six Nine, meant the officer was reporting the discovery of a body, that of an off-duty cop.

A "dead body," even of a cop, was not necessarily front-page news, but Mickey's ears perked up.

"Twenty-five A," the police radio operator called.

"Twenty-five A," the Twenty-fifth District sergeant on patrol responded. "What's that location?"

"300 West Luray Street."

"I got it," Twenty-five A announced. "En route."

And then Mickey's memory turned on.

Mickey glanced in his rearview mirror, hit the brakes, made a tire-squealing U-turn, and headed for 300 West Luray Street.

One of the unofficial perquisites of being the Commanding Officer of Highway Patrol was that of being picked up at your home and driven to work, normally a privilege accorded only to Chief Inspectors. A Highway car just seemed to be coincidentally in the neighborhood of the Commanding Officer every day at the time the Commanding Officer would be leaving for work. Captain David Pekach, however, normally chose to forgo this courtesy. He said that it would be inappropriate, especially since Inspector Peter Wohl, his superior, usually drove himself.

While this was of course true, Captain Pekach had another reason for waiving the privilege of being picked up at home and driven to work, and then being driven home again when the day's work was over. This was because it had been a rare night indeed, since he had met Miss Martha Peebles, that he had laid his weary head to rest on his own pillow in his small apartment.

He believed that any police supervisor—and he was Commanding Officer of Highway, which made him a special sort of supervisor—should set an example in both his professional and personal life for his subordinates. The officers of Highway would not understand that his relationship with Martha was love of the most pure sort, and a relationship which he intended to dignify before God and man in holy matrimony in the very near future.

He was painfully sensitive to the thoughts of his peers— the most cruel "joke" he had heard was that "the way to get rich was to have a dong like a mule and find yourself a thirty-five-year-old rich-as-hell virgin"—and if they, his friends, his fellow captains, were unable to understand what he and Martha shared, certainly he could not expect more from rank-and-file officers.

Obviously, if he was picked up and dropped off every day at Martha's house, there would be talk. So he drove himself. And it was nobody's business but his own that he had arranged with the telephone company to have the number assigned to his apartment transferred to Martha's house, so that if anyone called his apartment, he would get the call in Chestnut Hill.

In just five weeks, he thought as he got into his assigned Highway Patrol car and backed it out of the five-car garage behind Martha's house, the problem would be solved, and the deception no longer necessary. They would be married.

They would already be married if they were both Catholic or, for that matter, both Episcopal. Both Martha and his mother had climbed up on a high horse about what was the one true faith. His mother said she would witness her son getting married in a heathen ceremony over her dead body, and Martha had said that she was sorry, she had promised her late father she would be married where he had married, and his father before him, in St. Mark's Church in Center City Philadelphia.

Her father would, she said, tears in her eyes, which really hurt Dave Pekach, turn over in his grave if she broke her word to him, and worse, were married according to the rules of the Church of Rome, which would have required her to promise any children of their union to be raised in the Roman Catholic faith.

Extensive appeals through the channels of the Archdiocese of Philadelphia, lasting months, had resulted in a compromise. After extensive negotiations, with the prospective groom being represented by Father Kaminski, his family's parish priest, and the prospective bride by Brewster Cortland Payne II, Esq., the compromise had been reached in a ninety-second, first-person conversation between the Cardinal of the Archdiocese of Philadelphia and his good friend the Bishop of the Episcopal Diocese of Philadelphia, with enough time left over to schedule eighteen holes at Merion Golf Course and a steak supper the following Wednesday.

It had been mutually agreed that the wedding would be an ecumenical service jointly conducted by the Episcopal Bishop and a Roman Catholic Monsignor, and the prospective bride would be required only to promise that she would raise any fruit of their union as "Christians."

Mother Pekach had been, not without difficulty, won over to the compromise by Father Kaminski, who reminded her what St. Paul had said about it being better to marry than to burn, and argued that if the Cardinal himself was going to send Monsignor O'Hallohan, the Chancellor of the Archdiocese, himself, to St. Mark's Church for the wedding, it really couldn't be called a heathen ceremony in a heathen church.

There would be a formal announcement of their engagement the day after tomorrow, at a party, with the wedding to follow a month later.

Captain Pekach drove out the gates of the Peebles' estate

at 606 Glengarry Lane in Chestnut Hill, and tried to decide the best way to get from there to Frankford and Castor avenues at this time of the morning. He decided he would have a shot at going down North Broad, and then cutting over to Frankford. There was no *good* way to get from here to there.

He reached under the dashboard without really thinking about it and turned on both of the radios with which his car, and those of half a dozen other Special Operations/Highway Patrol cars, were equipped.

As he approached North Broad and Roosevelt Boulevard, the part of his brain which was subconsciously listening to the normal early-morning radio traffic was suddenly wide awake.

"Give me a supervisor at this location. This is a Five Two Nine Two, an off-duty Three Six Nine."

"Twenty-five A," the police radio operator called.

"Twenty-five A," the Twenty-fifth District sergeant on patrol responded. "What's that location?"

"300 West Luray Street."

300 West Luray Street? My God, that's Jerry Kellog's address. Jerry Kellog? Dead? Jesus, Mary and Joseph!

"I got it," Twenty-five A announced. "En route."

Without really being aware of what he was doing, Captain Pekach reached down and turned on the lights and siren and pushed the accelerator to the floor.

It took him less than three minutes to reach 300 West Luray Street, but that was enough time for him to have second thoughts about his rushing to the scene.

For one thing, it's none of my business.

But on the other hand, anything that happens anywhere in the City of Philadelphia is Highway's business, and I'm the Highway Commander.

That's bullshit and you know it.

But Jerry Kellog is one of my guys.

Not anymore he's not. You're no longer a Narcotics Lieutenant, but the Highway Captain.

Yeah, but somebody has to notify Helene, and who better than me?

Jesus, I heard there was bad trouble between them. You don't think . . .

There was a Twenty-fifth District RPC at the curb, and as Pekach got out of his car, a Twenty-fifth District sergeant's car pulled up beside him.

"Good morning, sir," the Sergeant said, saluting him. He was obviously surprised to see Pekach. "Sergeant Manning, Twenty-fifth District."

"I heard this on the radio," Pekach said. "Jerry Kellog used to work for me in Narcotics. What's going on?"

"I seen him around," Sergeant Manning said. "I didn't know he was working Narcotics."

The front door of the house opened and a District uniform came out and walked up to them. And he too saluted and looked at Pekach curiously.

"He's in the kitchen, Sergeant," he said.

"Anything?"

"No. When I got here—"

"What brought you here?" Pekach interrupted.

"He wasn't answering his phone, sir. Somebody from Narcotics asked us to check on him." Pekach nodded. "When I got here, the back door was open, and I looked in and saw him."

"You check the premises?" the Sergeant asked.

"Yeah. Nobody was inside."

"You should have asked for backup," the Sergeant said, in mild reprimand.

"I'm going to have a look," Pekach announced.

Pekach went through the open front door. He found the body, lying on its face, between the kitchen and the "dining area," which was the rear portion of the living room.

Kellog was on his stomach, sprawled out. His head was in a large pool of blood, now dried nearly black. Pekach recognized him from his chin and mustache. The rest of his head was pretty well shattered.

Somebody shot him, maybe more than once, in the back of his head. Probably *more than once.*

What the hell happened here? Was Narcotics involved? Christ, it has to be.

"Well," Sergeant Manning said, coming up behind Pekach, "he didn't do that to himself. I'm going to call it in to Homicide."

"I've got to get to a phone myself," Pekach said, thinking out loud.

"Sir?"

No, I don't. You're not going to call Bob Talley and volunteer to go with him to tell Helene that Jerry's dead.

"I'm going to get out of everybody's way. If Homicide wants a statement from me, they know where to find me."

"Yes, sir," Sergeant Manning said.

Dave Pekach turned and walked out of the house and got back in his car.

TWO

When the call came into the Homicide Unit of the Philadelphia Police Department from Police Radio that Officer Jerome H. Kellog had been found shot to death in his home in the Twenty-fifth District, Detective Joseph P. D'Amata was holding down the desk.

D'Amata took down the information quickly, hung up, and then called, "We've got a job."

When there was no response, D'Amata looked around the room, which is on the second floor of the Roundhouse, its windows opening to the south and overlooking the parking lot behind the building. It was just about empty.

"Where the hell is everybody?" D'Amata, a slightly built, natty, olive-skinned thirty-eight-year-old, wondered aloud.

D'Amata walked across the room and stuck his head in the open door of Lieutenant Louis Natali's office. Natali, who was also olive-skinned, dapper, and in his mid-thirties,

looked something like D'Amata. He was with Sergeant
Zachary Hobbs, a stocky, ruddy-faced forty-four-year-old.
Both looked up from whatever they were doing on Natali's
desk.

"We've got a job. In the Twenty-fifth. A cop. A plainclothes narc by the name of Kellog."

"What happened to him?"

"Shot in the back of his head in his kitchen."

"And?" Natali asked, a hint of impatience in his voice.

"Joe said his name was Kellog, Lieutenant," Hobbs said
delicately.

"Kellog?" Natali asked. And then his memory made the
connection. "Jesus Christ! Is there more?"

D'Amata shook his head.

There was a just-perceptible hesitation.

"Where's Milham?"

Hobbs shrugged.

"Lieutenant, there's nobody out there but me," D'Amata
said.

"Is Captain Quaire in his office?"

"Yes, sir," D'Amata said.

"Hobbs, see if you can find out where Milham is," Natali
ordered. "You get out to the scene, Joe. Right now. We'll get
you some help."

"Yes, sir."

Natali walked to Captain Henry C. Quaire's office, where
he found him at his desk, visibly deep in concentration.

"Boss," Natali said. It took a moment to get Quaire's attention, but he finally looked up.

"Sorry. What's up, Lou?"

"Radio just called in a homicide. In the Twenty-fifth. The
victim is a police officer. Jerome H. Kellog. The name mean
anything to you?"

"He worked plainclothes in Narcotics?"

Natali nodded. "He was found with at least one bullet
wound to the head in his house."

"You don't think . . .?"

"I don't know, Boss."

"We better do this one by the book, Lou."

"Yes, sir. D'Amata was holding down the desk. He's on his way." He gestured across the room to where D'Amata was taking his service revolver from a cabinet in a small file room. "And so am I."

"Give me a call when you get there," Quaire ordered.

"Yes, sir."

There were two Twenty-fifth District RPCs, a District van, a Twenty-fifth District sergeant's, and a battered un-marked car D'Amata correctly guessed belonged to East Detectives in front of Kellog's house when D'Amata turned onto West Luray Street.

A Twenty-fifth District uniform waved him into a parking spot at the curb.

Joe got out of his car and walked to the front door, where a detective D'Amata knew, Arnold Zigler from East Detectives, was talking to the District uniform guarding the door. Joe knew the uniform's face but couldn't recall his name. Zigler smiled in recognition.

"Well, I see that East Detectives is already here, walking all over my evidence," D'Amata said.

"Screw you, Joe," Zigler said.

"What happened?"

"What I hear is that when he didn't show up at work, somebody in Narcotics called the Twenty-fifth, and they sent an RPC—Officer Hastings here—over to see if he over-slept or something. The back door was open, so Hastings went in. He found him on the floor, and called it in."

"Hastings, you found the *back* door was open?"

"Right."

Kellog's row house was about in the middle of the block. D'Amata decided he could look at the back door from the inside, rather than walk to the end of the block and come in that way.

D'Amata smiled at Officer Hastings, touched his arm, and went into the house.

"Hey, Joe," Sergeant Manning said. "How are you?"

Again D'Amata recognized the face of the Sergeant but could not recall his name.

"Underpaid and overworked," D'Amata said with a smile. "How are you, pal?"

"Underpaid, my ass!" the Sergeant snorted.

D'Amata squatted by Kellog's body long enough to determine that there were two entrance wounds in the back of his skull, then carefully stepped over it and the pool of blood around the head, and went into the kitchen.

The kitchen door was open. There were signs of forced entry.

Which might mean that someone had forced the door. Or might mean that someone who had a key to the house—an estranged wife, for example—wanted the police to think that someone had broken in.

Without consciously doing so, he put *We Know For Sure Fact #1* into his mental case file: Officer Jerome H. Kellog was intentionally killed, by someone who fired two shots into his skull at close range.

He looked around the kitchen. The telephone, mounted on the wall, caught his eye. There were extra wires coming from the wall plate. He walked over for a closer look.

The wires led to a cabinet above the sink.

D'Amata took a pencil from his pocket and used it to pull on the cabinet latch. Inside the cabinet was a cassette tape recorder. He stood on his toes to get a better look. The door of the machine was open. There was no cassette inside. There was another machine beside the tape recorder, and a small carton that had once held an Economy-Pak of a half-dozen Radio Shack ninety-minute cassette tapes. It was empty.

He couldn't be sure, of course, and he didn't want to touch it to get a better look until the Mobile Crime Lab guys went over it for prints, but he had a pretty good idea that the second machine was one of those clever gadgets you saw in Radio Shack and places like that that would turn the recorder on whenever the telephone was picked up.

There were no tapes in the cabinet, nor, when he carefully opened the drawers of the lower cabinets, in any of them, either. He noticed that, instead of being plugged into a wall outlet, the tape recorder had been wired to it.

Probably to make sure nobody knocked the plug out of the wall.

But where the hell are the tapes?

What the hell was on the tapes?

"Joe?" a male voice called. "You in here?"

"In the kitchen," D'Amata replied.

"Jesus, who did this?" the voice asked. There were hints of repugnance in the voice, which D'Amata now recognized as that of a civilian police photographer from the Mobile Crime Lab.

"Somebody who didn't like him," D'Amata said.

"What is that supposed to be, humor?"

"There's a tape recorder in the kitchen cabinet. I want some shots of that, and the cabinets," D'Amata said. "And make sure they dust it for prints."

"Any other instructions, Detective?" the photographer, a very tall, very thin man, asked sarcastically.

"What have I done, hurt your delicate feelings again?"

"I do this for a living. Sometimes you forget that."

"And you wanted to be a concert pianist, right?"

"Oh, fuck you, Joe," the photographer said with a smile. "Get out of my way."

"Narcotics, Sergeant Dolan," Dolan, a stocky, ruddy-faced man in his late forties, answered the telephone.

"This is Captain Samuels, of the Twenty-fifth District. Is Captain Talley around? He doesn't answer his phone."

"I think he's probably in the can," Sergeant Dolan said. "Just a second, here he comes."

Samuels heard Dolan call, "Captain, Captain Samuels for

you on Three Six," and then Captain Robert F. Talley, the Commanding Officer of the Narcotics Bureau, came on the line.

"Hello, Fred. What can I do for you?"

"I've got some bad news, and a problem, Bob," Samuels said. "They just found Officer Jerome Kellog's body in his house. He was shot in the head."

"Jesus Christ!" Talley said. "Self-inflicted?"

Talley, like most good supervisors, knew a good deal about the personal lives of his men, often more than he would have preferred to know. He knew in the case of Officer Jerome Kellog that he was having trouble, serious trouble, with his wife. And his experience had taught him the unpleasant truth that policemen with problems they could not deal with often ate their revolvers.

"No. Somebody shot him. Twice, from what I hear."

"Do we know who?"

"No," Samuels said. "Bob, you know the routine. He lived in my district."

Talley knew the routine. In the case of an officer killed on the job, the body was taken to a hospital. The Commanding Officer of the District where the dead officer lived drove to his home, informed his wife, or next of kin, that he had been injured, and drove her to the hospital.

By the time they got there, the Commissioner, if he was in the City, or the senior of the Deputy Commissioners, and the Chief Inspector of his branch of the Police Department—and more often than not, the Mayor—would be there. And so would be, if it was at all possible to arrange it, the dead officer's parish priest, or minister, or rabbi, and if. not one of these, then the Departmental Chaplain of the appropriate faith. They would break the news to the widow or next of kin.

"And you can't find his wife?" Talley asked.

"No. Bob, there's some unpleasant gossip—"

"All of it probably true," Talley interrupted.

"You've heard it?"

"Yeah. Fred, where are you? In your office?"

"Yeah. Bob, I know that you and Henry Quaire are pretty close—"

Captain Henry Quaire was Commanding Officer of the Homicide Unit.

"I'll call him, Fred, and get back to you," Talley said. He broke the connection with his finger, and started to dial a number. Then, sensing Sergeant Dolan's eyes on him, quickly decided that telling him something of what he knew made more sense than keeping it to himself, and letting Dolan guess. Dolan had a big mouth and a wild imagination.

"They just found Jerry Kellog shot to death in his house," he said.

"Jesus, Mary, and Joseph!" Dolan said. "They know who did it?"

"All I know is what I told you," Talley said. "I'm going to call Captain Quaire and see what I can find out."

"You heard the talk?" Dolan asked.

"Talk is cheap, Dolan," Talley said shortly. He walked across the room to his office, closed the door, and dialed a number from memory.

"Homicide, Sergeant Hobbs."

"Captain Talley, Sergeant. Let me talk to Captain Quaire. His private line is always busy."

"Sir, the Captain's tied up at the moment. Maybe I could help you?"

"I know what he's tied up with, Hobbs. Tell him I need to talk to him."

"Captain, Chief Lowenstein's in there with him."

"Tell him I'd like to talk to him," Talley repeated.

"Yes, sir. Hang on a minute, please."

Sergeant Hobbs walked through the outer office to the office of the Commanding Officer and knocked at it.

The three men inside—Captain Henry Quaire, a stocky, balding man in his late forties; Chief Inspector of Detectives Matt Lowenstein, a stocky, barrel-chested man of fifty-five;

and Lieutenant Louis Natali—all looked at him with annoyance.

"It's Captain Talley," Sergeant Hobbs called, loud enough to be heard through the door.

"I thought we might be hearing from him," Chief Lowenstein said, then raised his voice loud enough to be heard by Hobbs. "On what, Hobbs?"

"One Seven Seven, Chief," Hobbs replied.

Lowenstein turned one of the telephones on Quaire's desk around so that he could read the extension numbers and pushed the button marked 177.

"Chief Lowenstein, Talley. I guess you heard about Officer Kellog?"

"Yes, sir. Captain Samuels of the Twenty-fifth called. He's—"

"Having trouble finding the Widow Kellog?"

"Yes, sir."

"Detective Milham, who's working a job, has been asked to come in to see Captain Quaire and myself to see if he might be able to shed light on that question. If he can, I will call Captain Samuels. And for your general fund of information, Detective Milham was not up for the Kellog job. Does that answer all the questions you might have?"

Sergeant Harry McElroy, a wiry, sandy-haired thirty-eight-year-old, had been "temporarily" assigned as driver to Chief Matt Lowenstein three years before. He had then been a detective, assigned to East Detectives, and didn't want the job. Like most detectives, he viewed the Chief of Detectives with a little fear. Lowenstein had a well-earned reputation for a quick temper, going strictly by the book, and an inability to suffer fools.

The term "driver" wasn't an accurate description of what a driver did. In military parlance, a driver was somewhere between an aide-de-camp and a chief of staff. His function was to relieve his chief of details, sparing him for more important things.

During Harry's thirty-day temporary assignment, Lowenstein had done nothing to make Harry think he had made a favorable impression on him. He had been genuinely surprised when Lowenstein asked him how he felt about "sticking around, and not going back to East."

Since that possibility had never entered Harry's mind, he could not—although he himself had a well-earned reputation for being able to think on his feet—think of any excuse he could offer Lowenstein to turn down the offer.

Over the next eleven months, as he waited for his name to appear on the promotion list to sergeant—he had placed sixteenth on the exam, and was fairly sure the promotion would come through—he told himself that all he had to do was keep his nose clean and all would be well. He had come to believe that Lowenstein wasn't really as much of a sonofabitch as most people thought, and when his promotion came through, he would be reassigned.

He would, so to speak, while greatly feeling the threat of evil, have safely passed through the Valley of Death. And he knew that he had learned a hell of a lot from his close association with Lowenstein that he could have learned nowhere else.

McElroy learned that his name had come up on a promotion list from Chief Lowenstein himself, the morning of the day the list would become public.

"There's a vacancy for sergeant in Major Crimes," Lowenstein had added. "And they want you. But what I've been thinking is that you could learn more staying right where you are. Your decision."

That, too, had been totally unexpected, and by then he had come to know Lowenstein well enough to know that when he asked for a decision, Lowenstein wanted it right then, that moment.

"Thank you, Chief," Harry had said. "I'd like that."

McElroy now had his own reputation, not only as Lowenstein's shadow, but for knowing how Chief Lowenstein thought, and what he was likely to do in any given situation.

His telephone often rang with conversations that began, "Harry, how do you think the Chief would feel about . . ."

He did, he came to understand, really have an insight into how Lowenstein thought, and what Lowenstein wanted.

Usually, Harry went wherever Lowenstein went. This morning, however, he sensed without a hint of any kind from Lowenstein that he would not be welcome in Captain Henry Quaire's office when the Chief went in there to discuss the murder of Officer Jerome H. Kellog with Quaire and Lieutenant Natali.

He got himself a cup of coffee and stationed himself near the entrance to the Homicide Unit, where he could both keep an eye on Quaire's office and intercept anybody who thought they had to see the Chief.

Chief Lowenstein came suddenly out of Quaire's office and marched out of Homicide. As he passed Harry, he said, "I've got to go see the Dago."

"Yes, sir."

The Dago was the Mayor of the City of Philadelphia, the Honorable Jerry Carlucci.

They rode down to the lobby in the elevator, and out the door to where Harry had parked the Chief's official Oldsmobile, by the CHIEF INSPECTOR DETECTIVE BUREAU sign at the door.

The police band radios came to life with the starting of the engine, and there was traffic on the command band:

"Mary One, William Five, at the Zoo parking lot," one metallic voice announced.

"A couple of minutes," a second metallic voice replied.

"Mary One" was the call sign of the limousine used by the Mayor of Philadelphia, "William" the identification code assigned to Special Operations.

"Who's William Five?" Sergeant McElroy asked thoughtfully.

"Probably Tony Harris," Lowenstein said. "Washington is William Four. But what I'd really like to know is why Special Operations is meeting the Mayor, or vice versa, in the

Zoo parking lot. I wonder what wouldn't wait until the Mayor got to his office."

"Yeah," McElroy grunted thoughtfully.

"Well, at least we know where to wait for the Mayor. City Hall, Harry."

"Yes, sir."

"Did Weisbach call in this morning?"

"No, sir."

"When we get to City Hall, you find a phone, get a location on Weisbach, call him, and tell him to stay wherever he is until I get back to him."

"Yes, sir."

When the mayoral Cadillac limousine rolled onto the sidewalk on the northeast corner of Philadelphia City Hall, which sits in the middle of the junction of Broad and Market streets in what is known as Center City, Chief Lowenstein was leaning against the right front fender of his Oldsmobile waiting for him.

He knew that Police Commissioner Taddeus Czernich habitually began his day by waiting in Mayor Carlucci's office for his daily orders, and he wanted to see Mayor Carlucci alone.

Lowenstein walked quickly to the side of the long black Cadillac, reaching it just as Lieutenant Jack Fellows pulled the door open. He saw that his presence surprised Fellows, and a moment later, as he came out of the car, Mayor Carlucci as well.

"'Morning, Matt," Carlucci said. He was a tall, large-boned, heavyset man, wearing a well-tailored, dark blue suit, a stiffly starched, bright-white shirt, a dark, finely figured necktie, and highly polished black wing-tip shoes.

He did not seem at all pleased to see Lowenstein.

"I need a minute of your time, Mr. Mayor."

"Here, you mean," Carlucci said, on the edge of unpleasantness, gesturing around at the traffic circling City Hall.

A citizen recognized His Honor and blew his horn. Carlucci smiled warmly and waved.

"Yes, sir," Lowenstein said.

Carlucci hesitated a moment, then got back in the limousine and waved at Lowenstein to join him. Fellows, after
hesitating a moment, got back in the front seat. The Mayor
activated the switch that raised the divider glass.

"OK, Matt," Carlucci said.

"A police officer has been shot," Lowenstein began.

"Dead?" the Mayor interrupted. There was concern and
indignation in the one word.

"Yes, sir. Shot in the back of his head."

"Line of duty?"

"His name is Kellog, Mr. Mayor. He was an undercover
officer assigned to the Narcotics Unit. He was found in his
home about an hour ago."

"By who?"

"When he didn't show up for work, they sent a Twenty-
fifth District car to check on him."

"He wasn't married?"

"Separated."

"Has she been notified?"

"They are trying to locate her."

"Get to the goddamned point, Matt."

"The story is that she's moved in with another detective."

"Oh, Jesus! Do you know who?"

"Detective Wallace J. Milham, of Homicide."

"Isn't he the sonofabitch whose wife left him because she
caught him screwing around with her sister?"

Mayor Carlucci's intimate knowledge of the personal
lives of police officers was legendary, but this display of in-
stant recall surprised Lowenstein.

"Yes, sir."

"Is what you're trying to tell me that this guy, or the wife,
is involved?"

"We don't know, sir. That is, of course, possible."

"You realize the goddamned spot this puts me in?" the

Mayor asked rhetorically. "I show up, or Czernich shows up, to console the widow, and there is a story in the goddamned newspapers, and the day after that it comes out—and wouldn't the *Ledger* have a ball with that?—that she's really a tramp, shacked up with a Homicide detective, and they're the doers?"

"Yes, sir. That's why I thought I'd better get to you right away with this."

"And if I don't show up, or Czernich doesn't, then what?" the Mayor went on. He turned to Lowenstein. "So what are you doing, Matt?"

"Detective Milham is on the street somewhere. They're looking for him. A good man, Joe D'Amata, is the assigned detective. Lou Natali's already on his way to the scene, and probably Henry Quaire, too."

"You ever hear the story of the fox protecting the chicken coop?" Carlucci asked nastily. "If you haven't, you can bet that the *Ledger* has."

"Henry Quaire is a straight arrow," Lowenstein said.

"I didn't say he wasn't. I'm talking about appearances. I'm talking about what the *Ledger*'s going to write."

"I don't think Wally Milham has had anything to do with this. I think we're going to find it's Narcotics-related."

"A man who would slip the salami to his wife's sister is capable of anything," the Mayor said. "I have to think that maybe he did. Or the wife did, and if he's shacked up with her . . ."

"So what do you want me to do, give it to Peter Wohl?"

"Wohl's got enough on his back right now," the Mayor said.

You mean running an investigation of corruption that I'm not even supposed to know about, even though I'm the guy charged with precisely that responsibility?

"What's the name of that mousy-looking staff inspector? Weis-something?"

"Mike Weisbach?"

"Him. He's good, and he's a straight arrow."

You used to think I was a straight arrow, Jerry. What the hell happened to change your mind?

"What are you going to do? Have him take over the investigation?"

"The Commissioner's going to tell him to *observe* the investigation, to tell you every day what's going on, and then you tell me every day what's going on."

The Mayor pushed himself off the cushions and started to crawl out of the car, over Lowenstein. He stopped, halfway out, and looked at Lowenstein, whose face was no more than six inches from his.

"I hope, for everybody's sake, Matt, that your Homicide detective who can't keep his pecker in his pocket isn't involved in this."

Lowenstein nodded.

The Mayor got out of the limousine and walked briskly toward the entrance to City Hall. Lieutenant Fellows got quickly out of the front seat and ran after him.

Lowenstein waited until the two of them disappeared from sight, then got out of the limousine, walked to his Oldsmobile, and got in the front seat beside Harry McElroy.

"You get a location on Weisbach?"

"He's in his car, at the Federal Courthouse, waiting to hear from you."

Lowenstein picked a microphone up from the seat.

"Isaac Fourteen, Isaac One."

"Fourteen."

"Meet me at Broad and Hunting Park," Lowenstein said.

"En route."

Staff Inspector Michael Weisbach's unmarked year-old Plymouth was parked on Hunting Park, pointing east toward Roosevelt Boulevard, when Chief Inspector Lowenstein's Oldsmobile pulled up behind it.

"We'll follow you to the scene," Lowenstein said to Harry McElroy as he opened the door. "You know where it is?"

"I'll find out," McElroy said.

Lowenstein walked to Weisbach's car and got in beside him.

"Good morning, Chief," Weisbach said.

He was a slight man of thirty-eight, who had started losing his never-very-luxuriant light brown hair in his late twenties. He wore glasses in mock tortoise frames, and had a slightly rumpled appearance. His wife, Natalie, with whom he had two children, Sharon (now eleven) and Milton (six), said that thirty minutes after putting on a fresh shirt, he looked as if he had been wearing it for three days.

"Mike," Lowenstein replied, offering his hand. "Follow Harry."

"Where are we going?"

"A police officer named Kellog was found an hour or so ago shot in the back of his head."

"I heard it on the radio," Weisbach said as he pulled into the line of traffic.

"You are going to—*observe* the investigation. You are going to report to me once a day, more often if necessary, if anything interesting develops." He looked at Weisbach and continued. "And I will report to the Mayor."

"What's this all about?"

"It seems that Officer Kellog's wife—he's been working plainclothes in Narcotics, by the way—moved out of his bed into Detective Milham's."

"Wally Milham's a suspect?" Weisbach asked disbelievingly.

"He's out on the street somewhere. Quaire is looking for him. I want you to sit in on the interview."

"Then he is a suspect?"

"He's going to be interviewed. The Mayor doesn't want to be embarrassed by this. He wants to be one step ahead of the *Ledger*. If a staff inspector is involved, he thinks it won't be as easy for the *Ledger* to accuse Homicide, the Department—him—of a cover-up."

"Why me?" Weisbach asked.

"What the Mayor said was, 'He's good and he's a straight

arrow,'" Lowenstein replied, and then he met Weisbach's eyes and smiled. "He knows that about you, but he doesn't know your name. He referred to you as 'that mousy-looking staff inspector, Weis-something.'"

Weisbach chuckled.

"He knows your name, Mike," Lowenstein said. "What we both have to keep in mind is that the real name of the game is getting Jerry Carlucci reelected."

"Yeah," Weisbach said, a tone that could have been either resignation or disgust in his voice.

Staff Inspector Michael Weisbach, who was one of the sixteen staff inspectors in the Philadelphia Police Department, had never really wanted to be a cop until he had almost five years on the job.

His father operated a small, mostly wholesale, findings store, Weisbach's Buttons and Zipper World, on South Ninth Street in Center City Philadelphia, and the family lived in a row house on Higbee Street, near Oxford Circle. By the time he had finished high school, Mike had decided, with his parents' approval, that he wanted to be a lawyer.

He had obtained, on a partial scholarship, in just over three years, a bachelor of arts degree from Temple University, by going to school year round and supporting himself primarily by working the graveyard shift managing a White Tower hamburger emporium on the northwest corner of Broad and Olney. The job paid just a little more than his father's business could afford to pay, and there was time in the early-morning hours, when business was practically nonexistent, to study.

Sometime during this period, Natalie had changed from being the Little Abramowitz Girl Down the Block into the woman with whom Michael knew he wanted to share his life. And starting right then—when he saw her in her bathing suit, he thought of the Song of Solomon—not after he finished law school and took the bar exams and managed to build a practice that would support them.

The thing for them to do, he and Natalie decided, was for

him to get a job. Maybe a day job with the City, or the Gas Company, that would pay more than he was making at White Tower, not require a hell of a lot of work from him, and permit him to go to law school at night. With what she could earn working in her new job as a clerical assistant at the Bursar's Office of the University of Pennsylvania, there would be enough money for an apartment. That was important, because they didn't want to live with his family or hers.

He filed employment applications with just about every branch of city government, and because there didn't seem to be a reason not to, took both the Police and Fire Department entrance examinations.

When the postcard came in the mail saying that he had been selected for appointment to the Police Academy, they really hadn't known what to do. He had never seriously considered becoming a cop, and his mother said he was out of his mind, as big as he was, what was going to happen if he became a cop was that some six foot four Schwartzer was going to cut his throat with a razor; or some guy on drugs would shoot him; or some gangster from the Mafia in South Philly would stand him in a bucket full of concrete until it hardened and then drop him into the Delaware River.

Michael graduated from the Philadelphia Police Academy and was assigned to the Seventh District, in the Far Northeast region of Philadelphia. For the first year, he was assigned as the Recorder in a two-man van, transporting prisoners from the District to Central Lockup in the Roundhouse, and carrying people and bodies to various hospitals.

The second year he spent operating an RPC, turning off fire hydrants in the summer and working school crossings. He took the examination for promotion to detective primarily because it was announced two weeks after he had become eligible to take it. At the time, he would have been much happier to take the corporal's exam, because corporals, as a rule of thumb, handled administration inside districts. But there had been no announcement of a corporal's exam, so he took the detective's examination.

If he passed it, he reasoned, there would be the two years of increased pay while he finished law school.

Detective Michael Weisbach was assigned first to the Central Detective District, which covers Center City. There, almost to his surprise, he not only proved adept at his unchosen profession, but was actually happy to go to work, which had not been the case when he'd been working the van or walking his beat in the Seventh District.

His performance of duty attracted the attention of Lieutenant Harry Abraham, whose rabbi, it was said, was then Inspector Matt Lowenstein of Internal Affairs. When Abraham was promoted to captain and assigned to the Major Crimes Unit, he arranged for Weisbach to be transferred with him.

Detective Weisbach was promoted to sergeant three weeks before he passed the bar examination. With it came a transfer to the office of just-promoted Chief Inspector Matt Lowenstein, who had become Chief of the Detective Division.

It just made sense, he told Natalie, to stick around the Department for a little longer. If he was going to go into private practice, they would need a nest egg to furnish an office, pay the rent, and to keep afloat until his practice reached the point where it would support them.

By then, although he was really afraid to tell even Natalie, much less his mother, he was honest enough to admit to himself that the idea of practicing law, handling people's messy divorces, trying to keep some scumbag from going to prison, that sort of thing, did not have half the appeal for him that being a cop did.

When he passed the lieutenant's examination, Chief Lowenstein actually took him out and bought him lunch and told him that if he kept up the good work, there was no telling how high he could rise in the Department. Natalie said that Chief Lowenstein was probably just being polite. But when the promotion list came out, and he was assigned to the Intelligence Unit, instead of in uniform in one of the districts, he told Natalie he knew Lowenstein had arranged it, and that he had meant what he said.

There had been a shake-up in the Department, massive retirements in connection with a scandal, and he had made captain much sooner than he had expected to. With that promotion came an assignment in uniform, to the Nineteenth District, as commanding officer. The truth was that he rather liked the reflection he saw in the mirror of Captain Mike Weisbach in a crisp white shirt, and captain's bars glistening on his shoulders, but Natalie said she liked him better in plain clothes.

More vacancies were created two years later in the upper echelons of the Department, as sort of an aftershock to the scandal and the retirements the original upheaval had caused. Three staff inspectors, two of whom told Mike they had never planned to leave the Internal Affairs Division, were encouraged to take the inspector's examination. That of course meant there were now three vacancies for staff inspectors, and Mike had already decided to take the exam even before Chief Lowenstein called him up and said that it would be a good idea for him to do so.

And like the men he had replaced, Mike Weisbach thought he had found his final home in the Department. He had some vague notion that, a couple of years before his retirement rolled around, if there was an inspector's exam, he would take it. There would be a larger retirement check if he went out as an inspector, but he preferred to do what he was doing now to doing what the Department might have him do—he didn't want to wind up in some office in the Roundhouse, for example—if he became an inspector now.

Staff inspectors, who were sometimes called—not pejoratively—"supercops," or "superdetectives," had, Weisbach believed, the most interesting, most satisfying jobs in the Department. They handled complicated investigations, often involving prominent government officials. It was the sort of work Mike Weisbach liked to do, and which he knew he was good at.

He still went to work in the morning looking forward to what the day would bring. It was only rarely that he was handed a job he would rather not do.

This "observation" of a Homicide investigation fell into that category. It was the worst kind of job. The moment he showed up on the scene, whichever Homicide detective had the job—for that matter, the whole Homicide Unit—would immediately and correctly deduce that they were not being trusted to do their job the way it should be done.

And he would feel their justified resentment, not Lowenstein or Mayor Carlucci.

As he followed Harry McElroy, crossing over Old York Road and onto Hunting Park Avenue, then onto Ninth Street, he tried to be philosophical about it. There was no sense moaning over something he couldn't control.

The street in front of Officer Kellog's home was now crowded with police vehicles of all descriptions, and Mike was not surprised to see Mickey O'Hara's antenna-festooned Buick among them.

"I don't have to tell you what to do," Chief Lowenstein said as he got out of the car. "Call me after the Milham interview."

"Yes, sir," Mike said, and walked toward the District cop standing at the door of the row house.

The cop looked uncomfortable. He recognized the unmarked Plymouth as a police vehicle, and was wise enough in the ways of the Department to know that a nearly new unmarked car was almost certain to have been assigned to a senior white-shirt, but this rumpled little man was a stranger to him.

"I'm Staff Inspector Weisbach. I know your orders are to keep everybody out, but Chief Lowenstein wants me to go in."

"Yes, sir."

Captain Henry Quaire and Lieutenant Lou Natali were in the kitchen, trying to stand out of the way of the crew of laboratory technicians.

*They don't have any more business here than I do. You
don't get to be a Homicide detective unless you know just
about everything there is to know about working a crime
scene. Homicide detectives don't need to be supervised.*

"Good morning, Henry, Lou."

"Hello, Mike," Quaire replied. His face registered his surprise, and a moment later his annoyance, at seeing Weisbach.

"Inspector," Natali said.

Weisbach looked at the body and the pool of blood and
quickly turned away. He was beyond the point of becoming
nauseous at the sight of a violated body, but it was very unpleasant for him. His brief glance would stay a painfully
clear memory for a long time.

"Shot twice, it looks, at close range," Quaire offered.

"I don't suppose you know who did it?" a voice behind
Mike asked.

Mike turned to face Mr. Michael J. O'Hara of the *Bulletin.*

"Not yet, Mickey," Quaire said. "The uniform was told to
keep people out of here."

"I have friends in high places, Henry," O'Hara said. "Not
only do I know Staff Inspector Weisbach here well enough
to ask him what the hell he's doing here, but I know the legendary Chief Lowenstein himself. Lowenstein told the uniform to let me in, Henry. He wouldn't have, otherwise."

"He's out there?" Quaire asked.

O'Hara nodded.

"Talking to Captain Talley."

"I want to talk to Talley too," Quaire said, and walked toward the front door.

"So what are you doing here, Mike?" O'Hara asked.

" 'Observing,' " Weisbach said. He saw the displeased reaction on Lieutenant Lou Natali's face.

"Is that between you and me, or for public consumption?"
O'Hara asked.

"Spell my name right, please."

" 'Observing'? Or 'supervising'?"

"Observing."

"Exactly what does that mean?"

"Why don't you ask Chief Lowenstein? I'm not sure, myself."

"OK. I get the picture. But—this is for both of you, off the record, if you want—do you have any idea who shot Kellog?"

"No," Natali said quickly.

"I just got here, Mike."

"Is there anything to the story that the Widow Kellog is—how do I phrase this delicately?—*personally involved* with Wally Milham?"

"I don't know how to answer that delicately," Natali said.

"Mike?"

"I heard that gossip for the first time about fifteen minutes ago," Weisbach said. "I don't know if it's true or not."

His eye fell on something in the open cabinet behind Natali's head.

"What's that?" he asked, and pushed by Natali for a closer look.

"It's a tape recorder. With a gadget that turns it on whenever the phone is used," Weisbach said. "Has that been dusted for prints, Lou?"

"Yes, sir."

Weisbach pulled the recorder out of the cabinet and saw that there was no cassette inside.

"Anything on the tape?" he asked.

"There was no tape in it when D'Amata found it," Natali said. "And no tape anywhere around it. There was an empty box for tapes, but no tapes."

"That's strange," Weisbach thought out loud. "The thing is turned on." He held it up to show the red On light. "Did the lab guys turn it on?"

"D'Amata said you can't turn it off, it's wired to the light socket."

"Strange," Weisbach said.

"Yeah," Mickey O'Hara agreed. "Very strange."

A uniformed officer came into the kitchen.

"Lieutenant, the Captain said that Detective Milham is on his way to the Roundhouse."

"Thank you," Natali said.

"I want to sit in on the interview," Weisbach said.

"You're going to question Milham?" Mickey O'Hara asked.

"Yes, sir," Natali said, not quite succeeding in concealing his displeasure.

"Routinely, Mick," Weisbach said. "If there's anything, I'll call you. All right?"

O'Hara thought that over for a second.

"You have an honest face, Mike, and I am a trusting soul. OK. And in the meantime, I will write that at this point the police have no idea who shot Kellog."

"We don't," Weisbach said.

THREE

Detective Wallace J. Milham, a dapper thirty-five-year-old, who was five feet eleven inches tall, weighed 160 pounds, and adorned his upper lip with a carefully manicured pencil-line mustache, reached over the waist-high wooden barrier to the Homicide Unit's office and tripped the lock of the door with his fingers.

He turned to the left and walked toward the office of Captain Henry C. Quaire, the Homicide commander. When he had come out of the First Philadelphia Building, Police Radio had been calling him. When he answered the call, the message had been to see Captain Quaire as soon as possible.

Quaire wasn't in his office. But Lieutenant Louis Natali was, and when he saw Milham, waved at him to come in.

Milham regarded Natali, one of five lieutenants assigned to Homicide, as the one closest to Captain Quaire, and in effect, if not officially, his deputy. He liked him.

41

"I got the word the Captain wanted to see me," Milham said as he pushed open the door.

"Where were you, Wally? We've been looking for you for an hour."

"At the insurance bureau in the First Philadelphia Building," Milham replied, then when he sensed Natali wanted more information, went on: "On the Grover job."

A week before, Mrs. Katherine Grover had hysterically reported to Police Radio that there had been a terrible accident at her home in Mt. Airy. When a radio patrol car of the Fourteenth District had responded, Officer John Sarabello had found Mr. Arthur Grover, her husband, dead against the wall of their garage. Mrs. Grover told Officer Sarabello that her foot had slipped off the brake onto the accelerator, causing their Plymouth station wagon to jump forward.

Neither Officer Sarabello, his sergeant, or the Northwest Detective Division detective who further investigated the incident were completely satisfied with Mrs. Grover's explanation of what had transpired, and the job was referred to the Homicide Unit. Detective Milham got the job, as he was next up on the wheel.

"I know she did it," Detective Milham went on. "And she knows I know she did it. But she is one tough little cookie."

"The insurance turn up anything?"

"Nothing here in the last eighteen months. They're going to check Hartford for me."

While it might be argued that the interest of the insurance industry in a homicide involving someone whose life they have insured may be more financial than moral—if it turned out, for example, that Mrs. Grover had feloniously taken the life of her husband, they would be relieved of paying her off as the beneficiary of his life insurance policy—the industry for whatever reasons cooperates wholeheartedly with police conducting a homicide investigation.

"You weren't listening to the radio?"

Milham shook his head.

"You know a cop named Kellog?"

Milham nodded.

"They found him, this morning, in the kitchen of his house," Natali said. "Somebody shot him, twice, in the back of his head."

"Jesus Christ!"

"He'd probably been dead about six hours."

"Who did it?"

"They had trouble finding his wife. She apparently didn't live with him. So the neighbors say. They just found her a half an hour ago."

"She works for the City," Milham said. "The neighbors should have known that."

"I think that's where they finally got it, from the neighbors," Natali said. "Where were you last night, Wally, from, say, midnight to six in the morning?"

"So that's what this is all about."

"Where were you, Wally?"

"He was an asshole, Lieutenant. I think he was also dirty. But I didn't shoot the sonofabitch."

"So tell me where you were last night from midnight on."

"Jesus Christ, Lieutenant! I was home."

"Were you alone?"

"No."

"Was she with you?"

Milham looked at Natali for a moment before replying.

"Yeah, she was."

"She wouldn't make a very credible alibi, Wally."

"I told you I didn't do it."

·"I didn't think *you* did," Natali said.

"She was with me, I told you that."

"You wouldn't make a very credible witness either, Wally, under the circumstances."

"So we're both suspects? Is that what you're telling me?"

"Of course you are," Natali said. "Think about it, Wally."

"So what are you telling me?"

"You're going to have to give a formal statement. Joe

D'Amata was up on the wheel for the job. I'll do the interview. You know Mike Weisbach?"

"Sure."

"He'll sit in on it. Chief Lowenstein has assigned him to 'observe' the investigation. He's upstairs with the Captain and Chief Coughlin. They ought to be here in a minute."

"OK."

"Unless you want to claim the Fifth."

"If I do?"

"You know how it works, Wally."

"I'm not claiming the Fifth. I didn't do it."

"I don't think you did, either."

"What's with Weisbach?"

"I guess they want to make sure we do our job. I don't like that any more than you like being interviewed. You want a little advice?"

"Sure."

"Go through the motions. Don't lose your temper in there. And then go back to work and forget about it."

Milham met Natali's eyes.

"I start midnights tonight," he said absently.

"I don't think that anybody thinks you had anything to do with it. We're just doing this strictly by the book."

"A staff inspector 'observing' is by the book?"

STATEMENT OF: Detective Wallace J. Milham Badge 626

DATE AND TIME: 1105 AM May 19, 1975

PLACE: Homicide Unit, Police Admin. Bldg. Room A.

CONCERNING: Death by Shooting of Police Officer Jerome H. Kellog

IN PRESENCE OF:
    Det. Joseph P. D'Amata, Badge 769
    Staff Inspector Michael Weisbach

INTERROGATED BY: Lieutenant Louis Natali Badge 233

RECORDED BY: Mrs. Jo-Ellen Garcia-Romez, Clerk/Typist

I AM Lieutenant Natali and this is Inspector Weisbach, Detective D'Amata and Mrs. Garcia-Romez, who will be recording everything we say on the typewriter.

We are questioning you concerning your involvement in the fatal shooting of Police Officer Jerome H. Kellog.

We have a duty to explain to you and to warn you that you have the following legal rights:

A. You have the right to remain silent and do not have to say anything at all.

B. Anything you say can and will be used against you in Court.

75-331D (Rev.7/70)   **Page 1**

C. You have a right to talk to a lawyer of your own choice before
we ask you any questions, and also to have a lawyer here with
you while we ask questions.

D. If you cannot afford to hire a lawyer, and you want one, we
will see that you have a lawyer provided to you, free of charge,
before we ask you any questions.

E. If you are willing to give us a statement, you have a right to
stop anytime you wish.

1. Q. Do you understand that you have a right to keep quiet and
do not have to say anything at all?
   A. Yes, of course.

2. Q. Do you understand that anything you say can and will be
used against you?
   A. Yes.

3. Q. Do you want to remain silent?
   A. No.

4. Q. Do you understand you have a right to talk to a lawyer
before we ask you any questions?
   A. Yes, I do.

5. Q. Do you understand that if you cannot afford to hire a
lawyer, and you want one, we will not ask you any questions until
a lawyer is appointed for you free of charge?
   A. Yes, I do.

6. Q. Do you want to talk to a lawyer at this time, or to have a
lawyer with you while we ask you questions?
   A. I don't want a lawyer, thank you.

7. Q. Are you willing to answer questions of your own free will,
without force or fear, and without any threats and promises having been made to you?
   A. Yes, I am.

75-331D (Rev.7/70)   Page 2

8. Q. State your name, city of residence, and
    employment?
    A. Wallace J. Milham, Philadelphia. I am a
    detective.

9. Q. State your badge number and duty assignment?
    A. Badge Number 626. Homicide Unit.

10. Q. Did you know Police Officer Jerome H. Kellog?
    A. Yes.

11. Q. Was he a friend of yours?
    A. No.

12. Q. What was the nature of your relationship to
    him?
    A. He was married to a friend of mine.

13. Q. Who is that?
    A. Mrs. Helene Kellog.

14. Q. What is the nature of your relationship to
    Mrs. Helene Kellog?
    A. We're very good friends. She is estranged
    from her husband.

(Captain Henry C. Quaire entered the room and became
    an additional witness to the interrogation at
    this point.)

15. Q. (Captain Quaire) Wally, you have any problem
    with me sitting in on this?
    A. No, Sir. I'd rather have you in here than
    looking through the mirror.

16. Q. Would it be fair to categorize your relation-
    ship with Mrs. Kellog as romantic in nature?
    A. Yes.

17. Q. You seemed to hesitate. Why was that?
    A. I was deciding whether or not to answer it.

18. Q. Was Officer Kellog aware of your relationship with his wife?
A. I suppose so. I never had a fight with him about it or anything. But I think, sure, he knew. She moved out on him.

19. Q. How long have you had this relationship with Mrs. Kellog?
A. About a year. A little less.

20. Q. You are aware that Officer Kellog was found shot to death in his home this morning?
A. I am.

21. Q. How did you first learn of his death?
A. Lieutenant Natali informed me of it a few minutes ago.

22. Q. That is Lieutenant Louis Natali of the Homicide Unit?
A. Yes.

23. Q. Did you shoot Officer Kellog?
A. No.

24. Q. Do you have any knowledge whatsoever of the shooting of Officer Kellog?
A. No. None whatsoever.

25. Q. How would you categorize the relationship of Officer Kellog and his wife?
A. They were estranged.

26. Q. Do you know where Mrs. Kellog went to live when she left the home of her husband?
A. With me.

27. Q. Do you have a department-issued firearm, and if so, what kind?
A. Yes, a .38 Special Caliber Colt snub nose.

28. Q. Where is this firearm now?
A. In the gun locker.

29. Q. Would you be willing to turn this firearm
    over to me now for ballistics and other testing
    in connection with this investigation?
    A. Captain, I go on at midnight. When would I
    get it back?

(Captain Quaire) I've got a Cobra in my desk. You
    can use that.

30. Q. Do you own, or have access to, any other
    firearms?
    A. Yes, I have several guns at my house.

31. Q. You have stated that Mrs. Kellog resides in
    your home. That being the case, would Mrs. Kel-
    log have access to the firearms you have stated
    you have in your home?
    A. Yes.

32. Q. Precisely what firearms do you have in your
    home?
    A. I've got a .45. An Army Model 1911A1 automat-
    ic. And an S & W Chief's Special. And a Savage
    .32 automatic. And there's a .22, a rifle. A
    Winchester Model 12 shotgun, 12 gauge. And a
    Remington Model 70 .30-06 deer rifle.

33. Q. And Mrs. Kellog has had access to these
    firearms?
    A. Yes.

34. Q. Do you believe Mrs. Kellog had anything what-
    soever to do with the shooting of her husband?
    A. I do not.

35. Q. Would you be willing to turn over any or all
    of the firearms in your home to me for ballistic,
    and other testing in connection with this inves-
    tigation?
    A. Yes.

36. Q. Would you be willing to do so immediately
    after this interview is completed? Go there with
    myself or another detective and turn them over?
    A. Yes.

37. Q. Where were you between the hours of six pm
last evening and ten o'clock this morning?
A. I don't remember where I was at six, but from
seven to about eight-thirty, I was interviewing
people in connection with the Grover job.

38. Q. You were on duty, conducting an official
investigation?
A. Right.

39. Q. And then what happened? When you went off
duty at half past eight?
A. I went home, had some dinner, watched TV, and
went to bed.

40. Q. Were you alone?
A. No. Helene, Mrs. Kellog was with me. She was
home when I got there.

41. Q. Mrs. Kellog was with you all the time?
A. Yes. From the time I got home, a little
before nine, until we went to work this morning.

42. Q. You were not out of each other's company from
say nine pm until say 8 am this morning?
A. Correct.

43. Q. Did you see anyone else during that period, 9
pm last night until 8 am today?
A. No.

44. Q. Is there anything at all that you could tell
me that might shed light on the shooting death
of Officer Kellog?
A. No.

45. Q. You have no opinion at all?
. A. He was working Narcotics. If you find who did
this, I'd bet it'll have something to do with
that.

46. Q. Can you expand on that?
A. I don't know anything, if that's what you
mean. But I've heard the same talk you have.

47. Q. Captain Quaire?
A. (Captain Quaire) I can't think of anything.
Anybody else?
(There was no reply.)

```
48. Q. Thank you, Detective Milham.
    A. Captain, I'm going to probably need some
    vacation time off.
    A. (Capt. Quaire) Sure, Wally. Just check in.
    A. (Det. Milham) I don't like sitting in here
    like this.
    A. (Capt. Quaire) None of us like it, Wally.


75-331D (Rev.7/70)                                Page 7
```

"Thanks, Henry," Staff Inspector Mike Weisbach said, taking a cup of coffee from Captain Henry Quaire in Quaire's office.

Quaire made a "It's nothing, you're welcome" shrug, and then met Weisbach's eyes. "Is there anything else we can do for you, Inspector?"

"Tell me how you call this, Henry," Weisbach said. "Out of school."

"I don't think Wally Milham's involved."

"And the Widow Kellog?"

Quaire shrugged. "I don't know her."

"Would it be all right with you if I went with D'Amata when he interviews her?"

"What if I said no, Mike?" Quaire asked, smiling.

"Then I would go anyway, and you could go back to calling me 'Inspector,' " Weisbach said, smiling back. "Can I presume that you have finally figured out that I don't want to be here any more than you want me to?"

"Sometimes I'm a little slow. It made me mad. My guys would throw the Pope in Central Lockup if they thought he was a doer, and Lowenstein knows it, and he still sends you in here to look over our shoulder."

"That came from the Mayor."

"The Mayor knows that my people are straight arrows."

"I think he's trying to make sure the *Ledger* has no grounds to use the word 'cover-up.' "

"That means he thinks it's possible that we would."

"I don't think so, Henry. I think he's just covering his behind."

Quaire shrugged.

"I know you didn't ask for the job," he said.

Weisbach guessed the Widow Kellog was twenty-eight, twenty-nine, something like that, which would make her three years younger than the late Officer Kellog. She was a slender, not-unattractive woman with very pale skin—her lipstick was a red slash across her face, and her rouge did little to simulate the healthy blush of nature.

She was wearing a black suit with a white blouse, silk stockings, high heels, a hat with a veil, and sunglasses. No gloves, which gave Weisbach the opportunity to notice that she was wearing both a wedding and an engagement ring. They had obviously gotten here, to her apartment, just in time. She was on her way out.

"Mrs. Kellog," Joe D'Amata said, showing her his badge, "I'm Detective D'Amata and this is Inspector Weisbach."

She looked at both of them but didn't reply.

"We're very sorry about what happened to your husband," D'Amata said. "And we hate to intrude at a time like this, but I'm sure you understand that the sooner we find out who did this to Jerry, the better."

"Did you know him?" she asked.

"Not well," D'Amata said. "Let me ask the hard question. Do you have any idea who might have done this to him?"

"No."

"Not even a suspicion?"

"It had something to do with drugs, I'm pretty sure of that."

"When was the last time you saw your husband?"

"A couple of weeks ago."

"You didn't see him at all yesterday?"

"No."

"Just for the record, would you mind telling me where you were last night? Say, from six o'clock last night."

"I was with a friend."

"All that time? I mean, all night?"

She nodded.

"Would you be willing to give me that friend's name?"

"I was with Wally Milham. I think you probably already knew that."

"I hope you understand we have to ask these questions. What, exactly, is your relationship with Detective Milham?"

"Jerry and I were having trouble, serious trouble. Can we leave it at that?"

"Mrs. Kellog," Weisbach said. "When we were in your house, where we found Officer Kellog, we noticed a tape recorder."

D'Amata doesn't like me putting my two cents in. But the last thing we want to do is make her angry. And she would have been angry if he had kept pressing her. And for what purpose? Milham told us they're sleeping together.

"What about it?" Mrs. Kellog asked.

"I just wondered about it. It turned on whenever the phone was picked up, right?"

"He recorded every phone call," she said. "It was his, not mine."

"You mean, he used it in his work?"

"Yes. You know that he did."

"Do you happen to know where he kept the tapes?"

"There was a box of them in the cabinet. They're gone?"

"We're trying to make sure we have all of them," Weisbach said.

"All the ones I know about, he kept right there with the recorder."

"Did your husband ever talk to you about what he did?" Weisbach asked. "I mean, can you think of anything he ever said that might help us find whoever did this to him?"

"He never brought the job home," she said. "He didn't want to tell me about what he was doing, and I didn't want to know."

"My wife's the same way," Weisbach said.

"And you don't work Narcotics," she said. "Listen, how long is this going to last? I've got to go to the funeral home and pick out a casket."

"I think we're about finished," Weisbach said. "Can we offer you a lift? Is there anything else we can do for you?"

"I've got a car, thank you."

"Thank you for your time, Mrs. Kellog," Weisbach said. "And again, we're very sorry that this happened."

"We had our problems," she said. "But he didn't deserve to have this happen to him."

Detective Anthony C. "Tony" Harris, after thinking about it, decided that discretion dictated that he park the car in the parking garage at South Broad and Locust streets and walk to the Bellvue-Stratford Hotel, even though that meant he would have to get a receipt from the garage to get his money back, and that he would almost certainly lose the damned receipt, or forget to turn it in, and have to pay for parking the car himself.

Things were getting pretty close to the end, and he didn't want to blow the whole damned thing because one of the Vice scumbags—they were, after all, cops—spotted the unmarked Ford on the street, or in the alley behind the Bellvue-Stratford, where he had planned to leave it, and started wondering what it was doing around the hotel at that hour of the night.

Tony Harris was not a very impressive man physically. He was a slight and wiry man of thirty-six, already starting to bald, his face already starting to crease and line. His shirt collar and the cuffs of his sports jacket were frayed, his tie showed evidence of frequent trips to the dry cleaners, his trousers needed to be pressed, and his shoes needed both a shine and new heels.

He enjoyed, however, the reputation among his peers of being one of the best detectives in the Philadelphia Police Department, where for nine of his fifteen years on the job he had been assigned to the Homicide Unit. It had taken him five years on the job to make it to Homicide—an unusually short time—and he would have been perfectly satisfied to spend the rest of his time there. Eighteen months ago, over his angry objections, he had been transferred to the Special Operations Division.

He had mixed emotions about what he was doing now. Bad guys are supposed to be bad guys, not fellow cops, not guys you knew for a fact were—or at least had been—good cops.

On one hand, now that he had been forced to think about it, he was and always had been a straight arrow. And just about all of his friends were straight arrows. He personally had never taken a dime. Even when he was fresh out of the Academy, walking a beat in the Twenty-third District, he had been made uncomfortable when merchants had given him hams and turkeys and whiskey at Christmas.

Taking a ham or a turkey or a bottle of booze at Christmas wasn't really being on the take, but even then, when he was walking a beat, he had drawn the line at taking cash, refusing with a smile the offer of a folded twenty-dollar bill or an envelope with money in it.

There was something wrong, he thought, in a cop taking money for doing his job.

What these sleazeballs were doing was taking money, big-time money, for *not* doing their jobs. Worse, for doing crap behind their badges they knew goddamned well was dirty.

That was one side—they were dirty, and they deserved whatever was going to happen to them.

The other side was, they were cops, brother officers, and doing what he was doing made him uncomfortable.

When Tony had been on the sauce, brother officers had turned him loose a half-dozen times when they would have locked up a civilian for drunken driving, or belting some guy in a bar and making a general asshole of himself.

It wasn't, in other words, like he was Mr. Pure himself.

Washington, Sergeant Jason Washington, his longtime

partner in Homicide, and now his supervisor, was Mr. Pure. And so was Inspector Wohl, who was running this job. About the only thing they had ever taken because they were wearing a badge was the professional courtesy they got from a brother officer who stopped them for speeding.

And the kids he was supervising now were pure too. Payne would never take money because he didn't have to, he was rich, and Lewis was pure because he'd got that from his father. Lieutenant Foster H. Lewis, Jr., was so pure and such a straight arrow that they made jokes about it; said that he would turn himself in if he got a goober stuck in his throat and had to spit on the sidewalk.

Tony knew that what he was doing was right, and that it had to be done. He just wished somebody else was doing it.

He entered the Bellvue-Stratford Hotel by the side entrance on Walnut Street, into the cocktail lounge. He stood just inside the door long enough to check for a familiar face at the bar, and then, after walking through it, checked the lobby before walking quickly across to the bank of elevators. He told the operator to take him to twelve.

He tried the key he had to 1204, but it was latched—as it should have been—from inside, and he had to wait until Officer Foster H. Lewis, Jr., who was an enormous black kid, six three, two hundred twenty, two hundred thirty even, came to it and peered through the cracked door and then closed it to take the latch off and let him in.

When he opened the door, Lewis was walking quickly across the room to the window, a set of earphones on his head still connected by a long coiled cord to one of the two reel-to-reel tape recorders set up on the chest of drawers.

"What's going on, Tiny?" Harris asked, and then before Lewis could reply, "Where's Payne?"

Tiny replied by pointing, out the window and up.

Harris crossed the room, noticing as he did a room-service cart with a silver pot of coffee and what looked like the leftovers from a room-service steak dinner.

Payne, of course. It wouldn't occur to him to take a quick

*trip to McDonald's or some other fast-food joint and bring
a couple of hamburgers and some paper cups full of coffee
to the room. He's in a hotel room, call room service and
order up a couple of steaks, medium rare. Fuck what it
costs.*

Detective Tony Harris looked out the window and saw
Detective Matthew M. Payne.

"Jesus H. Christ!" he exclaimed. "What the fuck does he
think he's doing?"

"The lady opened the window," Officer Lewis replied,
"which dislodged the suction cup."

"Did she see the wire?" Harris wondered out loud, and
was immediately sorry he had.

Dumb question. If she had seen the wire, Payne would not
be standing on a twelve-inch ledge thirteen floors up, trying
to put the suction cup back on the window.

"I don't think so," Tiny said.

"Did we get anything?"

"If we had a movie camera instead of just a microphone,
we would have a really blue movie," Tiny Lewis said.

"Is he crazy or what, to try that?"

"I told him he was. He said he could do it."

"How did he get out there?"

"There have been no lights in Twelve Sixteen all night.
Two doors down from Twelve Eighteen. He said he thought
he could get in."

"You mean pick the lock?" Harris asked, and again without giving Officer Lewis a chance to reply, went on. "What
if someone had seen him in the corridor?"

"For one thing, from what was coming over the wire before the lady knocked the mike off, we didn't think the Lieutenant was quite ready to go home to his wife and kiddies,
and for another, Matt's wearing a hotel-maintenance uniform, and says he doesn't think the Lieutenant knows him
anyway."

"Yeah, but what if he had?"

"He's got it!" Lewis said.

He took the earphones from his head and held them out to Tony Harris.

Harris took them and put them on.

The sounds of sexual activity made Harris uncomfortable.

"I've been wondering if the fact that I find some of that rather exciting makes me a pervert," Tiny said.

"We're trying to catch him with one of the mobsters, not with his cock in some hooker's mouth."

"Unfortunately, at the moment, all we have is him and the lady. Maybe Martinez and Whatsisname will get lucky when they relieve us," Tiny said, and then added: "He's back inside. I agree with you, that was crazy."

"Your pal is crazy," Harris said.

"I think he prefers to think of it as devotion to duty," Tiny said. "You know, 'Neither heat, nor rain, nor thirteen stories off the ground will deter this courier . . .'"

"Oh, shit," Harris said, chuckling. "I'd never try something like that."

"Neither would I. But I don't want to be Police Commissioner before I'm forty."

Harris looked at him and smiled.

"You think that's what he wants? Really?"

"I don't know. Sometimes I think he's just playing cop . . ."

Harris snorted.

"Other times, I think he takes the job as seriously as my old man. You know, the thin blue line, protecting the citizens from the savages. We know he's not doing it for the money."

There was a knock at the door.

"What did he do? Run back?" Harris asked.

"Hay-zus, more likely," Tiny said, and went to the door.

It was in fact Detective Jesus Martinez, a small—barely above departmental minimums for height and weight—olive-skinned man with a penchant for gold jewelry and sharply tailored suits from Krass Brothers.

"What's up?" he said by way of greeting.

"X-rated audiotapes," Tiny said.

"And your buddy's been playing Supercop."

There was no love lost between Detectives Payne and Martinez, and Tony Harris knew it.

"Where is he?"

"The last we saw him, he was on a ledge outside the love-nest," Tony said.

"Doing what?"

"Putting the mike back. The hooker opened the window and knocked the suction cup off."

Martinez went to the window and looked out.

"No shit? Is it working now?"

"Yeah. The Lieutenant's having a really good time," Tiny said, offering Martinez the headset.

Martinez took the headset and held one of the phones to his ear. He listened for nearly a minute, then handed it back.

"Payne really went out on that ledge to put it back?"

" 'Neither heat nor rain . . .' " Tiny began to recite, stopping when there was another knock at the door.

Martinez opened it.

Detective Matthew M. Payne stood there. He was a tall, lithe twenty-five-year-old with dark, thick hair and intelligent eyes, wearing the gray cotton shirt and trousers work uniform of the hotel-maintenance staff.

"What do you say, Hay-zus?" Payne said. "Strangely enough, I'm delighted to see you."

Martinez didn't respond.

"Is it working?" Payne asked Tiny Lewis. Lewis nodded.

"Tony, now that Detective Martinez is here," Payne said, "and the goddamned microphone is back where it's supposed to be, can I take off?"

Harris did not respond directly. He looked at Tiny Lewis.

"Anything on what you have so far?"

"You mean in addition to the grunts, wheezes, and other sighs of passion? No. No names were mentioned, and the subject of money never came up."

"Washington will want to hear them anyway," Harris said, and turned to Payne. "You take the tapes to Washington, and you can take off. Let Martinez know where you are."

"OK, it's a deal."

"Going out on that ledge was dumb," Harris said.

"The Lieutenant's inamorata knocked the microphone off," Payne replied. "No ledge, no tape."

"The Lieutenant's what?" Tiny asked.

"I believe the word is defined as 'doxy, paramour, lover,' " Payne said.

"In other words, 'hooker'?"

"A hooker, by definition, does it for money," Payne said. "We can't even bust this one for that. No money has changed hands. The last I heard, accepting free samples of available merchandise is not against the law. When you think about it, for all we know, it was true love at first sight between the Lieutenant and the inamorata."

Harris laughed.

"Get out of here, Payne," Harris said. "You want to take off, Tiny, I'll stick around until the other guy—what the hell is his name?—gets here."

"Pederson," Martinez furnished. "Pederson with a *d*."

"I'll wait. I find this all fascinating."

"You're a dirty young man, Tiny," Payne said. "I'm off."

FOUR

At just about the same time—9:35 P.M.—Detective Matthew M. Payne left the Bellvue-Stratford Hotel by the rear service entrance and walked quickly, almost trotted, up Walnut Street toward his apartment on Rittenhouse Square, Mr. John Francis "Frankie" Foley walked, almost swaggered, into the Reading Terminal Market four blocks away at Twelfth and Market streets.

Mr. Foley was also twenty-five years of age, but at six feet one inch tall and 189 pounds, was perceptibly larger than Detective Payne. Mr. Foley was wearing a two-toned jacket (reddish plaid body, dark blue sleeves and collar) and a blue sports shirt with the collar open and neatly arranged over the collar of his jacket.

Mr. Foley walked purposefully through the Market, appreciatively sniffing the smells from the various food counters, until he reached the counter of Max's Cheese Steaks.

Waiting for him there, sitting on a high, backless stool, facing a draft beer, a plate of french-fried potatoes, and one of
Max's almost-famous cheese steak sandwiches, was Mr.
Gerald North "Gerry" Atchison, who was forty-two, five
feet eight inches tall, and weighed 187 pounds.

Mr. Atchison, who thought of himself as a businessman
and restaurateur—he owned and operated the Inferno
Lounge in the 1900 block of Market Street—and believed
that appearances were important, was wearing a dark blue
double-breasted suit, a crisp white shirt, a finely figured silk
necktie, and well-polished black wing-tip shoes.

Both gentlemen were armed, Mr. Atchison with a Colt
Cobra .38 Special caliber revolver, carried in a belt holster,
and Mr. Foley with a .45 ACP caliber Colt Model 1911A1
semiautomatic pistol that he carried in the waistband of his
trousers at the small of his back. Mr. Atchison was legally
armed, having obtained from the Sheriff of Delaware
County, Pennsylvania, where he maintained his home, a license to carry a concealed weapon for the purpose of personal protection.

Mr. Atchison had told the Chief of Police that he often left
his place of business late at night carrying large sums of
cash and was concerned with the possibility of being
robbed. The Chief of Police knew that the 1900 block of
Market Street was an unsavory neighborhood and that Mr.
Atchison was not only a law-abiding citizen, but a captain in
the Pennsylvania Air National Guard, in which he was himself an officer, and granted the license to carry.

It is extremely difficult in Philadelphia for any private citizen to get a license to carry a concealed weapon, but
Philadelphia honors concealed-weapons permits issued by
other police jurisdictions. Mr. Atchison, therefore, was in violation of no law for having his pistol.

Mr. Foley, on the other hand, did not have a license to
carry a concealed weapon. He had applied for one, with the
notion that all the cops could say was "no," in which case he
would be no worse off than he already was. And for a while,

it looked as if he might actually get the detective to give him one. The detective he had talked to when he went to fill out the application forms had a USMC *Semper Fi!* decalcomania affixed to his desk and Frankie had told him he'd been in the Crotch himself, and they talked about Parris Island and Quantico and 29 Palms, and the detective said he wasn't promising anything because permits were goddamned hard to get approved—but maybe something could be worked out. He told Frankie to bring in his DD-214, showing his weapons qualifications, so a copy of that could be attached to the application; that might help.

Frankie explained that while he would be happy to bring in his Form DD-214, which showed that he had qualified as Expert with the .45, there was a small problem. A fag had come on to him in a slop chute at 29 Palms, and he had kicked the shit out of him, and what his Form DD-214 said about the character of his release from service was "Bad Conduct," which was not as bad as "Dishonorable," but wasn't like "Honorable" either.

Frankie could tell from the way the detective's attitude had changed when he told him he'd gotten a "Bad Conduct" discharge from the Crotch that bringing in his DD-214 would be a waste of fucking time, so he never went back.

He was, therefore, by the act of carrying a concealed firearm, in violation of Section 6106 of the Crimes Code of Pennsylvania, and Sections 907 (Possession of Instrument of Crime), and 908 (Possession of Offensive Weapon) of the Uniform Firearms Act, each of which is a misdemeanor of the first degree punishable by imprisonment of not more than five years and/or a fine of not more than $10,000.

Mr. Foley was not concerned with the possible ramifications of being arrested for carrying a concealed weapon. Primarily, he accepted the folklore of the streets of Philadelphia that on your first bust you got a walk, unless your first bust was for something like raping a nun. The prisons were crowded, and judges commonly gave first offenders a talking-to and a second chance, rather than put them behind

bars. Frankie had never been arrested for anything more serious than several traffic violations, once for shoplifting, and
once for drunk and disorderly.

And even if that were not the case, he trusted Mr. Atchison, who did carry a gun, about as far as he could throw the
sonofabitch—*what kind of a shitheel would hire somebody
to kill his own wife?*—and he was not going to be around
him anywhere at night without something to protect himself.

More important, the purpose of their meeting was to fi-
nalize the details of the verbal contract they had made between themselves, the very planning of which, not to
mention the execution, was a far more serious violation of
the Crimes Code of Pennsylvania than carrying a gun without a permit.

In exchange for five thousand dollars, half to be paid now
at Max's, and the other half when the job was done, Mr.
Foley had agreed to "eliminate" Mrs. Alicia Atchison, Mr.
Atchison's twenty-five-year-old wife, who Mr. Atchison
said had been unfaithful to him, and Mr. Anthony J. Marcuzzi, fifty-two, Mr. Atchison's business partner, who, Mr.
Atchison said, had been stealing from him.

Frankie wasn't sure whether Marcuzzi had really been
stealing from the Inferno—it was more likely that Atchison
just wanted him out of the way. Maybe *he* was stealing from
Marcuzzi, and was afraid Marcuzzi was catching on—but he
was sure that his wife's fucking around on him wasn't the
reason Atchison wanted her taken care of. Atchison had another broad Frankie knew about, another young one, and
probably he figured that since he was having Marcuzzi
taken care of, he might as well get rid of them both at once.
Or maybe he thought it would look more convincing if she
got knocked off when Marcuzzi got it. Or maybe there was
insurance on her or something.

But whatever his reasons, it wasn't because he was really
pissed off that she had let somebody get into her pants. Two
weeks after Frankie had met Gerry Atchison, *before* Atchison had talked to him about taking care of his wife and Mar-

cuzzi, he had just about come right out and said that if Frankie wanted to fuck Alicia, that was all right with him.

Frankie had been tempted—Alicia wasn't at all bad-looking, nice boobs and legs—but had decided against it, as it wasn't professional. He didn't want to get involved with somebody he was going to take out.

On his part, Mr. Foley had not been entirely truthful with Mr. Atchison, either. He was not, as he had led Mr. Atchison, and others, to believe, an experienced hit man who accepted contracts from the mob in Philadelphia (and elsewhere, like New York and Las Vegas) that for one reason or another they would rather not handle themselves.

This job, in fact, would be his first.

It was, as he thought of it, putting his foot on the ladder to a successful criminal career. He'd given it a lot of thought when they'd thrown him out of the Crotch. There was a lot of money to be made as a professional criminal. The trouble was, you had to start out doing stupid things like breaking in someplace, or stealing a truck. If you got caught, you spent a long time in jail. And even if you didn't get caught, unless you had the right connections, you didn't get shit—a dime on the dollar, if you were lucky—for what you stole.

You had to get on the inside, and to do that, you needed a reputation. The most prestigious member of the professional criminal community, Frankie had concluded, was the guy who everybody knew took people out. Nobody fucked with a hit man. So clearly the thing to do was become a hit man, and the way to do that was obviously to hit somebody.

The problem there was to find somebody who wanted somebody hit and was willing to give you the job. Frankie was proud of the way he had handled that. He knew a guy, Sonny Boyle, from the neighborhood, since they were kids. Sonny was now running numbers; only on the edges of doing something important, but he knew the important people.

Frankie picked up their friendship again, hanging out in bars with him, and not telling Sonny what he was doing to pay the rent, which was working in the John Wanamaker's warehouse, loading furniture on trucks. He let it out to Sonny that he had been kicked out of the Crotch for killing a guy—actually it had been because they caught him stealing from wall lockers—and when Sonny asked what he was doing told him he was in business, and nothing else.

And then the next time he had seen in the newspapers that the mob had popped somebody—the cops found a body out by the airport with .22 holes in his temples—he went to Sonny Boyle and told him he needed a big favor, and when Sonny asked him what, he told Sonny that if the cops or anybody else asked, they had been together from ten at night until at least three o'clock in the morning, and that they hadn't gone anywhere near the airport during that time.

And when Sonny had asked what he'd been doing, he told Sonny he didn't want to know, and that if he would give him an alibi, he would owe him a big one.

That got the word spreading—Sonny had diarrhea of the mouth, and always had, which is what Frankie had counted on—and then he did exactly the same thing the next time the mob shot somebody, and there was one of them "police report they believe the murder had a connection to organized crime" crime stories by Mickey O'Hara in the *Bulletin*; he went to Sonny and told him he needed an alibi.

Three weeks after that happened, Sonny took him to the Inferno Lounge and said there was somebody there, the guy who owned it, Gerry Atchison, that he wanted him to meet.

He'd known right off, from the way Atchison charmed him and bought him drinks, shit, even as much as told him he could have a shot at fucking his wife, that Sonny had been telling Atchison about his pal the hit man and that Atchison had swallowed it whole.

There were to be other compensations for taking the contract in addition to the agreed-upon five thousand dollars. Frankie would become sort of a mixture of headwaiter and bouncer at the Inferno Lounge. The money wasn't great, not much more than he was getting from Wanamaker's, but he told Atchison that he was looking for a job like that, not for the money, but so he could tell the cops, when they asked, that he had an honest job.

That would be nice too. He could quit the fucking Wanamaker's warehouse job and be available, where people could find him. Frankie Foley was sure that when the word spread around, as he knew it would, that he'd done a contract on Atchison's wife and Marcuzzi, his professional services would be in demand.

Mr. Foley slid onto the backless high stool next to Mr. Atchison. Atchison seemed slightly startled to see him.

"You got something that belongs to me, Gerry?" Frankie Foley asked Gerry Atchison, whereupon Mr. Atchison handed Mr. Foley a sealed, white, business-size envelope, which Mr. Foley then put into the lower left of the four pockets on his two-tone jacket.

"We got everything straight, right?" Mr. Atchison inquired, somewhat nervously.

Mr. Foley nodded.

Mr. Atchison did not regard the nod as entirely satisfactory. He looked around to see that the counterman was wholly occupied trying to look down the dress of a peroxide blonde, and then leaned close to Frankie.

"You will come in for a drink just before eleven," he said softly. "I'll show you where you can find the ordnance. Then you will leave. Then, just after midnight, you will walk down Market, and look in the little window in the door, like you're wondering why the Inferno's closed. If all you see is me, then you'll know I sent Marcuzzi downstairs to count the cash, and her down to watch him, and that I left the back door open."

"We been over this twenty times," Mr. Foley said, getting off the stool. "What you should be worried about is whether you can count to twenty-five hundred. Twice."

"Jesus, Frankie!" Mr. Atchison indignantly protested the insinuation that he might try to shortchange someone in a business transaction.

"And you lay off the booze from right now. Not so much as another beer, understand?" Mr. Foley said, and walked away from Max's Cheese Steaks.

Mr. Paulo Cassandro, who was thirty-six years of age, six feet one inches tall, and weighed 185 pounds, and was President of Classic Livery, Inc., had dined at the Ristorante Alfredo, one of the better restaurants in Center City Philadelphia, with Mr. Vincenzo Savarese, a well-known Philadelphia businessman, who was sixty-four, five feet eight inches tall and weighed 152 pounds.

Mr. Savarese had a number of business interests, including participation in both Ristorante Alfredo and Classic Livery, Inc. His name, however, did not appear anywhere in the corporate documents of either, or for that matter in perhaps ninety percent of his other participations. Rather, almost all of Mr. Savarese's business participations were understandings between men of honor.

Over a very nice veal Marsala, Mr. Cassandro told Mr. Savarese that he had a small problem, one that he thought he should bring to Mr. Savarese for his counsel. Mr. Cassandro said that he had just learned from a business associate, Mrs. Harriet Osadchy, that an agreement that had been made between Mrs. Osadchy and a certain police officer and his associates was no longer considered by the police officer to be adequate.

"As I recall that agreement," Mr. Savarese said, thoughtfully, "it was more than generous."

"Yes, it was," Mr. Cassandro said, and went on: "He said that his expenses have risen, and he needs more money."

Mr. Savarese shook his head, took a sip of Asti Fumante from a very nice crystal glass, and waited for Mr. Cassandro to continue.

"Mrs. Osadchy feels, and I agree with her, that not only is a deal a deal, but if we increase the amount agreed upon, it will only feed the bastard's appetite."

Mr. Cassandro was immediately sorry. Mr. Savarese was

a refined gentleman of the old school and was offended by profanity and vulgarity.

"Excuse me," Mr. Cassandro said.

Mr. Savarese waved his hand in acceptance of the apology for the breach of good manners.

"It would be, so to speak, the nose of the camel under the flap of the tent?" Mr. Savarese asked with a chuckle.

Mr. Cassandro smiled at Mr. Savarese to register his appreciation of Mr. Savarese's wit.

"How would you like me to handle this, Mr. S?"

"If at all possible," Mr. Savarese replied, "I don't want to terminate the arrangement. I think of it as an annuity. If it is not disturbed, it will continue to be reasonably profitable for all concerned. I will leave how to deal with this problem to your judgment."

"I'll have a word with him," Mr. Cassandro said. "And reason with him."

"Soon," Mr. Savarese said.

"Tonight, if possible. If not tonight, then tomorrow."

"Good," Mr. Savarese said.

Mr. Cassandro was fully conversant not only with the terms of the arrangement but with its history.

Mrs. Harriet Osadchy, a statuesque thirty-four-year-old blonde of Estonian heritage, had come to Philadelphia from Hazleton, in the Pennsylvania coal region, four years before, in the correct belief that the practice of her profession would be more lucrative in Philadelphia. Both a decrease in the demand for anthracite coal and increasing mechanization of what mines were still in operation had substantially reduced the work force and consequently the disposable income available in the region.

She had first practiced her profession as a freelance entrepreneur, until, inevitably, her nightly presence in the lounges of the better Center City hotels had come to the attention of the plainclothes vice officers assigned to the Inspector of Central Police Division.

Following her third conviction, which resulted in a thirty-day sentence at the House of Correction for violation of Sections 5902 (Prostitution) and 5503 (Disorderly Conduct) of the Crimes Code of Pennsylvania, she realized that she would either have to go out of business or change her method of doing business. By then, she had come to know both many of her fellow freelance practitioners of the world's oldest profession, and several gentlemen who she correctly believed had a certain influence in certain areas in Philadelphia.

With a high degree of tact, she managed to get to meet Mr. Cassandro, and to outline her plan for the future. If it would not interfere in any way with any similar arrangement in which any of Mr. Cassandro's friends and his associates had an interest, she believed the establishment of a very high-class escort service would fill a genuine need in Philadelphia.

Since she was unaware of how things were done in Philadelphia, and was a woman alone, she would require both advice, in such things as finding suitable legal and medical services, and protection from unsavory characters who might wish to prey upon her. She said she believed that ten percent of gross receipts would be a fair price to pay for such advice and protection.

Mr. Cassandro had told Mrs. Osadchy that he would consider the question, make certain inquiries, and get back to her.

He then sought an audience with Mr. Savarese and reported the proposal to him. After thinking it over for several days Mr. Savarese told Mr. Cassandro that he believed Mrs. Osadchy's proposal had some merit, and that he should encourage her to cautiously proceed with it.

It was agreed between them as men of honor that Mr. Savarese would receive twenty-five percent of the ten percent of gross proceeds Mrs. Osadchy would pay to Mr. Cassandro, in payment for his counsel.

The business prospered from the start. Mrs. Osadchy chose both her work force and her clientele with great care.

She also understood the absolute necessity of maintaining good relations with the administrative personnel of the hotels—not limited to security personnel—where her work force practiced their profession.

For example, if she anticipated a large volume of business from, say, a convention of attorneys, or vascular surgeons, or a like group of affluent professionals, she would engage a room (or even, for a large convention, a small suite) in the hotel for the duration of the convention. No business was conducted *in* the room. But between professional engagements, her work force would use it as a base of operations. This both increased efficiency and eliminated what would otherwise have been a parade of unaccompanied attractive young women marching back and forth through the hotel lobby.

And Mrs. Osadchy was of course wise enough to be scrupulously honest when it came to making the weekly payments of ten percent of gross income to Mr. Cassandro.

For his part, Mr. Cassandro introduced Mrs. Osadchy to several attorneys and physicians who could be relied upon to meet the needs of Mrs. Osadchy and her work force with both efficacy and confidentiality. And, more important, he let the word get out that Mrs. Osadchy was a very good friend of his, and thus entitled to a certain degree of respect. An insult to her would be considered an insult to him.

It was a smooth-running operation, and everybody had been happy with it.

And now this fucking cop was getting greedy, which could fuck everything up, and was moreover a personal embarrassment to Mr. Cassandro, who had not liked having to go to Mr. Savarese with the problem.

I should have known, when he started wanting to help himself to the hookers, Mr. Cassandro thought angrily, *that this sonofabitch was going to cause me trouble.*

He's a real sleazeball, and now it's starting to show. And cause me trouble.

What I have to remember, because I keep forgetting it, is

that Lieutenant Seymour Meyer is a cop, a cop on the take, and not a businessman, and consequently can be expected to act like an asshole.

When Mr. Cassandro left Mr. Savarese in the Ristorante Alfredo, instead of getting into the car that was waiting for him outside, he walked to the Benjamin Franklin Hotel on Chestnut Street and entered a pay telephone booth in the lobby.

He telephoned to Mrs. Harriet Osadchy and told her that he was working on their problem, that he had been given permission to deal with it.

"I'm really glad to hear that," Mrs. Osadchy replied. "He's really getting obnoxious."

"Financially speaking, you mean?" Mr. Cassandro asked, laughing. "Or generally speaking?"

"He called up about an hour ago, and asked what the room number was at the Bellvue. So I told him. And then he said the reason he wanted to know was because it was a slow night, and he was a little bored, so why didn't I send Marianne over there, so they could have a little party."

"He's a real shit, Harriet," Mr. Cassandro sympathized.

"It's not just the money that he don't pay the girls and I have to. He's a sicko with the girls. I had a hard time making Marianne go."

"He's a real shit," Mr. Cassandro repeated, and then he had a pleasant thought. "Harriet, why don't you call over there?"

"What?"

"Tell her to keep him there. I want to talk to him. That's as good a place as any."

"I'll call her," Harriet said dubiously. "But I don't want her involved in anything, Paulo."

"Trust me, Harriet," Mr. Cassandro said, and hung up.

Detective Matt Payne turned off the Parkway into the curved drive of a luxury apartment building and stopped with a squeal of tires right in front of the door. The uniformed doorman standing inside looked at him in annoyance.

The car was a silver Porsche 911. It had been Matt's graduation present, three years before, when he had finished his undergraduate studies, cum laude, at the University of Pennsylvania.

Miss Penelope Detweiler, who was his fiancée in everything but formal announcement and ring-on-her-finger, frequently accused him, with some justification, of showering far more attention on it than he did on her.

He was still wearing the gray cotton uniform of the Bellvue-Stratford Hotel Maintenance Staff. By the time he had gone from the hotel to his apartment on Rittenhouse Square, which is five blocks west of the Bellvue-Stratford Hotel, to get the car, he had concluded (a) the smart thing for him to have done was to have prevailed yet again on Tiny Lewis's good nature and asked him to take the damned tapes to Washington, and (b) that since he had failed to do so he was going to be so late that changing his clothing was out of the question. He had gone directly to the basement garage and taken his car.

"I'll just be a minute," he said to the doorman, who, accustomed to Payne's frequent, brief, nocturnal visits, simply grunted and picked up his telephone to inform Ten Oh Six that a visitor was on his way up.

Mrs. Martha Washington, a very tall, lithe, sharply featured woman, who looked, Matt often thought, like one of the women portrayed on the Egyptian bas-reliefs in the museum, opened the door to him. She was wearing a loose, ankle-length silver lamé gown.

"He's not here, Matt," she said, giving him her cheek to kiss. "I just opened a nice bottle of California red, if you'd like to come in and wait. He was supposed to be here by now."

"I'm already late for dinner, thank you," he said. "Would you give him this, please?"

He handed her a large, sealed manila envelope.

"Dinner, dressed like that?" she said, indicating his maintenance department uniform. "It looks like you've been fixing stopped-up sinks. What in the world have you been up to?"

She saw the uncomfortable look on his face, and quickly added: "Sorry, forget I asked."

"I'll take a rain check on the California red," Matt said. "I don't know where we're going for dinner, but I'll be home early if he wants me."

"I'll tell him."

Ten minutes later, Matt pulled the Porsche to a stop at the black painted aluminum pole, hinged at one end, which barred access to a narrow cobblestone street in Society Hill, not far from Independence Hall and the Liberty Bell. A neatly lettered sign reading "Stockton Place—Private Property—No Thoroughfare" hung on short lengths of chain from the pole. A Wachenhut Private Security officer came out of a Colonial-style redbrick guard shack and walked to the Porsche.

"May I help you, sir?"

"Matthew Payne, to see Mr. Nesbitt."

"One moment, sir, I'll check," the Wachenhut Security officer said, and went back into his shack.

It was said that, before renovation, the area known as Society Hill, not far from the Delaware River, had been going downhill since Benjamin Franklin—whose grave was nearby in the Christ Church Cemetery at Fifth and Arch streets—had walked its narrow streets. Before renovation had begun, it was an unpleasant slum.

Now it was an upscale neighborhood, with again some of the highest real estate values in Philadelphia. The Revolutionary-era buildings had been completely renovated—often the renovations consisted of discarding just about everything but the building's facades—and turned into luxury apartments and town houses.

One of the developers, while doing title research, had

been pleasantly surprised to learn that a narrow alley between two blocks of buildings had never been deeded to the City. That provided the legal right for them to bar the public from it, something they correctly suspected would have an appeal to the sort of people they hoped to interest in their property.

They promptly dubbed the alley "Stockton Place," closed one end of it, and put a Colonial-style guard shack at the other.

Having been informed that Mr. Chadwick Thomas Nesbitt IV, who with his wife occupied Number Nine B Stockton Place—an apartment stretching across what had been the second floor of three Revolutionary-era buildings—did in fact expect a Mr. Payne to call, the Wachenhut Security officer pressed a switch on his control console which caused the barrier pole to rise.

Matt drove nearly to the end of Stockton Place, carefully eased the right wheels of the Porsche onto the sidewalk, walked quickly into the lobby of Number Nine, and then quickly up a wide carpeted stairway to the second floor.

The door to Nine B opened as he reached the landing. Standing in it, looking more than a little annoyed, was Miss Penelope Detweiler, who was twenty-four, blond, and just this side of beautiful. She was wearing a simple black dress, adorned with a string of pearls and a golden pin, a representation of a parrot.

"Where the *hell* have you been?" Miss Detweiler asked, and then, seeing how Detective Payne was attired, went on: "Matt, for Christ's sake, we're going to dinner!"

"Hi!" Detective Payne said.

"Don't 'Hi' me, you bastard! We had reservations for nine-thirty, you're not even here at nine-thirty, and when you finally show up, you're dressed like that!"

He tried to kiss her cheek; she evaded him, then turned and walked ahead of him into the living room of the apartment. Wide glass windows offered a view of the Benjamin Franklin Bridge, the Delaware River, and an enormous sign atop a huge brick warehouse on the far—New Jersey—side of the river showing a representation of a can of chicken soup and the words NESFOODS INTERNATIONAL.

"I would hazard to guess, old buddy, that you are on the lady's shitlist," said Mr. Chadwick Thomas Nesbitt IV, who was sprawled on a green leather couch. Sitting somewhat awkwardly beside him was his wife, the former Daphne Elizabeth Browne, who was visibly in the terminal stages of pregnancy.

A thick plate-glass coffee table in front of the couch held a bottle of champagne in a glass cooler.

"What are we celebrating?" Matt asked.

"Look at how he's dressed!" Penny Detweiler snapped.

"Never fear, Chadwick is here, the problem will be solved," Chad Nesbitt said, waving his champagne glass as he rose from the couch. "Will you have a little of this, Matthew?"

"What are we celebrating?" Matt asked again.

"I am no longer peddling soup store by store," Nesbitt said. "I will tell you all about it as you change out of your costume."

Chadwick Thomas Nesbitt IV and Matthew Mark Payne had been best friends since they had met, at age seven, at Episcopal Academy. They had been classmates and fraternity brothers at the University of Pennsylvania, and Matt had been Chad's best man when he married.

Nesbitt grabbed the champagne bottle from its cooler by its neck, snatched up a glass, handed it to Matt, then led him down a corridor to his bedroom. There he gestured toward a walk-in closet and arranged himself against the headboard of his king-sized bed.

"What the hell are you dressed up for?" he asked. "Or as?"

"I was on the job."

"Unstopping toilets?"

"That's not original. I was asked the same question just

fifteen minutes ago," Matt said as he selected a shirt and tie from Chad Nesbitt's closet.

"In other words, it's secret police business, right? Not to be shared with the public?"

"Right."

"I wouldn't count on dipping your wick tonight, Matthew. Penny's really pissed."

"I told her I didn't know when I could get here," Matt said.

"Your tardy appearance is a symptom of what she's pissed about, not the root cause."

"So what else is new?"

"How long are you going to go on playing cop?"

"I am not playing cop, goddamn it! And you. This is what I do. I'm good at it. I like it. Don't you start, too."

"I'm afraid I have contributed to the lady's discontent," Nesbitt said. "The champagne is because you are looking at the newest Assistant Vice President of Nesfoods International."

"Really?"

"Yeah. I hate to admit it, but the old man was right. The whole goddamned business does ride on the shoulders of the guys who are out there every day fighting for shelf space. And the only way to really understand that is to go out on the streets and do it yourself."

The business to which Mr. Nesbitt referred was Philadelphia's largest single employer, Nesfoods International. Four generations before, George Detweiler had gone into partnership with Chadwick Thomas Nesbitt to found what was then called The Nesbitt Potted Meats & Preserved Vegetables Company. It was now Nesfoods International, listed just above the middle of the Fortune 500 companies and still tightly held. C. T. Nesbitt III was Chairman of the Executive Committee and H. Richard Detweiler, Penny's father, was President and Chief Executive Officer.

"Newest Assistant Vice President of what?" Matt asked.

"Merchandising."

"Congratulations," Matt said.

"A little more enthusiasm would not be out of order," Chad said. "Vice President, even *Assistant* Vice President, has a certain ring to it."

Matt threw a pair of Nesbitt's trousers and a tweed sports coat on the bed, then started to take his gray uniform trousers off. He had trouble with the right leg, which he finally solved by sitting on the bed, pulling the trousers leg up, and unstrapping an ankle holster.

"Doesn't that thing bother your leg?" Chad asked.

"Only when I'm taking my pants off. I meant it, Chad. Congratulations."

"Penny was already here when I got home," Chad said. "When I made the grand announcement, her response was, 'And Matt is still childishly playing policeman,' or words to that effect."

"If I had gone into the Marine Corps with you, I would just be finishing my first year in law school," Matt replied. "I wonder what she would call that."

"Sensible," Chad said. "Your first foot on the first rung of your ladder to legal and/or corporate success. Anyway, if she is bitchy tonight, you know who to blame."

"I don't want to be a lawyer, and I don't—especially don't—want to work for Nesfoods International."

" '*Especially don't*'? What are you going to do when you marry Penny? It's a family business, for Christ's sake."

"Your family. Her family. Not mine."

"That's bullshit and you know it," Chad said. "She's an only child. I don't know how much stock she owns now, but . . ."

"Let it go, Chad!"

". . . eventually, she'll inherit . . ."

"Goddamn it, quit!"

"Your old man sits on the board," Chad went on. "Mawson, Payne, Stockton, McAdoo and Lester's biggest client is Nesfoods."

"Just for the record, it is not," Matt said. "Now, are you

going to quit, or do you want to celebrate your vice presidency all by yourself?"

Nesbitt sensed the threat wasn't idle.

"One final comment," he said. "And then I'll shut up. Please?"

After a moment, as he closed the zipper of Chad's gray flannel slacks, Matt nodded.

"I liked the Marine Corps. I was, I thought, a damned good officer. I really wanted to stay. But I couldn't, Matt. For the same reasons you can't ignore who you are, and who Penny is. I think they call that maturity."

"You're now finished, I hope?"

"Yeah."

"Good. Now we'll go out and celebrate your vice-presidency. I can handle you alone, or Penny, but not the both of you together."

"OK."

"Where are we going?"

"There's a new Italian place down by the river. Northern Italian. I think that means without tomato sauce."

Matt pulled up his trousers leg and strapped his ankle holster in place.

"You really have to carry that with you all the time?" Chad asked.

"I'm a cop," Matt said. "Write that on the palm of your hand."

Mr. John Francis "Frankie" Foley checked his watch as he circled City Hall and headed west on Kennedy Boulevard. It was ten forty-five. He had told Mr. Gerald North "Gerry" Atchison "between quarter of eleven and eleven," so he was right on time.

Mr. Foley considered that a good omen. It was his experience that if things went right from the start, whatever you were doing would usually go right. If little things went wrong, like for example you busted a shoelace or spilled spaghetti sauce on your shirt, or the car wouldn't start, whatever, so that you were a little late, you could almost count on the big things being fucked up, too.

And he felt good about what he was going to do, too, calm, *professional.* He'd spent a good long time thinking the whole thing through, trying to figure out what, or who, could fuck up. His old man used to say, "No chain is stronger than its weakest link," and say what you want to say about that nasty sonofabitch, he was right about that.

And the weak link in this chain, Mr. Foley knew, was Mr. Gerry Atchison. For one thing, Frankie was pretty well convinced that he could trust Atchison about half as far as he could throw the slimy sonofabitch. I mean, what kind of a shitheel would offer somebody you just met a chance to fuck his wife, even if you were planning to get rid of her for business purposes?

The first thing that Frankie thought of was that maybe what Atchison was planning on doing was letting him do the wife and the business partner, and then he would shoot Frankie. That would be the smart thing for him to do. He would have his wife and partner out of the way, and if the shooter was dead, too, with the fucking gun in his hand, Atchison could tell the cops that when he heard the shots in the basement office he went to investigate and shot the dirty sonofabitch who had shot his wife and his best friend and business partner. And with Frankie dead, not only couldn't he—not that he would, of course—tell the cops what had really happened, but Atchison wouldn't have to come up with the twenty-five hundred Frankie was due when he did the wife and the business partner.

Frankie didn't think Atchison would have the balls to do that, but the sonofabitch was certainly smart enough to figure out that he *could* do something like that. So he'd covered those angles, too. For one thing, the first thing he was going to do when he saw Atchison now was make sure that sonofabitch had the other twenty-five hundred ready, and the way he had asked for it, in used bills, nothing bigger than a twenty.

If he didn't have the dough ready, then he would know the fucker was trying to screw him. He really hoped that wouldn't happen, he wanted this whole thing to happen, and if Atchison didn't have the dough ready, he didn't know what he'd do about it, except maybe smack the sonofabitch alongside his head with the .45.

But Atchison could have the dough ready, Frankie reasoned, and still be planning to do him after he had done the wife and the partner. He had figured out the way to deal with the whole thing: first, make sure that he had the dough, and second, when he came back to do the contract, either make sure that Atchison didn't have a gun, or, which is what most likely would happen, make sure that he always had the drop on Atchison.

All he had to be was calm and professional.

Frankie steered his five-year-old Buick convertible into the left lane, turned left off Kennedy Boulevard onto South Nineteenth Street, crossed Market Street, and then made another left turn into the parking lot at South Nineteenth and Ludlow Street. During the day, you had to pay to park there, but not at this time of night. There were only half a dozen cars in the place. He got out of the car, walked back to Market Street, and turned right.

He caught a glimpse of himself reflected in a storefront window. He was pleased with what he saw. There was nothing about the way he was dressed (in a brown sports coat with an open-collared maroon sports shirt and light brown slacks) that made him look any different from anyone else walking up Market Street to have a couple of drinks and maybe try to get laid. No one would remember him because he was dressed flashy or anything like that.

He pushed open the door to the Inferno Lounge and walked in. There were a couple of people at the bar, and in the back of the place he saw Atchison glad-handing a tableful of people.

"Scotch, rocks," Frankie said to the bartender as he slid onto a bar stool.

The bartender served the drink, and when Frankie didn't decorate the mahogany with a bill, said, "Would you mind settling the bill now, sir? I go off at eleven."

"You mean you're closing at eleven?"

"The guy who works eleven 'til closing isn't coming in tonight. The boss, that's him in the back, will fill in for him," the bartender said.

"Hell, you had me worried. The night's just beginning," Frankie said, and took a twenty—his last—from his wallet and laid it on the bar.

So far, so good. Atchison said tonight was the late-night bartender's night off.

Frankie pushed a buck from his stack of change toward the bartender and then picked up his drink. There was a mirror behind the bar, but he couldn't see Atchison in it, and he didn't want to turn around and make it evident that he was looking for him.

Frankie wondered where whatsername, the wife— *Alicia*—was, and the partner.

I wonder if I should have fucked her. She's not bad-looking.

Goddamn it, you know better than that. That would have really been dumb.

"What do you say, Frankie?" Gerry Atchison said, laying a hand on his shoulder. Frankie was a little startled; he hadn't heard or sensed him coming up.

"Gerry, how are you?"

"I got something for you."

"I-hoped you would. How's the wife, Gerry?"

Atchison gave him a funny look before replying, "Just fine, thanks. She'll be here in a little while. She went somewhere with Tony."

Tony is the partner, Anthony J. Marcuzzi. What did he do, send her off to fuck the partner?

"Tommy," Gerry Atchison called to the bartender. "Stick around a couple of minutes, will you? I got a little business with Mr. Foley here."

There was nothing Tommy could do but fake a smile and say sure.

Atchison started walking to the rear of the Inferno. Frankie followed him. They went down a narrow flight of stairs to the basement and then down a corridor to the office.

Atchison closed and bolted the office door behind them, then went to a battered wooden desk, and unlocked the right-side lower drawer. He took from it a small corrugated paper box and laid it on the desk.

He unwrapped dark red mechanic's wiping towels, exposing three guns. One was a Colt .38 Special caliber revolver with a five-inch barrel. The second was what Frankie thought of as a cowboy gun. In this case it was a Spanish copy of a Colt Peacemaker, six-shot, single-action .44 Russian caliber revolver. The third was a Savage Model 1911 .32 ACP caliber semiautomatic.

"There they are," he announced.

"Where's the money?" Frankie asked.

"In the desk. Same drawer."

"Let's see it."

"You don't trust me?" Atchison asked with a smile, to make like it was a joke.

"Let's see the money, Gerry," Frankie said.

He picked up the Colt and opened the cylinder and dumped the cartridges in his hand. Then he closed the cylinder and dry-snapped the revolver. The cylinder revolved the way it was supposed to.

The noise of the dry snapping upset Gerry Atchison.

"What are you doing?"

"Making sure these things work."

"You didn't have to do that. I checked them out."

Yeah, but you don't know diddly-shit about guns. You just think you do.

The Colt was to be the primary weapon. He would do both the wife and the partner with the Colt. The cowboy gun was the backup, in case something went wrong. Better safe than sorry, like they say. The Savage was to wound Atchison in the leg. Frankie would have rather shot him with the .38 Special Colt, but Atchison insisted on the smaller .32 ACP Savage.

Atchison held out an envelope to Frankie.

"You get this on delivery, you understand?"

Frankie took the envelope and thumbed through the thick stack of bills.

"You leave it in the desk," Frankie ordered, handing the envelope back to Atchison. "If it's there when I come back, I do it."

Frankie next checked the functioning of the .44 Russian cowboy six-shooter, and finally the .32 Savage automatic.

He put them back in the corrugated paper box and folded the mechanic's rags back over them.

"I sort of wish you'd take those with you," Atchison said. "What if somebody comes down here and maybe finds them?"

"You see that don't happen. I'm not going to wander around Center City with three guns."

Atchison looked like he was going to say something, but changed his mind.

"I'll show you the door," he said.

Frankie followed him out of the office and farther down the corridor to the rear of the building. There a shallow flight of stairs rose toward a steel double door.

With Frankie watching carefully, Atchison removed a chain-and-padlock from the steel doors, then opened the left double door far enough to insert the padlock so that there would be room for Frankie's fingers when he opened the door from the outside.

"Be careful when you do that. You let the door slip, you'll never get it open."

"I'm always careful, Gerry," Frankie said.

Atchison took the corrugated paper box with the pistols from Frankie and put it on the top stair, just below the steel door.

He turned and sighed audibly. Then he smiled and put out his hand to Frankie.

"Jesus!" Frankie said with contempt. "Make sure that envelope is where it's supposed to be," he said, then turned and walked purposefully down the narrow corridor toward the stairs.

FIVE

Detective Wallace H. Milham reported for duty in the Homicide Unit in the Roundhouse at midnight as his duty schedule called for. The alternative, he knew, was sitting around his apartment alone with a bottle of bourbon. Or sitting around in a bar somewhere, alone, which he thought would be an even dumber thing to do than getting plastered all by himself in his apartment.

It had been a really lousy day.

Wally told himself that he should have expected something lousy to happen—not something as lousy as this, but something—the other shoe to drop, so to speak, because things lately had been going so damned well. For eighteen months, things had really been lousy.

In what he was perfectly willing to admit was about the dumbest thing Wally had ever done in his life, he had gotten involved with his wife Adelaide's sister, Monica. Monica lived in Jersey, in Ocean City. Her husband was a short fat guy who sold insurance. Adelaide's and Monica's mother and dad owned a cottage close to the beach in Wildwood.

Everybody in the family—Adelaide's family; Wally was an only child—got to use the cottage. Adelaide had one other sister besides Monica, and two brothers. The Old Man—Adelaide's father—wouldn't take any money when anybody used it, which sort of bothered Wally, who liked to pay his own way and not be indebted to anybody. So when the place needed a paint job, he volunteered to do that. He told the Old Man that the way his schedule worked, there were often two or three days he had off in the middle of the week, when Adelaide was working in the library, and he would rather do something useful with that time than sit around the house watching the TV.

Which was true. When he offered to paint the cottage in Wildwood, that was all he had in mind, pay his way. Monica didn't come into his thinking at all.

But Charles, Monica's husband, got in the act. He said that if Wally was going to drive all the way over from Philly to do the labor, the least he could do was provide the materials. So he did. And Monica drove the paint down in their station wagon because Charles of course was at work.

And he didn't think about that either. The first two days he spent painting the cottage, he used up most of the paint that Charles had Monica drive down to give him, so he told Adelaide to call Monica to ask Charles if he wanted to provide more paint, or have Wally get it, in which case he would have to know where he'd gotten the first three gallons, so they could mix up some more that would match.

Adelaide told him that Charles said that the paint would be there waiting for him the next time he went to Wildwood. It wasn't, so he started painting with what was left, and just before noon Monica showed up with the paint, and said that Charles had told her to take him out to lunch, and not to take no for an answer, it was the least they could do for him.

So they went out for lunch, and he was surprised when

Monica tossed down three martinis, one after the other. He had never seen her take more than one drink at a time. And she started talking—women with a couple of drinks in them tend to do that—and she started out by saying that she was a little jealous of Adelaide because Adelaide was married to a man who had an exciting career, catching murderers, and Charles was a bore.

In more ways than one, she said, if Wally took her meaning.

And he told her that being a Homicide detective wasn't as exciting as people who didn't know thought it was, that most of it was pretty ordinary stuff, just asking questions until somebody came up with the answer.

She said, yeah, but he got to meet interesting, exciting people, and she asked him if he ever met any exciting women, and he told her no, but she said he was just saying that, and she'd bet that if he told her the truth, he got to meet a lot of exciting women.

That's when he realized what was going on, and if he had had half the sense he was born with, he would have stopped it right there, but he'd had three martinis too.

In her car on the way back to the Old Man's cottage, she kept letting her hand fall on his leg, and ten minutes after they got back to the cottage, they were having at it in the Old Man's and Grandma's bed.

Afterward, Monica told him she didn't know what had come over her, it must have been the martinis, and they could never let anything like that happen again. But the way she stuck her tongue down his throat when she kissed him good-bye, he knew that was what she was saying, not what she meant.

So far as he was concerned, that was it, the one time. It would be a long time before he ever let himself be alone with her again.

Two weeks after that, at eleven o'clock in the morning, he had just gotten out of bed and made himself a cup of coffee when the doorbell at the house rang and there was Monica.

She was in Philly to do some shopping, she said, and she thought she would take a chance and see if maybe Adelaide hadn't gone to work at the library and they could go together.

He told her no, Adelaide had gone to work, and wouldn't be home until five, five-thirty.

And she asked what about the kids, and he told her they were both at school and wouldn't be home until quarter to four.

And then she said that she just couldn't get him out of her mind, and since he hadn't called her or anything, she had come to see him.

Three weeks after that, Adelaide walked in on them and caught them in her bed, right in the middle of doing it.

The way Adelaide saw it, it was all his fault, and maybe, he thought, in a way it was. He had known what was going on.

Adelaide said she hoped that he would at least have the decency to get a civilized divorce, so that nobody in her family knew that it was Monica he was taking advantage of, and ruin her life too. She said that she would hate to tell the children what an unmitigated immoral sonofabitch their father was, and hoped he wouldn't make her.

There was a clause in the divorce that said he had to pay a certain amount to her, in addition to child support, so that she could learn a trade or a profession. She decided she would go back to college and get a degree in library science, and get a better job than the one she had, which was "clerical assistant," which meant that he would be giving her money for two years, maybe three. Or more. She was going only part time.

And then she met Greg. Greg was a great big good-looking guy who sold trucks for a living, and who made a hell of a lot more money doing that than Wally had ever made, even in Homicide.

Adelaide started to spend nights in Greg's apartment whenever Wally had the kids over the weekend or she could get the Old Man and Grandma to take them. Wally knew that, because he sometimes drove by Greg's apartment at midnight and saw her car, and then drove past again at three in the morning, and again at seven, and it was still there.

But she wasn't going to marry Greg, because the minute she married him, that was the end of her training for a new career at his expense. She as much as told him that, and let him know if he made any trouble for her about how she conducted her private affairs, she would have to tell the kids what a sonofabitch he was, seducing her own sister, caring only for himself and not for his family.

And then Adelaide had really surprised him two and a half months before by calling him up—she sounded like she was half in the bag on the phone—and telling him she had just come back from Elkton, Maryland, where she and Greg had tied the knot.

Which meant that he could stop paying for her career education and move out of the one-room apartment, which was all he could afford on what was left of his pay, into something at least decent.

And then he went to Lieutenant Sackerman's funeral, and met Helene. Jack Sackerman was an old-time Homicide detective, a good one. When Wally had first gone to Homicide, he had taken him under his wing and showed him how to operate. Wally thought that if it hadn't been for Jack Sackerman, he probably never would have gotten to stay in Homicide.

When Jack had started thinking about retirement, he knew he had to leave Homicide. Homicide detectives make good money, damned good money, because of all the overtime, but when they retire, they get the same retirement pay as any other detective, and that's not much. So Jack had taken the examination for sergeant, and passed that, and they assigned him to Narcotics. Then he took the lieutenant's examination, and passed that, and they kept him in Narcotics. He was getting ready for the captain's examination when they discovered the cancer. And that, of course, was that.

Everybody from Narcotics was at Jack's viewing, of course, and that's when he met Helene and her husband. Captain Talley, the Narcotics Commander, introduced them. Her husband, Officer Kellog, had on a suit and a tie, but he still looked like a bum. Anybody who worked Plainclothes Narcotics had to dress like he was part of the drug business, so it was understandable—when Lieutenant Pekach, who was now a Captain in Special Operations, was running Undercover Narcotics, he actually had a pigtail—but he still looked like a bum.

He met Helene first at the viewing, and then the next day at the reception at Sackerman's house after the funeral, and a third time at Emmett's Place bar, where a bunch of the mourners went after they left Sackerman's house. Jack had had a lot of friends.

Her husband wasn't with her at Emmett's Place, but they seemed to wind up together and started talking. Wally was attracted to her, but didn't come on to her. Only a stupid bird dirties his own nest, and she was married to a cop.

After that, they kept bumping into each other. She worked for the City in the Municipal Services Building in Center City, and he was always around the City Hall courtrooms or the DA's Office, in the same area, so that was understandable. Wally ran into Helene one time on his way to the Reading Terminal Market for lunch and asked her if she wanted a cheese steak or something, and she said yes and went with him.

After that, they started meeting once or twice a week for lunch, or sometimes dinner, and she let him understand that things weren't perfect with her husband, but she never told him—and he didn't ask—what specifically was wrong between them. He told her about Adelaide, what had happened. And absolutely nothing happened between them, he didn't so much as try to hold her hand, until the night she called him, three days after he'd moved into the new apartment, and sounded as if she was crying.

Wally asked her what the matter was, and she said she

was calling from the Roosevelt Motor Inn, on Roosevelt Boulevard, that what had happened was that she had finally left the sonofabitch—he remembered that she had used that word, because it was the first time she had ever said anything nasty about him—and needed to talk to somebody.

He said sure, and did she want him to come out there and pick her up and they could go somewhere for a drink, and she said it wouldn't look right, in case somebody saw them, for him to pick her up at a motel. And as far as that went, it wouldn't look right if somebody saw them having a drink someplace the very night she moved out on her husband.

So Wally had asked her, did she maybe want to come to his apartment, and Helene said she didn't know, what did he think, and she didn't want to impose or anything.

So he told her to get in a taxi and come down. And she did. And before she got there, he went to a Chinese restaurant and got some takeout to go with the bottle of wine he knew he had somewhere at home. He didn't want to offer her a drink of whiskey, to keep her from getting the wrong idea. All he wanted to be was a friend, offering her something to eat and wine, and a sympathetic ear.

She didn't even take the wine when he offered it to her, but she wolfed down the Chinese, and he was glad he thought of that, and while he watched her eat, he decided that if she wanted to talk about her husband, fine, and if she didn't, fine, too.

When she finished, she smiled at him and asked him if he thought she would be terrible if she asked for a drink. She really needed a drink.

So he made her one and handed it to her, and she started to take a sip and then started crying and he put his arm around her, and one thing led to another, and that was the way they started.

Whatever was wrong between her and her husband wasn't that she was frigid, or anything like that.

And she told him, afterward, that the truth of the matter was that she had been thinking about him and her like that from the very first time she saw him, at Lieutenant Sackerman's viewing; that he was really an attractive man.

So at five o'clock in the morning, he took her back to the Roosevelt Motor Inn on Roosevelt Boulevard, and met her in City Hall at noon, after she'd talked to a lawyer, and they went to his apartment so they could talk without worrying about people at the next table in a restaurant listening in. They didn't do much talking about what the lawyer said, except that it was going to be harder getting a divorce than she thought it would be.

She took a tiny apartment so that her family wouldn't ask questions, but from the first they lived together, and they got along just fine, and without coming right out and talking about it, they understood that as soon as she got him to agree to the divorce, they would get married. With what they made between them, they could live pretty well. They talked about getting a larger apartment, maybe even a house, so there would be room for his kids when he had them on weekends or whenever.

They never talked much about what bad had happened between her and Kellog, but he got the feeling it had something to do with Kellog being dirty on the job. She knew something, and Wally knew if he pressed her, he could get it out of her.

But then what? For one thing, she might not know what she was talking about, and for another, dirty cops are Internal Affairs' business, not his. If he learned something he felt he had to tell somebody about, it would come out that he and Helene were living together, and it would look as if he was trying to frame the sonofabitch.

And then the sonofabitch gets himself shot. And guess who they think had something to with it?

Kellog was in Narcotics. If they ever found out who the doer, or doers, were, it was ten-to-one it would have something to do with Narcotics. But they might not ever find the doers, and until they did, Helene was going to be a suspect, and so was he.

The interview in Homicide was the most humiliating thing that Wally could remember ever having to go through. Except maybe being driven to his apartment by Ken Summers to pick up his guns, and having Ken look around "professionally" to see what he could see that might connect him with the Kellog shooting.

And when he finally got to see Helene, he could see that she had been crying, and she told him that D'Amata and Staff Inspector Weisbach had been to see her, and that she thought it would be better for everybody concerned if they didn't see each other until things settled down, at least until after the funeral, and that she was going to the apartment right then to pick up her things and take them to her apartment. And that she thought it would be better if he didn't try to see her, or even telephone, until she thought it would be all right, and when she thought it would be she would telephone him.

She didn't even kiss him before she walked away.

Wally did the only thing he could think of doing. He worked on the Grover job. And nothing. Not from interviewing neighbors or friends, or what he learned from New Haven. She did not have an insurance policy on her husband, except for the ones she told him about. And neither did anyone else.

But she did him. Wally was sure about that. Somehow, he was going to get her.

He went to the apartment about six and had a beer and made himself a hamburger, and it was pretty goddamned lonely. Then he tried to sleep, setting the alarm for eleven. With nothing else to do, he might as well go to work.

He woke up at nine-thirty, alone in their bed, and couldn't get back to sleep, and got up and drank a beer, and then he thought about going to a bar and having a couple of drinks, and fuck going to work. Captain Quaire had told him to take off what time he needed.

But he knew that would be dumb, so he just had the one

beer, and took a shower and a shave and left the apartment at half past eleven for the Roundhouse.

A new Plymouth sedan slowed to a near stop in front of the Delaware Valley Cancer Society Building on Rittenhouse Square, and then slowly and carefully put the right-side wheels on the curb, finally stopping equidistant between two signs announcing that this was a No Parking At Any Time Tow Away Zone.

The door opened and a very large, black, impeccably dressed gentleman got out. He was Sergeant Jason Washington of the Special Operations Division of the Philadelphia Police Department, known—behind his back, of course—to his peers as "the Black Buddha."

He believed himself to be the best investigator in the Philadelphia Police Department. This opinion was shared by a number of others, including the Honorable Jerome H. "Jerry" Carlucci, Mayor of the City of Brotherly Love, by Inspector Peter Wohl, Commanding Officer of the Special Operations Division, for whom Washington worked, and by Detective Matthew M. Payne, who worked for Sergeant Washington.

Sergeant Washington was wearing a light gray pin-striped suit. His Countess Mara necktie was fixed precisely in place at the collar of a custom-made crisply starched white Egyptian cotton shirt, and gold cuff links bearing his initials gleamed at the shirt's cuffs.

For most of their married life, Jason Washington and his wife had lived frugally, although their combined income had been above average. He had spent most of his career in Homicide, where overtime routinely meant a paycheck at least as large as an inspector's, and Martha had a very decent salary as an artist for a Center City advertising agency.

They had put money away faithfully for the education of their only child, a daughter, and they had invested what they could carefully, and, it turned out, wisely.

In the last three or four years, they had become affluent.

Their daughter had married (much too young, they agreed) an electrical engineer, at whom (they also agreed) RCA in Cherry Hill seemed to throw money. Her marriage had, of course, relieved them of the expense of her college education, and at about the same time, what had begun as Martha's dabbling in the art market had suddenly blossomed into the amazingly profitable Washington Galleries on Chestnut Street.

They could afford to live well, and did.

Sergeant Washington walked to the plate-glass door of the Cancer Society Building and waited until it was opened to him by the rent-a-cop on duty.

"Is Supercop at home?" Sergeant Washington greeted him. The rent-a-cop was a retired police officer whom Washington had known for years.

"Came in about ten minutes ago. What's he done now?"

"Since he works for me, I'm embarrassed to tell you," Washington said, and then had a sudden thought: "Did he come home alone?"

"For once," the rent-a-cop said.

"Good. I would not like to redden the ears of his girlfriend with what I have to say to him," Washington said, smiling, as he got into the elevator.

He rode to the third floor, then pushed a doorbell beside a closed door.

"Yes?" A voice came over an intercom.

"Would you please let me in, Matthew?"

"Hey, Jason, sure."

The door's solenoid buzzed and Washington opened the door. He climbed a steep, narrow flight of stairs. Matt Payne waited for him, smiling.

"Don't smile," Washington said. "I just had a call from Tony Harris vis-à-vis your human-fly stunt, you goddamned fool! What the hell is the matter with you?"

"The Lieutenant's lady friend opened the window and knocked the mike suction cup loose. We weren't getting anything at all."

"These people are not plotting the overthrow of Christian

society as we know it, you damned fool! We have some dirty cops, that's all. Not one of them, not this whole investigation, is worth risking your life over."

"Yes, sir."

"Good God, Matt! What were you thinking?"

Matt didn't reply.

"I would hate to think that you were trying to prove your all-around manhood," Washington said.

It was a reference to one of the reasons offered for a nice young man from the Main Line electing to follow a police career instead of a legal one. He had failed, at the last minute before entering upon active duty, the Marine Corps' Pre-Commissioning Physical Exam. He had then, the theory went, joined the Police Department as a means to prove his masculinity.

"I was thinking I could put the mike back without getting hurt," Matt said coldly. "And I did."

Washington saw in his eyes that he had gotten through to him. He fixed him with an icy glance for another thirty seconds, which seemed much longer.

Then he smiled, just a little.

"It would seem to me, considering the sacrifice it has meant for me to come here at this late hour to offer you my wise counsel, that the least you could do would be to offer me a small libation. Perhaps some of the Famous Grouse scotch?"

"Sure, sorry," Matt said, smiling. He went into his kitchen. As he opened first one, and then another over-the-sink cabinet, he called, "What are you doing out this late?"

"Our beloved Mayor has been gracious enough to find time to offer me *his* wise counsel."

"Really?"

"Specifically, he is of the opinion that we should go to Officers Crater and Palmerston and offer them immunity from prosecution in exchange for their testimony against Captain Cazerra and Lieutenant Meyer."

"Jason," Matt said, "I can't find a bottle of any kind of scotch. Not even Irish."

"I am not surprised," Washington said. "It's been one of those days. Get your coat. We will pub crawl for a brief period."

"There's some rum and gin. And vermouth. I could make you a martini."

"Get your coat, Matthew," Washington said. "I accept your kind offer of a drink at the Rittenhouse Club bar."

"Oh, thank you, kind sir," Matt said, mockingly, and started shrugging into Chad Nesbitt's tweed jacket. "I think the Mayor's idea stinks."

"Why?"

"Because any lawyer six weeks out of law school could tear them up on the stand, and we know Cazerra and Meyer's lawyers will be good."

"Armando C. Giacomo, Esquire," Washington agreed, citing the name of Philadelphia's most competent criminal lawyer. "Or someone of his ilk. Perhaps even the legendary Colonel J. Dunlop Mawson, Esquire."

Matt laughed. "No way. My father would go ballistic. I'm ready."

"I made that point to His Honor," Washington said as he pushed himself out of one of Matt's small armchairs.

"And?"

"And as usual got nowhere. Or almost nowhere. We have two weeks to get something on Cazerra and Meyer that will stand up in court. He wants those two in jail."

"Or what?"

"We work Crater and Palmerston over, figuratively speaking of course, with a rubber hose."

"What does Wohl say?" Matt asked as he waved Washington ahead of him down the stairs.

"I haven't told him yet. I figured I would ruin tomorrow for him by doing that first thing in the morning."

The Rittenhouse Club was closed when they got there.

"What do we do now?" Matt asked.

"Why don't we take a stroll down Market Street?"

Washington replied. "It will both give us a chance to see how the other half lives, and trigger memories of those happy days when Officer Washington was walking his first beat."

"You walked a beat on Market Street?" Matt asked. It was difficult for him to imagine Washington in a police officer's uniform, patrolling Market Street.

Officer Friendly Black Buddha, he thought, *impeccably tailored and shined, smiling somewhat menacingly as he slapped his palm with his nightstick.*

"Indeed I did. Under the able leadership of Lieutenant Dennis V. Coughlin. And on *our* watch," Washington announced sonorously, "the thieves and mountebanks plied their trade in someone else's district."

"Police Emergency," David Meach said into his headset.

"This is the Inferno Lounge," his caller announced. "1908 Market. There's been a shooting, and somebody may be dead."

"Your name, sir, please?"

"Shit!" the caller responded and hung up.

David Meach had been on the job six years, long enough to be able to unconsciously make judgments regarding the validity of a call, based on not only what was said, but how it was said. Whether, for example, the caller sounded mature (as opposed to an excited kid wanting to give the cops a little exercise) and whether or not there was excitement or tension or a certain numbness in his voice. This call sounded legitimate; he didn't think he'd be sending police cars racing through downtown Philadelphia for no purpose.

He checked to see what was available.

RPC Nine Ten seemed closest to the scene. Meach pressed a key to send two short attention beeps across the airways, then activated his microphone:

"All cars stand by. 1908 Market Street, the Inferno

Lounge, report of a shooting and a hospital case. Nine Ten, you have the assignment."

The response was immediate.

"Nine Ten, got it," Officer Edward Schirmer called into the microphone of Radio Patrol Car Number Ten of the Ninth District, as Officer Lewis Roberts, who was driving the car down Walnut Street, reached down to the dashboard and activated the siren and flashing lights.

"Nine Seven in on that," another voice reported, that of Officer Frederick E. Rogers, in RPC Nine Seven.

"Highway Thirteen, in on the 1908 Market," responded Officer David Fowler.

"Nine Oh One, got it," responded Officer Adolphus Hart, who was riding in one of the two vans assigned to the Ninth District.

Nine Oh One had five minutes before left the Police Administration Building at Eighth and Race streets, after having transferred two prisoners from the holding cells at the Ninth District to Central Lockup.

Officer Thomas Daniels, who was driving Nine Oh One, had for no good reason at all elected to drive up Market Street and was by happenstance able to be the first police vehicle responding to the "Shooting and Hospital Case" call to reach the scene.

There was nothing at all unusual about the location when they pulled to the curb. The Inferno Lounge's neon-flames sign was not illuminated, and the establishment seemed to be closed for the night.

He stopped just long enough to permit Officer Hart to jump out of the van and walk quickly to the door of the Inferno, and to see if Hart could open the door. He couldn't. Then he turned left on Ludlow Street, so that he could block the rear entrance.

Two civilians, a very large black man and a tall young white man, both very well dressed, were walking down Nineteenth Street, toward Market. They could have, Officer

Daniels reasoned, just come out of the alley behind the Inferno.

Officer Daniels, sounding his horn, drove the van into the alley, blocking it, and jumped out of the van.

"Hold it right there, please!" he called out.

His order proved to be unnecessary. The two civilians had stopped, turned, and were looking at him with curiosity.

While a Pedestrian Stop was of course necessary, Officer Daniels made the snap judgment that it was unlikely that these two had anything to do with whatever—if anything—had happened at the Inferno. They hadn't run, for one thing, and they didn't look uncomfortable.

Officer Daniels had an unkind thought: This area was an unusual place to take a stroll after midnight, unless, of course, the two were cruising for women. Or men. Maybe they had just found each other.

"Excuse me, sir," Daniels said. "May I please see some identification?"

The younger man laughed. Daniels glowered at him.

"We're police officers," the black man said. "What have you got?"

The younger one exhibited a detective's badge.

"What's going on here, Officer?" the black man asked.

Officer Daniels hesitated just perceptibly before replying: "Shooting and hospital case inside the Inferno."

"Was the front door open?" the black man asked.

"No."

"I'll go block the front," the black man said. "The rear door to this place is halfway down the alley. There's usually a garbage can full of beer bottles, and so on." He turned to the young white man. "You go with him, Matt."

The young man sort of stooped, and when he stood erect again, there was a snub-nose revolver in his hand.

Officer Daniels looked dubiously at the black man.

"I told you to go with him," the black man said to Officer Daniels, a tone of command in his voice. Then he started to trot toward Market Street.

Officer Daniels ran after the young white man and caught up with him.

"Who is that guy?" he asked.

"That is Sergeant Jason Washington. He just told me he used to walk this beat."

"He doesn't have any authority here."

"You tell him that," Matt said, chuckling as he continued down the alley.

The sound of dying sirens and the squeal of tires announced the arrival of other police vehicles.

The alley between the buildings was pitch dark, and twice Matt stumbled over something he hadn't seen. There was more light when he reached the end of the alley, coming down what had been in Colonial times a cobblestone street but was now not much more than a garbage-littered alley.

He found the Inferno Lounge's garbage cans. As Jason had said they would be, they were filled to overflowing with kitchen scraps and beer bottles.

He went to a metal door and tried it. It opened.

If there was somebody in here, they're probably gone. The door would ordinarily be locked.

He stepped to one side, hiding, so to speak, behind the bricks of the building, and then pulled the door fully open.

"Police officers!" he called.

There was no response.

He looked very carefully around the bricks. There was no one in sight, but he could see a corridor dimly illuminated by the lights burning in the kitchen, and beyond that, in the public areas of the bar, or restaurant, or whatever the hell this place was.

"Stay here," he ordered Officer Daniels, and then entered the building and started down the corridor. Halfway down it, he saw a flight of stairs leading to the basement, and saw lights down there. It was possible that someone was down in the basement; he was pleased with himself for having told the wagon uniform to stay at the back door.

He went carefully through the kitchen, and then into the public area of the restaurant. There was banging on the closed front door of the place, and someone—not Jason, but to judge by the depth of his voice, not the young guy in the wagon, either—was calling, not quite shouting, "Police, open up."

The door was closed with a keyed dead bolt. There were keys in it. It was hard to unlock. Matt had shoved his pistol in his hip pocket and used both hands to get it open.

There was a uniformed sergeant standing there, and two Highway Patrolmen. Behind them Matt could see Jason Washington looking for all the world like a curious civilian.

"What have you got, Payne?" one of the Highway Patrolmen said. Matt recalled having met him somewhere. He couldn't recall his name.

"Nothing yet. I figured I'd better let you guys in."

"How'd you get in?"

"Back door was unlocked. The wagon guy's covering it."

"Who are you?" the uniformed sergeant asked.

"He's Detective Payne of Special Operations," Jason answered for him. "And I am Sergeant Washington. Nothing, Matt?"

"Nothing on the floor. There's a basement, I didn't get down there."

"I think we should have a look," Washington said, and moving with a quick grace, suddenly appeared in front of the two Highway Patrolmen and the uniformed sergeant. "Lead on, Matthew!"

Matt turned and walked quickly back through the bar, the restaurant, and the kitchen to the corridor, then started down the stairs. Washington stopped him with a massive hand on his shoulder.

"Announce your arrival," he said softly. "You don't know what you're going to find down there, and if the proprietor, for example, is down there, you want to be sure he knows the man coming down the stairs is a police officer."

"Police!" Matt called.

"Down here!" a male voice called.

The stairs led to a narrow corridor, and the corridor to a small office.

The first thing Matt saw was a somewhat stocky man in his forties sitting behind a battered desk, in the act of taking a pull from the neck of a bottle of Seagram's VO. There was a Colt Cobra revolver lying on the desk.

The next thing Matt saw, as he entered the office, was a young female, white, sitting in a chair. Her head was hanging limply back. Her eyes were open and her head, neck, and chest were covered with blood. She was obviously dead. On the floor, lying on his side in a thick pool of blood, was the body of a heavy man. His arm was stretched out, nearly touching the desk.

Matt looked at the man behind the desk.

"What happened here?"

"I was held up," the man said.

"By who?"

Matt looked at the office door and saw that Jason Washington and one of the Highway Patrolmen had stepped inside the office.

"Two white guys."

"Are you all right?"

"I was shot in the leg," the man said.

Matt crossed to him and saw that he had his right leg extended, and that the trouser leg between the knee and the groin was soaked in blood.

"Can you describe the men?" Matt asked.

"There was two of them," the man said. "One was a short, stocky sonofabitch, and the other was about as big as I am."

"How were they dressed?"

"The little fucker was in a suit; the other one was wearing a zipper jacket."

"Mustaches, beards, anything like that?"

The man shook his head.

Jason Washington turned to the Highway Patrolman standing beside him.

"Get out a flash on that," he said softly. "And tell Police Radio that Sergeant Washington and Detective Payne of Special Operations are at the scene of what appears to be an armed robbery and double homicide."

SIX

"That was interesting," Sergeant Edward McCarthy of the Homicide Unit said to Detective Wallace J. Milham as he walked up to a desk where Milham was trying to catch up with his paperwork. Milham looked at McCarthy with mingled curiosity and annoyance at having been disturbed.

"Radio just told me we have a *double* homicide at the Inferno Lounge," McCarthy said. "No names on the victims yet, but the report came from Police by radio. A Ninth District van, relaying a message from none other than Sergeant Jason Washington of Special Operations, who is apparently on the scene."

"I wonder what that's all about." Milham chuckled. "That neighborhood, and especially that joint, is not the Black Buddha's style. Who's got the job?"

"You're the assigned detective, Detective Milham," McCarthy said.

106

"Give me thirty seconds," Milham said. "Let me finish this page."

"Take your time. The victims aren't going anywhere," McCarthy said, and added, "I'm going to see if I can find the Captain."

Captain Henry C. Quaire, Commanding Officer of the Homicide Unit, was located attending a social function—the annual dinner of the vestry of St. John's Lutheran Church—in the Bellvue-Stratford Hotel with his wife when Sergeant McCarthy reached him.

"Where are you, Mac?"

"In the Roundhouse."

"Pick me up outside. I'll be waiting for you."

"Yes, sir."

Preoccupied with his concern about what his wife would say when he told her she would have to drive herself home—a dire prediction of tight lips and a back turned coldly toward him in their bed when he finally got home, a prediction that was to come true—Captain Quaire neglected to inquire of Sergeant McCarthy whether or not he had gotten in touch with Chief Inspector Matthew Lowenstein. The Chief liked to be notified of all interesting jobs, no matter what the hour, and a double willful killing would qualify by itself. With Washington somehow involved, he would be even more interested.

He would, he decided, try to get on a phone while waiting for McCarthy to pick him up. That idea went out the window when he stepped off the elevator and saw Mac's car waiting for him outside on South Broad Street.

"I don't suppose you got in touch with the Chief?" he asked as he got in the car.

McCarthy turned on the flashing lights and the siren and made a U-turn on Broad Street.

"I didn't have to," McCarthy replied. "I got a call from Radio, saying the Chief was going in on this, and would somebody call his wife and tell her he was delayed."

"Who are the victims? Do we know yet?"

"I'm praying that it was a family dispute," McCarthy said.

Quaire chuckled. Sergeant McCarthy was not referring to a disagreement between husband and wife, but to one between members of Philadelphia's often violent Mafia.

"Who's assigned?" Quaire asked.

"Wally Milham. You didn't say anything . . ."

"Sure. He was up, he got the job. I don't think he had anything to do with Kellog."

"I wonder who did that."

"Nothing's turned up?"

"Not a thing."

By the time Detective Milham pulled up in front of the Inferno Lounge, there were nine police vehicles, including three unmarked cars, parked on Market Street. Without consciously doing so, he picked out the anomaly. The three unmarked cars were battered and worn. Therefore, none of them belonged to Sergeant Jason Washington, whose brand-new unmarked car had been the subject of much conversation in the Homicide Unit.

Wally wondered if McCarthy had been pulling his chain about Washington being in on this; or if someone had been pulling McCarthy's chain.

There was a uniformed cop standing at the door who recognized Milham and let him in. Inside the Inferno, Milham saw three detectives whom he knew: David Rocco of the Central Detective Division; John Hanson of the Major Theft Unit; and Wilfred "Wee Willy" Malone, a six-foot-four-inch giant of a man assigned to the Intelligence Unit. That explained the three unmarked cars.

Rocco and Hanson gave him a wave. Wee Willy looked at him strangely. Wally wondered if he had heard about Kellog; that he had been interviewed and that they were checking his guns at Ballistics.

"We're glad you're here," Rocco said. "*Sergeant* Washington is with the victims, protecting the scene until the arrival of the hotshots—one of which presumably is you, Wally—of Homicide."

"If you less important people would learn not to walk all over our evidence, that wouldn't be necessary," Wally replied, and then, not seeing Washington: "Where's the Black Buddha?"

"Oh, shit," Hanson said, and laughed and then pointed. "There's a stairway off the corridor in back. There's an office downstairs."

Wally found the stairs and went down them. Washington heard him coming, and turned with an impatient look on his face until he recognized him.

"Good morning, Detective Milham," Washington said.

"Hello, Jason. What have we got?"

"Have you the acquaintance of Detective Payne?"

"Only by reputation," Milham said, and offered the young detective his hand.

"Detective Payne and myself, by pure coincidence," Washington went on, "were taking the air on Nineteenth Street when the first police vehicle to respond to the call—Officers Adolphus Hart and Thomas Daniels, in Wagon Nine Oh One, they are upstairs—arrived. In the absence of anyone more senior, I took charge of the scene, and being aware that the front door of the premises was steel and locked, ordered Detective Payne to attempt to enter the building from the rear, and sent Officer Daniels with him. Detective Payne was able to gain entrance. He left Officer Daniels to guard the rear door, proceeded through the building, and opened the front door, which was locked from the inside, and admitted me. With Detective Payne leading the way, we searched the building, and came upon the scene of the crime.

"We found Mr. Gerald Atchison, one of the proprietors of this establishment, sitting behind the desk. Mr. Atchison told us he was in the bar upstairs when he heard the sound, a popping noise, of what he now presumes was gunfire. When he went to investigate, he encountered in the corridor upstairs two white males, armed—a flash has gone out with their descriptions—who fired upon him, striking him in the leg. He drew his own pistol . . ."

Jason paused.

"Matthew, give Detective Milham the pistol, please."

Matt turned to a filing cabinet. Carefully placing his fingers on the checkered wooden handles, he picked up a Colt Cobra revolver and extended it to Milham. Wally took a plastic bag from his jacket pocket and held it open until Matt dropped the revolver into it.

". . . which Mr. Atchison is licensed by the Sheriff of Delaware County to carry," Washington went on, "and a gun battle during which Mr. Atchison suffered the wound to his leg ensued. Mr. Atchison fell to the floor. He lay there he doesn't know how long."

"It's starting to hurt," Atchison said.

"A police wagon is outside, Mr. Atchison," Washington said. "In just a moment, you will be transported to a hospital. Have I reported the essence of your discussion with Detective Payne accurately?"

"A short fucker and big one did this," Atchison replied.

"After he knows not how long he laid on the floor, Mr. Atchison reports that he recovered sufficiently to become aware that his assailants were no longer present. He then descended the stairs to the office, where he found the bodies of his wife and his business partner. He thereupon sat down at his desk, called Police Emergency to report what had happened, and then took a drink of whiskey against the pain of his wound. Am I still correct, Mr. Atchison?"

"I knew they were dead," Mr. Atchison said.

"Yes, of course, you could see that," Washington said, and then continued: "I then instructed a Highway officer to report to Police Radio that I had come upon evidence of a double homicide. I then secured the scene of the crime, pending the arrival of someone from the Homicide Unit. No one but Detective Payne and myself have entered the scene. And un-

less there is some other question you would like to ask of either of us, Detective Payne and myself will now be on our
way. Barring stringent objections, we will prepare state-
ments regarding our involvement in this incident, and have
them at Homicide Unit before noon tomorrow. Do you have
any questions, Wally?"

"No, Jason," Milham said, smiling. "That covers everything neatly."

The day Wally had reported for duty as a Homicide detective, during his "welcome aboard" interview with then
Lieutenant Quaire, Quaire had pulled a Homicide Investigation binder from the file and handed it to him.

"Don't let him know I showed you this, Milham, his ego
is bad enough as it is, but this is what you should try for."

"What is it, sir?"

"It's a real Homicide report, Detective Jason Washington's, of a homicide in the course of an armed robbery, but
it's also a textbook example of what a completed Homicide
binder should be. Everything is in it, in the right sequence,
there's no ambivalence, there's no duplication, there's no
procedural errors, no spelling or grammatical mistakes, and
if there are any type-overs, I can't find one."

"That being the case, Wally, I leave this matter in your capable hands. Shall we be on our way, Matt?"

"I got to get medical attention," Mr. Atchison said. "My
goddamned leg is starting to hurt."

"We regret the delay, Mr. Atchison," Washington said.
"But I am sure that you are even more interested than we are
in apprehending the people who murdered your wife and
business associate, and it was necessary for me to put what
information I have regarding this tragic incident in the hands
of the police officer who will be in charge of the investigation."

"Yeah. I want those bastards caught. And fried."

"Good night, sir," Washington said. "Thank you for your
patience."

He turned, and met Wally Milham's eyes. Then he wrinkled his nose, as if smelling something rotten.

"Good night, Detective Milham," he said, and took Matt's arm and propelled him out of the room.

There were well over a dozen police vehicles of all kinds, among them Chief Inspector Matthew Lowenstein's Oldsmobile sedan, parked on the street and on the sidewalk in front of the Inferno Lounge, when Captain Quaire and Sergeant McCarthy arrived.

Captain Thomas Curran of the Central Detective Division was standing on the sidewalk with Staff Inspector Michael Weisbach and Captain Alexander Smith of the Ninth District, but neither Chief Lowenstein nor his driver was anywhere in sight.

"The Chief is inside," Curran explained. "Enter at your own risk. He told us to wait out here, and Weisbach was with him when he drove up. He is not in a good mood."

"Washington's in there?" Quaire asked.

"Which may explain his mood." Curran nodded. "Washington, and that kid, Payne, who shot the rapist. And Milham. Milham just got here."

"You better wait, too, Mac," Quaire said, and walked to the entrance of the Inferno Lounge, where a uniform pulled the door open for him.

Quaire found Chief Lowenstein not where he expected to find him, wherever the bodies were, but in the restaurant area of the Inferno, sitting at a table with Sergeant Jason Washington and Detective Matthew M. Payne.

"Good evening, sir," Quaire said.

"Sergeant Washington's sole function in this has been to keep Highway from walking all over the evidence," Lowenstein said. "The bodies are downstairs. Milham's down there."

"Who are the victims?" Quaire asked.

"One white female, Alicia Atchison," Washington answered. "The wife of the proprietor, one Gerry Atchison.

And Mr. Atchison's business partner, one Anthony J. Marcuzzi. Mr. Atchison contends that two white males shot them in the course of a robbery, during which he was himself shot, as he bravely attempted to defend his wife, his property, and his friend and business associate."

He pinched his nose with his thumb and his index finger, which might have been a simple, innocent gesture, or might have been an indication that he believed Mr. Atchison's version of what had transpired smelled like rotten fish.

"I'll go have a look," Quaire said.

"Take Detective Payne with you," Lowenstein said. "He might be useful—he was first on the scene—and he might learn something."

Matt Payne, looking a little surprised, stood up.

Chief Lowenstein waited until Quaire and Payne were out of earshot, then turned to Washington.

"Jason, we've been friends for a long time."

" 'Uh-oh,' the Apache warrior said, aware that he was about to be schmoozed by the Big Chief,' " Washington said.

Lowenstein smiled, and then the smile vanished.

"I know what you're doing, Jason."

"Excuse me?"

"And for what it's worth, if I had to pick somebody to do it, it would be you. Or Peter Wohl. Or the both of you, which is the way I hear it is."

"Chief, we have been friends a long time, and what you're doing is putting me on a hell of a spot."

"Yeah, and I know it. But goddamn it . . ."

Washington looked at him, met his eyes, but said nothing.

"I'm going to ask you some questions. If you feel you can answer them, answer them. If you feel you can't, don't."

Washington didn't reply, but after a moment, nodded his head.

"How bad is it?"

Washington, after ten seconds, which seemed like much longer, said, "Bad."

"How high does it go?"

"There's a captain involved."

"Suspicion, or something that can be proved?"

Washington thought that question over before replying.

"There will be indictments."

Lowenstein met his eyes and exhaled audibly.

"Anybody I know?"

"Chief, you know a lot of people."

"If I ran some names by you, would you nod your head?"

"No."

"Mike Weisbach heard some talk abut Vito Cazerra."

Washington didn't reply.

"He's working on it. Weisbach's a damned good investigator."

Washington remained silent, his face fixed.

"The name of Seymour Meyer also came up."

"Chief, we're not having this conversation," Washington said. "If we were, I'd have to report it."

Lowenstein met Washington's eyes.

"How much time do I have?"

Washington shrugged, then said, "Very little."

"Are you going to tell the Mayor I cornered you and we had this little chat?"

"What little chat?"

"OK, Jason," Lowenstein said. "Thanks."

Washington made a deprecating gesture.

Lowenstein stood up and looked down at Washington.

"Does Denny Coughlin know what's going on?" he asked.

It was a moment before Washington, just perceptibly, shook his head no.

Lowenstein considered that, nodded his head, and turned and walked out of the Inferno Lounge.

Wally Milham was not surprised to see Captain Henry Quaire come into the basement office of the Inferno Lounge. Quaire routinely showed up at the scene of an interesting murder, and this double murder qualified. Wally was surprised and annoyed, however, to see Detective Payne with him.

"What have we got, Wally?" Quaire asked.

Wally told him, ending his synopsis with the announcement that he was about to have Mr. Atchison transported to Hahnemann Hospital for treatment of his leg wound.

"You're ready for the technicians?" Quaire asked. "They're here."

"Yes, sir."

"I'll go get them," Quaire said. "We want to do this by the book. Chief Lowenstein's here, too. Keep me posted on this one, Wally."

"Yes, sir."

Since Detective Payne had arrived with Captain Quaire, Detective Milham reasonably presumed that he would leave with him. He didn't.

What the hell is he hanging around for?

"I've been thinking that maybe I better talk to my lawyer," Mr. Atchison said. "With something like this happening, I'm not thinking too clear."

"Certainly," Wally said. "I understand."

"How long do you think it will take at the hospital?" Mr. Atchison asked.

"No telling," Wally replied. "An hour, anyway. There'd be time for him to meet you there, if that's what you're thinking."

"And I'm going to need a ride home," Mr. Atchison said. "I can't drive with my leg like this."

"Have you got his number? Would you like me to call him for you?" Wally asked solicitously.

"I'll call him," Atchison said, and, grunting, sat up and moved toward the desk.

"It would be better if you didn't use that phone, sir," Matt said, and when Atchison looked at him, continued: "We'd like our technicians to see if there are any fingerprints on it. That would be helpful, when we find the men who did this to you, to prove that they were here in this room."

What's this "we" shit? This is my job, pal, not yours. Butt the hell out.

"Yeah, sure."

"There will be a telephone in the hospital, I'm sure," Matt went on. "Or, if you would like us to, we can get word to him to meet you at Hahnemann Hospital."

More of this "we" shit! Just who the hell do you think you are, Payne?

"That's very nice of you," Atchison said. "His name is Sidney Margolis. I got his number here in the card file."

He started to reach for it, and Matt stopped him.

"It would be better, Mr. Atchison, if you didn't touch that, either, until the technicians have done their thing. Is he in the phone book? Or is his number unlisted?"

"I remember it," Atchison said, triumphantly calling it forth from his memory.

"If you give that to me again," Matt said, "I'd be happy to call him for you."

"Would you, please? Tell him what happened here, and ask him to meet me at Hahnemann."

Matt took a small notebook from his pocket and wrote the number down.

"Can I see you a minute, Payne?" Wally said, and took Matt's arm and led him out of the office. "Be right with you, Mr. Atchison."

He led Matt a dozen steps down the corridor, then stopped.

"I don't know who the hell you think you are, Payne," he snapped. "But shut your fucking mouth. This is my job. When I want some help, I'll ask for it."

"Sorry," Matt said. "I was just trying to help."

"Do me a favor. Don't."

"OK. Sorry."

Wally's anger had not subsided.

"I'll tell you what I do want you to do," he said. "First, give me that lawyer's phone number, and then get your ass down to the Roundhouse and wait for me there. I want your

statement. I may have to put up with that 'I'll get my statement to you in the morning' shit from Washington, but I
don't have to put up with it from you."

Matt, his face red, tore the page with the phone number
from his notebook and handed it to Wally. Wally took it and
went back down the corridor.

Matt watched him a moment, then went up the stairs, as
two uniformed officers, one carrying a stretcher, came down
them.

Chief Lowenstein was gone. Jason Washington, alone at
the table where they had been sitting, stood up when he saw
Matt.

"Well, did you learn anything?"

"A," Matt replied, "Detective Milham has all the charm
of a constipated alligator, and B, he wants my statement
tonight, not tomorrow."

Washington's right eyebrow rose in surprise.

"Shall I have a word with him?"

"No. No, thanks. Now that I think of it, I'd just as soon
get it over with now. I've got a busy day tomorrow."

"All right. Walk me back to your place, and I'll drop you
off at the Roundhouse on my way home. Or you can get
your car."

"I'll take the ride, thanks. And catch a cab home later."

Jason Washington was surprised and just a little alarmed
when he quietly let himself into his apartment to see that
there were lights on in the living room.

*Not only is the love of my life angry, but angry to the point
where she has decided that marital justice demands that she
wait up for me to express her displeasure personally, immediately, and in some detail.*

As he walked down the corridor, he heard Martha say,
somewhat formally, "I think that's him."

*Someone's with her. Someone she doesn't know well.
Who? And who else would it be at this hour of the morning?*

He walked into the living room. Martha, in a dressing

gown, was sitting on the couch. There was a coffee service on the coffee table. And a somewhat distraught-looking woman sitting in one of the armchairs, holding a coffee cup in her hands.

"Martha, I'm sorry to be so late. I was tied up."

"That happens, doesn't it?" Martha replied, the tone of her voice making it clear she thought he had been tied up by a slow-moving bartender.

"Good evening," Jason said to the distraught-looking woman.

"More accurately, 'good morning,'" Martha said. "Jason, this is Mrs. Kellog."

"How do you do?" Jason said.

Kellog? As in Officer Kellog?

"I'm sorry to have come here like this," Mrs. Kellog said. "But I just had to."

"How may I help you, Mrs. Kellog?"

"Jerry Kellog was my husband," she said.

That's precisely what I feared. And what are you doing here, in my home?

"May I offer my condolences on your loss, Mrs. Kellog?"

"I didn't have anything to do with him being killed," she said. "And neither did Wally."

Washington nodded sympathetically.

"Martha, I'm sure you're tired," he said.

"No. Not at all," Martha said, smiling sweetly, letting Jason know that even if this was business he wasn't going to dismiss her so lightly in her own home.

"Wally told me, not only Wally, but Lieutenant Sackerman, too, especially him, that you're not only the best Homicide detective . . ."

"That was very gracious of Jack Sackerman," Washington said, "we were friends for a long time."

". . . but the only cop you *know* is honest."

"That's very kind, but I cannot accept the blanket indictment of the rest of the Police Department," Washington said.

"I like to think we're something like Ivory Soap: ninety-nine and forty-four one hundredths pure."

Helene Kellog ignored him.

"That's why I came to you," she said. "I didn't know where else to go." She looked at him, took a deep breath, and went on: "Jerry was dirty. I know that. And—what happened to him—had something to do with that. They're all dirty, the whole Five Squad is dirty."

"Mrs. Kellog, when you were interviewed by detectives investigating the death of your husband, did you tell any of them what you just told me?"

She snorted.

"Of course not. They all acted like they think that I had something to do with it. Or that Wally did. I wouldn't be a bit surprised if they were in on it."

"In on what?"

"Covering up. Maybe trying to pin it on Wally or me. Wally *and* me."

"Does Detective Milham know that you've come to see me?"

"Of course not!"

"Why do you think anyone would want to 'pin' what happened to your husband on you? Or Detective Milham?"

"I just told you! To cover up. To protect themselves. They're all dirty. The whole damned Five Squad is dirty! That's probably why Jerry was killed. He never really wanted to get involved with that. They made him! And maybe he was going to tell somebody or do something."

"By dirty, you mean you believe your husband was taking money from someone?"

"Yes, of course."

"Did he tell you he was?"

"No. He wouldn't talk about it at all."

"Then how do you know?"

"He was getting the money from someplace."

"What money?"

"All of the money. All of a sudden we've got lots of

money. You're a cop. You know how much a cop, even with overtime, makes."

"And Jerry had large sums of money?"

"We—*he*—bought a condo at the shore, and there's a boat. And he paid cash. He didn't get that kind of money from the Police Department."

"Did you ask him where the money came from?"

"He wouldn't tell me. That's when we started to have trouble, when he wouldn't tell me."

"Have you told anything about this to Detective Milham?"

"No."

"May I ask why not?"

"Because if I did, he would have done something about it. He's an honest cop."

"Then wouldn't he logically be the person to tell?"

"I didn't want Jerry to go to jail," she said. "And besides, what would it look like, coming from me? Me living with Wally. I'd look like a bitch of a wife trying to make trouble."

"Did you come to me for advice, Mrs. Kellog?" Washington asked.

"For help. For advice."

"If what you told me is true . . ."

"Of course it's true!" she interrupted.

". . . then the information you have should be placed in the hands of the people who can do something about it. I'm sure you know that we have an Internal Affairs Division . . ."

"If I thought I could trust Internal Affairs, I wouldn't be here," she said. "They're all in on it."

"Mrs. Kellog, I can understand why you're upset, but believe me, you can trust Internal Affairs."

At this moment, unfortunately, I'm not absolutely sure that's true. And neither am I sure that what I so glibly said before, that the Department is ninety-nine and forty-four one hundredths percent pure is true, either.

She snorted.

"If I gave you the name of a staff inspector in Internal Affairs whom I can personally vouch for . . ."

Helene Kellog stood up.

"I guess I should have known better than to come here," she said, on the edge of tears. "I'm sorry to have wasted your time." She turned to Martha Washington. "Thank you."

"Mrs. Kellog, there's really nothing I can do to help you. I have nothing to do with either Homicide or Narcotics or Internal Affairs."

"Like I said, I'm sorry I wasted your time," she said. "That's the way out, right?"

"I'll see you to the door," Washington said, and went with her.

At the door, she turned to him.

"Do me one favor, all right? Don't tell Wally that I came to see you."

"If you wish, Mrs. Kellog."

She turned her back on him and walked down the corridor to the elevator.

Martha was waiting for him in the living room.

"I'm sorry about that, honey," he said.

"I think she was telling the truth."

"She believed what she was saying," Jason said after a moment. "That is not always the same thing as the whole truth."

"I felt sorry for her."

"So did I."

"But you're not going to do anything about what she said?"

"I'll do something about it," he said.

"What?"

"I haven't decided that yet. I don't happen to think that Wally Milham had anything to do with her husband's murder; he's not the type. I saw him tonight, by the way. That's where I was."

"Excuse me?"

"I went to see Matt. We tried to go to the Rittenhouse

Club for a drink, but it was closed, so we took a walk, and walked up on a double homicide. On Market Street. And we got involved in that. Wally Milham had the job."

"You mean, you were involved in a shooting?"

"No. We got there after the fact."

"What was so important that you had to see Matt at midnight?" Martha asked. "And be warned that 'police business' will not be an acceptable reply."

He met her eyes, smiled, and shook his head.

"We're conducting a surveillance. Earlier tonight, the microphone we had in place on a hotel window was dislodged. I learned from Tony Harris that Matt climbed out on a ledge thirteen floors up to replace the damned thing."

"My God! At the Bellvue? When he was here, he was wearing a Bellvue maintenance uniform."

Jason ignored the question.

"I wanted to bawl him out for that. And alone."

"So you went to the bar at the Rittenhouse Club?"

"That was after I bawled him out."

"After you bawled him out, you felt sorry for him?"

"I felt sorry for myself. I wanted a drink, and he didn't have anything."

"I'm going to give you the benefit of the doubt," Martha said, "and accept that story."

"Thank you."

"Do want something to eat? Coffee? Another drink?"

"If I told you what I really want, you'd accuse me of . . ."

"Oddly enough, I was thinking along those lines myself," Martha said. "Why don't you get one of those champagne splits from the fridge, while I turn off the lights."

When Detective Wallace J. Milham walked into the Homicide Division, he saw Detective Matthew M. Payne sitting at an unoccupied desk reading the *Daily News*. When Payne saw him, he closed the newspaper and stood up.

Wally beckoned to him with his finger and led him into one of the interview rooms, remembering as he passed through the door that he had the previous morning given a statement of his own in the same goddamn room.

Milham sat down in the interviewee's chair, a steel version of a captain's chair, firmly bolted to the floor, with a pair of handcuffs locked to it through a hole in the seat.

He motioned for Payne to close the door.

Payne handed him two sheets of typewriter paper.

"I didn't know how you wanted to handle this," Payne said. "But I went ahead and typed out this."

Milham read Matt's synopsis of what had happened at the Inferno Lounge. It wasn't up to Washington's standards, but he was impressed with the clarity, organization, and completeness. And with the typing. There were no strike-overs.

Why the hell am I surprised? He works for Washington.

"What do you do for Washington?" he wondered aloud.

Payne looked uncomfortable.

"Whatever he tells me to do," he said. "That wasn't intended to be a flip answer."

He doesn't want to talk about what he does for Washington. That shouldn't surprise me either. I don't know what they've got Jason doing, but whatever it is, somebody thinks it's more valuable to the Department than his working Homicide. And this guy works for him.

"Payne, I'm sorry I jumped on your ass at the Inferno. I had a really bad day yesterday, but I shouldn't have taken it out on you."

"No. I was out of line. You were right."

There was a knock at the door. Wally pushed himself out of the steel captain's chair and went to it and opened it.

A portly detective Matt recognized stood there.

"Mr. Atchison and his attorney, Mr. Sidney Margolis, are here," he said formally, and then he recognized Matt. "Whaddayasay, Payne?"

Summers shrugged, a gesture Milham interpreted to mean *Fuck you, too,* and went out of the interview room.

"You know Summers?"

"The sonofabitch and another one named Kramer had me

in here when I shot Stevens. The way they acted, I thought they were his big brothers."

"When you did what? 'Shot Stevens'?"

"Charles D. Stevens, a.k.a. Abu Ben Mohammed. He was one of the, quote, Arabs, unquote, on the Goldblatt Furniture job."

"I remember that," Wally said. "He tried to shoot his way out of an alley in North Philly when they went to pick him up?"

"Right."

"And shot a cop, who then put three rounds in him? That was you?"

Matt nodded. "I took a ricochet off a wall."

"I didn't make the connection with you," Wally said. And then, surprising himself, he added, "You hear about the plainclothes Narcotics guy getting shot?"

"Washington said something about it."

"Summers had me in here earlier today. 'What did you know about the death of Officer Jerome H. Kellog?' "

"I heard."

"Kellog's wife—they were separated—and I are pretty close. They had me in here. Sitting in that chair is a real bitch."

"Yeah," Matt agreed.

"And you took out the North Philly Serial Rapist, too, didn't you?" Wally said, remembering.

Matt nodded.

Jesus, Wally thought, *as long as I've been on the job, I've never once had to use my gun. And this kid has twice saved the City the price of a trial.*

"If I give you Boy Scout's Honor to keep my runaway mouth shut, could I hang around here?" Matt asked.

"Why would you want to do that?"

"Washington said you're a damned good investigator. I'd like to see you work."

Washington said that about me? I'll be damned!

"Sure. Be my guest."

"Where has, quote, the victim, unquote, been up to now?"

"Probably in the Hahnemann Hospital parking lot being told what not to say by his lawyer. Or deciding if it would be smarter to take the Fifth."

"Wouldn't he be? I had the feeling Jason Washington didn't believe what he had to say."

"Oh, this guy did it," Milham responded matter-of-factly. "Or had it done. There's not much question about that. *Proving* it is not going to be easy. He's smart, and tough, and he's got a good lawyer. But I think I'll nail the sonofabitch."

"Is that intuition on your part? Or Jason's? Or did I miss something?"

"I don't know about Washington. He sees things, senses things, that the rest of us miss. But what I saw was first of all a guy who didn't seem all that upset to be sitting around across a desk from his wife, who had just had her brains blown out. And there's his business partner on the floor, with bullet holes in him, too. I didn't hear one word about 'poor whatsisname.' Did you?"

"Marcuzzi, Anthony J." Matt furnished, shaking his head, no.

" 'Poor Tony, he was more than a business partner. We were very close friends. I loved him,' " Milham said mockingly.

Matt chuckled.

"On the way to Hahnemann Hospital," Milham went on, "I guess he thought about that: 'Jesus, I should remember that I'm supposed to be sorry as hell about this!' He started crying in the wagon. He wasn't all that bad, either. I almost felt sorry for him."

"Do you think he knows that you suspect him?"

"I don't know," Milham replied thoughtfully. "Probably about now, yeah, I think he's realized we haven't swallowed his bullshit. There's always something you forget when you set up something like this. I don't know what the hell he forgot, not yet, but he knows. I'd say right about now, he's getting worried."

"What I wondered about..." Matt said. "When I got hit, it hurt like hell. He didn't seem to be hurting much."

"I was not surprised when the bullet they took out of him at Hahnemann," Wally said, and dug in his pocket and came out with a plastic bag, handed it to Matt, then continued, "turned out to be a .32. Or that he had been shot only once. Whoever shot the wife and the partner made damned sure they were dead."

Matt examined the bullet and handed the plastic envelope back.

"And I won't be surprised, judging by the damage they caused, when we get the bullets in the bodies from the Medical Examiner, if they are *not* .32s. At least .38s, maybe even .45s, which do more damage. If I were a suspicious person, which is what the City pays me to be, I would wonder about that. How come the survivor has one small wound in the leg, and..."

"Yeah," Matt said thoughtfully.

"I think it's about time we ask them to come in," Wally said. "You want to stick around, stick around."

Milham got out of the captain's chair and went to the door and opened it.

"Would you please come in, Mr. Atchison?" he asked politely.

A moment later, Atchison, his arm around the shoulder of a short, portly, balding man, appeared in the interview-room door.

"Feeling a little better, Mr. Atchison?" Wally asked.

"How the fuck do you think I feel?" Atchison said.

Margolis looked coldly, but without much curiosity, at Matt.

"Howareya?" he said.

Matt noticed that despite the hour—it was reasonable to presume that when Milham called him, he had been in bed—Margolis was freshly shaven and his hair carefully arranged in a manner he apparently thought best concealed his deeply receded hairline. His trousers were mussed, however, and did not match his jacket, and his white shirt was not fresh. He was not wearing a tie.

Margolis led Atchison to the captain's chair and eased him down into it.

Matt saw that Atchison was wearing a fresh shirt and other—if not fresh—trousers. There were no bloodstains on the ones he was wearing.

"I object to having my client have to sit in that goddamned chair like you think he's guilty of something. He just suffered a gunshot wound, for Christ's sake!" Margolis said.

"We really don't have anything more comfortable, Mr. Atchison," Wally said. "But I'll ask Detective Payne to get another chair in here so you can rest your leg on it. Would that be satisfactory?"

"It wouldn't hurt. Let's get this over, for God's sake," Atchison said. "My leg is starting to throb."

"We'll get through this as quickly as we can," Matt heard Wally say as he went in search of another chair. "We appreciate your coming in here, Mr. Atchison."

Matt found a straight-back chair and carried it into the interview room. He arranged it in front of the captain's chair, and with a groan, Atchison lifted his leg up and rested it on it.

Matt glanced at Atchison. Atchison was examining him carefully, and Matt remembered what Wally had just said about "I think he's realized we haven't swallowed his bullshit."

When Matt looked at Milham, Milham, with a nod of his head, told him to stand against the wall, behind Atchison in the captain's chair.

A slight, gray-haired woman, carrying a stenographer's notebook in one hand and a metal folding chair in the other, came into the room.

"This is Mrs. Carnelli," Milham said. "A police stenographer. She'll record this interview. Unless, of course, Mr. Atchison, you have an objection to that?"

Atchison looked at Margolis.

"Let's get on with it," Margolis said.

"Thank you," Milham said. He waited to see that Mrs. Carnelli was ready for him, and then spoke, slightly raising his voice. "This is an interview conducted in the Homicide Unit May 20, at 2:30 A.M. of Mr. Gerald N. Atchison, by Detective Wallace J. Milham, badge 626, concerning the willfully caused deaths of Mrs. Alicia Atchison and Mr. Anthony Marcuzzi. Present are Mr. Sidney Margolis, Mr. Atchison's attorney, and Detective Payne...first name and badge number, Payne?"

"Matthew M. Payne, badge number 701," Matt furnished.

"Mr. Atchison, I am Detective Milham of the Homicide Unit," Milham began. "We are questioning you concerning the willful deaths of Mrs. Alicia Atchison and Mr. Anthony Marcuzzi."

SEVEN

Mrs. Martha Washington was not surprised, when she woke up, that her husband was not in bed beside her. They had been married for more than a quarter century and she was as accustomed to finding herself alone in bed—even after a romantic interlude—as she was to the witticisms regarding her married name. She didn't like either worth a damn, but since there was nothing she could do about it, there was no sense in feeling sorry for herself.

She was surprised, when she looked at her bedside clock, to see how early it was: twenty minutes past seven. She rarely woke that early. And then she had the explanation: the sound of a typewriter clattering in the living room. *Her* typewriter, an IBM Electric, brought home from the Washington Galleries, Inc., when IBM wouldn't give her a decent trade-in when she'd bought new Selectrics.

"Damn him!" she said.

She pushed herself out of bed and, with a languorous, unintentionally somewhat erotic movement, pulled her nightgown over her head and tossed it onto the bed. Naked, showing a trim, firm figure that gave her, at forty-seven, nothing whatever to be unhappy about, she walked into the marble-walled bathroom and turned on the faucets in the glass-walled shower.

When she came out of the shower, she toweled her short hair vigorously in front of the partially steamed-over mirror. She had large dark eyes, a sharp, somewhat hooked nose, and smooth, light brown skin. After Matt had made the crack that she looked like the women in the Egyptian bas-reliefs in the collection of the Philadelphia Art Museum, she had begun to consider that there might actually be something to it, if the blood of an Egyptian queen—or at least an Egyptian courtesan; some of the women in those bas-reliefs looked as though they knew the way to a man's heart wasn't really through his stomach—might really flow in her veins.

She wrapped herself in a silk robe and went through the bedroom into the living room. Her red IBM Electric and a tiny tape recorder were on the plate-glass coffee table before the couch. Her husband, a thin earplug cord dangling from his ear, was sitting—somewhat uncomfortably, she thought—on the edge of the leather couch before it, his face showing deep concentration.

She went to the ceiling-to-floor windows overlooking the Art Museum, the Schuylkill River, and the Parkway and threw a switch. With a muted hum, electric motors opened the curtains.

"How many times have I asked you not to put things on the coffee table? Heavy things?"

"How many times have I told you that I called and asked how much weight this will safely support?" her husband replied, completely unabashed.

He was nearly dressed to go to work. All he would have to do to be prepared to face the world would be to put on his shoulder holster (on the coffee table beside the IBM Selectric) and his jacket (on the couch).

"Am I allowed to ask what you're doing?"

"Ask? Yes. Am I going to tell you? No."

"You can make your own coffee."

"I already have, and if you are a good girl, you may have a cup."

"You wouldn't like me if I was a good girl."

"That would depend on what you were good at," he said. "And there are some things, my dear, at which you are very good indeed."

The typewriter continued to clatter during the exchange. She was fascinated with his ability to do two things, several things, at once. He was, she realized, listening to whatever was on the tapes, selecting what he wanted to type out, and talking to her, all at the same time.

"I really hate to see you put the typewriter there," Martha said.

"Then don't look," he said, and leaving one hand to tap steadily at the keyboard, removed the earplug, took the telephone receiver from its cradle, and dialed a number from memory with the other. "Stay in bed."

She went into the kitchen and poured coffee.

"Good morning, Inspector," she heard him say. "I hope I didn't wake you."

The Inspector, Martha felt, was probably Peter Wohl. Whatever Wohl replied, it caused her husband to chuckle, which came out a deep rumble.

"I have something I think you ought to see and hear, and as soon as possible," she heard her husband say. "What would be most convenient for you?"

I wonder what that's all about? What wouldn't wait until he saw Wohl in his office?

"This won't take long, Peter," Washington said.

And then Martha intuited what this was all about. She walked to the kitchen door and looked at him.

"I'll be outside waiting for you," Jason said. Then he dropped the telephone in its cradle.

He looked up at her.

"Did you tape-record that pathetic woman last night?"

Jason didn't reply.

"You did," Martha said, shock and disgust in her voice. "Jason, she came to you in confidence."

"She came to me looking for help. That's what I'm trying to do."

"That's not only illegal—and you're an officer of the law—it's disgusting! She wouldn't have told you what she did if she knew you were recording it!"

He looked at her a long moment.

"I wanted to make sure I really understood what she said," he said. "Watch!"

He pushed the Erase button on the machine.

"No tape, Martha," he said. "I just wanted to make sure I had it all."

He stood up and started to put on his shoulder holster.

She turned angrily and went back to the stove.

He appeared in the kitchen door, now fully dressed. She recognized his jacket as a new one, a woolen tweed from Uruguay, of all places.

"You ever hear about the ancient custom of killing the messenger who bears the bad news?" Jason replied. "Be kind to me, Martha."

"Don't try to be clever. Whatever it is, Peter Wohl won't blame you."

"I'm talking about the Mayor."

She met his eyes for a moment, turned away from him, and then back again, this time offering a mug of coffee.

"Do you have time for this?" she asked. "Or is the drawing and quartering scheduled in the next five minutes?"

"It's not a hearty meal, but the condemned man is grateful nonetheless."

He took the coffee, took a sip, and then set it down.

"What's all this about?" Martha asked. "What that woman said last night? Dirty cops in Narcotics?"

"We're working on dirty cops elsewhere in the Department."

"I thought Internal Affairs was supposed to police the Police Department."

"They are."

She considered that a moment.

"Oh, which explains why you and Peter are involved."

He nodded.

"And now this. I think Mrs. Kellog was telling the truth. It will not make the Mayor's day."

Martha shook her head.

"Am I going to be honored with your company later today?" Martha asked. "At any time later today? Or maybe sometime this week?"

"I know what you should do. You should go back to bed and try this again. This time, get up with a smile, and with nothing in your heart but compassion for your overworked and underappreciated husband."

"We haven't had any time together for weeks. And even when you're here, you're not. You're working."

"I know. This will be over soon, Martha. And we'll go to the shore for a couple of days."

"I've heard that before," she said, but she went to him and kissed his cheek. "Get that stuff off my table. Put the damned typewriter back where you found it."

"Yes, Ma'am," Jason said. He put the typewriter back where he had found it, in a small closet in the kitchen, and then, carrying the tape recorder, left the apartment, pausing only long enough to pat his wife on her rump.

"Good morning, Jason," Wohl said as Washington got into the front seat of Wohl's car.

"I'm sorry about this, but I really thought I should get this to you as soon as I could."

"What's up?"

"About midnight last night, Matt and I walked up on a double homicide on Market Street."

"Really? What in the world were you two doing walking on Market Street at midnight?"

"For a quick answer, the bar at the Rittenhouse Club was closed."

"Tell me about the homicide."

"Two victims. What looks like large-caliber-bullet wounds to the cranium. One victim was the wife of one of the owners of the Inferno Lounge..."

"I know where it is."

"And the other the partner. It was called in by the other partner, who suffered a small-caliber-bullet wound in what he says was an encounter with the doers, two vaguely described white males."

He didn't call me here to tell me this. Why? Because he thinks that it wasn't an armed robbery, that the husband was the doer? And the Homicide detective is accepting the husband's story?

"We got there right after a Ninth District wagon responded to the call. Chief Lowenstein also came to the scene, and then got me alone. He knows what's going on."

I knew that he wouldn't have bothered me if it wasn't important!

"His finding out was inevitable. How much did you have to tell him?"

"Not much. He knows the names. Most of them. I told him I couldn't talk about it. The only time he really leaned on me was to ask how much time he had."

"What did you tell him?"

"Quote, not much, unquote."

"That's true, isn't it?"

"Yes, sir. Peter, I told him that we didn't have the conversation, that if we had it, I would have to report it."

"Is that what you're doing?"

"That's up to you, Peter. I'll play it any way you want me to."

"I like Matt Lowenstein. There has been absolutely nothing to suggest he's done anything wrong. What purpose would it serve to go to Carlucci with this?"

"You heard what the Mayor said, Peter. If anyone came to you or me asking—asking *anything*—about the investigation, he wanted to know about it."

"The call is yours, Jason. Was Chief Lowenstein—what word am I looking for?—*pissed* that you wouldn't tell him anything?"

"No. He seemed to understand he was putting me on a spot."

"My gut reaction, repeating the call is yours, is that you didn't talk to Chief Lowenstein about anything but the double homicide."

"OK. That's it. We didn't have this conversation, either."

"What conversation?" Wohl asked, with exaggerated innocence.

"I'm not through, I'm afraid," Washington said.

"What else?" Wohl asked tiredly as he pulled the door shut again.

"Chief Lowenstein got rid of Matt, so that he could talk to me, by sending him to the crime scene—the victims were in a downstairs office—with Henry Quaire when Quaire came to the scene. I don't know what happened between Matt and Milham, but Milham pulled the rule book on him and insisted on getting Matt's statement that night—God, that's something else I have to do this morning, get my statement to Homicide—so Matt went to the Roundhouse, and I went home, and when I got there the Widow Kellog was there."

"The widow of the undercover Narcotics guy?"

Washington nodded.

"Who was found with two bullets in his head in his house. Detective Milham's close friend's estranged husband."

"She was at your place?" Wohl asked, surprised.

"Right. And she is convicted that her husband's death is connected with drugs . . ."

"You don't think Milham had anything to do with it, do you?"

"No. I don't think so. But the Widow Kellog thinks it was done by somebody in Narcotics, because they—they being the Five Squad—are all dirty."

"The Narcotics Five Squad, according to Dave Pekach, are knights in shining armor, waging the good war against controlled substances. A lot of esprit de corps, which I gather means they think they're better than other cops, including the other four Narcotics squads. In other words, a bunch of hotshots who do big buys, make raids, take doors, that sort of thing. They're supposed to be pretty effective. It's hard to believe that any of them would be dirty, much less kill one of their own."

"That's what the lady is saying."

"You believe her?"

"She said there's all kinds of money floating around. She said she, she and her husband, bought a house at the shore and paid cash for it."

"That could be checked out, it would seem to me, without much trouble. Did she tell Homicide about this? Or anybody else?"

"No. She thinks everybody's dirty."

"What did you tell her?"

"I told her I knew a staff inspector I knew was honest, and she should go to him; that I would set it up."

"And she doesn't want to go to him?"

"No," Washington said. "Absolutely out of the question."

"You believe her?"

"I think she's telling the truth. My question is, what do we do with this?"

"If you take it to Internal Affairs..." Wohl said.

"Yeah."

"Let me read this," Wohl said, opening the envelope.

Wohl grunted twice while reading the three sheets of paper the envelope contained, then stuffed them back into the envelope.

"This has to go to the Mayor," he said. "As soon as you can get it to him. And then I think you had better have a long talk with Captain Pekach about the Narcotics Five Squad."

Washington nodded.

"Can I tell him I'm doing so at your orders?"

"Everything you do is at my orders. Dave Pekach knows that. Are you getting paranoid, Jason?"

"Simply because one is paranoid doesn't mean that people aren't really saying terrible things about one behind one's back," Washington said sonorously.

Wohl laughed.

"No cop likes the guy who asks the wrong questions about other cops. Me included. I especially hate being the guy who asks the questions," Washington said.

"I know," Wohl said sympathetically. "Please don't tell me there's more, Jason."

"That's enough for one morning, wouldn't you say?"

At five minutes to eight, Sergeant Jason Washington drove into the parking lot of what had been built in 1892 at Frankford and Castor avenues as the Frankford Grammar School, and was now the headquarters of the Special Operations Division of the Philadelphia Police Department.

He pulled into a parking spot near the front entrance of the building marked with a sign reading INSPECTORS. He regarded this as his personal parking space. While he was sure that there were a number of sergeants and lieutenants annoyed that he parked his car where it should not be, and who almost certainly had complained, officially or unofficially about it, nothing had been said to him.

There was a certain military-chain-of-command–like structure in the Special Operations Division. Only one's immediate superior was privileged to point out to one the errors of one's ways. In Jason Washington's case, his immediate superior was the head man, Inspector Peter Wohl, the Commanding Officer of Special Operations. Peter Wohl knew where he parked his car and had said nothing to him.

That was, Jason had decided, permission to park by inference.

Sergeant Jason Washington and Inspector Peter Wohl had a unique relationship, which went back to the time Detective Wohl had been assigned to Homicide and been placed under the mentorship of Detective Washington. At that time, Jason Washington—who was not burdened, as his wife often said, with crippling modesty—had decided that Wohl possessed not only an intelligence almost equal to his, but also an innate skill to find the anomalies in a given situation—which was really what investigation was all about, finding what didn't fit—that came astonishingly close to his own extraordinary abilities in that regard.

Washington had predicted that not only would Detective Wohl remain in Homicide (many detectives assigned to Homicide did not quite cut the mustard and were reassigned to other duties) but he would have a long and distinguished career there.

Homicide detectives were the elite members of the Detective Bureau. For many people, Jason Washington among them, service as a Homicide detective represented the most challenging and satisfying career in the Police Department, and the thought of going elsewhere was absurd.

Detective Wohl had not remained in Homicide. He had taken the sergeant's examination, and then, with astonishing rapidity, became the youngest sergeant ever to serve in the Highway Patrol; a lieutenant; the youngest captain ever; and then the youngest staff inspector ever.

And then Special Operations had come along.

It had been formed several years before, it was generally, and essentially correctly, believed as a response to criticism of the Police Department—and by implication, of the Mayor—by the Philadelphia *Ledger*, one of the city's four major newspapers.

Mr. Arthur J. Nelson, Chairman of the Board and Chief Executive Officer of the Daye-Nelson Corporation, which owned the *Ledger* and twelve other newspapers, had never been an admirer of the Hon. Jerry Carlucci, and both the *Ledger* and the Daye-Nelson Corporation's Philadelphia television and radio stations (WGHA-TV, Channel Seven; WGHA-FM 100.2 MHz; and WGHA-AM, 770 KC) had opposed him in the mayoral election.

The dislike by Mr. Nelson of Mayor Carlucci had been considerably exacerbated when Mr. Nelson's only son, Jerome Stanley Nelson, had been found murdered—literally butchered—in his luxurious apartment in a renovated Revolutionary War–era building on Society Hill.

Considering the political ramifications of the case, no one had been at all surprised when the job had been given to Detective Jason Washington, who had quickly determined the prime suspect in the case to be Mr. Jerome Nelson's live-in companion, a twenty-five-year-old black homosexual who called himself "Pierre St. Maury."

When this information had been released to the press by Homicide Unit Lieutenant Edward M. DelRaye—who shortly afterward was transferred out of Homicide, for what his superiors regarded as monumentally bad judgment—it had been published in the *Inquirer*, the *Bulletin*, and the *Daily News*, Philadelphia's other major newspapers, and elsewhere.

Mrs. Arthur J. Nelson suffered a nervous breakdown, which Mr. Nelson attributed as much to the shame and humiliation caused her by the publication of their son's lifestyle as by his death. And if the police had only had the common decency to keep the sordid facts to themselves, rather than feed them to the competition in vindictive retribution for his support of the Mayor's opponent in the mayoral election, of course this would not have happened.

Almost immediately, the *Ledger*'s reporters had begun to examine every aspect of the operation of the Philadelphia Police Department with a very critical eye, and on its editorial page there began a series of editorials—many of them, it was suspected, written by Mr. Nelson himself—that called the public's attention to the Department's many failings.

The Highway Patrol, a special unit within the Department, were often referred to as "Carlucci's Commandos," for example, and in one memorable editorial, making reference to the leather puttees worn by Highway Patrolmen since its inception, when the unit was equipped with motorcycles, they became "Philadelphia's Jackbooted Gestapo."

A splendid opportunity for journalistic criticism of the Police Department presented itself to Mr. Nelson and his employees at this time with the appearance of a sexual psychopath whose practice it was to abduct single young women, transport them to remote areas in his van, and there perform various imaginatively obscene sexual acts on their bodies. The Department experienced some difficulty in apprehending this gentleman, who had been quickly dubbed "the Northwest Philadelphia Serial Rapist."

The *Ledger*, sparing no expense in their efforts to keep the public informed, turned up a rather well-known psychiatrist who said that there was no question in his mind that inevitably the Northwest Philadelphia Serial Rapist would go beyond humiliation of his victims, moving into murder and perhaps even dismemberment.

A lengthy interview with this distinguished practitioner of the healing arts was published in the *Ledger*'s Sunday supplement magazine, under a large banner headline asking, "Why Are Our Police Doing Nothing?"

The Monday after the Sunday supplement article appeared, Police Commissioner Taddeus Czernich summoned to the Commissioner's Conference Room in the Police Administration Building the three deputy commissioners and six of the dozen chief inspectors. There he announced a reorganization of certain units within the Police Department. There would be a new unit, called Special Operations Division. It would report directly to the Deputy Commissioner for Operations. It would deal, as the name suggested, with special situations. Its first task would be to apprehend the Northwest Philadelphia Serial Rapist. Special Operations would be commanded by Staff Inspector Peter Wohl, who would be transferred from the Staff Investigation Bureau of the Internal Affairs Division.

That was the first anomaly. Staff inspectors, who ranked between captains and inspectors in the departmental hierarchy, were regarded as sort of super-detectives whose superior investigative skills qualified them to investigate the most complex, most delicate situations that came up, but they did not serve in positions of command.

Staff Inspector Peter Wohl had recently received some very flattering press attention—except, of course, in the *Ledger*—following his investigation of (and the subsequent conviction of) Superior Court Judge Moses Findermann for various offenses against both the law and judicial ethics.

And Highway Patrol, Commissioner Czernich announced, would be transferred from the bureaucratic command of the Traffic Division and placed under Special Operations. As would other elements and individuals from within the Department as needed to accomplish the mission of the Special Operations Division.

Among those to be immediately transferred, Commissioner Czernich announced, would be newly promoted Captain David Pekach of the Narcotics Bureau. He would replace Captain Michael J. Sabara, the present Highway Patrol Commander, who would become Staff Inspector Wohl's deputy.

In response to the question "What the hell is that all about?" posed by Chief Inspector Matt Lowenstein of the Detective Division, Commissioner Czernich replied:

"Because the Mayor says he thinks Mike Sabara looks like a concentration camp guard and Pekach looks like a Polish altar boy. He's thinking public image, OK?"

There were chuckles. Captain Sabara, a gentle, kindly man who taught Sunday school, did indeed have a menacing appearance. Captain Pekach, who until his recent promotion had spent a good deal of time working the streets in filthy clothing, a scraggly beard, and pigtail, would, indeed, shaved, bathed, and shorn, resemble the Polish altar boy he had once been.

Chief Lowenstein had laughed.

"Don't laugh too quick, Matt," Commissioner Czernich said. "Peter Wohl can have any of your people he thinks he needs for as long as he thinks he needs them. And I know he thinks Jason Washington is the one guy who can catch the rapist."

Lowenstein's smile had vanished.

The assignment of any detective outside the Detective Bureau was another anomaly, just as extraordinary as the assignment of a staff inspector as a commanding officer. Lowenstein looked as if he was going to complain over the loss to Special Operations of Detective Jason Washington, whom he—and just about everyone else—considered to be the best Homicide detective, but he said nothing. There was no use in complaining to Commissioner Czernich. This whole business was not Czernich's brainstorm, but the Mayor's, and Lowenstein had known the Mayor long enough to know that complaining to him would be pissing in the wind.

The next day, Detective Washington and his partner, Detective Tony Harris, over their bluntly expressed objections, had been "temporarily" transferred to Special Operations for the express purpose of stopping the Northwest Serial Rapist.

They had never been returned to Homicide.

Peter Wohl had treated both of them well. There was as much overtime, without question, as they had in Homicide. They were now actually, if not officially, on a five-day-a-week day shift, from whenever they wanted to come in the morning to whenever they decided to take off in the afternoon.

They were each provided with a new unmarked car for their sole use. New unmarked cars usually went to inspectors and up, and were passed down to lesser ranks. Wohl had implied—and Washington knew at the time he had done so that he believed—that the investigations they would be as-

signed to perform would be important, interesting, and challenging.

That hadn't come to pass. It could be argued, of course,
that bringing down police officers who were taking money
from the Mafia in exchange for not enforcing the law was
important. And certainly, if challenging meant difficult, this
was a challenging investigation. But there was something
about investigating brother police officers—vastly com-
pounded when it revealed the hands of at least a captain and
a lieutenant were indeed covered with filth—that Washington found distasteful.

The hackneyed phrase "It's a dirty job, but someone has
to do it!" no longer brought a smile to Washington's face.

Washington got out of his car and entered the building.
He first stopped at the office of the Commanding Officer,
which looked very much as it had when it had been the Principal's Office of the Frankford Grammar School.

Officer Paul Thomas O'Mara, Inspector Wohl's administrative assistant, attired in a shiny, light blue suit Washington suspected had been acquired from the Bargain Basement
at J. C. Penney's, told him that Captain Mike Sabara, Wohl's
deputy, had not yet come in.

"Give me a call when he does come in, will you,
Tommy?" Washington asked, left the Principal's Office, and
climbed stone stairs worn deeply by seventy-odd years of
children's shoes to the second floor, where he entered what
had been a classroom, over the door of which hung a sign:
INVESTIGATION SECTION.

There he found Detective Matthew M. Payne on duty.
Payne was attired in a sports coat Jason knew that Detective
Payne had acquired at a Preferred Customer 30% Off Sale at
Brooks Brothers, a button-down-collar light blue shirt, the
necktie of the Goodwill Rowing Club, and well-shined
loafers.

He looked like an advertisement for Brooks Brothers,
Jason thought. It was a compliment.

"Good morning, Detective Payne," Jason said. "You need a shave."

"I woke late," Payne said, touching his chin. "And took a chance you wouldn't get here until I could shave."

"What happened? Did Milham keep you at Homicide?"

"I was there. But he didn't keep me. He let me sit in on interviewing Atchison."

Washington's face showed that he found that interesting, but he didn't reply.

"We can't have you disgracing yourself and our unit with a slovenly appearance when you meet the Mayor," Washington said.

"Am I going to meet the Mayor?" Payne asked.

"I think so," Jason replied, already dialing a number.

There was a brief conversation with someone named Jack, whom Detective Payne correctly guessed to be Lieutenant J. K. Fellows, the Mayor's bodyguard and confidante, and then Washington hung up.

"Get in your car," he ordered, handing Matt Payne the large envelope. "Head for the Schuylkill Expressway. When you get there, call M-Mary One and get a location. Then either wait for them or catch up with them, and give Lieutenant Fellows this."

"What is it?"

"When I got home last night, Officer Kellog's widow was waiting for me. There is no question in her mind that her husband's death has something to do with Narcotics. She also made a blanket indictment of Five Squad Narcotics. She says they're all dirty. That's a transcript, almost a verbatim one, of what she said."

"You believe her?"

Washington shrugged. "I believe she believes what she told me. Wohl said to get it to the Mayor as soon as we can."

Washington dialed the unlisted private number of the Commanding Officer, Highway Patrol from memory. It was answered on the second ring.

"Captain Pekach."

"Sergeant Washington, sir."

"Honest to God, Jason, I was just thinking about you."

"I was hoping you could spare a few minutes for me, sir."

"That sounds somehow official."

"Yes, sir. Inspector Wohl asked me to talk to you."

"You're in the building?"

"Yes, sir."

"Come on, then. You've got me worried."

When Washington walked into Captain Pekach's office, Pekach was in the special uniform worn only by the Highway Patrol, breeches and boots and a Sam Browne belt going back to the days when the Highway Patrol's primary function had been to patrol major thoroughfares on motorcycles.

Washington thought about that as he walked to Pekach's desk to somewhat formally shake Pekach's offered hand: *They used to be called "the bandit chasers"; now they call them "Carlucci's Commandos." Worse, "The Gestapo."*

"Thank you for seeing me, sir."

"Curiosity overwhelms me, *Sergeant*," Pekach said. "Coffee, Jason?"

"Thank you," Washington said.

Pekach walked around his desk to a small table holding a coffee machine, poured two mugs, handed one to Washington, and then, waving Washington into one of the two upholstered armchairs, sat down in the other and stretched his booted legs out in front of him.

"OK, what's on your mind?"

"Officer Kellog. The Narcotics Five Squad," Washington said. "The boss suggested I talk to you about both."

"What's our interest in that?"

"This is all out of school," Washington said.

Pekach held up the hand holding his mug in a gesture that meant, *understood*.

"The Widow Kellog came to my apartment last night,"

Washington said. "She is convinced that her husband's death is Narcotics-related."

"She came to your apartment?" Pekach asked, visibly surprised, and without waiting for a reply, went on: "I think that's a good possibility. Actually, when I said I was thinking about you just before you called, I was going to ask you if Homicide had come up with something along that line. I figured you would know if they had come up with something."

"She is also convinced that Officer Kellog was, and the entire Narcotics Five Squad is, dirty," Washington went on.

This produced, as Washington feared it would, an indignant reaction. Pekach's face tightened, and his eyes turned cold.

"Bullshit," he said. "Jerry Kellog worked for me before he went on the Five Squad. A good, smart, hardworking, *honest* cop. Which is how he got onto the Five Squad. I recommended him."

"How much do you know about the Five Squad?"

"Enough. Before I got promoted, I was the senior lieutenant in Narcotics...no I wasn't, Lieutenant Mikkles was. But I filled in for Captain Talley enough to know all about the Five Squad. Same thing—good, smart, hardworking, *honest* cops."

Washington didn't reply.

"Christ, Jason, the Narcotics Five Squad is—" He looked for a comparison, and found one: "—the Highway Patrol of Narcotics. The best, most experienced, hardworking people. A lot of pride, esprit de corps. They're the ones who make the raids, take the doors, stick their necks out. Where did Wohl get the idea they're dirty?"

"From me, I'm afraid," Washington said.

Pekach looked at him in first surprise and then anger.

"I'm not saying they're dirty," Washington said. "I don't know—"

"Take my word for it, Jason," Pekach interrupted.

"What I told the Boss was that I believed Mrs. Kellog believed what she was saying."

"She's got an accusation to make, tell her to take it to Internal Affairs."

"She's not willing to do that. She doesn't trust Internal Affairs."

"I suppose both you and Wohl have considered that she might be trying to take the heat off her boyfriend?" Pekach challenged. "What's his name? Milham?"

"That, of course, is a possibility."

"What I think you should do—and if you don't want to tell Wohl, by God, I will—is turn this over to Internal Affairs and mind our own business."

Washington didn't reply.

Pekach's temper was now aroused.

"You know what Internal Affairs would find? Presuming that they didn't see these wild accusations for what they are—a desperate woman trying to turn the heat off her boyfriend—and conducted an investigation, they'd find a record of good busts, busts that stood up in court, put people away, took God only knows how much drugs off the street."

"We can't go to Internal Affairs with this right now," Washington said.

"Why not?" Pekach demanded, looking at him sharply. "Oh, is that what you've all been up to, that nobody's talking about? Investigating Internal Affairs? Is that why you can't take this to them?"

"You're putting me on a spot, Captain," Washington said. "I can't answer that."

"No, of course you can't," Pekach said sarcastically. "But let me tell you this, Jason: If anybody just happened to be investigating Internal Affairs, say, for example, the Mayor's personal detective bureau, I'd say they have a much better chance of finding dirty cops there than anyone investigating the Narcotics Five Squad would find there."

Washington was aware that his own temper was beginning to flare. He waited a moment.

"Captain, I do what the Boss tells me. He told me to have a long talk with you about the Narcotics Five Squad. That's what I'm doing."

"Oh, Christ, Jason, I know that. It just burns me up, is all, that the questions would be asked. I know those guys. I didn't, I really didn't, mean to jump on you."

Washington didn't reply.

"And I'll tell you something else, just between us," Pekach said. "I guess my nose is already a little out of joint. I'm supposed to be the Number Three man in Special Operations, and I don't like not knowing what you and your people are up to. I know that's not your doing, but..."

"Just between you and me, Captain Sabara doesn't know either," Washington said. "And also, just between you and me, I know that the decision to keep you and Sabara in the dark wasn't made by Inspector Wohl, and he doesn't like it any more than you do."

"I figured it was probably something like that," Pekach said. "But thank you for telling me."

Washington shrugged.

"What else can I do for you, Jason?"

"I'm a little afraid to ask."

"Don't be."

"I don't know the first thing about how the Narcotics Five Squad operates. You do. Would you give some thought to how they could be dirty, and tell me?"

"Jesus Christ!" Pekach said bitterly, and then: "OK, Jason, I will."

"I'd appreciate it," Washington said, and stood up.

"Jason, I hope you understand why I'm sore. And that I'm not sore at you."

"I hope you understand, Captain, that I don't like asking the questions."

"Yeah, I do," Pekach said. "We're still friends, right? Despite my nasty Polish temper?"

"I really hope you still think of me as a friend," Washington said.

When Matt Payne went out the rear door into the parking lot, he saw that it was shift-change time. The lot was jammed with antenna-festooned Highway Patrol cars, somewhat less spectacularly marked Anti-Crime Team (ACT) cars, and a row of unmarked cars. Almost all of the cars were new.

There was more than a little resentment throughout the Department about Special Operations' fleet of new cars. In the districts, radio patrol car odometers were commonly on their second hundred thousand miles, seat cushions sagged, windows were cracked, heaters worked intermittently, and breakdowns of one kind or another were the rule, not the exception.

The general belief held by most District police officers was that Inspector Wohl was the fair-haired boy of the Department, and thus was able to get new cars at the expense of others who did not enjoy his status. Others felt that Special Operations had acquired so many new vehicles because it was the pet of Mayor Carlucci, and was given a more or less blank check on the Department's assets.

The truth, to which Matt Payne was privy—he had been then Staff Inspector Wohl's administrative assistant before becoming a detective—had nothing to do with Inspector Wohl or the fact that Special Operations had been dreamed up by the Mayor, but rather with the Congress of the United States.

Doing something about crime-in-the-streets had, about the time the Mayor had come up with his idea for Special Operations, been a popular subject in Congress. It was a legitimate—that is to say, one the voters were getting noisily concerned about—problem, and Congress had reacted in its usual way by throwing the taxpayers' money at it.

Cash grants were made available to local police departments to experiment with a new concept of law enforcement. This was called the Anti-Crime Team concept, which carried with it the acronym ACT. It meant the flooding of high-crime areas with well-trained policemen, equipped with the very latest equipment and technology, and teamed with special assigned prosecutors within the District Attorney's Office who would push the arrested quickly through the criminal justice system.

The grants were based on need. Philadelphia qualified on a need basis on two accounts. Crime was indeed a major problem in Philadelphia, and Philadelphia needed help. Equally important, the Hon. Jerry Carlucci was a political force whose influence extended far beyond the Mayor's office. Two Senators and a dozen or more Congressmen seeking continued employment needed Jerry Carlucci's influence.

Some of the very first, and most generous, grants were given to the City of Philadelphia. There was a small caveat. Grant money was to be used solely for new, innovative, experimental police operations, not for routine police expenditures. So far as Mayor Carlucci was concerned, the Special Operations Division was new, innovative and experimental. The federal grants could thus legally be, and were, expended on the pay of police officers transferred to Special Operations for duty as Anti-Crime Team police, and for their new and innovative equipment, which of course included new, specially equipped police cars. Since it was, of course, necessary to incorporate the new and innovative ACT personnel and equipment into the old and non-innovative Police Department, federal grant funds could be used for this purpose.

Until investigators from the General Accounting Office had put a stop to it, providing the Highway Patrol, in its new, innovative, and experimental role as a subordinate unit of the new, innovative, and experimental Special Operations Division, with new cars had been, in Mayor Carlucci's opinion, a justifiable expenditure of federal grant funds.

More senior police officers, lieutenants and above, usually, the "white shirts," who understood that money was money, and that if extra money from outside bought Special Operations and Highway cars, then the money which would ordinarily have to eventually be spent for that purpose could be spent elsewhere in the Department, were not as resentful. But this rationale was not very satisfying to a cop in a district whose battered radio patrol car wouldn't start at three o'clock in the morning.

Detective Payne went to a row of eight new, unmarked Ford sedans, which so far as the federal government was concerned were involved in new, innovative, and experimental activities under the ACT concept, and got in one of them. It was one of four such cars assigned to the Investigation Section. Sergeant Jason Washington had one, and Detective Tony Harris the second, on an around-the-clock basis. The two other cars were shared by the others of the Investigation Section.

He drove out of the parking lot and headed up Castor Avenue toward Hunting Park Avenue. He turned off Hunting Park Avenue onto Ninth Street and off Ninth Street onto the ramp for the Roosevelt extension of the Schuylkill Expressway, and then turned south toward the Schuylkill River.

At the first traffic light, he took one of the two microphones mounted just about out of sight under the dash.

"Mary One, William Fourteen."

"You have something for me, Fourteen?" Lieutenant Jack Fellows's voice came back immediately.

"Right."

"Where are you now?"

"Just left Special Operations."

There was a moment's hesitation as Lieutenant Fellows searched his memory for time-and-distance.

"Meet us at the Zoo parking lot," he said.

"On the way," Matt said, and dropped the microphone onto the seat.

Then he reached down and threw a switch which caused both the brake lights and the blue and white lights concealed behind the grille of the Ford to flash, and stepped hard on the accelerator.

The Mayor is a busy man. He doesn't have the time to waste sitting at the Zoo parking lot waiting for a lowly detective. This situation clearly complies with the provisions of paragraph whatever the hell it is of Police Administrative Regulations restricting the use of warning lights and sirens to those clearly necessary situations.

There were a number of small pleasures involved with being a policeman, and one of them, Matt Payne had learned, was being able to turn on warning lights and the siren when you had to get somewhere in a hurry.

He had thought of this during dinner the previous evening, during a somewhat acrimonious discussion of his—their—future with Miss Penelope Detweiler.

It was her position (and that of Mr. and Mrs. Chadwick Thomas Nesbitt IV, who allied themselves with Miss Detweiler in the Noble Cause of Talking Common Sense to Matt) that it was childish and selfish of him, with his education, potential, and background, to remain a policeman, working for peanuts, when he should be thinking of *their* future.

He had known that it would not have been wise to have offered the argument "Yeah, but if I'm not a cop, I won't be able to race down Roosevelt Boulevard with the lights on." She would have correctly decided that he was simply being childish again.

There were other satisfactions in being a policeman, but for some reason, he seemed to become instantly inarticulate whenever he tried to explain them to her. In his own mind, he knew that he had been a policeman long enough so that it was in his blood, and he would never be happy at a routine job.

He reached the Schuylkill River, crossed it, and turned east toward Center City. Then he reached down and turned off the flashing lights. The traffic wasn't that heavy, and if Mary One, the mayoral limousine, beat him to the Zoo parking lot, he wasn't entirely sure if the Mayor would agree with his decision that turning on the lights was justified.

From what he'd heard of the Mayor's career as a policeman, he'd been a really by-the-book cop.

When he got to the Zoo parking lot, he stopped and picked up his microphone.

"Mary One, William Fourteen, at the Zoo."

"A couple of minutes," Lieutenant Fellows's voice came back.

Matt picked the envelope off the floor, and got out of the car and waited for the Mayor.

Two minutes later the limousine pulled up beside him. Matt walked to the front-seat passenger door as the window whooshed down and Lieutenant Fellows came into view.

"Good morning, sir," Matt said, and handed him the envelope.

"Thank you, Payne," Fellows said, and the window started back up. Then the rear window rolled down and he heard the Mayor of the City of Philadelphia order:

"Hold it a minute, Charley," and then the rear door opened and the Mayor got out.

"Long time no see," the Mayor said, offering his hand. "How are you, Matt?"

"Just fine, Mr. Mayor. Thank you."

"Good to see you, Matt," the Mayor said. "And say hello to your mother and dad for me."

"Yes, sir. I will. Thank you."

The Mayor patted his shoulder and got back in the limousine, and in a moment it rolled out of the parking lot.

EIGHT

Matt got back in the unmarked Ford and drove out of the Zoo parking lot, wondering where the hell he was going to find a drugstore and buy the razor he had been ordered to buy.

It had been nice of the Mayor, he thought, to get out of his car to say hello. It was easy to accuse the Mayor of being perfectly willing to wrap his arm around an orangutan and inquire as to the well-being of his parents if that would get him one more vote, but the truth, Matt realized, was that after he had wrapped his arm around *your* shoulder, it made you feel good, and you were not at all inclined to question his motives.

While it was said, and mostly believed, that the Mayor knew the name of every cop in the Department, this was not true. There were eight thousand policemen in the Department, and the Mayor did not know the name or even the face of each of them. But he did know the faces and sometimes the names of every cop who was someone, or who had ever done something, out of the ordinary.

Matt qualified on several counts. One of them was that the Mayor knew his parents, but the most significant way Matt Payne had come to the Mayor's attention was as a cop.

Shortly after the formation of Special Operations, as Detective Washington was getting close enough to the Northwest Serial Rapist to have a cast of his tire tracks and a good description of his van, Mr. Warren K. Fletcher, thirty-one, of Germantown, had attempted to run down Matt with his van when he approached it.

That gave Matt (although he was so terrified at the time that this legal consideration had not entered his mind) the justification to use equal—deadly—force in the apprehension of a suspect. He had drawn his service revolver and fired five times at the van. One of the bullets found and exploded Mr. Fletcher's brain all over the windshield of his van.

It didn't matter that finding what looked like it could possibly be the van could be described only as blind luck, or that when Matt had fired his revolver he had been so terrified that hitting Mr. Fletcher had been pure coincidence. What mattered was that Mr. Fletcher, at the time of his death, had Mrs. Naomi Schneider, thirty-four, of Germantown, in the back of his van, stripped naked, trussed neatly with telephone wire, and covered with a tarpaulin, and shortly before their trip was interrupted had been regaling her with a description of what he had planned for them as soon as they got somewhere private.

What also mattered a good deal was that Matt Payne was assigned to Special Operations. Even the imaginatively agile minds on the editorial floor of the *Ledger* building had trouble finding Police Department incompetence in the end of Mr. Fletcher's career. The *Ledger* just about ignored the story. The other papers gave it a good deal of play, most of them running a front-page picture of the Mayor at the shooting scene with his arm wrapped cordially around the shoulder of Special Operations Division plainclothes officer Matthew M. Payne.

Several months after that, following a robbery, brutal assault, and senseless murder at Goldblatt's Furniture Store in South Philadelphia, the Special Operations Division was asked by the Detective Bureau to assist them in the simultaneous arrest of eight individuals identified as participants in the robbery-murder.

The eight, who identified themselves as members of something called the Islamic Liberation Army, were at various locations in Philadelphia. Seven of them, in what the press—save again the *Ledger*—generally agreed was a well-planned, perfectly carried out maneuver, were placed in custody without incident. The eighth suspect, in trying to escape, drew a .45 Colt pistol and attempted to shoot his way through officers in an alley. In the process, he wounded a police officer, who drew and fired his service revolver in self-defense, inflicting upon Abu Ben Mohammed (also known as Charles D. Stevens) several wounds which proved to be fatal.

And again there were photographs of Officer Matthew M. Payne on the front pages of the *Daily News*, the *Inquirer*, and the *Bulletin* (but not in the *Ledger*), this time showing him with his face bandaged in a hospital bed and Mayor Carlucci's approving arm around his shoulders.

It was said at the time by senior white shirts that, considering the favorable publicity he had engendered for the Special Operations Division, and thus the Mayor, the young police officer had found a home in Special Operations. The only way he was going to get out of Special Operations was when he either retired or was carried to his grave. Or resigned, when he tired of playing cop.

Matt had heard the stories at the time, but had not been particularly concerned. He planned to take, as soon as he was eligible, the examination leading to promotion to detective. He was reasonably confident that he would pass it, and be promoted. And since the only places that detectives could be assigned within the Police Department were in one of the subordinate units of the Detective Division, that's where they would have to assign him. In the meantime, he liked working for Staff Inspector Wohl as his administrative assistant.

And that came to pass. Police Officer Matthew M. Payne took the Examination for Promotion to Detective, passed it, and with a high enough score (he placed third) so as to earn promotion very soon after the results were published.

He was duly transferred to the East Detective Division, which is on the second floor of the building housing the Twenty-fourth and Twenty-fifth Districts at Front and Westmoreland streets, and there began his career as a detective under the tutelage of Sergeant Aloysius J. Sutton.

His initial war of detection against crime wherever found had consisted almost entirely of investigating recovered stolen vehicles. This, in turn, consisted of going to where the stolen vehicle had been located, and then filling out a half-dozen forms in quadruplicate. None of these forms, he had quickly come to understand, would—once they had passed Sergeant Sutton's examination of them for bureaucratic perfection—ever be seen by human eyes again.

Almost all stolen and then recovered vehicles had been taken either by kids who wished to take a joyride and had no vehicle of their own in which to do so or by kids who wished to remove the tires, wheels, radios from said vehicles with the notion of selling them for a little pocket money. Or a combination of the foregoing.

Stolen and never-recovered vehicles were almost always stolen by professional thieves who either stripped the car to its frame or got it on the boat to Asunción, Paraguay, before the owner realized it was gone.

Theft of an automobile is a felony, however, and investigation of felonies, including the return of recovered stolen property, is a police responsibility. Detective Payne learned in EDD that this responsibility, when the recovered property was an automobile, is normally placed in the hands of the member of the detective squad whose time is least valuable.

There was a sort of sense to this, and he told himself that investigating recovered vehicles was both sort of on-the-job training for more important investigations, and a rite-of-passage. Every new detective went through it.

And he was prepared to do whatever was asked of him.

But then his assignment to EDD came to an abrupt end. He was reassigned to Special Operations. In theory it was a simple personnel matter, the reassignment of a detective from a unit where his services weren't really required to a unit which had need of his services. Matt quickly learned that he had been reassigned to Special Operations because the Mayor had suggested to Commissioner Czernich that this might be a wise thing to do.

There he found that the table of organization now provided for an investigation section. The supervisor of the investigation section was newly promoted Sergeant Jason Washington. Under him were personnel spaces for five detectives, three of whom had been assigned: Tony Harris, Jesus Martinez, and Matthew M. Payne.

Tony Harris was an experienced homicide detective recruited (Harris and Washington both used the term "shanghaied") from Homicide when they were trying to catch up with Warren K. Fletcher, and kept over their objections because Peter Wohl felt his extraordinary investigative skills would almost certainly be needed in the future.

Jesus Martinez was another young police officer, although far more experienced than Matt. He had begun his police career working undercover in the Narcotics Unit, under then Lieutenant David Pekach. He and another young plainclothes officer named Charles McFadden had—"displaying professional skill and extraordinary initiative far beyond that expected of officers of their rank and experience" according to their departmental citations—located and run to earth "with complete disregard of their personal safety" one Gerald Vincent Gallagher, who had shot to death Captain Richard C. "Dutch" Moffitt during an armed robbery.

The resultant publicity had destroyed their ability to function as undercover Narcotics officers, and for that reason, and as a reward for their effective closing of the case of Captain Moffitt's murder (Mr. Gallagher had been cut into several pieces when run over by a subway train as Officers McFadden and Martinez chased him down the subway tracks), they had been transferred to Highway Patrol.

Highway Patrol was considered a very desirable assignment, and officers were normally not considered for Highway Patrol duty until they had from five to seven years of exemplary service. Inasmuch as Captain Moffitt had been Commanding Officer of Highway at the time of his murder, it was generally agreed that the assignment of Officers McFadden and Martinez to Highway was entirely appropriate, their semi-rookie status notwithstanding.

Officer Martinez had ranked seventh on the Examination for Promotion to Detective when he and several hundred other ambitious police officers had taken it, and had been on the same promotion list which elevated Officer Payne to detective. Officer McFadden had not done nearly as well on the examination, and had been pleasantly surprised to find his the last name on the promotion list when it came out.

Detective Payne and Detective McFadden were friends, as were, of course, Detectives Martinez and McFadden. Detective Payne and Detective Martinez were not friends. Privately, Detective Payne thought of Detective Martinez as a mean little man with a chip on his shoulder, and Detective Martinez thought of Detective Payne as a rich kid with a lot of pull from the Main Line who was playing cop.

Usually—but by no means all the time—Detectives Payne and Martinez kept their dislike for one another under control.

The fourth Detective Personnel space was filled "temporarily" by Police Officer Foster H. Lewis, Jr., twenty-three, who had been on the job even less time than Detective

Payne. Officer Lewis, who stood well over six feet tall and weighed approximately 230 pounds and was thus inevitably known as "Tiny," knew more about the workings of the Police Department than either Detective Payne or Detective Martinez. Not only was his father a policeman, but Tiny had, from the time he was eighteen, worked nights and weekends as a police radio operator in the Police Administration Building. He had been in his first year at Temple University Medical School when he decided that what he really wanted to be was a cop, and not a doctor. This decision had pained and greatly annoyed his father, Lieutenant Foster H. Lewis, Sr.

Lieutenant Lewis was also displeased, for several reasons, with Officer Lewis's assignment to the investigations section of the Special Operations Division. He suspected, for one thing, that because of the growing attention being paid to racial discrimination, his son was the token nigger in Special Operations. Jason Washington might have—indeed, almost certainly had—been selected for his professional ability and not because of the color of his skin, but Lieutenant Lewis could think of no reason but his African heritage that had seen his son assigned to Special Operations practically right out of the Police Academy.

And in plain clothes, with an assigned unmarked car, and what looked like unlimited overtime, which caused his take-home pay (Tiny had somewhat smugly announced) to almost equal that of his father.

Lieutenant Lewis believed that officers should rise within the Department, both with regard to rank and desirable assignment, only after having touched all the bases. Rookies went to work in a district, most often starting out in a van, and gained experience on the street dealing with routine police matters, before being given greater responsibilities. He himself had done so.

The fifth personnel space for a detective with the investigations sections of the Special Operations Division was unfilled.

Detective Payne found a drugstore, purchased a Remington battery-powered electric razor and bottles of Old Spice pre-shave and after-shave lotion, and went back to his car.

This was, he thought, the fifth electric razor he had bought in so many months. While certainly his fellow law-enforcement officers were not thieves, it was apparently true that when they found an unaccompanied electric razor in the men's room at the schoolhouse and it was still there two hours later, they chose to believe that the Beard Fairy had intended it as a present for them.

The black Cadillac limousine provided by the taxpayers of Philadelphia to transport their mayor, the Honorable Jerry Carlucci, about in the execution of his official duties came north on South Broad Street, circled City Hall, which sits in the middle of the intersection of Broad and Market streets in the center of America's fourth-largest city, and turned onto the Parkway, which leads past the Philadelphia Museum of Art to, and then along, the Schuylkill River.

The Mayor was wearing a dark blue suit, a stiffly starched, bright-white shirt, a dark, finely figured necktie, highly polished black shoes, and a Smith & Wesson "Chief's Special" .38 Special caliber revolver in a cutaway leather holster attached to his alligator belt.

He shared the backseat of the limousine with his wife, Angeline, who was wearing a simple black dress with a single strand of pearls and a pillbox hat which she had chosen with great care, knowing that what she chose had to be appropriate for both the events on tonight's social calendar.

The evening had begun with the limousine taking them from their home in Chestnut Hill, in the northwest corner of Philadelphia, to the Carto Funeral Home at 2212 South Broad Street in South Philadelphia.

City Councilman the Hon. Anthony J. Cannatello, a long-time friend and political ally of Mayor Carlucci, had been called to his heavenly home after a long and painful battle with prostate cancer, and an appearance at both the viewing and at the funeral tomorrow was considered a necessary expenditure of the Mayor's valuable and limited time. He had planned to be at Carto's for no more than thirty minutes, but it had been well over an hour before he could break free from those who would have felt slighted if there had not been a chance to at least shake his hand.

Councilman Cannatello's many mourners, the Mayor was fully aware, all voted, and all had relatives who voted, and the way things looked—especially considering what was going to be a front-page story in the Monday editions of Philadelphia's four newspapers—the *Bulletin*, the *Ledger*, the *Inquirer*, and the *Daily News*—he was going to need every last one of their votes.

They were now headed back to Chestnut Hill for an entirely different kind of social gathering, this one a festive occasion at which, the Mayor had been informed, the engagement of Miss Martha Peebles to Mr. David R. Pekach would be announced.

It was going from one end of Philadelphia to the other in both geographical and social terms. The invitations, engraved by Bailey, Banks & Biddle, the city's most prominent jewelers and social printers, requesting "The Pleasure of the Company of The Honorable The Mayor of Philadelphia and Mrs. Jerome H. Carlucci at dinner at 606 Glengarry Lane at half past eight o'clock" had been issued in the name of Mr. and Mrs. Brewster Cortland Payne II.

Mr. Payne, a founding partner of Mawson, Payne, Stockton, McAdoo & Lester, arguably Philadelphia's most prestigious law firm, had been a lifelong friend of Miss Peebles's father, the late Alexander F. Peebles. He had been Alex Peebles's personal attorney, and Mawson, Payne, Stockton, McAdoo & Lester served as corporate counsel to Tamaqua Mining, Inc. In Mr. Peebles's obituary in the *Wall Street Journal*, it was said Mr. Peebles's wholly-owned Tamaqua Mining, Inc., not only owned approximately 11.5 percent of the known anthracite coal reserves in the United States, but had other substantial holdings in petrochemical assets and real estate.

A year after Mr. Peebles's death, it was reported by the *Wall Street Journal* that a suit filed by Mr. Peebles's only son, Stephen, challenging his father's last will and testament, in which he had left his entire estate to his daughter, had been discharged with prejudice by the Third United States Court of Appeals, sitting *en banc*.

As was the case in the Mayor's visit to the viewing of the late City Councilman Cannatello at Carto's, the Mayor had both a personal and a political purpose in attending Martha Peebles's dinner. There would certainly be a larger than ordinary gathering of Philadelphia's social and financial elite there, who not only voted, and had friends and relatives who voted, but who were also in a position to contribute to the Mayor's reelection campaign.

Considering what was going to be in Monday's newspapers, it was important that he appear to Martha Peebles's friends to be aware of the situation, and prepared—more important, competent—to deal with it.

Personally, while he did not have the privilege of a close personal friendship with Miss Peebles, he was acquainted with the groom-to-be, Dave Pekach, and privately accorded him about the highest compliment in his repertoire: Dave Pekach was a hell of a good cop.

The Mayor had a thought.

I think Mickey O'Hara's going to be at the Peebles place, but I don't know. And Mickey's just about as good as I am, getting his hands on things he's not supposed to have. I want him to get this straight from me, not from somebody else, and then have him call me and ask about it. And the time to get it to him is now.

He pushed the switch that lowered the sliding glass partition between the passenger's and chauffeur's sections of the limousine, and slid forward off the seat to get close to the opening.

There was a passenger-to-chauffeur telephone in the limousine, but after trying it once to see if it worked, the Mayor had never used it again. He believed that when you can face somebody when you're talking to them, that's the best way.

The very large black man on the passenger side in the chauffeur's compartment, who carried a photo-identification card and badge in a leather folder stating he was Lieutenant J. K. Fellows of the Philadelphia Police Department, had turned when he heard the dividing glass whoosh downward.

"Mayor?"

"Get on the radio and see if you can get a location on Mickey O'Hara," the Mayor ordered.

Lieutenant Fellows nodded, and reached for one of the two microphones mounted just under the dashboard.

As the Mayor slid back against the cushions, his jacket caught on the butt of his revolver. With an easy gesture, as automatic as checking to see that his tie was in place, he knocked the offending garment out of the way.

Jerry Carlucci rarely went anywhere without his pistol.

There were several theories why he did so. One held that he carried it for self-protection; there was always some nut running loose who wanted to get in the history books by shooting some public servant. The Department had just sent off to Byberry State Hospital a looney-tune who thought God had ordered him to blow up the Vice President of the United States. A perfectly ordinary-looking guy who was a Swarthmore graduate and a financial analyst for a bank, for God's sake, who had a couple of hundred pounds of high explosive in his basement and thought God talked to him!

The Mayor did not like to think how much it had cost the Department in just overtime to put that fruitcake in the bag.

A second theory held that he carried it primarily for public relations purposes. This theory was generally advanced by the Mayor's critics, of whom he had a substantial number. "He's never without at least one cop-bodyguard with-a-gun, so what does he need a gun for? Except to get his picture in the papers, 'protecting us,' waving his gun around as if he thinks he's Wyatt Earp or somebody."

The only person who knew the real reason the Mayor elected to go about armed was his wife.

"Do you need that thing?" Angeline Carlucci had asked several years before, in their bedroom, as she watched him deal with the problem, Where does one wear one's revolver when wearing a cummerbund?

"Honey," the Mayor had replied, "I carried a gun for twenty-six years. I feel kind of funny, sort of half-naked, when I don't have it with me."

Mayor Carlucci had begun his career of public service as a police officer, and had held every rank in the Philadelphia Police Department except policewoman before seeking elective office.

Mrs. Carlucci accepted his explanation. So far as she knew, her husband had never lied to her. If she thought that there were perhaps other reasons—she knew it did not hurt him with the voters when his picture, with pistol visible, at some crime site, was published in the papers—she kept her opinion to herself.

"Mary One," Lieutenant Fellows said into the microphone of the Command Band radio.

The response from Police Radio was immediate.

"Mary One," a pleasant, female-sounding voice replied.

"We need a location on Mickey O'Hara," Lieutenant Fellows said.

"Stand by," Police Radio said, and Lieutenant Fellows hung the microphone up as the dividing glass whooshed back into place.

Police Radio, in the person of thirty-seven-year-old Janet Grosse, a civilian with thirteen years on the job, was very familiar with Mr. O'Hara, as well as with what the Mayor's bodyguard—she had recognized Lieutenant Fellows's voice—wanted. He wanted a location on Mickey O'Hara, that and nothing more. He expected her to be smart enough not to go on the air and inquire of every radio-equipped police vehicle in Philadelphia if they had seen Mickey, and if so, where.

Janet had the capability of doing just that, and if it got down to that, she would have to, the result of which would be that the police frequencies would be full with at least a dozen reports of the last time anyone had seen Mickey's antenna-festooned Buick. While he didn't know every cop in Philadelphia, every cop knew him.

And Mickey would be monitoring his police band radios and would learn that they were looking for him. Fellows had said the Mayor wanted a location on him, not that he wanted Mickey to know he wanted to know where he was.

Janet thought a moment and then threw a switch on her console which caused her voice to be transmitted over the Highway Band. Only those vehicles assigned to Highway Patrol, plus a very few in the vehicles of the most senior white shirts, were equipped with Highway Band radios.

"William One," she said.

William One was the call sign of Inspector Peter Wohl. Janet knew that his official vehicle—an unmarked new Ford, which he customarily drove himself—was equipped with an H-Band radio.

There was no answer, which did not surprise Janet, as she had a good hunch where he was, and what he was doing, and consequently that he would not be listening to his radio. Neither was she surprised when a voice came over the H-Band:

"Radio, this is Highway One. William One is out of service. I can get a message to him."

Highway One was the call sign of the vehicle assigned to the Commanding Officer of the Highway Patrol, which was a subordinate unit of the Special Operations Division.·

I thought that would happen. William One, Highway One, and just about every senior white-shirt not on duty is in Chestnut Hill tonight. Wohl is having Highway One take his calls.

"Highway One, are you in Chestnut Hill?"

"Right."

"Is Mickey O'Hara there, too?"

"Right."

Bingo! I am a clever girl. Look for a gathering of white-shirts where the free booze is flowing, and there will be Mickey O'Hara.

"That will be all, Highway One. Thank you," Janet said. She switched to the Command Band.

"Mary One."

"Mary One."

"The gentleman is in Chestnut Hill at a party," Janet reported. "Do you need an address?"

"That was quick," Fellows said, laughter in his voice. "No, thanks, I'm sure we can find him with that. Thank you."

"Have a good time," Janet said, and sat back and waited for another call.

"Mayor, Mickey's already at the party."

Mayor Carlucci nodded.

"When we get there, find him. Give me a couple of minutes to circulate, and then ask Mickey if he has a moment for me," the Mayor said, "and bring him over."

"Yes, sir."

There were uniforms—white hats from the Traffic Division, not policemen from the Fourteenth District, which included Chestnut Hill—directing traffic on Glengarry Lane in Chestnut Hill. The mayoral limousine was quickly waved to the head of the line of cars waiting to pass through the ornate gates of the five-acre estate. As the Cadillac rolled past, each uniform saluted and got a wave from the Mayor in return.

The long, curving drive to the turn-of-the-century Peebles mansion was lined with parked cars, and there a cluster of chauffeurs gathered around a dozen limousines—including three Rolls Royces, Jerry Carlucci noticed—parked near the mansion itself.

If is wasn't for what's going to be on the front page of every newspaper in town tomorrow, the Mayor thought, *tonight would be a real opportunity. Now all I can hope for is to minimize the damage, keep these people from wondering whether they're betting on the wrong horse.*

There was a man in a dinner jacket collecting invitations just outside the door. He didn't ask for the Mayor's, confirming the Mayor's suspicion that he looked familiar, and was probably a retired police officer, now working as a rent-a-cop for Wachenhut Security, or something like that.

The reception line consisted of Mr. and Mrs. Brewster Cortland Payne II, Miss Martha Peebles, and Mr.—Captain—David Pekach.

"Mrs. Carlucci, Mr. Mayor," Payne said. "How nice to see you."

Payne and Pekach were wearing dinner jackets.

Probably most everybody here will be wearing a monkey suit but me, the Mayor thought. *But it couldn't be helped. I couldn't have shown up at Tony Cannatello's viewing wearing a monkey suit and looking like I was headed right from the funeral home to a fancy party.*

"We're happy to be here, Mr. Payne."

"You know my wife, don't you? And Miss Peebles?"

"How are you, Angeline?" Mrs. Patricia Payne said. "I like your dress."

Patricia Payne and Martha Peebles were dressed similarly, in black, off-the-shoulder cocktail dresses. The Peebles woman had a double string of large pearls reaching to the valley of her breasts, and Mrs. Payne a single strand of pearls.

Nice chest, the Mayor thought, vis-à-vis Miss Peebles. *Nice-looking woman. She'd be a real catch for Dave Pekach even without all that money.*

And then, slightly piqued: *Yeah, of course I know your wife. I've known her longer than you have. I carried her first husband's casket out of St. Dominic's when we buried him. And as long as we've known each other, isn't it about time you started calling me "Jerry"?*

"How is it, Patricia," Angeline Carlucci spoke truthfully, "that you still look like a girl?"

The Mayor had a sudden clear mental image of the white, grief-stricken face of the young widow of Sergeant John X. Moffitt, blown away by a scumbag when answering a silent alarm at a gas station, as they lowered his casket into the ground in St. Dominic's cemetery.

A long time ago. Twenty-five years ago. I was Captain of Highway when Jack Moffitt got killed.

Angie's right. She does look good. Real good. She's a Main Line lady now, a long way from being a cop's widow living with her family off Roosevelt Boulevard.

"I'm so glad you could come," Martha Peebles said to Angeline Carlucci.

"Oh, Jerry wouldn't have missed it for the world," Angeline said.

"No, I wouldn't," the Mayor agreed. "Thank you for having us, Miss Peebles."

"Oh, Martha, please," she said as she took his hand.

Then the Mayor put his hand out to Captain Pekach.

"Don't you look spiffy, Dave," he said.

"Mr. Mayor."

"There's a rumor going around that some unfortunate girl who doesn't know what she's getting into has agreed to marry you. Anything to it?"

Martha Peebles giggled. Dave Pekach looked at her and smiled uneasily at the Mayor but didn't reply.

A waiter in a white jacket stood at the end of the reception line holding a tray of champagne glasses. Angeline took one. The waiter, seeing the indecision on the Mayor's face, said, "There is a bar in the sitting room to your left, Mr. Mayor."

"A little champagne will do just fine," the Mayor said, and took a glass. "But thank you."

NINE

It took the Mayor five minutes to work his way through the entrance foyer to the bar in the sitting room, and another five to find somebody he could leave Angie with and then to reach his destination.

In descending order of importance, he wished to have a word with Chief Inspector Dennis V. Coughlin, Chief Inspector Matthew Lowenstein, and Inspector Peter Wohl. It would have been his intention to first find Denny or Matt and then send Fellows to fetch the others, but luck was with him. The three were standing together in a corner of the sitting room—*not surprising, birds of a feather, et cetera*—and there was a bonus. With them were Chief Inspector (Retired) August Wohl, Detective Matthew M. Payne, and Mr. Michael J. O'Hara of the *Bulletin*.

Chiefs Coughlin, Lowenstein, and Wohl were in business suits. Inspector Wohl and Detective Payne were in monkey suits. Mr. O'Hara was wearing a plaid sports coat of the type worn by the gentlemen who offer suggestions on the wagers one should make at a racetrack.

Not surprising, the Mayor thought. *Dave Pekach works for Peter Wohl, and Peter would have probably rented a monkey suit for this if he didn't have one, and he probably has his own, because he's a bachelor, and doesn't have a family to support and can afford a monkey suit. And Detective Payne not only is also a bachelor with no family to support, but doesn't have to worry about living on a detective's pay anyway. His father—what was the way they put it? His* adoptive father, *he adopted him when he married Patty Moffitt—is Brewster Cortland Payne II.*

The Mayor handed Inspector Wohl his champagne glass.

"Get rid of this for me, will you, Mac?" he asked, as if he thought anybody in a monkey suit had to be a waiter. "Get me a weak scotch, and get my friends another round of whatever they're drinking."

"Good evening, Mr. Mayor," Peter Wohl said, as the others laughed.

"My God, my mistake!" the Mayor said in mock horror. "What we have here is a cop in a monkey suit. I would never have recognized him."

"Two, Jerry," Chief Wohl said. "Three counting Dave Pekach. The Department's getting some class."

As Mayor Carlucci had risen through the ranks of the Police Department he had had Chief Inspector Wohl as his mentor and protector. The phrase used was that "Wohl was Carlucci's rabbi." It was said, quietly of course, but quite accurately, that Chief Wohl had not only helped Carlucci's career prosper, but had on at least two occasions kept it from being terminated.

And Inspector, and then Chief Inspector, and then Deputy Commissioner and ultimately Commissioner Carlucci had been rabbi to Chiefs Coughlin and Lowenstein as they had worked their way up in the hierarchy. Detective Payne, it was universally recognized, had two rabbis, Chief Coughlin and Inspector Wohl.

Payne's relationship with Wohl was the traditional one.

Wohl saw in him a good cop, one who, with guidance and experience, could become a good senior police official. His relationship with Chief Dennis V. Coughlin was something different. Coughlin had been John Francis Xavier Moffitt's best friend since they had been at the Police Academy. He had been the best man at his wedding, and he had gone to tell Patricia Moffitt, pregnant with Matt, that her husband had been killed. Just about everyone—including Jerry Carlucci—had thought it certain that after a suitable period, the Widow Moffitt would marry her late husband's best friend. You didn't have to be Sherlock Holmes to tell from the way he looked at her, and talked about her, how he felt about her.

Patty Moffitt had instead met Brewster Cortland Payne II, an archetypical Main Line WASP, in whose father's law firm she had found work as a typist. He had been widowed four months previously when his wife had died in a traffic accident returning from their summer cottage in the Poconos.

Their marriage had enraged both families. Having lost a mate was not considered sufficient cause to marry hastily, and across a vast chasm of social and religious differences. It was generally agreed that the marriage would not, could not, last, and that was the reason many offered for Denny Coughlin never having married: he was still waiting for Patty Moffitt.

The marriage endured. Payne adopted Matthew Mark Moffitt and gave him his name and his love. Denny Coughlin never married. He and Brewster Payne became friends, and he was Uncle Denny to all the Payne children.

The Mayor shook everybody's hand. A waiter appeared. The Mayor gave him his champagne glass and asked for a weak scotch. Inspector Wohl and Detective Payne both took champagne from the waiter's tray.

"How ya doing, Mayor?" Mickey O'Hara asked.

"Take a look at this," the Mayor said as he took a newspaper clipping from his pocket and handed it to O'Hara, "and make a guess."

O'Hara read the story, then handed it back to the Mayor, who handed it to Chief Wohl.

"You all better read it," the Mayor said.

MORE UNSOLVED MURDERS; NO ARRESTS AND 'NO COMMENT'

BY CHARLES E. WHALEY
PHILADELPHIA LEDGER STAFF WRITER

Capt. Henry O. Quaire, commanding officer of the Homicide Unit of the Philadelphia Police Department, refused to comment on rumors circulating through the police department that a homicide detective is under investigation for the brutal murder of Police Officer Jerome H. Kellog. Chief Inspector Matthew Lowenstein, who heads the Detective Bureau of the Police Department, was "out of town on official business" when this reporter attempted to contact him.

Kellog, 33, who was assigned to the Narcotics Unit, was found Friday morning in his home at 300 West Luray Street in the Feltonville section, dead of multiple gunshot wounds to the head. His death has been classified as "a willful death," which is police parlance for murder.

Rumors began almost immediately to circulate that an unnamed Homicide Unit detective, who is allegedly involved with Officer Kellog's estranged wife, is a prime suspect in the killing.

Although a large number of his fellow police officers called to pay their last respects to Officer Kellog at the John F. Fluehr & Sons Funeral Home this afternoon, including more than a dozen middle-ranking police supervisors, none of the police department's most senior officers were present.

Their absence fueled another rumor, that Officer Kellog was not to be accorded the elaborate funeral rites, sometimes called an "Inspector's Funeral," normally given to a police officer killed in the line of duty.

Capt. Robert F. Talley, Commanding Officer of the Narcotics Unit, who made a brief appearance at the funeral home visitation, accompanying Officer Kellog's widow, refused comment.

Captain Quaire, when asked if the denial to Officer Kellog of an "Inspector's Funeral" suggested that his death was not in the line of duty, said that as far as he knew, no decision had been made in the matter. He stated that Police Commissioner Taddeus Czernich was the official who authorized, or denied, an official police funeral, and that all questions on the subject should be referred to him.

Commissioner Czernich's office, when contacted, said the Commissioner was out of the office, and they had no idea when he would be available to answer questions from the press.

Kellog will be buried tomorrow in Lawnview Cemetery, in Rockledge, following funeral services at the Memorial Presbyterian Church of Fox Chase.

Quaire also said that the Homicide Unit was "actively involved" in the investigation of the murders of Mrs. Alicia Atchison and Anthony J. Marcuzzi in a downtown restaurant shortly after midnight last night, but the police as yet have been unable to identify, much less arrest, the two men who were identified by Gerald N. Atchison, Mrs. Atchison's husband, and the proprietor of the restaurant, as the murderers.

"Why are you surprised?" O'Hara asked. "You know the *Ledger*'s after you."

"I don't care if they go after me," the Mayor said, "but putting in the paper that his widow has been messing around, that's pretty goddamned low. Did you hear those rumors?"

O'Hara nodded.

"Did you write about them?" the Mayor asked. "Or feel your readers had the right to know that the widow was carrying on with some cop?"

O'Hara shook his head.

"There you go, Mick," the Mayor said with satisfaction. "In that one goddamn story, that sonofabitch writes that the widow is a tramp..."

"That's a little strong, Jerry," Chief Wohl protested.

"What do you call a married woman who sleeps with another man?" the Mayor asked sarcastically. "And while we're on that subject, Lowenstein, how is it that neither you nor Quaire told Detective Milham to keep his pecker in his pocket?"

Chief Lowenstein's face colored.

"Jerry, I don't consider that sort of thing any of my business," he said.

"Maybe you should," the Mayor snapped. "I don't know if I'd want a detective around me whose wife divorced him for carrying on with her sister, and the next thing you know is playing hide-the-salami with a brother officer's wife. It says something about his character, wouldn't you say?"

Lowenstein's face was now red.

Chief Wohl touched Lowenstein's arm to stop any response. The worst possible course of action when dealing with an angry Jerry Carlucci was to argue with him.

"Take it easy, Jerry," Chief Wohl said.

Matt Payne glanced at Chief Coughlin. Coughlin made a movement with his head that could have been a signal for him to leave the group. He was considering this possibility when his attention was diverted by the Mayor's angry voice:

"Who the hell are you to tell me to take it easy?"

"Well, for one thing, I'm bigger than you are," Chief Wohl said with a smile, "and for another, smarter. And better-looking."

Carlucci glowered at him.

"Matty," Chief Coughlin said. "Your girlfriend's looking daggers at you. Maybe you better go pay some attention to her."

Matt looked around but could not find Penny Detweiler. He wasn't surprised. Coughlin was telling him a lowly detective should not be here, where he would be privy to what looked like a major confrontation between senior white-shirts and the Mayor of Philadelphia.

"Excuse me," he said.

"You've been doing some good work, Payne," the Mayor said. "It hasn't gone unnoticed."

Carlucci waited until Matt was out of earshot.

"You know what that young man did? Not for publication, Mickey?"

"No," O'Hara replied with a chuckle. "What did that young man do, not for publication?"

"Peter here's been running a surveillance operation," Carlucci began.

"Surveilling who?" O'Hara interrupted.

"I'll get to that in a minute. Anyway, they had a microphone mounted on a window, and it got knocked off. The window was on the thirteenth floor, I forgot to say. So what does Payne do? He goes to the room next door to the one where the mike fell off, goes out on a ledge, and puts it back in place. How's that for balls, Mickey?"

"I hadn't heard about that," Chief Coughlin said, looking at Peter Wohl.

"Either had I," Peter said.

"He knew what had to be done, and he did it," the Mayor said approvingly. "That's the mark of a good cop."

"Or a damned fool," O'Hara said. "It was that important?"

"What the hell could be that important? He could have killed himself," Coughlin said.

"The way it turned out, it was that important," Carlucci said. "If he hadn't put the mike back, we wouldn't have got what we got after he put it back. Tony Harris told me that when he gave me the tapes this morning."

"Which is what?" Coughlin asked.

"Enough, Tony Callis tells me, to just about guarantee a true bill from the grand jury and an indictment."

The Hon. Thomas J. "Tony" Callis was the District Attorney for Philadelphia County.

"Of who?" O'Hara asked.

"Not yet, Mickey, but you will be the first to know, trust me. The warrants are being drawn up. Peter, I think you should let Payne go with you when you and Weisbach serve them; he's entitled."

When I and Weisbach serve them? Wohl thought. *What the hell is that all about?*

"Serve them on who?" O'Hara asked.

"I told you, Mickey, you'll be the first to know, but not right now. For right now, you can have this." The Mayor reached in his pocket and handed O'Hara a folded sheet of paper. "I understand the first of these will be given out first thing in the morning. You don't know where you got that," he said.

O'Hara unfolded the sheet of paper. It was a press release.

POLICE DEPARTMENT

CITY OF PHILADELPHIA

FOR IMMEDIATE RELEASE:

Police Commissioner Taddeus Czernich today announced a major reorganization of the self-policing functions of the Police Department, to take effect with the retirement of Chief Inspector Harry Allgood, presently the Commanding Officer of the Internal Affairs Division. Chief Allgood's retirement will become effective tomorrow.

"The public's faith in the absolute integrity of its police department is our most important weapon in the war against crime," Commissioner Czernich declared.

"A new unit, the Ethical Affairs Unit (EAU), has been formed. It will be commanded by Staff Inspector Michael Weisbach, who will report directly to me on matters concerning any violation of the high ethical standards of behavior demanded of our police officers by the public, myself and Mayor Carlucci," Commissioner Czernich went on.

"I have directed Inspector Peter Wohl, Commanding Officer of the Special Operations Division, to make available to Staff Inspector Weisbach whatever he requires to accomplish his new mission from the assets of Special Operations, which includes the Highway Patrol, the Anti-Crime Teams, and the Special Operations Investigation Section.

"Internal Affairs will continue to deal with complaints from the public regarding inappropriate actions on the part of police officers," Commissioner Czernich concluded.

"What is that, Jerry?" Chief Wohl asked.

"Show it to him, Mickey," the Mayor replied. O'Hara handed it to him.

"I can use this now, or am I supposed to sit on it until everybody else gets it?" O'Hara asked.

"You can use what? I didn't give you anything," Carlucci said.

"OK," O'Hara replied. "I would like to be there, Peter, when you and Weisbach serve your warrants."

"I'm sure Peter can arrange that, Mickey," the Mayor said. "Can't you, Peter?"

"Yes, sir," Wohl said as he took the press release from his father and started to read it.

"I wouldn't be at all surprised if you could find Staff Inspector Weisbach at Peter's office in the morning," the Mayor said.

"I got to go find a phone," O'Hara said.

"Matt," Carlucci said to Chief Lowenstein, "are you having problems with Commissioner Czernich's reorganization plan?"

"'*Commissioner Czernich's* reorganization plan'?" Lowenstein quoted mockingly. "Hell no, Jerry. I know where the Commissioner gets his ideas, and I wouldn't dream of questioning his little inspirations."

Chief Wohl chuckled.

"But I would like to know what the hell's going on," Lowenstein added.

"Well, apparently the Commissioner thought that since Allgood decided to retire, Internal Affairs needed some reorganization."

"Why?" Lowenstein pursued.

"To put a point on it, Matt, because it wasn't doing the job it's supposed to do."

"You got something specific?"

"Yeah, I got something specific," Carlucci said unpleasantly. "That surveillance Peter has been running, that tape I got this morning, because Payne climbed out on a ledge and put the microphone back? It recorded a conversation between Lieutenant Seymour Meyer of Central Police Division's Vice Squad—your friend, Matt—and Paulo Cassandro. You know who Paulo Cassandro is, right?"

"Take it easy, Jerry," Chief Wohl said.

"I know who Paulo Cassandro is," Lowenstein said softly.

"What they were talking about, Matt, was that Meyer and his good buddy, Captain Vito Cazerra—you know Cazerra, don't you, Matt? He commands the Sixth District?"

Lowenstein didn't reply.

"I asked you if you know Captain Cazerra," the Mayor said nastily.

"Yeah. I know him," Lowenstein said.

"As I was saying, we now have a tape of Meyer telling Cassandro that he and Cazerra don't think they're getting a big enough payoff from the mob for letting a Polack whore from Hazleton named Harriet Osadchy run a call-girl operation in our better hotels. You know Harriet Osadchy, Matt?"

"No, I don't know her," Lowenstein said.

"We also have what must be a couple of *miles* of tape of your friend Meyer in the sack with a half-dozen of Harriet Osadchy's whores."

"Jesus!" Lowenstein said.

"Now, I know and you know and Commissioner Czernich knows how hard it is to catch somebody actually taking money. But the Commissioner was very disappointed to learn that Internal Affairs didn't take a close look at Meyer even after they got an anonymous call about the sonofabitch screwing Osadchy's whores in every hotel in Center City."

"They get all kinds of anonymous—"

"Goddamn it, Matt," Carlucci flared, "don't you start to make excuses."

"—calls," Lowenstein went on, undaunted. "A lot of them from disgruntled people just trying to make trouble."

"Yeah, well, this disgruntled person—Peter thinks he's a

retired cop working as hotel security—was so disgruntled that after he called Internal Affairs twice and nothing happened, he wrote me a letter."

"And you put your own private detective bureau to work on it," Lowenstein said bitterly.

"My own detective bureau?" Carlucci replied icily. "I don't know what you're talking about, Lowenstein. But if you have a problem with Commissioner Czernich asking Special Operations to look into something I gave him that neither your detective bureau nor Internal Affairs seem to even have heard about, why don't you ask for an appointment with the Commissioner and discuss it with him?"

There was a tense moment when it looked as if Chief Lowenstein, who had locked eyes with the Mayor, was going to reply.

"Jerry, what's the relationship between EAU and Special Operations—I guess I mean between Peter and Weisbach—going to be under this reorganization?" Chief Wohl asked.

Did he ask that to change the subject to something safer? Peter Wohl wondered. *Or does he see it as a threat to my career?*

The question clearly distracted Mayor Carlucci. He glanced at Chief Wohl in confusion.

"Just a minute, Augie," Carlucci said, turning back to lock eyes with Lowenstein again.

"Lowenstein and I were talking about the Commissioner," he went on. "The Commissioner and I were discussing the Overnights this morning. When he can find the time, he brings them by my office, to keep me abreast of things."

It was common knowledge that at whatever time in the morning the Mayor of Philadelphia arrived at his office, he could expect to find the Police Commissioner of Philadelphia waiting for him in his outer office. The Police Commissioner's own day began when the Mayor was through with him.

"And the Commissioner had an idea. You saw the Overnights this morning, Chief Lowenstein?"

Lowenstein nodded.

"Excuse me? I didn't hear you, Chief."

"Yes, sir, I saw the Overnights," Lowenstein said.

"The double murder in the Inferno Lounge on Market Street? Did that catch your eye?"

"I was at the scene."

"Oh, yeah, that's right. Then you know that Detective Payne was the first police officer on the scene?"

"I saw that."

"Well, the Commissioner saw it too, and he asked me, what did I think of asking Peter, when he could spare him, of course, to send Payne over to Homicide to help Detective Milham on the investigation. Milham has the job, right? Your detective who can't keep his pecker in his pocket?"

"Detective Milham has the job," Lowenstein said, flat-voiced.

"Yeah, right. Well, the Commissioner said that maybe if Peter sent Payne over there, Payne might learn something about how a Homicide investigation is conducted. And he's a bright kid, he might learn some other things, too. About other investigations Homicide is running, for example. Things that would be of interest to Peter and Weisbach in carrying out their new responsibilities."

"You realize the hell of a spot you'd be putting the kid in, Jerry, sending him into Homicide that way? There'd be a lot of resentment," Chief Wohl said.

"Augie, I'm sure the Commissioner has considered that," the Mayor replied. "So anyway, I told the Commissioner that he's the Police Commissioner, he can run the Department any way he pleases, do what he wants. If the Commissioner does decide to ask Inspector Wohl to send Detective Payne over there, are you going to have any problem with that, Chief Lowenstein?"

Lowenstein now had his temper and voice under control.

"I have no problem, Mr. Mayor, with any decision of Commissioner Czernich," he said.

"Good," the Mayor said. "What do they call that? 'Cheerful, willing obedience'?" He turned to Chief Wohl. "You were asking, Augie, what Peter's relationship with the Ethical Affairs Unit is going to be?"

"That press release wasn't very clear about that."

"I thought it was perfectly clear. Peter and Weisbach have worked together before, and I can't imagine they'll have any problems."

Oh, shit! Peter thought. *What that means is that I'll be in the worst possible position. I'll have the responsibility, but no authority.*

"I thought I taught you years ago, Jerry," Chief Wohl said, as if he had been reading his son's mind, "that the worst thing you can do to a supervisor is give him responsibility without the necessary authority."

The Mayor's face suggested he didn't like to be reminded that anyone had ever taught him anything.

"Maybe you're right, Augie," Carlucci said. "Maybe that wasn't clear. I thought it was. Ethical Affairs Unit is under Special Operations. Weisbach reports directly to me, but he works for Peter. You understand that, Peter?"

"Yes, sir."

Carlucci looked around the room.

"Ah, there's Angie," he said. "I better go join her. She doesn't like it when I stay away too long."

He walked away from them.

"Jesus Christ!" Chief Lowenstein said when he was out of earshot.

"My sentiments exactly, Chief," Peter Wohl said.

"That crap about sending Payne to Homicide was a last-minute inspiration of his," Lowenstein said.

"That was to remind you who runs the Department," Chief Wohl said. "He thought maybe you'd forgotten."

"I know who runs the Department," Lowenstein said.

"You shouldn't have argued with him," Chief Wohl said.

"First about Seymour Meyer, and then about Wally Milham. He knows that Meyer is dirty, and thinks Milham is. And he's never wrong, especially when he's hot under the collar. You know that, Matt."

"Christ," Lowenstein said.

"That's what the whole business of sending Payne to Homicide is all about," Chief Wohl went on. "He couldn't think of anything, right then, that would piss you off more, and remind you who runs the Department."

"I'm sorry, sir," the stocky man in a dinner jacket said with a smile, as he saw two young formally dressed couples coming down the second-floor corridor of the Peebles mansion, "this part of the house has been closed off for the evening."

"It's all right," Matt Payne replied, "I'm a police officer, checking on the firearms collection."

The reply was clearly not expected by the stocky man.

"I'll have to see some identification, please," he said.

"Certainly," Matt said, showing his badge. "You're Wachenhut?"

Daffy (Mrs. Chadwick T.) Nesbitt IV giggled.

"Pinkerton," the stocky man said, stepping out of the way.

"Thank you," Matt said, putting his badge holder away and reclaiming the hand of Miss Penelope Detweiler. He led her and the Nesbitts almost to the end of the long corridor, and then opened a door to the right.

"You could fight a war with the guns in here," Matt said as he switched on the lights and signaled for Penny to walk in.

"Jesus," Chad said. "Look at them!"

"That was disgusting," Penny said.

"What was disgusting, love of my life?" Matt asked. There was a strain in his voice.

"We're not supposed to be in here," Penny said.

"Look," he said. "Chad wanted to see the guns. If we had gone to Martha—if we had been able to find Martha in that

mob downstairs—and asked her if we could look at the
guns, she would have said 'sure,' and we would have come
up here, and the Pinkerton guy wouldn't have let us in without written authorization, whereupon I would have showed
him my badge. OK?"

"You think that damned badge makes you something special," Penny said.

"Penny, sometimes you're a pain in the ass," Matt said.

"Hey!" Daffy said. "Stop it, you two!"

"The cabinets are locked," Chad said in disappointment.

"They lock up the crown jewels of England, too," Matt
said. "Something about them being valuable."

"Are these things valuable?" Penny asked.

"Some of the antiques are really worth money," Matt said.
"Museum stuff."

"But what did he do with all of them?" Penny asked.

"Looked at them," Matt said. "Just...took pleasure in having them."

"What the hell is this?" Chad asked, looking down into a
glass-topped, felt-lined display case. "It looks like a sniper
rifle, without a scope."

Matt went and looked.

"That one I know," he said. "The Great White Hunter
showed me that one himself. It's a .30 caliber—note that I
did not say .30-06—Springfield, Model of 1900. When Roosevelt, the first Roosevelt, came back from Cuba and got
himself elected President—"

"What in the world are you talking about?" Penny demanded.

"Turn your mouth off automatic, all right? I'm talking to
Chad."

"Screw you!"

"Before I was so rudely interrupted, Chad: When Roosevelt made the Ordnance Corps pay Mauser for a license to
manufacture bolt actions based on the Spanish 7mm they
used in Cuba, the Springfield Arsenal made a trial run.
Twenty rifles, I think he said. One of them they gave to Roo-

sevelt, who was then President. That's it. Christ only knows how much it's worth. Martha's father told me it took him three years to talk Roosevelt's daughter into selling it to him once he found out she had it."

"Are we finished here?" Penny asked.

"Penny!" Daffy said.

"We are not finished here, love of my life," Matt said, not at all pleasantly. "You may be, but I have just begun to give Chad the tour."

"I want to go back downstairs. I'm bored up here."

"And I'm bored down there."

"You didn't seem to be bored when you were sucking up to the Mayor."

"Have a nice time downstairs, Penelope," Matt said. "Don't let the doorknob hit you in the ass on your way out."

Penny extended her right hand, with the center finger in an extended upward position, the others folded, and walked out of the arms room.

"You're right, Matthew my boy," Chadwick Thomas Nesbitt IV said. "On occasion, and this is obviously one of them, our beloved Penny can be a flaming pain in the ass."

"I suspect it may be that time of the month," Matt said.

Chad laughed.

"The both of you are disgusting!" Daffy said. "I'm going with Penny."

"Mind what Matt said about the doorknob, darling," Chad said.

"You bastard!" Mrs. Nesbitt said, and marched out.

"I am tempted," Matt said, "to repeat the old saw that there would be a bounty on them, if they didn't have—"

"Don't!" Chad interrupted, laughing. "I'm too tired to have to fight to defend the honor of the mother-to-be of my children."

Ten minutes later, as Matt, having successfully gotten through the lock on one of the pistol cabinets, was showing Chad a mint-condition, low-serial-numbered Colt Model 1911 self-loader, Inspector Peter Wohl came into the gun room, trailed by Mrs. C. T. Nesbitt IV and Miss Penelope Detweiler.

"My God, she called the cops!" Matt said, the wit of which remark getting through only to Mr. Nesbitt.

"I asked Penny if she knew where you were," Wohl said. "Got a minute, Matt?"

"Yes, sir. Sure. You know Chad, don't you?"

"Hello, Nesbitt. How are you?"

"Inspector."

"Could you give us a minute?"

"Certainly," Chad said. "I'll be outside."

Wohl waited until they had gone and had closed the door behind them.

"You ever see one of these?" Matt asked, holding the Model 1911 out to Wohl.

"I just heard about you climbing out on the ledge at the Bellvue, you damned fool," Wohl said.

After a just-perceptible hesitation, Matt asked, "Who told you? Harris?"

"Actually, it was the Mayor. Harris told the Mayor and the Mayor told me."

"The Mayor?"

"The Mayor thinks it makes you a cop with great big balls," Wohl said. "I wanted to make sure you understand that in my book it makes you a goddamned fool."

Matt didn't reply for a moment.

"Inspector—"

"Just when I start to think that maybe you've started to grow up, you do something like that. Jesus H. Christ, Matt!"

"Are you willing to listen to me telling you that ledge was eighteen inches wide?"

"Be in my office at quarter to seven in the morning," Wohl said.

"Yes, sir."

"You and Staff Inspector Mike Weisbach are going to serve a warrant of arrest on Lieutenant Seymour Meyer."

"We are? All of a sudden? What happened? Who's Weis-bach?"

"This is in the nature of a reward," Wohl said. "I have been ordered by the Mayor to let you in on the arrest. He thinks your goddamned fool stunt on the ledge entitles you, because at two A.M., Paulo Cassandro and Meyer had an angry discussion, during which they mentioned names and specific sums and Meyer's oral sexual proclivities, all of which were recorded by the microphone you put back in place."

"No crap? We got 'em?"

"If it was up to me, tomorrow morning you'd be back on recovered stolen automobiles."

"Ah, come on, Inspector!"

"If you had fallen off that ledge, Supercop, or if you had been seen up there, all the time and money and effort we spent trying to get Meyer would have gone down the toilet. The conversation we got, or one just as incriminating, would have been repeated in a day or two. Don't you start patting yourself on the back. You acted like a goddamned fool, not like a detective with enough sense to find his ass with both hands."

He locked eyes with Matt until Matt gave in and shrugged his shoulders in chagrin.

"Quarter to seven, Detective Payne," Wohl said. "Have a nice night."

He walked out of the gun room.

Matt replaced the Colt Model 1911 in its cabinet, and was trying to put the cabinet lock back in place when Chad, Penny, and Daffy came back in the room.

"You are forgiven, Penelope," Matt said. "Out of the goodness of my heart. It will not be necessary for you to grovel in tears at my feet."

"What was that business about a ledge at the Bellvue?" Penny asked.

"Does he often call you a goddamned fool?" Chad inquired.

"No comment," Matt said, chuckling, trying desperately but not quite succeeding in making a joke of it.

"What was that all about?"

"He wants to see me at quarter to seven in his office, that's all."

"That's not what it sounded like, buddy." Chad chuckled.

"Tomorrow we're going to play golf!" Penny said. "Tomorrow's your day off. With Tom and Ginny."

"Tomorrow, like the man said, I will be in Wohl's office at quarter to seven. We'll just have to make our excuses to Tom and Ginny. Are they here?"

"We are going to be at Merion at nine," Penny said flatly.

"Chad, how do you feel about an early round?" Matt asked.

"Matt, I mean it!" Penny said.

"Or what, Penny? This is out of my control. I'm sorry, but I'm a cop."

"*You're sorry?* Your precious Inspector Wohl is not the only one who thinks you're a goddamned fool!" Penny said.

"Would you like the goddamned fool to take you home, Penny? I've had about all of you I can stand for one night."

"I'll get home by myself, thank you very much," Penny said.

"Oh, come on, you two," Daffy said.

"Come on, hell!" Penny said, and walked out of the gun room.

"You better go after her, Matt," Daffy said.

"Why? To get more of the same crap she's been giving me all night?"

"She's really angry with you, Matt."

"Frankly, my dear," Matt said, in decent mimicry of Clark Gable in *Gone With the Wind*, "I don't give a damn."

TEN

Chief Inspector Dennis V. Coughlin looked at Chief Inspector August Wohl (Retired) and then at Inspector Peter Wohl, shrugged, and said, "OK. I'll call him."

He leaned forward on Peter Wohl's white leather couch for the telephone. He stopped.

"I don't have his home phone," he said.

"I've got it," Peter Wohl said. "In my bedroom."

He pushed himself out of one of the two matching white leather armchairs and walked into his bedroom.

"I don't like this, Augie," Denny Coughlin said.

"It took place on his watch," Chief Wohl said. "He was getting the big bucks to make sure things like this didn't happen."

"Big bucks!" Coughlin snorted. "I wonder what's going to happen to him?"

"By one o'clock tomorrow afternoon, he will be trans-

189

ferred to Night Command. Unless the Mayor has one of his Italian tantrums again, in which case I don't know."

Peter Wohl came back in his living room with a sheet of paper and handed it to Coughlin.

"How did I wind up having to do this?" Coughlin asked.

"Peter's not senior enough, and the Mayor likes you," Chief Wohl said.

"Jesus," Coughlin said. He ran his finger down the list of private, official, home telephone numbers of the upper hierarchy of the Philadelphia Police Department, found what he was looking for, and dialed the number of Inspector Gregory F. Sawyer, Jr.

Inspector Sawyer was the Commanding Officer of the Central Police Division, which geographically encompasses Center City Philadelphia south of the City Hall. It supervises the Sixth and Ninth police districts, each of which is commanded by a captain. The Sixth District covers the area between Poplar Street on the north and South Street on the south from Broad Street east to the Delaware River, and the Ninth covers the area west of Broad Street between South and Poplar to the Schuylkill River. Its command is generally regarded as a stepping-stone to higher rank; both Chief Wohl and Chief Coughlin had in the past commanded the Central District.

"Barbara, this is Denny Coughlin," Chief Coughlin said into the telephone. "I hate to bother you at home, but I have to speak to Greg."

Chief Wohl leaned forward from his white leather armchair, picked up a bottle of Bushmills Irish whiskey, and generously replenished the glass in front of Denny Coughlin.

"Greg? Denny. Sorry to bother you at home with this, but I didn't want to take the chance of missing you in the morning. We need you, the Commanding Officer of the Sixth, Sy Meyer, a plainclothesman of his named Palmerston, and a Sixth District uniform named Crater at Peter Wohl's office at eight tomorrow morning."

"What's going on, Denny?" Inspector Sawyer inquired, loudly enough so that Chief Wohl and his son could hear.

"There was an incident," Coughlin began, visibly uncomfortable with having to lie, "involving somebody who had Jerry Carlucci's unlisted number. He wants a report from me by noon tomorrow. I figured Wohl's office was the best place to get everybody together as quietly as possible."

"An incident? What kind of an incident?"

"I don't know. I didn't hear about it myself until I saw the Mayor tonight. I guess we'll all find out tomorrow." He paused. "Greg, I probably don't have to tell you this, but don't start your own investigation tonight, OK?"

"Jesus Christ! I haven't heard a goddamned thing."

"Don't feel bad, either did I. Eight o'clock, Greg."

"I'll be there," Inspector Sawyer said.

"Good night, Greg."

"Good night, Denny."

Coughlin put the telephone back in its cradle and picked up his drink.

"Why the hell is my conscience bothering me?" he asked.

"It shouldn't," Chief Wohl said. "Not your conscience."

Officer Charles F. Crater, who lived with his wife Joanne and their two children (Angela, three, and Charles, Jr., eighteen months) in a row house at the 6200 block of Crafton Street in the Mayfair section of Philadelphia, was asleep at 7:15 a.m. when Corporal George T. Peterson of the Sixth District telephoned his home and asked to speak to him.

Mrs. Crater told Corporal Peterson that her husband had worked the four-to-twelve tour and it had been after two when he got home.

"I know, but something has come up, and I have to talk to him," Corporal Peterson replied. "It's important, Mrs. Crater."

Two minutes later, sleepy-eyed, dressed in a cotton bathrobe under which it could be seen that he had been sleeping in his underwear, Officer Crater picked up the telephone.

"What's up?" he asked.

"Charley, do you know where Special Operations Headquarters is?"

"Frankford and Castor?"

"Right. Be there at eight o'clock. See the Sergeant."

"Jesus," Crater said, looking at his watch. "It's quarter after seven. What's going on?"

"Wait a minute," Corporal Peterson said. "Charley, the Sergeant says to send a car for you. Be waiting when it gets there."

"What's going on?"

"Hold it a minute, Charley," Corporal Peterson said.

Sergeant Mario Delacroce came on the line.

"Crater, you didn't get this from me," he said. "All I know is that we got a call from Central Division saying to have you at Special Operations at eight this morning. What I *hear* is that Special Operations has got some operation coming off on your beat, and they want to talk to you."

"What kind of an operation?"

"Charley, Central Division don't confide in me, they just tell me what they want done. There'll be a car at your house in fifteen minutes. Be waiting for it. You want a little advice, put on a clean uniform and have a fresh shave."

"Right," Charley Crater said.

He put the telephone back in its cradle.

"What was that all about?" Joanne Crater asked, concern in her voice.

"Ah, those goddamned Special Operations hotshots are running some kind of operation on my beat, and they want to talk to me," Charley said.

"Talk to you about what?"

"Who knows?" Charley said. "They think their shit don't stink."

"I really wish you'd clean up your language, Charley."

"Sorry," he said. "Honey, I got to catch a quick shave and get dressed. Have I got a fresh uniform?"

"Yeah, there's one I picked up yesterday."

As he went up the stairs to his bedroom, Officer Crater had a very unpleasant thought: *Maybe it has something to do with...Nah, if it was something like that, I'd have been told, before I went off last night, to report to Internal Affairs.*

But what the hell does Special Operations want to ask me about?

Nine months before, a building contractor from Mc-Keesport, Pennsylvania, had telephoned the Eastern Pennsylvania Executive Escort Service, saying the service had been recommended to him by a client of the service. After first ascertaining that the building contractor did indeed know the client, and that he understood the price structure, Mrs. Osadchy dispatched to Room 517 of the Benjamin Franklin Hotel one of her associates, who happened to be an employee of the Philadelphia Savings Fund Society, whose husband had deserted her and their two children, and who worked on an irregular basis for the Eastern Pennsylvania Executive Escort Service to augment her income.

When she reached the building contractor's room, it was evident to her that he was very drunk, and when his behavior was unacceptably crude, she attempted to leave. The building contractor thereupon punched her in the face. She screamed, attracting the attention of the occupants of the adjacent room, who called hotel security.

The on-duty hotel security officer, a former police officer, was contacted as he stood on the sidewalk, chatting with Officer Charles F. Crater, of the Sixth District, who was walking his beat.

Officer Crater, ignoring the hotel security officer's argument that he could deal with the situation alone, accompanied him to the building contractor's room, where they found the building contractor somewhat aghast at the damage he had done to the face of the lady from the Eastern Pennsylvania Executive Escort Service, and the lady herself in the bathroom, trying to stanch the flow of blood from her mouth and nose, so that she could leave the premises without attracting horrified attention to herself.

The lady did not look like what Officer Crater believed hookers should look like. She was weeping. She told Officer Crater that her name was Marianne Connelly, and that her husband had deserted her and their two children, and that she had to do this to put food in their mouths. He believed her. She told him that if anyone at the Philadelphia Savings Fund Society heard about this, she would be fired, and then she didn't know what she would do. He believed her.

The building contractor said that he didn't know what had come over him, that he was a family man with children, and if this ever got back to McKeesport, he would lose his family and probably his business.

The hotel security officer suggested to Officer Crater that no real good would come from arresting the building contractor, since there were no witnesses to the assault, and the lady from the Eastern Pennsylvania Executive Escort Service wouldn't humiliate herself, and set herself up to surely get fired, by going to court to testify against him.

What harm would there be, the hotel security officer argued, if they settled this bad situation right here and now? The building contractor would give the lady from the Eastern Pennsylvania Executive Escort Service money, enough not only to pay for her medical bills and the damage to her clothing, but to compensate her for what the sonofabitch had done to her.

The sonofabitch produced a wallet stuffed with large-denomination bills to demonstrate his willingness to go along with this solution to the problem.

"Give it all to her," Officer Crater ordered.

"I got to keep out a few bucks, for Christ's sake!"

"Give it all to her, you sonofabitch!" Officer Crater ordered angrily, and watched as the building contractor gave the lady from the Eastern Pennsylvania Executive Escort

Service all the money in his wallet. Then he turned to the hotel security officer. "You'll see that she gets out of here and home all right, right?"

"Absolutely."

Officer Crater then turned and left the room.

The lady from the Eastern Pennsylvania Executive Escort Service went home and telephoned Mrs. Osadchy to report what had happened.

"How much did he give you, Marianne?"

"Six hundred bucks."

"You keep it, and I promise you, this will never happen again."

Mrs. Osadchy also reported the incident to Mr. Cassandro, who considered the situation a moment and then said, "I think, since the cop was so nice, that we ought to show our appreciation. Give the broad a couple of hundred and tell her to give it to the cop."

"I already told Marianne she could keep the dough she got from the john."

"Then you give her the money for the cop, Harriet. Consider it an investment. Trust me. Do it."

Two days later, while Officer Crater was walking his beat, the lady from the Philadelphia Savings Fund Society who moonlighted at the Eastern Pennsylvania Executive Escort Service approached him.

"I want to thank you for the other night," she said. "I really appreciate it."

"Aaaaaah," Officer Crater said, somewhat embarrassed.

"No, I really mean it," she said. "I really appreciate what you did for me."

"Forget it," Officer Crater said.

The lady handed him what looked like a greeting card.

"What's this?" Officer Crater asked.

"It's a thank-you card. I got it at Hallmark."

"You didn't have to do that," Officer Crater said. "All I was trying to do was make the best of a bad situation."

"You're sweet," the lady said. "What did you say your name was?"

"Crater."

"I mean your first name."

"Charley," Officer Crater replied.

"Mine's Marianne," she said. "Thanks again, Charley." She kissed Officer Crater on the cheek and walked away.

Officer Crater stuffed the Hallmark thank-you card in his pocket and resumed walking his beat. When he got home, he took another look at it. Inside the card were four crisp fifty-dollar bills.

"Jesus Christ!" Officer Crater said. He went to the bathroom and tore the thank-you card in little pieces and flushed the pieces down the toilet. His wife, he knew, would never understand. The two hundred he folded up and put in the little pocket in his wallet which, before he got married, he had used to hold a condom.

The next time he saw her, he told himself, he would give the money back to her. There was no point in making a big deal of the money; telling his sergeant about it would mean having to tell him what he had done in the first place.

A week after that, before he saw the lady again, he had a couple of drinks too many after work in Dave's Bar, at Third Street and Fairmount Avenue, with Officer William C. Palmerston, whom he had worked with in the Sixth District before Palmerston had been transferred to Vice.

He told him, out of school, about the thank-you card with the two hundred bucks in it, and that he intended to return it to the hooker the next time he saw her.

"Don't be a goddamned fool," Palmerston said. "Keep it."

"You're kidding, right?"

"It's not like she bribed you, is it? All you did was what you thought was the right thing to do in that situation, right? I mean, you didn't catch her doing something wrong, right? You didn't say, 'For two hundred bucks, I'll let you go,' did you?"

"No, of course not."

"You did her a favor, she appreciated it. Keep the money."

"You'd keep it?"

Officer Palmerston, in reply, extended his hand, palm upward, to Officer Crater.

"Try me."

"All right, goddamn you, Bill, I will," Officer Crater said, and took two of the fifties from the condom pocket in his wallet and laid them in Officer Palmerston's palm. Officer Palmerston stuffed the bills in his shirt pocket, then called for another round.

"I'll pay," Officer Palmerston said, and laid one of the fifties on the bar.

The next time, several days later, Officer Crater saw the lady from the Eastern Pennsylvania Executive Escort Service he could not, of course, give her the two hundred back, since he'd given half of it to Officer Palmerston.

She came up to him right after he started walking his beat, where he was standing on the corner of Ninth and Chestnut streets.

"Hi, Charley," she said. "How are you?"

"Hi," he replied, thinking again that Marianne didn't really look like a hooker.

"You ever get a break?" she asked. "For a cup of coffee or something?"

"Sure."

"I was about to have a cup of coffee. I'll buy," the lady said.

He seemed hesitant, and she saw this.

"Charley, all I'm offering is a cup of coffee," she said. "Come on."

Why not? Officer Crater reasoned. *I mean, what the hell is wrong with drinking a cup of coffee with her?*

They had coffee and a couple of doughnuts in a luncheonette. He never could remember afterward what they had talked about until Marianne suddenly looked at her watch and said she had to go. And offered her hand for him to shake, and he took it, and there was something in her hand.

"The lady I work for says thank you, too," Marianne said, and was gone before he could say anything else, or even look at what she had left in his hand.

When he finally looked, it was a neatly folded, crisp one-hundred-dollar bill.

"Jesus Christ!" he said aloud, before quickly putting the bill in his trousers pocket.

When he got off work that night, he went to Dave's Bar before going home, in the hope that he would run into Bill Palmerston.

Palmerston was already in Dave's Bar when he got there, and when he bought Palmerston a drink, he paid for it with the hundred-dollar bill.

Palmerston looked at the bill and then at Crater.

"Where'd you get that?"

"The same place I got the fifties," Crater said.

"Lucky you."

Palmerston watched as the bartender made change, and when he had gone, looked at Crater and asked, "Don't tell me your conscience is bothering you again?"

"A little," Officer Crater confessed.

Officer Palmerston reached toward the stack of bills on the bar and carefully pulled two twenties and a ten from it.

"Feel better?" he asked.

"Jesus, Bill, I don't like this."

"Don't be a damned fool," Palmerston said. "It's not like you're doing something wrong." Then Palmerston had a second thought. "Anybody see her give this to you?"

Crater shook his head.

"Then don't worry about it," Palmerston said. "Nobody's getting hurt. But I'll tell you what I'm going to do. I'm going to ask around."

"Ask around about what?"

"I wonder why this lady is being so nice to you. It sure

isn't because of the size of your cock. If I come up with something, I'll let you know."

Two weeks later, as Officer Crater was walking his beat, an unmarked car pulled to the curb beside him.

"Get in the back, Charley," Officer Palmerston, who was in the front passenger seat beside the driver, said.

Charley got in the backseat.

"This is Lieutenant Meyer," Palmerston said.

"How are you, Crater?"

"How do you do, sir?"

"I work for the Lieutenant, Charley," Palmerston said.

"Oh, yeah?"

"Bill tells me you're an all-right guy, Crater. Not too smart, but the kind of a guy you can trust."

Palmerston laughed.

"He also told me about your lady friend, the one you helped out, the one who's been showing her gratitude to you."

For a fleeting moment, Charley was very afraid that Bill Palmerston had turned him in for taking the hundred dollars from Marianne every week. But that passed. The Lieutenant wouldn't be talking the way he was if he was going to arrest him or anything like that.

"That's what I meant about you not being too smart, Charley," Lieutenant Meyer said.

"Sir?"

"You really don't know much about your lady friend's business, do you?"

"No, sir."

"Well, let me tell you what I found out after Bill came to me. What Bill and I found out. Your friend works for a woman named Harriet Osadchy. Her sheet shows three busts for prostitution here, and she has a sheet in Hazleton—you know where Hazleton is, Charley?"

"Out west someplace, in the coal regions."

"Right. Anyway, this Osadchy woman has a sheet as long as you are tall in Hazleton, mostly prostitution, some controlled-substance busts, all nol-prossed, even a couple of drunk and disorderlies. But she's smart. You got to give her that, right, Bill?"

"Yes, sir," Officer Palmerston said.

"We didn't even have a line on this Eastern Pennsylvania Executive Escort Service until you brought it to Bill's attention."

"The what?"

"The Eastern Pennsylvania Executive Escort Service. That's what she calls her operation."

"Oh."

"But like I was saying, now we have a line on her. She's got maybe twenty, twenty-five, maybe more hookers working for her. It's a high-class operation. The minimum price is a hundred dollars. That's for one hour."

"Damn!"

"Bill had a talk with your friend Marianne. She said the split is sixty-forty. For her forty percent, Harriet makes the appointments for the girls, and takes care of what has to be taken care of."

"Excuse me?"

"Her girls know that when they knock on some hotel door, they're not going to find some weirdo inside, or a cop, and that they'll get their money. They even take one of those credit card machines with them, in case—and you'd be surprised how often this happens—the john can put the girl on his expense account as secretarial services, or a rental car, or something like that."

"I didn't know they could use credit cards," Officer Crater confessed.

"There's a lot you don't know," Lieutenant Meyer said. "You got any idea how much money is involved here?"

"Not really. You said a hundred an hour."

"Right. Sometimes they stay more than an hour. Sometimes the john wants something more than a straight fuck. That costs more, of course. But the low side would be that a girl would work three johns a night. Let's say Harriet has twenty girls working. That's three times a hundred bucks times twenty girls."

"Six thousand dollars," Officer Crater said wonderingly.

"Right. Times seven nights a week. That's forty-two thousand gross. Harriet's share of that would come to almost seventeen thousand a week. It's a money machine. Now out of that, she has to pay her expenses. Three, four telephones. The rent on a little apartment she has on Cherry Street where the phones are. She has a couple of lawyers on retainer, and a couple of doctors who make sure the girls are clean, and she takes care of the people in the hotels who could make trouble for her. And then I'm sure she has some arrangement with the mob. Usually that's ten percent."

"With the mob? What for?"

"To be left alone. Years ago, the mob ran whorehouses. The Chinese still have a couple running. We keep shutting them down and they keep opening them up, but the mob found out that whorehouses are really more trouble than they're worth, so they went out of that business. Why the hell not, if they can take, like I said, ten percent of Harriet's forty-two thousand a week for doing nothing more than putting the word out on the street that Harriet is a friend of theirs? A freelance hooker can almost expect to get robbed, but even a really dumb sleazeball thug knows better than to mess with anyone who is a friend of the mob."

Officer Crater grunted.

"OK. So let's talk about where we fit in here," Meyer said. "The first thing you have to understand is that prostitution has been around a long time—they don't call it 'the oldest profession' for nothing—and there's absolutely no way to stop it. All we can do is control it. What the citizens don't want is hookers approaching people on the street, or in a bar. The citizens don't want disease. They don't want to see young girls—or, for that matter, young boys—involved. For the obvious reasons. And I think we do a pretty job of giving the citizens what they want.

"What the citizens also want, and I don't think most people understand this, or if they do, don't want to admit it, is somebody like Harriet Osadchy. The johns pay their money, they get what they want, they don't get a disease, they don't get robbed, nobody gets hurt, and nobody finds out that they're not getting what they should be getting at home."

"Yeah," Officer Crater said. "I see what you mean."

"And the Harriet Osadchys of this world don't give the police any trouble, either. They do their thing, and they do it clean, and we have the time to do what we're hired to do, protect the people. We close down the whorehouses, we keep the hookers from working the streets and the bars, we keep the people from getting a disease or robbed, or blackmailed, all those things."

"I see what you mean."

"So now we get back to you, and your friend Marianne. You did the right thing by her and the guy who beat her up. I mean, what good would it have done if you had run him in? Your friend Marianne would not have testified against him anyway, and he made it right by her by giving her a lot of money, right?"

"I think she would have really lost her job if the PSFS heard about that," Officer Crater said.

"Sure she would have," Lieutenant Meyer agreed. "And her john would have gotten in trouble with his wife, a lot of people would have been hurt, and you solved the problem all around. I would have done exactly the same thing myself."

"I thought it was the right thing to do," Officer Crater said.

"OK. So what happened next? Marianne told Harriet what happened, and Harriet knew that it would have been a real pain in the ass, really hurt her business, if you had gone strictly by the book and hauled either one of them in. So she was grateful, right, and she told Marianne to slip you a couple of hundred bucks right off, and a hundred a week regular after that. A little two-hundred-dollar present to say thank you for not running Marianne in, and a regular little hundred-dollar-a-week present just to remind you that being a good guy, doing what's right, sometimes gets you a little extra money. Nothing wrong with that, right?"

"Not the way you put it," Officer Crater said. "It bothered—"

"Wrong, you stupid shit!" Lieutenant Meyer snarled.

"Excuse me?"

"I explained to you, Crater, that Harriet Osadchy is personally pocketing *at least* seventeen thousand, seventeen thousand tax-free, by the way, each and every week, and you really pull her fucking chestnuts out of the fire, really save her ass, really save her big bucks, and she throws a lousy two hundred bucks at you? And figures she's buying you for a hundred a week? That's fucking *insulting*, Crater, can't you see that?"

Officer Crater did not reply.

"She's paying, as her cost of doing business, and happy to do it, some lawyer maybe a *thousand* a week, and some doctor another *thousand*, and slipping the mob probably *ten percent* of however the fuck much she takes in, and she slips you a lousy, what, a *total* of maybe *five hundred*, and you're not insulted?"

"I guess I never really thought about it," Officer Crater confessed.

"Right. You're goddamned right you didn't think about it," Meyer said.

"I don't know what you want me to say, Lieutenant," Crater said.

"You don't say anything, that's what I want you to say. We'll all be better off if you never open your mouth again. I will tell you what's going to happen, Crater. Your friend Marianne, the next time you see her, is going to give you another envelope. This one will have a thousand dollars in it. You will take two hundred for your trouble and give the rest to Bill. And every week the same goddamned thing. Am I getting through to you?"

"What do I have to do?"

"I already told you. Keep your mouth shut. That's all. And remember, if you're as stupid as I'm beginning to think you are, that if you start thinking about maybe going to Internal Affairs or something, it'd be your word against mine and Bill's. Not only would we deny this conversation ever took place, but Internal Affairs would have your ass for not coming to them the first time your friend Marianne gave you money."

Lieutenant Meyer took his arm off the back of the seat and faced forward and turned the ignition.

"Tell whatsisname he'd better get out of the car now, Bill," he said. "Unless he wants to go with us."

Staff Inspector Mike Weisbach turned off Frankford Avenue onto Castor and then drove into the parking lot of the Special Operations Division. He saw a parking slot against the wall of the turn-of-the-century school building marked RESERVED FOR INSPECTORS and steered his unmarked Plymouth into it.

I usually go on the job looking forward to what the day will bring, he thought as he got out of the car, *but today is different; today, I suspect, I am not going to like at all what the day will bring, and I don't mean because I'm not used to getting up before seven o'clock to go to work.*

He entered the building through the nearest door, above which "BOYS" had been carved in the granite, and found himself in what had been, and was now, a locker room. The difference was that the boys were now all uniformed officers, mostly Highway Patrolmen, and the room was liberally decorated with photographs of young women torn from *Playboy, Hustler*, and other literary magazines.

"How do I find Inspector Wohl's office?" Mike addressed a burly Highway Patrolman sitting on a wooden bench in his undershirt, scrubbing at a spot on his uniform shirt.

"I don't think you're supposed to be in here, sir," the Highway Patrolman said, using the word as he would use it to a civilian he had just stopped for driving twenty-five miles over the speed limit the wrong way down a one-way street. "Visitors is supposed to use the front door."

The Highway Patrolman examined him carefully.

"I know you?"

"I don't believe I've had the pleasure. My name is Mike Weisbach."

The Highway Patrolman stood up.

"Sorry, Inspector," he said. "I didn't recognize you. There's stairs over there. First floor. Used to be the principal's office."

"Thank you," Mike said, and then smiled and said, "Your face is familiar, too. What did you say your name was?"

"Lomax, sir. Charley Lomax."

"Yeah, sure," Mike said, and put out his hand. "Good to see you, Charley. It's been a while."

"Yes, sir. It has," Lomax said.

When he reached the outer office of the Commanding Officer of the Special Operations Division, Weisbach identified himself as Staff Inspector Weisbach to the young officer in plain clothes behind the desk.

"I know he's expecting you, Inspector. I'll see if he's free," the young officer said, and got up and walked to a door marked INSPECTOR WOHL, knocked, and went inside.

Mike's memory, which had drawn a blank vis-à-vis Officer Lomax, now kicked in about Wohl's administrative assistant.

His name is O'Mara, Paul Thomas. His father is Captain Aloysious O'Mara, who commands the Seventeenth District. His brother is Sergeant John F. O'Mara of Civil Affairs. His grandfather had retired from the Philadelphia Police Department. His transfer to Special Operations had been arranged because Special Operations was considered a desirable assignment for a young officer with the proper nepotistic connections.

That's not why I'm here. Lowenstein didn't arrange this transfer for me to enhance my career. I'm here to help Jerry Carlucci get reelected.

Peter Wohl, without a jacket, his sleeves rolled up and his tie pulled down, appeared at the door.

"Come on in, Mike," he said. "Can I have Paul get you a cup of coffee?"

"Please," Mike said.

"Three, Paul, please," Wohl ordered, and held the door open for Weisbach.

"Morning, Mike," Mickey O'Hara called as Weisbach entered the office.

He was sitting on a couch. On the coffee table in front of him was a tape recorder and a heavy manila paper envelope.

"What's good about it, Mick?" Weisbach asked.

"Peter's been telling me that the forces of virtue are about to triumph over the forces of evil," O'Hara replied. "I get an exclusive showing a dirty district captain and a dirty lieutenant on their way to the Central Cellroom. I like that, professionally and personally. So far as I'm concerned, that's not a bad way to start my day."

"Mick," Wohl asked, "how would you feel about going with Mike Sabara when he picks up Paulo Cassandro?"

"Instead of staying here, you mean?" O'Hara replied, and then went on without giving Wohl a chance to reply. "For one thing, Peter, the arrest of second- or third-level gangsters is not what gets on the front page. The arrest of a police captain, a district commander, is. And please don't tell him I said so, but Mike Sabara is not what you could call photogenic."

"It's your call, Mickey."

"I know what you're trying to do, Peter," Mickey said. "Keep a picture of a dirty captain getting arrested out of the papers. But it won't work. That's news, Peter."

"And you're here with Carlucci's blessing, right?"

"Yeah, I am, Peter. Sorry."

"OK. Let's talk about what's going to happen. Chief Coughlin will be here any minute. Inspector Sawyer and the others no later than eight. Sawyer comes in here. Coughlin plays the tape of Meyer and Cassandro for him—"

Wohl pointed to the tape machine.

"Coughlin's going to play the tape for him?" Mickey interrupted, sounding surprised.

"That was my father's idea. He and Coughlin choreographed this for me last night. The tape is damned incriminating. That should, I was told, keep Sawyer from loyally defending his men. And, Mickey, Carlucci's blessing or not, you are not going to be here when that happens."

"OK. Do I get to hear the tape?"

"Can you live with taking my word that it's incriminating?"

"Can I listen to it out of school?"

"OK. Why not?"

"Before?"

"After."

O'Hara shrugged his acceptance.

"Then we go to the Investigation Section, upstairs, where Cazerra, Meyer, and the two officers will be waiting. Inspector Sawyer will arrest Captain Cazerra. I will arrest Lieutenant Meyer. Their badges, IDs, and guns will be taken from them. Staff Inspector Weisbach, assisted by Detectives Payne and Martinez, will arrest the two officers, and take their guns and badges."

"Am I going to get to be there?" O'Hara asked.

"When Inspector Sawyer comes in here, you leave," Wohl said. "Wait outside. When we come out, we will be on our way upstairs. You can come with us."

"Thank you."

"The Fraternal Order of Police will be notified immediately after the arrests," Wohl went on. "It will probably take thirty minutes for them to get an attorney, attorneys, here. When that is over, I will take Captain Cazerra to the Police Administration Building in my car, which will be driven by Sergeant Washington. He will not be placed in a cell. Chief Coughlin has arranged for him to be immediately booked, photographed, fingerprinted, and arraigned. He will almost certainly be released on his own recognizance."

"Nice, smooth operation," O'Hara said.

"The same thing will happen with the others. Weisbach will take Lieutenant Meyer to the Roundhouse in his car, with Officer Lewis driving. Detectives Payne and Martinez will take the two officers in a Special Operations car."

"It would be nice if I could get a shot of Cazerra and Meyer in handcuffs," O'Hara said.

Wohl ignored him.

"It would be a good public relations shot, either one of them in cuffs," O'Hara pursued.

Wohl looked at him and shook his head.

"Mick," he said. "I am aware that there are certain public relations aspects to this, otherwise the Prince of the Fourth Estate would not be sitting in my office with egg spots on his tie and his fly open."

Mickey O'Hara glanced in alarm toward his crotch. His zipper was fastened.

"Screw you, Peter." He laughed. "Question: Don't you think the Mayor would be happier if Captain Cazerra were arrested by the new Chief of the Ethical Affairs Unit?"

"Why would that make the Mayor happier?"

"Maybe assisted by Detective Payne?" Mickey went on, not directly answering the question. "Handsome Matthew is always good copy. That picture, I'm almost sure, would make page one. Isn't that what Carlucci wants? More to the point, why he fixed it for me to be here?"

"I suggested last night that Mike make all the arrests."

"Thanks a lot, Peter," Mike Weisbach said sarcastically.

"Coughlin shot me down," Wohl went on. "There's apparently a sacred protocol here, and Coughlin wants it followed."

"Just trying to be helpful," Mickey said. "For purely selfish reasons. I want to get invited back the next time. I guess the Mayor will have to be happy with a picture of the Black Buddha standing behind Cazerra going into the Roundhouse. That should produce a favorable reaction from the voting segment of the black population, right?"

"Even if it does humiliate every policeman in Philadelphia," Wohl said bitterly. "Mike, you've heard it. See anything wrong with it?"

Weisbach shook his head.

"OK," Wohl said. "Then that's the way we'll do it."

"OK," Weisbach parroted.

"Afterward, Mike, you and I are going to have a long talk about the Ethical Affairs Unit."

"Right," Weisbach said.

Wohl's door opened and Chief Inspector Coughlin walked in.

"Morning," he said.

"Good morning, Chief," Wohl and Weisbach said, almost in unison.

"How are you, Mickey?" Coughlin said cordially, offering his hand.

"No problems," O'Hara said.

"Peter fill you in on what's going to happen?"

"Yep."

"Mick, just now, as I was driving over here, I wondered if you might not want to go with Captain Sabara when he arrests Cassandro."

"Nice try, Denny," O'Hara said. "But like I told Peter, a picture of a third-rate gangster in cuffs isn't news. A District captain getting arrested is."

Officer O'Mara put his head in the door.

"Inspector Sawyer is here, sir."

Wohl looked at Coughlin, who nodded.

"Ask him to come in," Peter said.

Inspector Gregory Sawyer, a somewhat portly, gray-haired man in his early fifties, came in the room.

He was visibly surprised at seeing Mickey O'Hara.

"I'll see you guys later," Mickey said. "How are you, Greg?"

He walked out of the room.

"Greg," Coughlin said. "I wasn't exactly truthful with you last night."

"Excuse me, Chief?"

"That thing ready?" Coughlin asked, pointing at the tape recorder.

"Yes, sir," Wohl said.

"Sit down, Greg," Coughlin said.

"Yes, sir."

"At the orders of the Commissioner, Inspector Wohl has been conducting an investigation of certain allegations involving Captain Cazerra, Lieutenant Meyer, and others in your division. A court order was obtained authorizing electronic surveillance of a room in the Bellvue-Stratford Hotel. What you are about to hear is one of the recordings made," Coughlin said formally. "Turn it on, please," he said, and then walked to Wohl's window and looked out at the lawn in front of the building.

ELEVEN

At 7:40 A.M. Miss Penelope Detweiler was sitting up in her canopied four-poster bed in her three-room apartment on the second floor of the Detweiler mansion when Mrs. Violet Rogers, who had been employed as a domestic servant by the Detweilers since Miss Detweiler was in diapers, entered carrying a tray with coffee, toast, and orange juice.

Miss Detweiler was wearing a thin, pale blue, sleeveless nightgown. Her eyes were open, and there was a look of surprise on her face.

There was a length of rubber medical tubing tied around Miss Detweiler's left arm between the elbow and the shoulder. A plastic, throwaway hypodermic injection syringe hung from Miss Detweiler's lower left arm.

"Oh, Penny!" Mrs. Rogers moaned. "Oh, Penny!"

She put the tray on the dully gleaming cherrywood hope chest at the foot of the bed, then stood erect, her arms folded disapprovingly against her rather massive breast, her full, very black face showing mingled compassion, sorrow, and anger.

And then she met Miss Detweiler's eyes.

"Oh, sweet Jesus!" Mrs. Rogers said, moaned, and walked quickly to the bed.

She waved a large, plump hand before Miss Detweiler's eyes. There was no reaction.

She put her hand to Miss Detweiler's forehead, then withdrew it as if the contact had burned.

She put her hands on Miss Detweiler's shoulders and shook her.

"Penny! Penny, honey!"

There was no response.

When Mrs. Rogers removed her hands from Miss Detweiler's shoulders and let her rest again on the pillows against the headboard, Miss Detweiler started to slowly slide to the right.

Mrs. Rogers tried to stop the movement but could not. She watched in horror as Miss Detweiler came to rest on her side. Her head tilted back, and she seemed to be staring at the canopy of her bed.

Mrs. Rogers turned from the bed and walked to the door. In the corridor, the walk became a trot, and then she was running to the end of the corridor, past an oil portrait of Miss Detweiler in her pink debutante gown, past the wide stairway leading down to the entrance foyer of the mansion, into the corridor of the other wing of the mansion, to the door of the apartment of Miss Detweiler's parents.

She opened and went through the door leading to the apartment sitting room without knocking, and through it to the closed double doors of the bedroom. She knocked at the left of the double doors, then went through it without waiting for a response.

H. Richard Detweiler, a tall, thin man in his late forties, was sleeping in the oversize bed, on his side, his back to his wife Grace, who was curled up in the bed, one lower leg outside the sheets and blankets, facing away from her husband.

Mr. Detweiler, who slept lightly, opened his eyes as Mrs. Rogers approached the bed.

"Mr. D," Violet said. "You better come."

"What is it, Violet?" Mr. Detweiler asked in mingled concern and annoyance.

"It's Miss Penny."

H. Richard Detweiler sat up abruptly. He was wearing only pajama bottoms.

"Jesus, now what?"

"You'd better come," Mrs. Rogers repeated.

He swung his feet out of the bed and reached for the dressing gown he had discarded on the floor before turning out the lights. As he put it on, his feet found a pair of slippers.

Mrs. Detweiler, a finely featured, rather thin woman of forty-six, who looked younger, woke, raised her head, and looked around and then sat up. Her breasts were exposed; she had been sleeping wearing only her underpants.

"What is it, Violet?" she asked as she pulled the sheet over her breasts.

"Miss Penny."

"What about Miss Penny?"

H. Richard Detweiler was headed for the door, followed by Violet.

"Dick?" Mrs. Detweiler asked, and then, angrily, "Dick!"

He did not reply.

Grace Detweiler got out of bed and retrieved a thick terry-cloth bathrobe from the floor. It was too large for her, it was her husband's, but she often wore it between the shower and the bed. She put it on, and fumbling with the belt, followed her husband and Violet out of her bedroom.

H. Richard Detweiler entered his daughter's bedroom.

He saw her lying on her side and muttered something unintelligible, then walked toward the canopied bed.

"Penny?"

"I think she's gone, Mr. D," Violet said softly.

He flashed her an almost violently angry glare, then bent over the bed and, grunting, pushed his daughter erect. Her head now lolled to one side.

Detweiler sat on the bed and exhaled audibly.

"Call Jensen," he ordered. "Tell him we have a medical emergency, and to bring the Cadillac to the front door."

Violet went to the bedside and punched the button that would ring the telephone in the chauffeur's apartment over the five-car garage.

H. Richard Detweiler stood up, then squatted and grunted as he picked his daughter up in his arms.

"Call Chestnut Hill Hospital, tell them we're on the way, and then call Dr. Dotson and tell him to meet us there," Detweiler said as he started to carry his daughter across the room.

Mrs. Arne—Beatrice—Jensen answered the telephone on the second ring and told Mrs. Rogers her husband had just left in the Cadillac to take it to Merion Cadillac-Olds for service.

"Mr. D," Mrs. Rogers said, "Jensen took the limousine in for service."

"Go get the Rolls, please, Violet," Detweiler said, as calmly as he could manage.

"Oh, my God!" Mrs. Grace Detweiler wailed as she came into the room and saw her husband with their daughter in his arms. "What's happened?"

"Goddamn it, Grace, don't go to pieces on me," Detweiler said. He turned to Violet.

"Not the Rolls, the station wagon," he said, remembering.

There wasn't enough room in the goddamned Rolls Royce Corniche for two people and a large-sized cat, but Grace had to have a goddamned convertible.

"What's the matter with her?" Grace Detweiler asked.

"God only knows what she took this time," Detweiler said, as much to himself as in reply to his wife.

"Beatrice," Violet said, "get the keys to the station wagon. I'll meet you by the door."

"Oh, my God!" Grace Detweiler said, putting her balled fist to her mouth. "She's unconscious!"

"Baxley has the station wagon," Mrs. Jensen reported. "He's gone shopping."

Baxley was the Detweiler butler. He prided himself that not one bite of food entered the house that he had not personally selected. H. Richard Detweiler suspected that Baxley had a cozy arrangement with the grocer's and the butcher's and so on, but he didn't press the issue. The food was a good deal better than he had expected it would be when Grace had hired the Englishman.

"Baxley's gone with the station wagon," Violet reported.

Goddamn it all to hell! Both of them gone at the same time! And no car, of five, large enough to hold him with Penny in his arms. And nobody to drive the car if there was one.

"Call the police," H. Richard Detweiler ordered. "Tell them we have a medical emergency, and to send an ambulance immediately."

He left the bedroom carrying his daughter in his arms, and went down the corridor, past the oil portrait of his daughter in her pink debutante gown and then down the wide staircase to the entrance foyer.

"Police Radio," Mrs. Leander—Harriet—Polk, a somewhat more than pleasingly plump black lady, said into the microphone of her headset.

"We need an ambulance," Violet said.

Harriet Polk had worked in the Radio Room in the Police Administration Building for nineteen years. Her long experience had told her from the tone of the caller's voice that this was a genuine call, not some lunatic with a sick sense of humor.

"Ma'am, what's the nature of the problem?"

"She's unconscious, not breathing."

"Where are you, Ma'am?"

"928 West Chestnut Hill Avenue," Violet said. "It's the Detweiler estate."

Harriet threw a switch on her console which connected her with the Fire Department dispatcher. Fire Department Rescue Squads are equipped with oxygen and resuscitation equipment, and manned by firemen with special Emergency Medical Treatment training.

"Unconscious female at 928 West Chestnut Hill Avenue," she said.

Then she spoke to her caller.

"A rescue squad is on the way, Ma'am," she said.

"Thank you," Violet said politely.

Nineteen years on the job had also embedded in Harriet Polk's memory a map of the City of Philadelphia, overlaid by Police District boundaries. She knew, without thinking about it, that 928 West Chestnut Hill Avenue was in the Fourteenth Police District. Her board showed her that Radio Patrol Car Twenty-three of the Fourteenth District was in service.

Harriet moved another switch.

"Fourteen Twenty-three," she said. "928 West Chestnut Hill Avenue. A hospital case. Rescue en route."

Police Officer John D. Wells, who also had nineteen years on the job, was sitting in his three-year-old Chevrolet, whose odometer was halfway through its second hundred thousand miles, outside a delicatessen on Germantown Avenue.

He had just failed to have the moral courage to refuse stuffing his face before going off shift and home. He had a wax-paper-wrapped Taylor-ham-and-egg sandwich in his hand, and a large bite from same in his mouth.

He picked up his microphone and, with some difficulty, answered his call: "Fourteen Twenty-three, OK."

He took off the emergency brake and dropped the gearshift into drive.

He had spent most of his police career in North Philadelphia, and had been transferred to "The Hill" only six months before. He thought of it as being "retired before retiring." There was far less activity in affluent Chestnut Hill than in North Philly.

He didn't, in other words, know his district well, but he knew it well enough to instantly recall that West Chestnut Hill Avenue was lined with large houses, mansions, on large plots of ground, very few of which had numbers to identify them.

Where the hell is 928 West Chestnut Hill Avenue?

Officer Wells did not turn on either his flashing lights or siren. There was not much traffic in this area at this time of the morning, and he didn't think it was necessary. But he pressed heavily on the accelerator pedal.

H. Richard Detweiler, now staggering under the hundred-and-nine-pound weight of his daughter, reached the massive oak door of the foyer. He stopped and looked angrily over his shoulder and found his wife.

"Grace, open the goddamned door!"

She did so, and he walked through it, onto the slate-paved area before the door.

Penny was really getting heavy. He looked around, and walked to a wrought-iron couch and sat down in it.

Violet appeared.

"Mr. D," she said, "the police, the ambulance, is coming," she said.

"Thank you," he said.

He looked down at his daughter's face. Penny was looking at him, but she wasn't seeing him.

Oh, my God!

"Violet, please call Mr. Payne and tell him what's happened, and that I'm probably going to need him."

Violet nodded and went back in the house.

● ● ●

Brewster Cortland Payne II, Esq., a tall, well-built—he
had played tackle at Princeton in that memorable year when
Princeton had lost sixteen of seventeen games played—man
in his early fifties, was having breakfast with his wife, Patricia, on the patio outside the breakfast room of his ram-
bling house on a four-acre plot on Providence Road in
Wallingford when Mrs. Elizabeth Newman, the Payne
housekeeper, appeared carrying a telephone on a long cord.

"It's the Detweilers's Violet," she said.

Mrs. Payne, an attractive forty-four-year-old blonde, who
was wearing a pleated skirt and a sweater, put her coffee cup
down as she watched her husband take the telephone.

"For you?" she asked, not really expecting a reply.

"Good morning, Violet," Brewster C. Payne said. "How
are you?"

"Mr. Detweiler asked me to call," Violet said. "He said he
will probably need you."

"What seems to be the problem?"

Payne, who was a founding partner of Mawson, Payne,
Stockton, McAdoo & Lester, arguably Philadelphia's most
prestigious law firm, was both Mr. H. Richard Detweiler's
personal attorney and his most intimate friend. They had
been classmates at both Episcopal Academy and Princeton.

Violet told him what the problem was, ending her recitation of what had transpired by almost sobbing, "I think
Penny is gone, Mr. Payne. He's sitting outside holding her in
his lap, waiting for the ambulance, but I think she's gone."

"Violet, when the ambulance gets there, find out where
they're taking Penny. Call here and tell Elizabeth. I'm leaving right away. When I get into Philadelphia, I'll call here
and Elizabeth can tell me where to go. Tell Mr. Detweiler
I'm on my way."

He broke the connection with his finger, lifted it and
waited for a dial tone, and then started dialing again.

"Well, what is it?" Patricia Payne asked.

"Violet went into Penny's room and found her sitting up
in bed with a needle hanging out of her arm," Payne replied,

evenly. "They're waiting for an ambulance. Violet thinks it's too late."

"Oh, my God!"

A metallic female voice came on the telephone: "Dr. Payne is not available at this time. If you will leave your name and number, she will return your call as soon as possible. Please wait for the tone. Thank you."

He waited for the tone and then said, "Amy, if you're there, please pick up."

"Dad?"

"Penny was found by the maid ten minutes ago with a needle in her arm. Violet thinks she's gone."

"Damn!"

"I think you had better go out there and deal with Grace," Brewster Payne said.

"Goddamn!" Dr. Amelia Payne said.

"Tell her I'm coming," Patricia said.

"Your mother said she's coming to Chestnut Hill," Payne said.

"All right," Amy said, and the connection went dead.

Payne waited for another dial tone and dialed again.

"More than likely by mistake," Matt's voice said metallically, "you have dialed my number. If you're trying to sell me something, you will self-destruct in ten seconds. Otherwise, you may leave a message when the machine goes bleep."

Bleep.

"Matt, pick up."

There was no human voice.

He's probably at work, Payne decided, and replaced the handset in its cradle.

"Elizabeth, please call Mrs. Craig—you'd better try her at home first—and tell her that something has come up and I don't know when I'll be able to come to the office. And ask her to ask Colonel Mawson to let her know where he'll be this morning."

Mrs. Newman nodded.

"Poor Matt," Mrs. Newman said.

"Good God!" Brewster Payne said, and then stood up. His old-fashioned, well-worn briefcase was sitting on the low fieldstone wall surrounding the patio. He picked it up and then jumped over the wall and headed toward the garage. His wife started to follow him, then stopped and called after him: "I've got to get my purse. And I'll try to get Matt at work."

She waited until she saw his head nod, then turned and went into the house.

Officer John D. Wells, in RPC Fourteen Twenty-three, slowed down when he reached the 900 block of West Chestnut Hill Avenue, a little angry that his memory had been correct.

There are no goddamned numbers. Just tall fences that look like rows of spears and fancy gates, all closed. You can't even see the houses from the street.

Then, as he moved past one set of gates, it began to open, slowly and majestically. He slammed on the brakes and backed up, and drove through the gates, up a curving drive lined with hundred-year-old oak trees.

If this isn't the place, I can ask.

It was the place.

There was a man on a patio outside an enormous house sitting on an iron couch holding a girl in her nightgown in his arms.

Wells got quickly out of the car.

"Thank God!" the man said, and then, quickly, angrily: "Where the hell is the ambulance? We called for an ambulance!"

"A rescue squad's on the way, sir," Wells said.

He looked down at the girl. Her eyes were open. Wells had seen enough open lifeless eyes to know this girl was dead. But he leaned over and touched the carotid artery at the rear of her ear, feeling for a pulse, to make sure.

"Can you tell me what happened, sir?" he asked.

"We found her this way, Violet found her this way."

There came the faint wailing of a siren.

"There was a needle in her arm," a large black woman said softly, earning a look of pained betrayal from the man holding the body.

Wells looked. There was no needle, but there was a purple puncture wound in the girl's arm.

"Where did you find her?" Wells asked the black woman.

"Sitting up in her bed," Violet said.

The sound of the ambulance siren had grown much louder. Then it shut off. A moment later the ambulance appeared in the driveway.

Two firemen got quickly out, pulled a stretcher from the back of the van, and, carrying an oxygen bottle and an equipment bag, ran up to the patio.

The taller of them, a very thin man, did exactly what Officer Wells had done, took a quick look at Miss Penelope Detweiler's lifeless eyes and concluded she was dead, and then checked her carotid artery to make sure.

He met Wells's eyes and, just perceptibly, shook his head.

"Sir," he said, very kindly, to H. Richard Detweiler, "I think we'd better get her onto the stretcher."

"There was, the lady said, a needle in her arm," Wells said.

H. Richard Detweiler now gave Officer Wells a very dirty look.

The very thin fireman nodded. The announcement did not surprise him. The Fire Department Rescue Squads of the City of Philadelphia see a good many deaths caused by narcotics overdose.

Officer Wells went to his car and picked up the microphone.

"Fourteen Twenty-three," he said.

"Fourteen Twenty-three," Harriet Polk's voice came back immediately.

"Give me a supervisor at this location. This is a Five Two Nine Two."

Five Two Nine Two was a code that went back to the time before shortwave radio and telephones, when police communications were by telegraph key in police boxes on street corners. It meant "dead body."

"Fourteen B," Harriet called.

Fourteen B was the call sign of one of two sergeants assigned to patrol the Fourteenth Police District.

"Fourteen B," Sergeant John Aloysius Monahan said into his microphone. "I have it. En route."

Officer Wells picked up a clipboard from the floor of the passenger side of his car and then went back onto the patio. The firemen were just finishing lowering Miss Detweiler onto the stretcher.

The tall thin fireman picked up a worn and spotted gray blanket, held it up so that it unfolded of its own weight, and then very gently laid it over the body of Miss Detweiler.

"What are you doing that for?" H. Richard Detweiler demanded angrily.

"Sir," the thin fireman said, "I'm sorry. She's gone."

"She's not!"

"I'm really sorry, sir."

"Oh, Jesus H. fucking Christ!" H. Richard Detweiler wailed.

Mrs. H. Richard Detweiler, who had been standing just inside the door, now began to scream.

Violet went to her and, tears running down her face, wrapped her arms around her.

"What happens now?" H. Richard Detweiler asked.

"I'm afraid I've got to ask you some questions," Officer Wells said. "You're Mr. Detweiler? The girl's father?"

"I mean what happens to...my daughter? I suppose I'll have to call the funeral home—"

"Mr. Detweiler," Wells said, "what happens now is that someone from the Medical Examiner's Office will come here and officially pronounce her dead and remove her body to the morgue. Under the circumstances, the detectives will have to conduct an investigation. There will have to be an examination of the remains."

"An autopsy, you mean? Like hell there will be."

"Mr. Detweiler, that's the way it is," Wells said. "It's the law."

"We'll see about that!" Detweiler said. "That's my daughter!"

"Yes, sir. And, sir, a sergeant is on the way here. And there will be a detective. There are some questions we have to ask. And we'll have to see where you found her."

"The hell you will!" Detweiler fumed. "Have you got a search warrant?"

"No, sir," Wells said. There was no requirement for a search warrant. But he did not want to argue with this grief-stricken man. The Sergeant was on the way. Let the Sergeant deal with it.

He searched his memory. John Aloysius Monahan was on the job. Nice guy. Good cop. The sort of a man who could reason with somebody like this girl's father.

Sergeant John Aloysius Monahan got out of his car and started to walk up the wide flight of stairs to the patio. Officer Wells walked down to him. Monahan saw a tall man in a dressing robe sitting on a wrought-iron couch, staring at a blanket-covered body on a stretcher.

"Looks like an overdose," Wells said softly. "The maid found her, the daughter, in her bed with a needle in her arm."

"In her bed? How did she get down here?"

"The father carried her," Wells said. "He was sitting on that couch holding her in his arms when I got here. He's pretty upset. I told him about the M.E., the autopsy, and he said 'no way.'"

"You know who this guy is?" Monahan asked.

Wells shook his head, then gestured toward the mansion. "Somebody important."

"He runs Nesfoods," Monahan said.

"Jesus!"

Monahan walked up the shallow stairs to the patio.
"Mr. Detweiler," he said.

It took a long moment before Detweiler raised his eyes to him.

"I'm Sergeant Monahan from the Fourteenth District, Mr. Detweiler," he said. "I'm very sorry about this."

Detweiler shrugged.

"I'm here to help in any way I can, Mr. Detweiler."

"It's a little late for that now, isn't it?"

"It looks that way, Mr. Detweiler," Monahan agreed. "I'm really sorry." He paused. "Mr. Detweiler, I have to see the room where she was found. Maybe we'll find something there that will help us. Could you bring yourself to take me there?"

"Why not?" H. Richard Detweiler replied. "I'm not doing anybody any good here, am I?"

"That's very good of you, Mr. Detweiler," Sergeant Monahan said. "I appreciate it very much."

He waited until Detweiler had stood up and started into the house, then motioned for Wells to follow them.

"What's your daughter's name, Mr. Detweiler?" Monahan asked gently. "We have to have that for the report."

"Penelope," Mr. Detweiler said. "Penelope Alice."

Behind them, as they crossed the foyer to the stairs, Officer Wells began to write the information down on Police Department Form 75-48.

They walked up the stairs and turned left.

"And who besides yourself and Mrs. Detweiler," Sergeant Monahan asked, "was in the house, sir?"

"Well, Violet, of course," Detweiler replied. "I don't know if the cook is here yet."

"Wells," Sergeant Monahan interrupted.

"I got it, Sergeant," Officer Wells said.

"Excuse me, Mr. Detweiler," Sergeant Monahan said.

Officer Wells let them get a little ahead of them, then, one at a time, he picked two of the half-dozen Louis XIV chairs that were neatly arranged against the walls of the corridor. He placed one over the plastic hypodermic syringe that both he and Sergeant Monahan had spotted, and the second over a length of rubber surgical tubing, to protect them.

Then he walked quickly after Sergeant Monahan and Mr. Detweiler.

Sergeant John Aloysius Monahan was impressed with the size of Miss Penelope Alice Detweiler's apartment. It was as large as the entire upstairs of his row house off Roosevelt Boulevard. The bathroom was as large as his bedroom. He was a little surprised to find that the faucets were stainless steel. He would not have been surprised if they had been gold.

And he was not at all surprised to find, on one of Miss Detweiler's bedside tables, an empty glassine packet, a spoon, a candle, and a small cotton ball.

He touched nothing.

"Is there a telephone I can use, Mr. Detweiler?" he asked.

Detweiler pointed to the telephone on the other bedside table.

"The detectives like it better if we don't touch anything," Monahan said. "Until they've had a look."

"There's one downstairs," Detweiler said. "Sergeant, may I now call my funeral director? I want to get...her off the patio. For her mother's sake."

"I think you'd better ask the Medical Examiner about that, Mr. Detweiler," Monahan said. "Can I ask you to show me the telephone?"

"All right," Detweiler said. "I was thinking of Penny's mother."

"Yes, of course," Monahan said. "This is a terrible thing, Mr. Detweiler."

He waited until Detweiler started out of the room, then followed him back downstairs. Officer Wells followed both of them. Detweiler led him to a living room and pointed at a telephone on a table beside a red leather chair.

"Officer Wells here," Monahan said, "has some forms that have to be filled out. I hate to ask you, but could you give him a minute or two?"

"Let's get it over with," Detweiler said.

"Officer Wells, why don't you go with Mr. Detweiler?" Monahan said, waited until they had left the living room, closed the door after them, went to the telephone, and dialed a number from memory.

"Northwest Detectives, Detective McFadden."

Detective Charles McFadden, a very large, pleasant-faced young man, was sitting at a desk at the entrance to the offices of the Northwest Detective Division, on the second floor of the Thirty-fifth Police District building at North Broad and Champlost streets.

"This is Sergeant Monahan, Fourteenth District. Is Captain O'Connor around?"

"He's around here someplace," Detective McFadden said, then raised his voice: "Captain, Sergeant Monahan on Three Four for you."

"What can I do for you, Jack?" Captain Thomas O'Connor said.

"Sir, I'm out on a Five Two Nine Two in Chestnut Hill. The Detweiler estate. It's the Detweiler girl."

"What happened to her?"

"Looks like a drug overdose."

"I'll call Chief Lowenstein," Captain O'Connor said, thinking aloud.

Lowenstein would want to know about this as soon as possible. For one thing, the Detweiler family was among the most influential in the city. The Mayor would want to know about this, and Lowenstein could get the word to him.

Captain O'Connor thought of another political ramification to the case: the Detweiler girl's boyfriend was Detective Matthew Payne. Detective Payne had for a rabbi Chief Inspector Dennis V. Coughlin. It was a toss-up between Coughlin and Lowenstein for the unofficial title of most important chief inspector. O'Connor understood that he would have to tell Coughlin what had happened to the Detweiler girl. And then he realized there was a third police officer who had a personal interest and would have to be told.

"You're just calling it in?" O'Connor asked.

"I thought I'd better report it directly to you."

"Yeah. Right. Good thinking. Consider it reported. I'll get somebody out there right away. A couple of guys just had their court appearances canceled. I don't know who's up on the wheel, but I'll see the right people go out on this job. And I'll go myself."

"The body's still on a Fire Department stretcher," Monahan said. "The father carried it downstairs to wait for the ambulance. I haven't called the M.E. yet."

"You go ahead and call the M.E.," O'Connor said. "Do this strictly by the book. Give me a number where I can get you."

Monahan read it off the telephone cradle and O'Connor recited it back to him.

"Right," Monahan said.

"Thanks for the call, Jack," O'Connor said, and hung up.

He looked down at Detective McFadden.

"Who's next up on the wheel?"

"I am. I'm holding down the desk for Taylor."

"When are Hemmings and Shapiro due in?"

Detective McFadden looked at his watch.

"Any minute. They called in twenty minutes ago."

"Have Taylor take this job when he gets here. I don't think you should."

McFadden's face asked why.

"That was a Five Two Nine Two, Charley. It looks like your friend Payne's girlfriend put a needle in herself one time too many."

"Holy Mother of God!"

"At her house. That's all I have. But I don't think you should take the job."

"Captain, I'm going to need some personal time off."

"Yeah, sure. As soon as Hemmings comes in. Take what you need."

"Thank you."

"I've seen pictures of her," Captain O'Connor said. "What a fucking waste!"

"Chief Coughlin's office. Sergeant Holloran."
"Captain O'Connor, Northwest Detectives. Is the Chief available?"
"He's here, but the door is closed. Inspector Wohl is with him, Captain."
"I think this is important."
"Hold on, Captain."
"Coughlin."
"Chief, this is Tom O'Connor."
"I hope this is important, Tom."
"Sergeant Monahan of the Fourteenth just called in a Five Two Nine Two from the Detweiler estate. The girl. The daughter. Drug overdose."
"Jesus, Mary, and Joseph," Chief Coughlin responded with even more emotion than O'Connor expected. Then, as if he had not quite covered the mouthpiece with his hand, O'Connor heard him say, "Penny Detweiler overdosed. At her house. She's dead." ⁄
"I'll be a sonofabitch!" O'Connor heard Inspector Peter Wohl say.
"Chief, I've been trying to get Chief Lowenstein. You don't happen to know where he is, do you?"
"Haven't a clue, Tom. It's ten past eight. He should be in his office by now."
"I'll try him there again," O'Connor said.
"Thanks for the call, Tom."
"Yes, sir."

At 7:55 A.M., Police Commissioner Taddeus Czernich, a tall, heavyset, fifty-seven-year-old with a thick head of silver hair, had been waiting in the inner reception room of the office of the Mayor in the City Hall Building when one of the telephones on the receptionist's desk had rung.
"Mayor Carlucci's office," the receptionist, a thirty-odd-

year-old, somewhat plump woman of obvious Italian extraction, had said into the telephone, and then hung up without saying anything else. Czernich thought he knew what the call was. Confirmation came when the receptionist got up and walked to the door of the Mayor's private secretary and announced, "He's entering the building."

The Mayor's secretary, another thirty-odd-year-old woman, also of obvious Italian extraction, who wore her obviously chemically assisted blond hair in an upswing, had arranged for the sergeant in charge of the squad of police assigned to City Hall to telephone the moment the mayoral limousine rolled into the inner courtyard of the City Hall Building.

Czernich stood up and checked the position of the finely printed necktie at his neck. He was wearing a banker's gray double-breasted suit and highly polished black wing-tip shoes. He was an impressive-looking man.

Three minutes later, the door to the inner reception room was pushed open by Lieutenant Jack Fellows. The Mayor marched purposefully into the room.

"Good morning, Mr. Mayor," the Police Commissioner and the receptionist said in chorus.

"Morning," the Mayor said to the receptionist and then turned to the Police Commissioner, whom he did not seem especially overjoyed to see. "Is it important?"

"Yes, Mr. Mayor, I think so," Czernich replied.

"Well, then, come on in. Let's get it over with," the Mayor said, and marched into the inner office, the door to which was now held open by Lieutenant Fellows.

"Good morning," the Mayor said to his personal secretary as he marched past her desk toward the door of his office. By moving very quickly, Lieutenant Fellows reached it just in time to open it for him.

Commissioner Czernich followed the Mayor into his office and took up a position three feet in front of the Mayor's huge, ornately carved antique desk. The Mayor's secretary appeared carrying a steaming mug of coffee bearing the logotype of the Sons of Italy.

The Mayor sat down in his dark green high-backed leather chair, leaned forward to glance at the documents waiting for his attention on the green pad on his desk, lifted several of them to see what was underneath, and then raised his eyes to Czernich.

"What's so important?"

Commissioner Czernich laid a single sheet of paper on the Mayor's desk, carefully placing it so that the Mayor could read it without turning it around.

"Sergeant McElroy brought that to my house while I was having my breakfast," Commissioner Czernich said, a touch of indignation in his voice.

The Mayor took the document and read it.

CITY OF PHILADELPHIA

MEMORANDUM

To: POLICE COMMISSIONER

From: COMMANDING OFFICER, DETECTIVE BUREAU

Subject: COMPENSATORY TIME/RETIREMENT

   1. The undersigned has this date placed himself on leave (compensatory time) for a period of fourteen days.
   2. The undersigned has this date applied for retirement effective immediately.
   3. Inasmuch as the undersigned does not anticipate returning to duty before entering retirement status, the undersigned's identification card and police shield are turned in herewith.

M. L. Lowenstein
Matthew L. Lowenstein
Chief Inspector

82-S-1AE (Rev. 3/59) RESPONSE TO THIS MEMORANDUM MAY BE MADE HEREON IN LONGHAND

"Damn!" the Mayor said.

Czernich took a step forward and laid a chief inspector's badge and a leather photo identification folder on the Mayor's desk.

"You did not see fit to let me know Chief Lowenstein was involved in your investigation," Czernich said.

"Damn!" the Mayor repeated, this time with utter contempt in his voice, and then raised it. "Jack!"

Lieutenant Fellows pushed the door to the Mayor's office open.

"Yes, Mr. Mayor?"

"Get Chief Lowenstein on the phone," the Mayor ordered. "He's probably at home."

"Yes, sir," Fellows said, and started to withdraw.

"Use this phone," the Mayor said.

Fellows walked to the Mayor's desk and picked up the handset of one of the three telephones on it.

"This makes the situation worse, I take it?" Commissioner Czernich asked.

"Tad, just close your mouth, all right?"

"Mrs. Lowenstein," Fellows said into the telephone. "This is Lieutenant Jack Fellows. I'm calling for the Mayor. He'd like to speak to Chief Lowenstein."

There was a reply, and then Fellows covered the microphone with his hand.

"She says he's not available," he reported.

"Tell her thank you," the Mayor ordered.

"Thank you, Ma'am," Lieutenant Fellows said, and replaced the handset in its cradle and looked to the Mayor for further orders.

"Take a look at this, Jack," the Mayor ordered, and pushed the memorandum toward Fellows.

"My God!" Fellows said.

"I had no idea this mess we're in went that high," Commissioner Czernich said.

"I thought I told you to close your mouth," the Mayor said, then looked at Fellows. "Jack, call down to the courtyard and see if there's an unmarked car down there. If there is, I want it. You drive. If there isn't, call Special Operations and have them meet us with one at Broad and Roosevelt Boulevard."

"Yes, sir," Fellows reported, and picked up the telephone again.

The Mayor watched, his face expressionless, as Fellows called the sergeant in charge of the City Hall detail.

"Inspector Taylor's car is down there, Mr. Mayor," Fellows reported.

"Go get it. I'll be down in a minute," the Mayor ordered.

"Yes, sir."

The Mayor watched Fellows hurry out of his office and then turned to Commissioner Czernich.

"How many people know about that memo?"

"Just yourself and me, Mr. Mayor. And now Jack Fellows."

"Keep—" the Mayor began.

"And Harry McElroy," Czernich interrupted him. "It wasn't even sealed. The envelope, I mean."

"Keep it that way, Tad. You understand me?"

"Yes, of course, Mr. Mayor."

The Mayor stood up and walked out of his office.

"Sarah," the Mayor of the City of Philadelphia said gently to the gray-haired, soft-faced woman standing behind the barely opened door of a row house on Tyson Street, off Roosevelt Boulevard, "I know he's in there."

She just looked at him.

She looks close to tears, the Mayor thought. *Hell, she has been crying. Goddamnitalltohell!*

"What do you want me to do, Sarah?" the Mayor asked very gently. "Take the door?"

The door closed in his face. There was the sound of a door chain rattling, and then the door opened. Sarah Lowenstein stood behind it.

"In the kitchen," she said softly.

"Thank you," the Mayor said, and walked into the house and down the corridor beside the stairs and pushed open the swinging door to the kitchen.

Chief Matthew L. Lowenstein, in a sleeveless undershirt, was sitting at the kitchen table, hunched over a cup of coffee. He looked up when he heard the door open, and then, when he saw the Mayor, quickly averted his gaze.

The Mayor laid Lowenstein's badge and photo ID on the table.

"What is this shit, Matt?"

"I'm trying to remember," Lowenstein said. "I think if you just walked in, that's simple trespassing. If you took the door, that's forcible entry."

"Sarah let me in."

"I told her not to. What's on your mind, Mr. Mayor?"

"I want to know what the hell this is all about."

Lowenstein raised his eyes to look at the Mayor.

"OK," he said. "What it's all about is that you don't need a chief of detectives you don't trust."

"Who said I don't trust you? For God's sake, we go back a long way together, twenty-five years, at least. Of course I trust you."

"That's why you're running your own detective squad, right? And you didn't tell me about it because you trust me? Bullshit, Jerry, you don't trust me. My character or my professional competence."

"That's bullshit!"

"And I don't have to take your bullshit, either. I'm not Taddeus Czernich. I've got my time on the job. I don't need it, in other words."

"What are you pissed off about? What happened at that goddamned party? Matt, for Christ's sake, I was upset."

"You were a pretty good cop, Jerry. Not as good as you think you were, but good. But that doesn't mean that nobody else in the Department is as smart as you, or as honest. I'm as good a cop, probably better—*I* never nearly got thrown out of the Department or indicted—than you ever were. So let me put it another way. I'm sick of your bullshit, I don't have to put up with it, and I don't intend to. I'm out."

"Come on, Matt!"

"I'm out," Lowenstein repeated flatly. "Find somebody else to push around. Make Peter Wohl Chief of Detectives. You really already have."

"So that's it. You're pissed because I gave Wohl Ethical Affairs?"

"That whole Ethical Affairs idea stinks. Internal Affairs, a part of the Detective Bureau, is supposed to find dirty cops. And by and large, they do a pretty good job of it."

"Not this time, they didn't," the Mayor said.

"I was working on it. I was getting close."

"There are political considerations," the Mayor said.

"Yeah, political considerations," Lowenstein said bitterly.

"Yeah, political considerations," Carlucci said. "And don't raise your nose at them. You better hope I get reelected, or you're liable to have a mayor and a police commissioner you'd *really* have trouble with."

"We don't have a police commissioner now. We have a parrot."

"That's true," the Mayor said. "But he takes a good picture, and he doesn't give you any trouble. Admit it."

"An original thought and a cold drink of water would kill the Polack," Lowenstein said.

"But he doesn't give you any trouble, does he, Matt?" the Mayor persisted.

"You give me the goddamned trouble. *Gave* me. Past tense. I'm out."

"You can't quit now."

"Watch me."

"The Department's in trouble. Deep trouble. It needs you. I need you."

"You mean you're in trouble about getting yourself re-elected."

"If I don't get reelected, then the Department will be in even worse trouble."

"Has it ever occurred to you that maybe the Department wouldn't be in trouble if you let the people who are supposed to run it actually run it?"

"You know I love the Department, Matt," the Mayor said. "Everything I try to do is for the good of the Department."

"Like I said, make Peter Wohl chief of detectives. He's already investigating everything but recovered stolen vehicles. Jesus, you even sent the Payne kid in to spy on Homicide."

"I sent the Payne kid over there to piss you off. I was already upset about these goddamned scumbags Cazerra and Meyer, and then you give me an argument about your detective who got caught screwing his wife's sister, and whose current girlfriend is probably involved in shooting her husband."

"That's bullshit and you know it."

"I wish I did know it."

Lowenstein looked at the Mayor and then shook his head.

"That's what Augie Wohl said. And Sarah said it, too. That you did that just to piss me off."

"And it worked, didn't it?" the Mayor said, pleased. "Better than I hoped."

"You sonofabitch, Jerry," Lowenstein said.

"Augie and Sarah are only partly right. Pissing you off wasn't the only thing I had in mind."

"What else?"

"I gave Ethical Affairs to Peter Wohl for political considerations, and even if you don't like the phrase, I have to worry about it. Peter's Mr. Clean in the public eye, the guy who put Judge Moses Findermann away. I needed something for the newspapers besides 'Internal Affairs is conducting an investigation of these allegations.' Christ, can't you see that? The papers, especially the *Ledger*, are always crying 'Police cover-up!' If I said that Internal Affairs was now investigating something they should have found out themselves, what would that look like?"

Chief Lowenstein granted the point, somewhat unwillingly, with a shrug.

"What's that got to do with Payne, sending him in to spy on Homicide?"

"Same principle. His picture has been all over the papers. Payne is the kind of cop the public wants. It's like TV and the movies. A good-looking young cop kills the bad guys and doesn't steal money."

There was a faint suggestion of a smile on Lowenstein's lips.

"So I figured if I send Payne to spend some time at Homicide (a) he can't really do any harm over there and (b) if it turns out your man who can't keep his dick in his pocket and/or the widow—and get pissed if you want, Matt, but that wouldn't surprise me a bit if that's the way it turns out—had something to do with Kellog getting himself shot, then what the papers have is another example of one of Mr. Clean's hotshots cleaning up the Police Department."

"I talked to Wally Milham, Jerry. I've seen enough killers and been around enough cops to know a killer and/or a lying cop when I see one. He didn't do it."

"Maybe he didn't, but if she had something to do with it, and he's been fucking her, which is now common knowledge, it's the same thing. You talk to her?"

"No," Lowenstein said.

"Maybe you should," the Mayor said.

"You're not listening to me. I'm going out. I'm going to move to some goddamned place at the shore and walk up and down the beach."

"We haven't even got around to talking about that."

"There's nothing to talk about."

"You haven't even heard my offer."

"I don't want to hear your goddamned offer."

"How do you know until you hear it?"

"Jesus Christ, can't you take no for an answer?"

"No. Not with you. Not when the Department needs you."
The kitchen door swung open.

"I thought maybe you'd need some more coffee," Sarah Lowenstein said a little nervously.

"You still got that stuff you bought to get rid of the rats?" Chief Lowenstein said. "Put two heaping tablespoons, three, in Jerry's cup."

"You two have been friends so long," Sarah said. "It's not right that you should fight."

"Tell him, Sarah," the Mayor said. "I am the spirit of reasonableness and conciliation."

"Four tablespoons, honey," Chief Lowenstein said.

TWELVE

Brewster Cortland Payne II had stopped in a service station on City Line Avenue and called his home. Mrs. Newman had told him there had been no call from Violet, the Detweiler maid, telling him to which hospital Penny had been taken.

If she hadn't been taken to a hospital, he reasoned, there was a chance that the situation wasn't as bad as initially reported; that Penny might have been unconscious—that sometimes happened when drugs were involved—rather than, as Violet had reported, "gone," and had regained consciousness.

If that had happened, Dick Detweiler would have been reluctant to have her taken to a hospital; she could be cared for at home by Dr. Dotson, the family physician, or Amy Payne, M.D., and the incident could be kept quiet.

He got back behind the wheel of the Buick station wagon and drove to West Chestnut Hill Avenue.

He realized the moment he drove through the open gates of the estate that the hope that things weren't as bad as reported had been wishful thinking. There was an ambulance and two police cars parked in front of the house, and a third car, unmarked, but from its black-walled tires and battered appearance almost certainly a police car, pulled in behind him as he was getting out of the station wagon.

The driver got out. Payne saw that he was a police captain.

"Excuse me, sir," the Captain called to him as Payne started up the stairs to the patio.

Payne stopped and turned.

"I'm Captain O'Connor. Northwest Detectives. May I ask who you are, sir?"

"My name is Payne. I am Mr. Detweiler's attorney."

"We've got a pretty unpleasant situation here, Mr. Payne," O'Connor said, offering Payne his hand.

"Just how bad is it?"

"About as bad as it can get, I'm afraid," O'Connor said, and tilted his head toward the patio.

Payne looked and for the first time saw the blanket-covered body on the stretcher.

"Oh, God!"

"Mr. Payne, Chief Inspector Coughlin is on his way here. Do you happen to know...?"

"I know the Chief," Payne said softly.

"I don't have any of the details myself," O'Connor said. "But I'd like to suggest that you..."

"I'm going to see my client, Captain," Payne said, softly but firmly. "Unless there is some reason...?"

"I'd guess he's in the house, sir," O'Connor said.

"Thank you," Payne said, and turned and walked onto the patio. The door was closed but unlocked. Payne walked through it and started to cross the foyer. Then he stopped and picked up a telephone mounted in a small alcove beside the door.

He dialed a number from memory.

"Nesfoods International. Good morning."

"Let me have the Chief of Security, please," he said.

"Mr. Schraeder's office."

"My name is Brewster C. Payne. I'm calling for Mr. Richard Detweiler. Mr. Schraeder, please."

"Good morning, Mr. Payne. How can I help you?"

"Mr. Schraeder, just as soon as you can, will you please send some security officers to Mr. Detweiler's home? Six, or eight. I think their services will be required, day and night, for the next four or five days, so I suggest you plan for that."

"I'll have someone there in half an hour, Mr. Payne," Schraeder said. "Would you care to tell me the nature of the problem? Or should I come out there myself?"

"I think it would be helpful if you came here, Mr. Schraeder," Payne said.

"I'm on my way, sir," Schraeder said.

Payne put the telephone back in its cradle and turned from the alcove in the wall.

Captain O'Connor was standing there.

"Dr. Amelia Payne is on her way here," Payne said. "As is my wife. They will wish to be with the Detweilers."

"I understand, sir. No problem."

"Thank you, Captain," Payne said.

"Mr. Detweiler is in there," O'Connor said, pointing toward the downstairs sitting room. "I believe Mrs. Detweiler is upstairs."

"Thank you," Payne said, and walked to the downstairs sitting room and pushed the door open.

H. Richard Detweiler was sitting in a red leather chair— his chair—with his hands folded in his lap, looking at the floor. He raised his eyes.

"Brew," he said, and smiled.

"Dick."

"Everything was going just fine, Brew. The night before

last, Penny and Matt had dinner with Chad and Daffy to celebrate Chad's promotion. And last night, they were at Martha Peebles's. And one day, three, four days ago, Matt came out and the two of them made cheese dogs for us. You know, you slit the hot dog and put cheese inside and then wrap it in bacon. They made them for us on the charcoal thing. And then they went to the movies. She seemed so happy, Brew. And now this."

"I'm very sorry, Dick."

"Oh, goddamn it all to hell, Brew," H. Richard Detweiler said. He started to sob. "When I went in there, her eyes were open, but I knew."

He started to weep.

Brewster Cortland Payne went to him and put his arms around him.

"Steady, lad," he said, somewhat brokenly as tears ran down his own cheeks. "Steady."

The Buick station wagon in which Amelia Payne, M.D., drove through the gates of the Detweiler estate was identical in model, color, and even the Rose Tree Hunt and Merion Cricket Club parking decalcomanias on the rear window to the one her father had driven through the gates five minutes before, except that it was two years older, had a large number of dings and dents on the body, a badly damaged right front fender, and was sorely in need of a passage through a car wash.

The car had, in fact, been Dr. Payne's father's car. He had made it available to his daughter at a very good price because, he said, the trade-in allowance on his new car had been grossly inadequate. That was not the whole truth. While Brewster Payne had been quietly incensed at the trade-in price offered for a two-year-old car with less that 15,000 miles on the odometer and in showroom condition, the real reason was that the skillful chauffeuring of an automobile was not among his daughter's many skills and accomplishments.

"She needs something substantial, like the Buick, something that will survive a crash," he confided to his wife. "If I could, I'd get her a tank or an armored car. When Amy gets behind the wheel, she reminds me of that comic-strip character with the black cloud of inevitable disaster floating over his head."

It was not that she was reckless, or had a heavy foot on the accelerator, but rather that she simply didn't seem to care. Her father had decided that this was because Amy had—always had had—things on her mind far more important than the possibility of a dented fender, hers or someone else's.

In the third grade when Amy had been sent to see a psychiatrist for her behavior in class (when she wasn't causing all sorts of trouble, she was in the habit of taking a nap) the psychiatrist quickly determined the cause. She was, according to the three different tests to which he subjected her, a genius. She was bored with the third grade.

At ten, she was admitted to a high school for the intellectually gifted operated by the University of Pennsylvania, and matriculated at the University of Pennsylvania at the age of thirteen, because of her extraordinary mathematical ability.

"Theoretical mathematics, of course," her father joked to intimate friends. "Double Doctor Payne is absolutely unable to balance a checkbook."

That was a reference to her two doctoral degrees, the first a Ph.D. earned at twenty with a dissertation on probability, the second an M.D. earned at twenty-three after she had gone through what her father thought of as a dangerous dalliance with a handsome Jesuit priest nearly twice her age. She emerged from this (so far as he knew platonic) relationship with a need to serve God by serving mankind. Her original intention was to become a surgeon, specializing in trauma injuries, but during her internship at the University of Pennsylvania Hospital, she decided to become a psychiatrist. She trained at the Menninger Clinic, then returned to

Philadelphia, where she had a private practice and taught at
the University of Pennsylvania School of Medicine.

She was now twenty-nine and had never married, although a steady stream of young men had passed through
her life. Her father privately thought she scared them off
with her brainpower. He could think of no other reason she
was still single. She was attractive, he thought, and charming, and had a sense of humor much like his own.

Amelia Payne, Ph.D., M.D., stopped the Buick in front of
the Detweiler mansion, effectively denying the use of the
drive to anyone else who wished to use it, and got out. She
was wearing a pleated tweed skirt and a sweater, and looked
like a typical Main Line Young Matron.

The EMT firemen standing near the blanket-covered
body were therefore surprised when she knelt beside the
stretcher and started to remove the blanket.

"Hey, lady!"

"I'm Dr. Payne," Amy said, and examined the body very
quickly. Then she pulled the blanket back in place and stood
up.

"Let's get this into the house," she said. "Out of sight."

"We're waiting for the M.E."

"And while we're waiting, we're going to move the body
into the house," Dr. Payne said. "That wasn't a suggestion."

The EMT firemen picked up the stretcher and followed
her into the house.

She crossed the foyer and opened the door to the sitting
room and saw her father and H. Richard Detweiler talking
softly.

"Are you all right, Uncle Dick?" she asked.

"Ginger-peachy, honey," Detweiler replied.

"Grace is upstairs, Amy," her father said.

"I'll look in on her," Amy said, and pulled the door
closed. She turned to the firemen. "Over there," she said. "In
the dining room."

She crossed the foyer, opened the door to the dining

room, and waited inside until the firemen had carried the stretcher inside. Then she issued other orders:

"One of you stay here, the other wait outside for the M.E. When he gets here, send for me. I'll be upstairs with Mrs. Detweiler, the mother."

"Yes, Ma'am," the larger of the two EMTs—whose body weight was approximately twice that of Amy's—said docilely.

Amy went quickly up the stairs to the second floor.

A black Ford Falcon with the seal of the City of Philadelphia and those words in small white letters on its doors passed through the gates of the Detweiler estate and drove to the door of the mansion.

Bernard C. Potter, a middle-aged, balding black man, tieless, wearing a sports coat and carrying a 35mm camera and a small black bag, got out and walked toward the door. Bernie Potter was an investigator for the Office of the Medical Examiner, City of Philadelphia.

This job, Potter thought, judging from the number of police cars—and especially the Fire Department rescue vehicle that normally would have been long gone from the scene— parked in front of the house, *is going to be a little unusual.*

And then Captain O'Connor, who Bernie Potter knew was Commanding Officer of Northwest Detectives, came out the door. This was another indication that something special was going on. Captains of Detectives did not normally go out on routine Five Two Nine Two jobs.

"What do you say, Bernie?"

"What have we got?" Bernie asked as they shook hands.

"Looks like a simple OD, Bernie. Caucasian female, early twenties, whose father happens to own Nesfoods."

"Nice house," Bernie said. "I didn't think these people were on public assistance. Where the body?"

"In the dining room."

"What are you guys still doing here?" Bernie asked the

Fire Department EMT on the patio. It was simple curiosity, not a reprimand.

The EMT looked uncomfortable.

"Like I told you," Captain O'Connor answered for him, "the father owns Nesfoods International." And then he looked down the drive at a new Ford coming up. "And here comes, I think, Chief Coughlin."

"Equal justice under the law, right?" Bernie asked.

"There's a doctor, a lady doctor, in there," the EMT said, "said she wanted to be called when you came."

"What does she want?" Bernie asked.

The EMT shrugged.

Chief Coughlin got out of his car and walked up.

"Good morning, Chief," Tom O'Connor said.

Coughlin shook his hand and then Bernie Potter's.

"Long time no see, Bernie," he said. "You pronounce yet?"

"Haven't seen the body."

"The quicker we can get this over, the better. You call for a wagon, Tom?"

"I didn't. I don't like to get in the way of my people."

"Check and see. If he hasn't called for one, get one here."

"Yes, sir."

"Where's the body?"

"In the dining room," the EMT said.

"I heard it was on the patio here."

"The lady doctor made us move it," the EMT said.

"Let's go have a look at it," Coughlin said. "I know where the dining room is. Tom, you make sure about the wagon."

"Yes, sir."

Coughlin led the way to the dining room.

"How did it get on the stretcher?" Bernie asked.

"What I hear is that the father carried it downstairs," the EMT said. "When we got here, he was sitting outside on one of them metal chairs, couches, holding it in his arms. We took it from him."

A look of pain, or compassion, flashed briefly over Chief Coughlin's face.

"Where did they find it?" Bernie asked.

Dr. Amelia Payne entered the dining room.

"In her bedroom," she answered the question. "In an erect position, with a syringe in her left arm."

"Dr. Payne, this is Mr. Potter, an investigator of the Medical Examiner's Office."

"How do you do?" Amy said. "Death was apparently instantaneous, or nearly so," she went on. "There is a frothy liquid in the nostrils, often encountered in cases of heroin poisoning. The decedent was a known narcotic-substance abuser. In my opinion—"

"Doctor," Bernie interrupted her uncomfortably, "I don't mean to sound hard-nosed, but you don't have any status here. This is the M.E.'s business."

"I am a licensed physician, Mr. Potter," Amy said. "The decedent was my patient, and she died in her home in not-unexpected circumstances. Under those circumstances, I am authorized to pronounce, and to conduct, if in my judgment it is necessary, any postmortem examination."

"Amy, honey," Chief Coughlin said gently.

"Yes?" She turned to him.

"I know where you're coming from, Amy. But let me tell you how it is. You may be right. You probably are. But while you're fighting the M.E. taking Penny's body, think what's going to happen: It's going to take time, maybe a couple of days, before even your father can get an injunction. Until he gets a judge to issue an order to release it to you, the M.E.'ll hold the body. Let's get it over with, as quickly and painlessly as possible. I already talked to the M.E. He's going to do the autopsy himself, as soon as the body gets there. It can be in the hands of the funeral home in two, three hours."

She didn't respond.

"Grace Detweiler's going to need you," Coughlin went on. "And Matt. That's what's important."

Amy looked at Bernie.

"There's no need for a postmortem," she said. "Everybody in this room knows how this girl killed herself."

"It's the law, Doctor," Bernie said sympathetically.

Amy turned to Dennis Coughlin.

"What about Matt? Does he know?"

"Peter Wohl's waiting for him on North Broad Street. He'll tell him. Unless..."

"No," Amy said. "I think Peter's the best one. They have a sibling relationship. And Peter obviously has more experience than my father. You think Matt will come here?"

"I would suppose so."

She turned to Bernie Potter.

"OK, Mr. Potter," she said. "She is pronounced at nine twenty-five A.M." She turned back to Chief Coughlin. "Thank you, Uncle Denny."

She walked out of the dining room.

Chief Coughlin turned to the EMT.

"The wagon's on the way. Wait in here until it gets here."

The EMT nodded.

"I'm going to have to see the bedroom, Chief," Bernie Potter said.

"I'll show you where it is," Chief Coughlin said. "You through here?"

"I haven't seen the body," Potter said.

He squatted beside the stretcher and pulled the blanket off. He looked closely at the eyes and then closed them. He examined the nostrils.

"Yeah," he said, as if to himself. Then, "Give me a hand rolling her over."

The EMT helped him turn the body on its stomach. Bernie Potter tugged and pulled at Penelope Alice Detweiler's nightdress until it was up around her neck.

There was evidence of livor. The lower back and buttocks and the back of her legs were a dark purple color. Gravity drains blood in a corpse to the body's lowest point.

"OK," he said. "No signs of trauma on the back. Now let's turn her the other way."

There was more evidence of livor when the body was again on its back. The abdominal area and groin were a deep purple color.

"No trauma here, either," Bernie Potter said. He picked up the left arm.

"It looks like a needle could have been in here," he said. "It's discolored."

"The maid said there was a syringe in her arm," Captain O'Connor said. "And the district sergeant saw one, and some rubber tubing, on the floor in the corridor upstairs. He put chairs over them."

Bernie Potter nodded. Then he put Penelope's arm back beside her body, tugged at the nightgown so that it covered the body again, replaced the blanket, and stood up.

"OK," he said. "Now let's go see the bedroom. And the needle."

Chief Coughlin led the procession upstairs.

"There it is," Tom O'Connor said when they came to the chairs in the middle of the upstairs corridor. He carefully picked up the chairs Officer Wells had placed over the plastic hypodermic syringe and the surgical rubber tubing and put them against the wall.

Bernie Potter went into his bag and took two plastic bags from it. Then, using a forceps, he picked up the syringe and the tubing from the carpet and carefully placed them into the plastic bags.

Coughlin then led him to Penelope's bedroom. Potter first took several photographs of the bed and the bedside tables, then took another, larger plastic bag from his bag and, using the forceps, moved the spoon, the candle, the cotton ball, and the glassine bag containing a white crystalline substance from Penelope's bedside table into it.

"OK," he said. "I've got everything I need. Let me use a telephone and I'm on my way."

"I'll show you, Bernie," Chief Coughlin said. "There's one by the door downstairs."

As they went down the stairs, the door to the dining room

opened and two uniformed police officers came through it, carrying Penelope's body on a stretcher. It was covered with a blanket, but her arm hung down from the side.

"The arm!" Chief Coughlin said.

One of the Fire Department EMTs, who was holding the door open, went quickly and put the arm onto the stretcher.

The policemen carried the stretcher outside and down the stairs from the patio and slid it through the already open doors of a Police Department wagon.

Chief Coughlin pointed to the telephone, then walked out onto the patio.

"Just don't give it to anybody," he called. "It's for Dr. Greene. He expects it."

"Yes, sir," one of the police officers said.

Coughlin went back into the foyer.

Bernie Potter was just hanging up the telephone.

"Thanks, Bernie," Coughlin said, and put out his hand.

"Christ, what a way to begin a day," Bernie said.

"Yeah," Coughlin said.

It would have been reasonable for anyone seeing Inspector Peter Wohl leaning on the trunk of his car, its right wheels off the pavement on the sidewalk, his arms folded on his chest, a look of annoyance on his face, to assume that he was an up-and-coming stockbroker, or lawyer, about to be late for an early-morning appointment because his new car had broken down and the Keystone Automobile Club was taking their own damned sweet time coming to his rescue.

The look of displeasure on his face was in fact not even because he was going to have to tell Matt Payne, of whom he was extraordinarily fond—his mother had once said that Matt was like the little brother she had never been able to give him, and she was, he had realized, right—that the love of his life was dead, but rather because it had just occurred to him that he was really a cold-blooded sonofabitch.

He would, he had realized, be as sympathetic as he could possibly be when Matt showed up, expressing his own personal sense of loss. But the truth of the matter was, he had just been honest enough with himself to admit that he felt Matt was going to be a hell of a lot better off with Penelope Detweiler dead.

It had been his experience, and as a cop, there had been a lot of experience, that a junkie is a junkie is a junkie. And in the case of Penelope Detweiler, if after the best medical and psychiatric treatment that money could, quite literally, buy, she was still sticking needles in herself, for whatever reason, that seemed to be absolutely true.

There would have been no decent future for them. If she hadn't OD'd this morning, she would have OD'd next week, or next month, or next year, or two years from now. There would have been other incidents, sordid beyond the comprehension of people who didn't know the horrors of narcotics addiction firsthand, and each of them would have killed Matt a little.

It was better for Matt that this had happened now, rather than after they had married, after they had children.

The fact that he felt sorry for Penelope Detweiler did not alter the fact that he was glad she had died before she could cause Matt more pain.

But by definition, Peter Wohl thought, *anyone who is glad a twenty-three-year-old woman is dead is a cold-blooded sonofabitch.*

He looked up as a car nearly identical to his flashed its headlights at him and then bounced up on the curb. Detective Jesus Martinez was driving. Detective Matt Payne, smiling, opened the passenger door and got out.

Martinez, annoyance on his face, hurried to follow him.

Why do those two hate each other?

The answer, obviously, is that opposites do not attract.

What do I say to Matt?

When all else fails, try the unvarnished truth.

"Don't tell me, you're broken down again?" Matt Payne said.

Gremlins—or the effects of John Barleycorn over the

weekend affecting Monday-morning Ford assembly lines—
had been at work on Inspector Wohl's automobiles. His gen-
erators failed, the radiators leaked their coolant, the
transmissions ground themselves into pieces, usually leaving him stranded in the middle of the night in the middle of
nowhere. Most of his subordinates were highly amused. He
was now on his third brand-new car in six months.

"Let's get in the car," Wohl said. "Jesus, give us a minute,
please?"

Matt looked curious but obeyed the order wordlessly. He
closed the door after him and looked at Wohl.

Wohl met Matt's eyes.

"Matt, Penny OD'd," he said.

Matt's face tightened. His eyebrows rose in question, as if
seeking a denial of what he had just heard.

Wohl shrugged, and threw his hands up in a gesture of
helplessness.

"Matt..."

"Oh, shit!" Matt said.

"The maid found her in her bed with a needle in her arm.
Death was apparently instantaneous."

"Oh, shit!"

"Tom O'Connor—he commands Northwest Detectives—
called Denny Coughlin when they called it in. I happened to
be in Denny's office when he got the call. He went out to the
house to see how he could help. By now the M.E. has the
body."

"Instantaneous?"

Wohl nodded. "So I'm told."

"Oh, shit, Peter!"

"I'm sorry, Matt," Wohl said, and put his arm around
Matt's shoulder. "I'm really sorry."

"We had a goddamned fight last night."

"This is not your fault, Matt. Don't start thinking that."

"Same goddamned subject. Our future. Me being a cop."

"If it hadn't been that, it would have been something else.
They find an excuse."

"Addicts, you mean?"

Wohl nodded.

"Has Amy been notified?" Matt asked. "This is going to wipe out Mrs. Detweiler."

His reaction is not what I expected. But what did I expect?

"I don't know," Wohl said, and then had a thought. He reached under the dash for a microphone.

"Isaac Three, William One."

"Isaac Three." It was the voice of Sergeant Francis Holloran, Chief Inspector Coughlin's driver.

"Tom, check with the Chief and see if Dr. Payne has been notified."

"She's here, Inspector."

"Thank you," Wohl said, and replaced the microphone. He looked over at Matt.

"I guess I'd better go out there," Matt said.

"Take the car and as much time as you need," Wohl said. "I'll take Martinez with me. Or why don't you give me the keys to your car, and I'll have Martinez or somebody bring it out there and swap."

"I'll go to the schoolhouse and get my car," Matt said. "I'm a coward, Peter. I don't want to go out there at all. With a little bit of luck, maybe I can get myself run over by a bus on my way."

"Matt, this isn't your fault."

Matt shrugged.

"I think I will take the car out there," he said. "Get it over with. I'll have it back at the schoolhouse in an hour or so."

"Take what time you need," Wohl said. "Is there anything else I can do, Matt?"

"No. But thank you."

"See me when you come to the schoolhouse."

Matt nodded.

"I'm really sorry, Matt."

"Yeah. Thank you."

They got out of the car and walked to Martinez.

"Are the keys in that?" Matt asked.

"Yeah, why?"

Without replying, Matt walked to the car, got behind the wheel, and started the engine.

Martinez looked at Wohl.

Matt bounced off the curb and, tires chirping, entered the stream of traffic.

"I should have sent you with him," Wohl thought aloud.

"Sir?"

"Penelope Detweiler overdosed about an hour ago."

"Madre de Dios!" Martinez said, and crossed himself.

"Yeah," Wohl said bitterly, then walked back to his car.

Martinez walked to the car but didn't get in.

"Get in, for Christ's sake," Wohl snapped, and was immediately sorry. "Sorry, Jesus. I didn't mean to snap at you."

Martinez shrugged, signaling that he understood.

"That poor sonofabitch," he said.

"Yeah," Wohl agreed.

"Sorry to have kept you waiting," Inspector Peter Wohl said to Staff Inspector Michael Weisbach as he walked in his office. "Something came up."

"The Detweiler girl?" Weisbach asked, and when Wohl nodded, added: "Sabara told me. Awful. For her—what was she, twenty-three, her whole life ahead of her—and for Payne. He was really up when you put out the call for him."

"Up? What for, for having put the cuffs on a crooked cop? He liked that?"

"No. I think he felt sorry for Captain Cazerra. I think he felt *vindicated.* He told me that you, and Washington and Denny Coughlin, had really eaten his ass out for going out on that ledge."

"I wasn't going to let it drop, either—it was damned stupid—until this...this goddamned overdose came along."

"I imagine he's pretty broken up?"

"I don't know. No outward emotion, which may mean he really has one of those well-bred stiff upper lips we hear about, or that he's in shock."

"Where is he?"

"Out at the estate. He's coming here. I'm going to see that he's not alone."

"There was a kid in here, McFadden, from Northwest Detectives, looking for him."

"Good. I was going to put the arm out for him. They're pals. You think he knows what happened?"

"I'm sure he does. When O'Mara told him Payne wasn't here, he said something about him probably being in Chestnut Hill, and that he would go there."

Wohl picked up his telephone and was eventually connected with O'Connor.

"Captain O'Connor. Inspector Wohl calling," he said, and then: "Peter Wohl, Tom. Need a favor."

Weisbach faintly heard O'Connor say, "Name it."

"If you could see your way clear to give your Detective McFadden a little time off, I'd appreciate it. He and my Detective Payne are friends, and for the next couple of days, Payne, I'm sure you know why, is going to need all the friends he has."

Weisbach heard O'Connor say, "I already told him to take whatever time he needed, Inspector."

"I owe you one, Tom."

"I owe you a lot more than one, Inspector. Glad to help. Christ, what a terrible waste!"

"Isn't it?" Wohl said, added, "Thanks, Tom," and hung up.

He had a second thought, and pushed a button on the telephone that connected him with Officer O'Mara, his administrative assistant.

"Yes, sir?"

"Two things, Paul. Inspector Weisbach and I need some coffee, and while that's brewing, I want you to call Special Agent Jack Matthews at the FBI. Tell him I asked you to tell him what happened in Chestnut Hill this morning, and politely suggest that Detective Payne would probably be grateful for some company. That latter applies to you, too. Why don't you stop by Payne's apartment on your way home?"

Weisbach heard O'Mara say, "Yes, sir."

Wohl looked at Weisbach as he hung up.

"Busy morning. I feel like it's two in the afternoon, and it's only ten to eleven."

"Busier even than I think you know. Did you hear about Lowenstein turning in his papers?"

"Jesus, no! Are you sure?"

The door opened and Paul O'Mara walked in with a tray holding two somewhat battered mugs of coffee, a can of condensed milk, and a saucer holding a dozen paper packets of sugar bearing advertisements suggesting they were souvenirs from McDonald's and Roy Rogers and other fast-food emporiums.

"That was quick," Wohl said. "Thank you, Paul." He waited until O'Mara had left, and then said, "Tell me about Lowenstein."

"The first thing this morning, Harry McElroy delivered Lowenstein's badge and a memorandum announcing his intention to retire to the Commissioner. I got that from McElroy, so that much I know for sure."

"God knows I'm sorry to hear that. But I'm not surprised that he's going out—"

Weisbach held up his hand, interrupting him.

"Just before I came out here," he said, "Lowenstein put out the arm for me. I met him at the Philadelphia Athletic Club on Broad Street. And not only did he not mention going out, but he didn't act like it, either."

"Interesting," Wohl said. "What did he want?"

"I got sort of a pep talk. He told me this Ethical Affairs Unit was a good thing for me, could help my career, and that all I had to do to get anything I wanted from the Detective Division was to ask."

"Lowenstein and the Mayor got into it at David Pekach's engagement party. Got into it bad. Did you hear about that?"

"The Mayor had just seen that Charley Whaley story in

the *Ledger*. The 'more unsolved murders, no arrests, no comment' story. You see that?"

"Yeah."

"For some reason, it displeased our mayor," Wohl said, dryly. "The Mayor then announced he wouldn't be surprised if Wally Milham was involved in the Kellog murder, primarily because he thinks that Milham's morals are questionable. You've heard that gossip, I suppose?"

"Milham and Kellog's wife? Yeah, sure."

"The Mayor asked Lowenstein why he hadn't spoken to him about his love life. Lowenstein told the Mayor he didn't think it was any of his business. Then, warming to the subject, defended Milham. And then, really getting sore, Lowenstein made impolitic remarks about, quote, the Mayor's own private detective squad, unquote."

"Ouch!"

"Whereupon the Mayor told him if he didn't like the way things were being run, he should talk it over with the Commissioner. And then—he was really in a lousy mood—to make the point to the Chief who was running the Department, he told him 'the Commissioner' was going to send Matt Payne, who knows zilch about Homicide, over to Homicide to (a) help with the double murder at that gin mill on Market Street—"

"The Inferno?"

"Right. And (b) to see what he could learn about other Homicide investigations, meaning, of course, how Homicide is handling the Kellog job."

"My God!"

"I thought Lowenstein was going to have a heart attack. Or punch out the Mayor. It was that bad. I'm not surprised, now that I hear it, that he turned in his papers."

"I got it from Harry McElroy that he did. But then he didn't act like it when he sent for me."

"OK. How's this for a scenario? Czernich ran to the Mayor with Lowenstein's retirement memorandum. The Mayor hadn't wanted to go that far with Chief Lowenstein.

Christ, they've been friends for years. He didn't want him to quit. So they struck a deal. Lowenstein would stay on the job if certain conditions were met. They apparently were. And since they almost certainly involve you and me, we'll probably hear about them sometime next month."

Weisbach considered what Wohl had said, then nodded his head, accepting the scenario.

"So what do I do this month? Peter, you can't be happy with me—the Ethical Affairs Unit—being suddenly dumped on you."

"I don't have any problems with it," Wohl said. "First of all, it, and/or you, haven't been dumped on me. All I have to do is support you, and I have no problem with that. I think the EAU is a good idea, that you are just the guy to run it, and I think your work is already cut out for you."

"You really think it's a good idea?" Weisbach asked, surprised. Wohl nodded. "And what do you mean my work is already cut out for me?"

"The Widow Kellog showed up at Jason Washington's apartment the night her husband was killed with the announcement that everybody in Five Squad in Narcotics—you know about Five Squad?"

"Not much. I've heard they're very effective." He chuckled, and added: "Sort of an unshaven Highway Patrol, in dirty clothes, beards, and T-shirts—concealing unauthorized weapons—reading 'Legalize Marijuana,' who cast fear into the drug culture by making middle-of-the-night raids."

"Everybody in Five Squad, according to the Widow Kellog, is dirty, and she implied that they did her husband."

"My God!"

"Washington believes her, at least about the whole Five Squad being dirty. Before all this crap happened, I was going to bring you in on it."

"That was nice of you."

"Practically speaking, our priorities are the Mayor's priorities. I don't think he wants to be surprised again by dirty Narcotics people the way he was with Cazerra and company.

Internal Affairs dropped the ball on that one, and I don't think we can give them the benefit of the doubt on this one. Yeah, it looks to me that you've got your work cut out for you."

"What kind of help can I have?"

"Anything you want. Washington and Harris, after getting their hands dirty on the Cazerra job, would love to work on a nice clean Homicide, especially of a police officer. And if there is a tie to Narcotics...Jesus!"

"What?"

"I forgot about the Mayor ordering Payne into Homicide," Wohl said. He reached for his telephone, pushed a button, and a moment later ordered, "Paul, would you get Chief Lowenstein for me, please?"

He put the telephone down.

"Drink your coffee, Mike," he said. "The first thing you're going to have to do is face the fact that your innocent, happy days as a staff inspector are over. You have just moved into the world of police politics, and you're probably not going to like it at all."

"That thought had already run through my mind," Weisbach said. He picked up his mug and, shaking his head, put it to his mouth.

The telephone rang. Wohl picked it up.

"Good morning, Chief," he said. "I wanted to check with you about sending Detective Payne to Homicide. Is that still on?"

He took the headset from his ear so that Weisbach could hear the Chief's reply.

"Denny Coughlin just told me what happened to the Detweiler girl," Lowenstein said. "I presume you're giving Matt some time off?"

"Yes, sir."

"Well, when he comes back, send him over whenever you can spare him. I've spoken to Captain Quaire. They're waiting for him."

"Yes, sir."

"And please tell him I'm sorry about what happened. That's really a goddamn shame."

"I'll tell him that, sir. Thank you."

"Nice talking to you, Peter," Chief Lowenstein said, and hung up.

"He didn't sound like someone about to retire, did he?" Weisbach said.

"No, he didn't."

One of the telephones on Wohl's desk rang.

"This is what happens when I forget to tell Paul to hold my calls," he said as he reached for it. "Inspector Wohl."

"Ah, Peter," Weisbach overheard. "How is the Beau Brummell of Philadelphia law enforcement this morning?"

"Why is it, Armando, that whenever I hear your voice, I think of King Henry the Sixth?"

"Peter, you are, as you well know, quoting that infamous Shakespearean 'kill all the lawyers' line out of context."

"Well, he had the right idea, anyhow. What can I do for you, Armando?"

"Actually, I was led to believe that Inspector Weisbach could be reached at your office."

"I'd love to know who told you that," Wohl said, and then handed the telephone to Weisbach. "Armando C. Giacomo, Esquire, for you, Inspector."

Giacomo, a slight, lithe, dapper man who wore what was left of his hair plastered to the sides of his tanned skull, was one of the best criminal lawyers in Philadelphia.

Wohl got up from his desk and walked to his window and looked out. He could therefore hear only Weisbach's side of the brief conversation.

"I'll call you back in five minutes," Weisbach concluded, and hung up.

Wohl walked back to his desk.

"Don't tell me," he said. "Giacomo has been asked to represent Mr. Paulo Cassandro."

"I'll bet that he has," Weisbach said. "But he didn't say so. What he said was that it would give him great pleasure if I would have lunch with him today at the Rittenhouse Club, during which he would like to discuss something which would be to our mutual benefit."

"I'd go, if I were you," Wohl said. "They set a very nice table at the Rittenhouse Club."

"Why don't you come with me?"

"I'm not in the mood for lunch, really, even at the Rittenhouse Club."

"He's looking for something, which means he's desperate. I'd like to have you there."

"Yeah," Wohl said, thoughtfully. "If he's looking for a deal, he would have gone to the District Attorney. It might be interesting."

He pushed the button for Paul O'Mara.

"Paul, call Armando C. Giacomo. Tell him that Inspector Weisbach accepts his kind invitation to lunch at the Rittenhouse Club at one, and that he's bringing me with him."

THIRTEEN

Peter Wohl pushed open the heavy door of the Rittenhouse Club and motioned for Mike Weisbach to go in ahead of him. They climbed a wide, shallow flight of carpeted marble stairs to the lobby, where they were intercepted by the club porter, a dignified black man in his sixties.

"May I help you, gentlemen?"

"Mr. Weisbach and myself as the guests of Mr. Giacomo," Peter said.

"It's nice to see you, Mr. Wohl," the porter said, and glanced at what Peter thought of as the Who's Here Board behind his polished mahogany stand. "I believe Mr. Giacomo is in the club. Would you please have a seat?"

He gestured toward a row of chairs against the wall, then walked into the club.

The Who's Here Board behind the porter's stand listed, alphabetically, the names of the three-hundred-odd members of the Rittenhouse Club. Beside each name was an inch-long piece of brass, which could be slid back and forth in a track. When the marker was next to the member's name, this indicated he was on the premises; when away from it that he was not.

Peter saw Weisbach looking at the board with interest. The list of names represented the power structure, social and business, of Philadelphia. Philadelphia's upper crust belonged to either the Rittenhouse Club or the Union League, or both.

Peter saw that Carlucci, J., an ex officio member, was not in the club. Giacomo, A., was. So was Mawson, J., of Mawson, Payne, Stockton, McAdoo & Lester, who competed with Giacomo, A., for being the best (which translated to mean most expensive) criminal lawyer in the city. Payne, B., Mawson, J.'s, law partner, was not.

And neither, Wohl noticed with interest, was Payne, M.

I didn't know Matt was a member. That's new.

Possibly, he thought, *Detweiler, H., had suggested to Payne, B., that they have a word with the Membership Committee. Since their offspring were about to be married, it was time that Payne, M., should be put up for membership. Young Nesbitt, C. IV, had become a member shortly before his marriage to the daughter of Browne, S.*

Wohl had heard that the Rittenhouse Club initiation fee was something like the old saw about how much a yacht cost: If you had to ask what it cost, you couldn't afford it.

The porter returned.

"Mr. Giacomo is in the bar, Mr. Wohl. You know the way?"

"Yes, thank you," Peter said, and led Weisbach into the club bar, a quiet, deeply carpeted, wood-paneled room, furnished with twenty or so small tables, at each of which were rather small leather-upholstered armchairs. The tables were spaced so that a soft conversation could not be heard at the tables adjacent to it.

Armando C. Giacomo rose, smiling, from one of the

chairs when he saw Wohl and Weisbach, and waved them over.

Wohl thought Giacomo was an interesting man. His family had been in Philadelphia from the time of the Revolution. He was a graduate of the University of Pennsylvania and the Yale School of Law. He had flown Corsairs as a Naval Aviator in the Korean War. He could have had a law practice much like Brewster Cortland Payne's, with clientele drawn from banks and insurance companies and familial connections.

He had elected, instead, to become a criminal lawyer, and was known (somewhat unfairly, Wohl thought) as the Mob's Lawyer, which suggested that he himself was involved in criminal activity. So far as Wohl knew, Giacomo's personal ethics were impeccable. He represented those criminals who could afford his services when they were hauled before the bar of justice, and more often than not defended them successfully.

Wohl had come to believe that Giacomo held the mob in just about as much contempt as he did, and that he represented them both because they had the financial resources to pay him, and also because he really believed that an accused was entitled to good legal representation, not so much for himself personally, but as a reinforcement of the Constitution.

Giacomo was also held in high regard by most police officers, primarily because he represented, *pro bono publico*, police officers charged with police brutality and other infractions of the law. He would not, in other words, represent Captain Vito Cazerra, because Cazerra could not afford him. But he would represent an ordinary police officer charged with the use of excessive force or otherwise violating the civil rights of a citizen, and do so without charge.

"Peter," Giacomo said. "I'm delighted that you could join us."

"I didn't want Mike to walk out of here barefoot, Armando, but thank you for your hospitality."

"I only talk other people out of their shoes, Peter, not my friends."

"And the check is in the mail, right?" Weisbach said, laughing as they shook hands.

A waiter appeared.

"I'm drinking a very nice California cabernet sauvignon," Giacomo said. "But don't let that influence you."

"A little wine would be very nice," Wohl said.

"Me, too, thank you," Weisbach said.

"The word has reached these hallowed precincts of the tragic event in Chestnut Hill this morning," Giacomo said. "What a pity."

"Yes, it was," Wohl agreed.

"If I don't have the opportunity before you see him, Peter, would you extend my sympathies to young Payne?"

"Yes, of course."

"He must be devastated."

"He is," Wohl said.

"And her mother and father..." Giacomo said, shaking his head sadly.

A waiter in a gray cotton jacket served the wine.

"I think we'll need another bottle of that over lunch, please," Giacomo said. He waited for the waiter to leave, and then said, "I hope you like that. What shall we drink to?"

Wohl shrugged.

"How about good friends?" Giacomo suggested.

"All right," Peter said, raising his glass. "Good friends."

"Better yet, Mike's new job."

"Better yet, Mike's new job," Wohl parroted. He sipped the wine. "Very nice."

"I'd send you a case, if I didn't know you would think I was trying to bribe you," Giacomo said.

"All gifts between friends are not bribes," Wohl said. "Send me a case, and I'll give Mike half. You can't bribe him, either."

"I'll send the both of you a case," Giacomo said, and then

added: "Would you prefer to hear what I'd like to say now, or over lunch?"

"Now, please, Armando," Wohl said. "I would really hate to have my lunch in these hallowed precincts ruined."

"I suspected you'd feel that way. They do a very nice mixed grill here, did you know that?"

"Yes, I do. And also a very nice rack of lamb."

"I represent a gentleman named Paulo Cassandro."

"Why am I not surprised?" Weisbach asked.

"Because you are both astute and perceptive, Michael. May I go on?"

"By all means."

"Mr. Cassandro was arrested this morning. I have assured Mr. Cassandro that once I bring the circumstances surrounding his arrest...Constitutionally illegal wiretaps head a long list of irregularities..."

"Come on, Armando," Weisbach said, laughing.

". . . to the attention of the proper judicial authorities," Giacomo went on, undaunted, "it is highly unlikely that he will ever be brought to trial. And I have further assured him that, in the highly unlikely event he is brought to trial, I have little doubt in my mind that no fair-minded jury would ever convict him."

"He's going away, Armando," Wohl said. "You know that and I know that."

"You tend to underestimate me, Peter. I don't hold it against you; most people do."

"I never underestimate you, Counselor. But that clanging noise you hear in the background is the sound of a jail door slamming," Peter said. "The choir you hear is singing, 'Bye, Bye, Paulo.' "

"If I may continue?"

"Certainly."

"However, this unfortunate business, this travesty of justice, comes at a very awkward time for Mr. Cassandro. It will force him to devote a certain amount of time to it, time he feels he must devote to his business interests."

"Freely translated, Peter," Weisbach said, "what Armando is telling us is that Paulo doesn't want to go to jail."

"I wondered what he was trying to say," Wohl said.

"What he wants to do is get this unfortunate business behind him as soon as possible."

"Tell him probably ten to fifteen years, depending on the judge. If he gets Hanging Harriet, probably fifteen to twenty," Weisbach said.

The Hon. Harriet M. McCandless, a black jurist who passionately believed that civilized society was based on a civil service whose honesty was above question, was famous for her severe sentences.

"You're not listening to me, Michael," Giacomo said. "I am quite confident that, upon hearing how the police department has so outrageously violated the rights of Mr. Cassandro, Judge McCandless, or any other judge, will throw this case out of court."

"God, you're wonderful," Peter said.

"As I was saying, with an eye to putting this unfortunate business behind him as soon as possible, my client would be..."

"Armando," Weisbach said, "even if I wanted to, we couldn't deal on this. You want to deal, try the District Attorney. But I'll bet you he'll tell you Cassandro has nothing to deal with. We have him cold and he's going to jail."

"I will, of course, discuss this matter with Mr. Callis. But frankly, it will be a good deal easier for me, when I do speak with him, if I could tell him that I had spoken to you and Peter, and that you share my belief that what I propose would serve the ends of justice."

"Armando," Wohl said, laughing, "not only do I like you, but you are about to not only send me a case of wine, but also buy me a very expensive lunch. What that entitles you to is this: If you will tell me what you want, and how Paulo Cassandro wishes to pay for it, I will give you my honest opinion of how hard Mr. Callis is going to laugh at you before he throws you out of his office."

"Mr. Cassandro, as a public-spirited citizen, is willing to testify against Captain Cazerra, Lieutenant Meyer, and the two police officers. All he asks in exchange is immunity from prosecution."

"Loudly," Weisbach said. "Mr. Callis is going to laugh very loudly when you go to him with that."

"He may even become hysterical," Wohl said.

"*And* against the lady," Giacomo went on. "The madam, what the hell is her name?"

I will be damned, Wohl thought. *He's flustered. Have we really gotten through to Armando C. Giacomo, shattered his famous rocklike confidence?*

"Her name is Osadchy, Armando," Wohl said. "If you have trouble remembering her last name, why don't you associate it with Hanging Harriet? Same Christian name."

"Very funny, Peter."

"By now, Armando, with the egg they have on their face about Mrs. Osadchy," Weisbach said, "I'll bet Vice is paying her a lot of attention. They'll find something, I'm sure, that they can take to the DA."

"Let's talk about that," Giacomo said. "The egg on the face."

"OK," Peter said. "The egg on whose face?"

"The Police Department's."

"Because we had a couple of dirty cops? There might be some egg on our face because of that, but I think we wiped off most of it this morning," Weisbach said.

"Not in a public relations sense, maybe. Let me put that another way. The egg you wiped off this morning is going to reappear when you try Captain Cazerra. The trial will last at least two weeks, and there will be a story in every newspaper in Philadelphia every day of the trial. People will forget that he was arrested by good cops; what they'll remember is that the Department had a dirty captain. And when his trial is over, we will have the trial of Lieutenant Meyer."

"I reluctantly grant the point," Peter said.

"On the other hand, for the sake of friendly argument, if

Captain Cazerra were to plead guilty and throw himself upon the mercy of the court because he became aware that Mr. Cassandro's public-spirited testimony was going to see him convicted . . ."

Or if the mob struck a deal with him, Peter thought. *"Take the fall and we'll take care of your family." Which is not such an unlikely idea. I wonder why it's so important that they keep Paulo out of jail. Has he moved up in the mob hierarchy? I'll pass this on to Intelligence and Organized Crime, anyway.*

". . . there would only be, on one day only," Giacomo went on, "a short story, buried in the back pages, that a dishonest policeman had admitted his guilt and had been sentenced. There are people who are wise in public relations, and I would include our beloved mayor among them, who would think that alternative would be preferable to a long and sordid public trial."

I'm agreeing with him again, which means that I am getting in over my head. I am now going to swim for shore before I drown.

"Before we go in for lunch, Armando, and apropos of nothing whatever, I would suggest that if Mr. Cassandro wants any kind of consideration at all from anybody you know, he's going to have to come up with more than a possible solution to a public relations problem."

"I understand, Peter," Armando said smoothly. "Such as what?"

"You've heard about the murder of Officer Jerry Kellog?" Wohl asked.

Giacomo nodded. "Tragic. Shot down in cold blood in his own house, according to the *Ledger.*"

"The *Ledger* also implied that a Homicide detective was involved," Wohl said. "My bet is that it's related to Narcotics. I would be grateful for any information that would lead the Department down that path."

"And then there's the double murder at the Inferno Lounge," Weisbach said. "Some people think that looks like a contract hit. I think the Department might be grateful for information that would help them there."

From the look on his face, Peter Wohl thought, *he thinks there is a mob connection.*

Confirmation came immediately.

"Those people, and you two know this as well as I do, have a code of honor . . ."

"Call it a code, if you like, but the word 'honor' is inappropriate," Peter said.

"Whatever you want to call it, turning in one of their own violates it," Giacomo said.

"They also don't fool around with each other's wives, either, do they?" Weisbach said. "And I wouldn't be at all surprised if they give a percentage of their earnings from prostitution and drugs to worthy causes and the church. Despite what you may have heard, they're really not bad people, are they, Armando?"

Giacomo looked very uncomfortable.

"A top-level decision would have to be made," Peter interrupted. "Who goes to jail? Who is more valuable? Paulo Cassandro or a hit man? Who goes directly to jail without passing 'go'?"

What the hell am I doing? Bargaining with the mob? Making a deal to have the mob do something the Police Department should be doing itself? Cassandro bribed some dirty cops. We caught them. They should all go to jail, not just the cops. Paulo Cassandro should not walk because it will increase Jerry Carlucci's chances of getting re-elected.

Wohl stood up.

"Is something wrong?" Giacomo asked.

"I'm not sure I want to eat lunch," he said. "And I know I have enough of this conversation."

Weisbach stood up. Giacomo looked up at them, and then stood up himself.

"I thank you for your indulgence," he said. "I would be deeply pained if this conversation affected our friendship."

Oddly enough, I believe him. Which probably proves I was right about getting in over my head.

"Please, let's not let this ruin a lunch with friends. Come and break bread with me, please," Giacomo said.

Wohl didn't reply for a moment.

"I was about to say, only if I can pay. But I can't pay in here, can I?"

"No. And it is an expulsable offense for a member to let a guest reimburse him. If that's important to you, Peter, would you like to go somewhere else?"

Wohl met his eyes for a moment.

"No," he said finally. "I think we understand each other, Armando. We can eat here."

South Rittenhouse Square—on the south side of Rittenhouse Square in Center City Philadelphia—is no wider than it was when it was laid out at the time of the American Revolution. There are a half-dozen NO PARKING AT ANY TIME—TOW AWAY ZONE signs, warning citizens that if they park there at any time, it is virtually certain that to reclaim their car, it will be necessary for them to somehow make their way halfway across Philadelphia to the Parking Authority impoundment lot at Delaware Avenue and Spring Garden Street and there both pay a hefty fine for illegal parking and generously compensate the City of Brotherly Love for the services of the Parking Authority tow truck that hauled their car away.

Despite this, when Amelia Payne, M.D., drove past the building housing the Delaware Valley Cancer Society, there were seven automobiles parked in front of it, all of them with their right-side wheels on the sidewalk. There was a new Oldsmobile sedan, a battered Volkswagen, a ten-year-old, gleaming Jaguar XK120, a new Mercedes convertible, a new Buick sedan, and two new sedans, a Ford and a Chevrolet.

There's not even room enough for me, Dr. Payne thought somewhat indignantly. Like most of her fellow practitioners of the healing arts, she was in the habit of interpreting rather loosely the privilege granted to physicians of ignoring NO PARKING AT ANY TIME signs when making emergency calls.

And she had intended to do so now, by placing her official PHYSICIAN MAKING CALL card on the dashboard of the Buick station wagon, because the basement garage of the Cancer Society Building, to which she had access, had a very narrow entrance passage that she had difficulty negotiating.

She continued past the Delaware Valley Cancer Society Building, noticing with annoyance the beat cop on the corner, his arms folded on his chest, calmly surveying his domain and oblivious to the multiple violations of parking laws.

Professional courtesy, she thought. *Damn the cops!*

She had recognized four of the cars—the Oldsmobile, the Volkswagen, the Jaguar, and the Mercedes—as belonging respectively to Chief Inspector Dennis V. Coughlin, Detective Charles McFadden, Inspector Peter Wohl, and Captain David Pekach, and had drawn, as the cop obviously had, the natural and correct conclusion that the rest of the cars were also the official or personal automobiles of other policemen (or in the case of Pekach, belonged to his fiancée, Miss Martha Peebles, which was just about the same thing) who regarded parking regulations as applying only to civilians.

She drove to South Nineteenth Street, where she turned right, and then made the next right, and ultimately reached the entrance of the underground garage, which, surprising her not at all, she failed to maneuver through unscathed. This time she scraped the right fender against a wall.

This served to further lower her morale. In addition to the early-morning horror at the Detweilers', she had just come from University Hospital, where a patient of hers, an attractive young woman whom she had originally diagnosed as suffering from routine postpartum depression, was manifesting symptoms of more serious mental illness that Amy simply could not fathom, nor could anyone else she had consulted.

She was not surprised, either, to find both of the reserved parking places she intended to use already occupied. One of them held a silver Porsche 911, and the other a Buick wagon identical to hers, save it was two years younger and unscratched and undented.

The Buick belonged to her father, who could be expected to offer some clever witticism about the dents in her Buick, and the Porsche to her brother. The Delaware Valley Cancer Society Building was owned by her father, and her brother occupied a tiny apartment in what had been the garret before the 1850s building had been gutted and converted into offices behind the original facade.

She parked the Buick—neatly straddling a marking line between spaces—and got out of the car. The elevator did not respond to her summons, and only after a while did she remember that it was late—she consulted her watch and saw that it was well after midnight—and remembered that at this hour, the elevator was locked. It would be necessary to call Matt's apartment by telephone, whereupon he could push a button activating the elevator.

And he took his damned sweet time answering the telephone, and when he did, it wasn't him, but a clipped, metallic voice she did not at first recognize.

"Yes?"

"This is Dr. Payne. Would you please push the elevator button?"

There was the sound of male laughter in the background.

"Just a moment, darlin'," the voice said. "I'll ask Matty how to work it."

She now recognized the voice to be that of Chief Inspector Dennis V. Coughlin. Normally, she did not mind his addressing her as "darlin'," but now it annoyed her.

The line went dead, and she stood there for a full minute, waiting for the sound of a buzzer, or whatever, which would bring the elevator to life. It gave her time to consider that what was going on upstairs was really an Irish wake, the males of the clan gathering to console one of their number who had suffered a loss.

She reached for the telephone again, then changed her mind and pushed the elevator button again. This time she was rewarded with the sound of the elevator moving.

It took her to the third floor. A closed door led to the narrow flight of stairs to Matt's apartment. She pushed the button, and in a moment, a solenoid buzzed and she was able to push the door open.

She was greeted again with the sound of male laughter, which for some reason annoyed her, although another part of her mind said that it was probably therapeutic.

She walked up the stairs.

The tiny apartment was jammed. In the living room, she saw Martha Peebles sitting on a small couch with Mary-Margaret McCarthy—Detective Charley McFadden's girl-friend—and a tall young man she recognized as Matt's friend Jack Matthews, an FBI agent. The small table in front of the couch was covered with jackets. It was hot in the apartment, and most of the men had taken off their jackets and pulled down their ties and rolled up their sleeves.

Which also served to reveal that most of them were armed. There were shoulder holsters and waist holsters, most of them carrying snub-nosed .38-caliber revolvers.

The tribal insignia, Amy thought, *like that little purse or whatever Scots wear hanging down over their kilts.*

Matt's two small armchairs held Captain David Pekach and Lieutenant Jack Malone, having what seemed to be a serious conversation; they didn't look at her.

Martha Peebles smiled and stood up when she saw her, and stepped over Mary-Margaret McCarthy and the FBI agent to come to her. Mary-Margaret and the FBI agent smiled at her.

"How's Grace?" Martha Peebles asked softly as she put her cheek next to Amy's.

"I stopped off earlier and gave her something to help her sleep," Amy said.

"How terrible for her!"

Amy nodded.

A large arm gently draped itself around Amy's shoulders. She looked up into the face of Chief Inspector Dennis V. Coughlin.

"I checked with the Medical Examiner," he said softly. "He released the body at noon. Kirk and Nice picked it up at half past twelve."

"I know, Uncle Denny," she said. "Thank you."

She looked around for Matt. He was in the kitchen, leaning against the refrigerator, holding a can of beer. He didn't seem drunk, which could or could not be a good thing. There was no sign that he was armed, but Amy knew better. Matt carried his .38 snub-nose in an ankle holster.

"It was the right way to go, darlin'," Coughlin said. "Thank you for trusting me."

"I always trust you, Uncle Denny," she said sincerely, and with a smile.

He squeezed her shoulder.

"Uncle Denny, I think it might be a good idea to get all these people out of here."

"I was thinking the same thing, darlin'."

"Getting him to take it might be a problem, but I'll try to give him something to help him sleep."

"I'll see to it," Coughlin said, and raised his voice. "David? See you a minute?"

Amy walked into the kitchen. Sitting at the small table, which was covered with whiskey bottles, empty cans, and the remnants of a take-out Chinese buffet were Inspector Peter Wohl, his father, Chief Inspector August Wohl (Retired), Captain Mike Sabara, Detective Charley McFadden, and her father.

"I agree with McFadden," Amy heard Chief Wohl say. "If he'd been hit in the head with a two-by-four, or something,

I'd say he walked in on a burglar, but two bullets in the back of the head? That makes it a hit."

Detective McFadden beamed to have the Chief agree with him.

Amy walked up to her brother, and resisted the temptation to kiss him. He looked desolate.

"How're you doing, Sherlock?"

He nodded and raised his beer can.

"OK. You want a beer?"

"Yes," she said after a moment's hesitation. "I think I would. Thank you."

"The beer's been gone for an hour," Peter Wohl said. "We can call and get some. Or would you like something stronger?"

"Hello, Peter," Amy said. "How are you?"

"Long time no see," he said evenly.

"There's scotch, bourbon, and gin, honey," Brewster C. Payne said. "And Irish."

"Yes, of course, Irish," Amy said. "An Irish, please. A short one, over the rocks. And then I think we should call off the wake."

Her father nodded and stood up to make the drink.

"Have you been out to Chestnut Hill?" he asked.

"Not since I saw you there. I gave Grace something to help her sleep, and I called a while ago and Violet said she'd gone to bed. I was tied up at the hospital."

"I left when Dick went to sleep," her father said.

In other words, passed out, Amy thought. *He was three-quarters drunk when I left there.*

"I'll go out there first thing in the morning," Amy said, and then turned to her brother. "I asked you how you're doing?"

He shrugged.

"What a goddamned waste," he said.

"I want a minute with you alone when everybody's gone," she said.

"None of your goddamned pills, Amy."

"I'm trying to help," she said.

"Yeah, I know."

"Your beer must be warm."

"Is that a prescription? Booze in lieu of happy pills?"

"It might help you sleep."

He met her eyes for a moment.

"Dad, could you make two of those, please?" he called.

Their father turned to look over his shoulder at her. She nodded, just perceptibly, and he reached for another glass.

"Charley," Mary-Margaret McCarthy called, "we're going."

There was a tone of command in her voice. She was a nurse, an R.N. who had gone back to school to get a degree, and was, she had once confided in Amy, thinking about going for an M.D.

McFadden immediately stood up.

Matt needs somebody like that, Amy thought. *A strong-willed young woman as smart as he is. He didn't need Penny.*

God, what a terrible thing to even think!

"We're going too," Martha Peebles announced. She already had her David—whom she usually called, to his intense embarrassment, "Precious"—in tow.

One by one, the men filed into the kitchen and shook Matt's hand.

"Circumstances aside, it was good to see you, Amy," Peter Wohl said, and offered her his hand.

"Thank you," she said.

He was almost at the top of the stairs when she went quickly after him.

"Peter, wait a moment," she called, and he stopped. "I'd like to talk to you," Amy said.

"Sure. When? Will it wait until morning?"

"I won't be with Matt more than a minute," she said.

"OK," he said with what she interpreted as reluctance, and then went down the stairs.

Her father touched her shoulder.

"You're the doctor. Is there anything I should be doing for Matt?"

"Just what you are doing," she said.

"Should I go out to Chestnut Hill in the morning, or is it better..."

"He's your friend, Dad," Amy said. "You'll have to decide."

"Yes, of course."

Finally, after a final hug from Denny Coughlin, Amy was alone with Matt.

He met her eyes, waiting for whatever she had to say.

"This was not your fault, Matt. She had a chemical addiction—"

"She was a junkie."

"—which she was unable to manage."

"And I wasn't a hell of a lot of help, was I?"

"What happened is not your fault, Matt."

"So everyone keeps telling me."

"The best thing you can do—an emotional trauma like this is exhausting—is to get a good night's sleep."

"And things will seem better in the morning, right?"

"I've got something to give you..."

"No, thank you."

". . . a mild sedative."

"In case you haven't noticed, I'm not climbing the walls, or hysterical, or . . ."

"It's inside, Matt, it's a pain. It will have to come out. The better shape you're in when it does, the better. That's why you need to sleep."

"You are your father's daughter, aren't you? You never know when to take no for an answer."

"OK. But people, even tough guys like you, have been known to change their minds. I'll leave the pills."

"Take two and call me in the morning?" Matt asked, now smiling.

"If you take two, you won't be able to use a telephone in

the morning. One, Matt, with water, preferably not on an empty stomach."

"My stomach is full of Chinese."

"I'll be at home until half past seven or so," Amy said. "If you want to talk."

"Amy, believe it or not, I'm touched by your concern," Matt said. "But all I need is to finish this"—he held up his whiskey glass—"and get in bed."

And then he surprised her by putting his arms around her.

"Who holds your hand when you need it, Doc?" he asked softly. "Don't you ever get it up to here with other people's problems?"

"Yeah," she said, surprised at her emotional reaction. "Just between thee, me, and the lamp pole, I do. But not with your problems, Matt. You're my little brother."

"Chronologically speaking only, of course."

She hugged him, and then broke away.

"Go to bed," she said. "I'll see you tomorrow."

She went down the narrow flight of stairs and turned at the bottom and looked up.

"Try to stay on the black stuff between parked cars, Amy," Matt called down to her with a wave.

"Wiseass," she called back, and closed the door to the stairs. She had just enough time to be surprised to find the landing empty when she heard the whine of the elevator.

That has to be Peter, she thought. *If he said he would wait for me, he will.*

And then she just had time to recognize the depth of her original disappointment when the elevator door opened. It was not Peter, it was Jason Washington.

Where the hell is Peter? Did he decide, "Screw her, I'm going home"?

"Good evening, Doctor," Washington said in his sonorous voice. "Or, more accurately, good morning."

"Mr. Washington."

"Do I correctly surmise from the look of disapproval on your face that now is not a good time to call on Matt?"

"No. As a matter of fact," Amy said with a nervous laugh—Jason Washington was a formidable male—"I think you'd be good for him. He said he was going to bed, but I don't believe him."

"I couldn't get here earlier," he said. "Inspector Wohl—he's with the security officer in the lobby—thought perhaps you . . ."

Peter did wait. Why are you so damned pleased?

"I think you're very kind to come at this hour, and that Matt will be delighted to see you."

"Thank you," Washington said, and waved her onto the elevator.

Peter did not smile when he saw her.

"Thank you for waiting," she said. "I really wanted to talk to you."

"So you said."

"Could we go somewhere for coffee? Or a drink?"

They locked eyes for a moment.

"Most of the places I'd take you to around here are closed."

"Would you have time to stop by my apartment?"

"Somehow I don't think that's an invitation to breakfast."

"Of course it wasn't," she snapped. "I want to talk about Matt. Nothing else."

"We tried the other, right, and it didn't work?"

"It didn't seem to, did it?"

"I'll meet you in your lobby," Peter said. "I hate to follow people."

"Thank you," she said, and got back on the elevator. By the time she turned around, he was already out the door.

"How are you holding up, Matthew?" Jason Washington asked as he reached the top of the steep flight of stairs.

"Most often by leaning against the wall," Matt replied.

"He said, masking his pain with humor. I am your friend, Matthew. Answer the question."

"You know the old joke: 'How is your wife?' and the

reply, 'Compared to what?' I don't know how I'm supposed to feel."

"Try a one-word reply."

"Empty," Matt said after a moment.

Washington grunted.

"I would suggest that is a normal reaction," he said. "I would have been here earlier, Matthew, but I was about the King's business, protecting our fair city from assorted mountebanks, scoundrels, and scalawags."

Matt chuckled. "Thanks for coming."

"I'm very sorry about Penny, Matt," Washington said.

"Thank you."

"It was originally my intention, and that of my fair lady, to come to add our voices to the chorus of those telling you that you are in no way responsible for what happened."

"Thank you."

"I mean that. I am not just saying it."

"I know," Matt said.

"My lesser half—who is a bitch on wheels when awakened from her slumber in the wee hours—is going to be mightily piqued when I finally show up at home and tell her I have been here alone."

Matt chuckled.

"Considering that sacrifice I have made—you have seen the lady in a state of pique and should be sympathetic—do you think you could find it in your heart to offer me one of whatever it is you're drinking?"

"Sorry," Matt said. "This is Irish. Is that all right?"

"Gaelic chauvinist's scotch will do nicely. Thank you," Washington said.

"You've been on the job?" Matt asked as he walked toward the kitchen.

"Indeed."

"I thought you'd be taking some time off, going to the Shore or something."

"There have been several interesting developments,"

Washington said. "What opinion did you form of Staff Inspector Weisbach?"

"I liked him. He's smart as hell."

"That's good, because he's our new boss."

"Really?"

"Would you be interested in his opinion of you?"

"Yeah."

"He said you need to be held on a tight leash."

"Is that what he said?"

"That's what he said."

"You said 'our new boss.' Are we going to be involved in this Ethical Affairs business?"

"I think we are the Ethical Affairs Unit."

"That sounds like Internal Affairs by another name."

Matt walked back into his living room and handed Washington the drink.

"Not precisely. Wohl and Weisbach have elected to lend a broad interpretation to their mandate."

"Wohl was here."

"I saw him in the lobby."

"He didn't say anything to me about . . . anything."

"Under the circumstances . . ."

"He did mention half a dozen times that what I have to do is put . . . what happened to Penny . . . behind me, and get on with my life."

"And so you should. Anyway, Armando C. Giacomo had Wohl and Weisbach as his guests for lunch at the Rittenhouse Club."

"He's representing Cassandro?"

"Uh-huh. And Mr. Cassandro really does not wish to go to jail. Mr. Giacomo proposed a deal: Cassandro testifies against Cazerra, Meyer, and company, in exchange for immunity from prosecution."

"They're not going to deal, are they? They don't need his testimony. We have the bastard cold."

"What Peter and Weisbach find interesting is why the deal was proposed. Giacomo can, if he can't get him off completely, delay his trial for forever and a day, and then keep him from actually going to jail, with one appeal or another, for another couple of years. So, what, in other words, is going on?"

"What is?"

"Weisbach and Wohl, taking a shot in the dark, told Giacomo that the only thing we're interested in, vis-à-vis Cassandro, that might accrue to his advantage would be help with the murder of Officer Kellog and what happened at the Inferno Lounge. According to Weisbach, Giacomo acted as if something might be worked out."

"The mob would give us one, or both, doers in exchange for Cassandro?"

Washington nodded. "Which, since that would constitute a gross violation of the Sicilian Code of Honor, again raises the question, Why is Cassandro not going to trial so important? And that is what Weisbach and I have been trying to find out."

"And?"

"Nothing so far."

"Anything turn up on the Inferno Lounge job?"

"No. But I suspect there may be a connection there. Rather obviously, it was a hit, not a robbery. If it was a contract hit, it was expensive. If they give us that doer, that means Cassandro not going to jail is really important, and we're back to why."

Matt grunted.

"Anyway, you'll be close to that one. You're still going to Homicide. Whenever you feel up to coming back on the job."

"If I had my druthers, I'd come back tomorrow morning. I really dread tomorrow."

"At something of a tangent," Washington said, "I have something to say which may sound cruel. But I think I should say it. My first reaction when I heard what happened was relief."

Matt didn't reply at first.

"I've also felt that," he said finally. "It makes me feel like a real sonofabitch."

"I've seen a good many murders, Matt. And more than my fair share of narcotics addicts. I hold the private opinion that a pusher commits a far more heinous crime than—for example—whoever shot Officer Kellog. Or Mrs. Alicia Atchison and Mr. Anthony J. Marcuzzi at the Inferno. For them, it was over instantaneously. It was brutal, but not as brutal as taking the life of a young woman, in painful stages, over a long period of time."

Matt did not reply.

"The point of this little philosophical observation, Matt, is that Penny was murdered the first time she put a needle in her arm. When you . . . became romantically involved . . . with one another, she was already dead. The man who killed her was the man who gave her her first hard drugs."

"I loved her."

"Yes, I know."

"We had a fight the last time I saw her. About me being a cop."

"If you had agreed to become the Nesfoods International Vice President in Charge of Keeping the Boss's Daughter Happy as of tomorrow morning, Matt," Washington said seriously, "she would have found some other excuse to seek narcotic euphoria. The addiction was out of her control. It had nothing to do with you. You've got to believe that, for the simple reason that it's true."

"I'll never know now, will I?"

Washington met his eyes, then set his drink down.

"Let's go bar-crawling."

"What?" Matt asked, surprised at the suggestion.

"How long have you been up here in the garret?"

Matt thought about that before replying.

"I got here about one-thirty."

"Twelve hours in a smoke-filled room. That's enough. Get your coat."

"Where are we going?"

"The Mall Tavern. At Tenth and Cherry. When I was an honest Homicide detective, I used to go there for a post-duty libation. Let's go listen to the gossip. Maybe we'll hear something interesting."

FOURTEEN

He doesn't look like a cop, Amy thought when she saw Peter talking to the night manager in the lobby of her apartment building. *Mr. Ramerez has put the well-cut suit and the Jaguar together and decided Dr. Payne is carrying on with a lawyer or a stockbroker.*

"Good evening, Doctor," Peter said.

"Thank you for coming at this hour," Amy replied. "Shall we go up?" She smiled at Mr. Ramerez. "Good evening, Mr. Ramerez."

It is obviously important to me that Mr. Ramerez understand that I am not carrying on with him, cop or stockbroker.

They rode in silence and somewhat awkwardly to Amy's apartment. She unlocked the door, and entered. He followed her.

"Coffee? Or a drink?" she asked.

"Neither, thank you. You said you wanted to talk about Matt."

"I think it important that he not be left alone."

"Tiny Lewis—he's a police officer . . ."

"I know who he is," Amy interrupted.

Peter nodded and went on: ". . . will be at Matt's apartment at seven-fifteen in the morning. If you think he should not be alone tonight, I can go back."

"I think he'll be all right tonight," she said. "Can you keep him busy? Especially for the next few days?"

Wohl nodded.

"He blames himself for Penny," Amy said.

"Yes, I know."

"I don't know if you appreciate it, but he is actually rather sensitive."

"I know."

"You know what he did tonight?" she asked, and went on without waiting for a reply. "He put his arms around me and asked who holds my hand when I need it."

"There has been at least one applicant for that job that I know about. As I recall, you didn't seem interested."

"Damn you, Peter, you're not making this easy."

"I don't know if you appreciate it, but I am actually rather sensitive," Wohl mockingly paraphrased what she had said about Matt.

"You bastard!" she said, but laughed. "Honest to God, Peter, I didn't want to hurt you."

He shrugged.

"I lied," Amy said.

"Not returning calls, not being in, having 'previous plans' when I finally got you on the phone is not exactly lying."

"I mean tonight," Amy said. "Certainly to you, and probably to myself. I knew that you, the Ancient and Honorable Order of Cops, were going to gather protectively around Matt and do more for him than I could."

Wohl looked at her, waiting for her to go on.

"I wanted somebody, to hold my hand. Penny Detweiler was my patient. I failed her."

He looked at her a moment.

"Somebody? Anybody? Or me?"

"I knew you would be there," Amy said.

Peter held his arms open. She took several hesitant steps toward him, and ultimately wound up with her face on his chest.

"Amy, you did everything that could be done for that girl," Peter said, putting his hand on the back of her head, gently caressing it. "Some people are beyond help. Or don't want it."

"Oh, God, Peter! I feel so lousy about it!"

He felt her back stiffen under his hand, and then tremble with repressed sobs.

"Tell you what I'm going to do, Doc," he said gently. "On one condition, I will accept your kind invitation to breakfast."

She pushed away from him and looked up at his face.

"I made no such invitation."

"That I cook breakfast. The culinary arts not being among your many other accomplishments."

"You think that would help?"

"I don't think it would hurt."

"I don't even know if there's anything in the fridge."

"So I'll open a can of spaghetti."

Amy tried to smile, failed, and put her head against his chest. She felt his arms tighten around her.

"Would you rather tear off my clothes here, or should we wait until we get into the bedroom?"

It was half past seven when the ringing of his door buzzer woke Matt Payne.

He fumbled on his bedside table for his wristwatch, saw the time, muttered a sacrilege, and got out of bed.

The buzzer went off again, for about five seconds.

"I'm coming, for Christ's sake," Matt said, although there was no possibility at all that anyone could hear him.

There was ten seconds of silence as he looked around for his discarded underpants—it being his custom to sleep in his birthday suit—and then another five seconds of buzzer.

He was halfway through the kitchen when the buzzer sounded again.

He found the button that activated the door's solenoid, pushed it, and then continued through the kitchen and the living room to the head of the stairs. When he looked down, the bulk of Officer Foster H. Lewis, Jr., attired in a nicely cut dark-blue suit, nearly filled the narrow stairway.

"Tiny, what the hell do you want?" Matt asked, far less than graciously.

"What I want to do is be home in my bed," Tiny Lewis replied. "What I have been told to do is not let you out of my sight."

"By who?"

"Wohl," Tiny said as he reached the head of the stairs. "God, are you always that hard to wake up? I've been sitting on that damned buzzer for ten minutes. I was about to take the door."

"I didn't get to bed until three," Matt said.

Tiny looked uncomfortable.

"Matt, I don't think booze is the solution."

"I was with Washington at the Mall Tavern."

"Doing what?"

"Ostensibly, it was so that he and I could listen to Homicide gossip. About the time he went home, I decided it was to introduce me socially to the Homicide guys; he was playing rabbi for me."

"My father said they're really going to be pissed that the Mayor sent you over there."

"I think their reaction, thanks to Washington, has been reduced from homicidal rage, pun intended, to bitter resentment by Washington's act of charity. Actually, they seemed to understand it wasn't my doing."

"I would have been here yesterday," Tiny said. "Personally, not because Wohl would have sent me. But Washington said there would be enough people here then, and I should come today." Tiny paused. "I'm sorry about what happened, Matt."

"Thank you."

"Anyway, you're stuck with me," Tiny said. "And apropos of nothing whatever, I haven't had my breakfast."

"See what's in the refrigerator while I have a shower," Matt said.

Matt came back into the kitchen ten minutes later to the smell of frying bacon and percolating coffee, and the sight of Tiny Lewis neatly arranging tableware on the kitchen table. He had taken off his suit jacket and put on an apron. It was a full-sized apron, but on Tiny's massive bulk it appeared much smaller. He looked ridiculous, and Matt smiled.

"I'll bet you can iron very well, too," he said.

"Fuck you, you don't get no breakfast," Tiny replied amiably.

"When you're through with that, you can vacuum the living room."

"Fuck you again," Tiny said. "Tell me about the double homicide at the Inferno."

Over breakfast, Matt told him.

"This Atchison guy is very good," he concluded. "Smart and tough. And his lawyer is good, too. Just when Milham was starting to get him, the lawyer—"

"Who's his lawyer?"

"A guy named Sidney Margolis."

Tiny snorted. "I know who he is. A real sleazeball. My father told me he's been reported to the bar association so often he's got his own filing cabinet."

"He's smart. He saw Milham was getting to Atchison, and said, 'Interview over. My client is in great pain.' "

"Was he?"

"After Margolis told him he was, he was. And that was it."

"I wish I could have seen the interview," Tiny said.

"Milham is very good."

"You heard about his lady friend's husband?"

"Yeah."

"Do you think he had anything to do with it?"

"No," Matt said immediately.

"Either does my father," Tiny said. "He said it's two-to-one it's something to do with Narcotics. Heading the long list of things I was absolutely forbidden to do when I came on the job was accept an assignment to Narcotics. He said those guys roll around on the pigsty floor so much, and there's so much money floating around that he's not surprised how many of them are dirty, but how many are straight."

"Charley and the Little Spic were undercover narcs, and so was Captain Pekach. They're straight."

"The exceptions that prove the rule," Tiny said. "So what do we do today?"

"I don't know what you're going to do, but I'm going out to Chestnut Hill in half an hour. Jesus, I hate to face that! The funeral is this afternoon."

"You mean, *we're* going to Chestnut Hill. I have heard my master's voice, and it said I'm not to let you out of my sight."

"Family and intimate friends only," Matt said. "I think it will be my family, the Detweilers, and the Nesbitts. And that's it."

"So what do I tell Wohl, since the riffraff aren't welcome?"

"I'll call him."

"Matt, I don't mind feeling unwelcome. With a suntan like mine, you get pretty used to it. If I can help some way . . ."

"You'd make a lousy situation worse, Tiny, but thanks," Matt said. He got up from the table and started toward the

telephone, then stopped. He touched Tiny's shoulder, and
Tiny looked up at him. "I appreciate that, pal," Matt said.

"Somehow saying I'm sorry about what happened doesn't
seem to be enough."

Matt picked up the telephone and dialed Wohl's home
number. When there was no answer, he called the headquarters of the Special Operations Division to see if, as he often
did, Wohl had come to work early. When Wohl's private line
was not answered by the fifth ring, the call was automati-
cally transferred to the line of the tour lieutenant.

"Special Operations, Lieutenant Suffern."

"Matt Payne, sir. Have you got a location on the Inspector?"

"Yeah. I got a number. Just a minute, Matt," Lieutenant
Suffern said, and then his voice changed: "Matt, I was sorry
to hear . . ."

"Thank you."

"If there's anything I can do?"

"I can't think of a thing, but thank you. I appreciate the
thought."

"Here it is," Suffern said, "One-thirty A.M. this morning
until further notice." He then read Matt the telephone number at which Inspector Wohl could be reached.

A look of mingled amusement and annoyance flickered
across Matt's face. The number he had been given was familiar to him. It was the one number in Greater Philadelphia
where calling Inspector Wohl at this time would be a very
bad idea indeed. It was that of the apartment of his sister,
Amelia Payne, M.D., Ph.D.

"Thank you, sir."

"When you feel up to it, Matt, we'll go hoist a couple."

"Thank you," Matt said. "I'd like to."

Matt hung up and turned to Tiny, a smile crossing his face
at his own wit.

"Wohl can't be reached right now," he said. "He's at the
doctor's."

"So what do we do?"

"When all else fails, tell the truth," Matt said. "You go to the schoolhouse and when Wohl shows up you tell him I said 'Thank you, but no thank you, I don't want any company.'"

"I don't know, Matt," Tiny said dubiously. "Wohl wasn't making a suggestion. He told me to sit on you."

"Oh, shit," Matt said, and dialed Amy's number.

"Dr. Payne is not available at this time," her answering machine reported. "If you will leave your name and number, she will return your call as soon as possible. Please wait for the tone. Thank you."

"Amy, I know you're there. I need to talk to Inspector Wohl."

A moment later, Wohl himself came on the line.

"What is it, Matt?"

"Tiny Lewis is here. Having him go with me to the Detweilers' is not such a good idea. The funeral is family and intimate friends only."

"So your sister has been telling me," Wohl said. "He's there? Put him on the line."

Matt held the phone up, and Tiny rose massively from the table and took it.

"Yes, sir?" he said.

Tiny's was the only side of the conversation Matt could hear, and he was curious when Tiny chuckled, a deep rumble, and said, "I would, too. That'd be something to see."

When he hung up, Matt asked, "What would be 'something to see'?"

"The Mayor's face when somebody tells him he can't get in. Wohl said he knows the Mayor's going to the funeral."

"This one he may not get to go to," Matt said. "My father said nobody's been invited, period."

"Wohl also said I was to drive you out there, if you wanted, and then to keep myself available. I was going to do that anyway."

"You can take me over to the Parkway as soon as I get dressed. I'm going to drive my sister out there, in her car."

"Yeah, sure. But listen to what I said. You need me, you know where to find me."

Inspector Peter Wohl was examining the hole gouged in his cheek by Amy Payne's dull razor—and from which an astonishing flow of blood was now escaping—when Amy appeared in the bathroom door.

She was in her underwear. It was white, and what there was of it was mostly lace. He found the sight very appealing, and wondered if that was her everyday underwear, or whether she had worn it for him.

That pleasant notion was immediately shattered by her tone of voice and the look on her face.

"It's for you," she said. "Again. Does everyone in Philadelphia know you're here?"

"Sorry," he said, and quickly tore off a square of toilet paper, pressed it to the wound, and went into her bedroom. He sat on the bed and grabbed the telephone.

"Inspector Wohl."

"I'm sorry to trouble you, sir," Jason Washington's deep, mellifluous voice said.

Washington's the soul of discretion. When he got this number from the tour lieutenant—and with that memory of his, he probably knows whose number it is—unless it was important, he would have waited until I went to work.

"No trouble. I'm just sitting here quietly bleeding to death. Good morning, Jason. What's up?"

"I just had an interesting call. An informant who has been reliable with what he's given me—which hasn't been much—in the past. He said the Inferno murders were a mob contract."

"Interesting. Did he give you a name?"

"Frankie Foley."

"Never heard of him."

Amy sat on the bed beside him and put her hand on his cheek. It was a gesture of affection, but only by implication. She had a cotton swab dipped in some kind of antiseptic.

She pulled the toilet paper bandage off and professionally swabbed his gouge.

"Either have I. And neither has Organized Crime or Intelligence."

"Even more interesting."

"What do you want me to do with it?"

It was a moment before Wohl replied.

"Give it to Homicide. And then see if you can make a connection to Cassandro."

"Yes, sir."

Wohl had an unpleasant thought. There was a strong possibility that he would have to remind Washington that a new chain of command was in effect. Washington was used to reporting directly to him. He might not like having to go through Weisbach.

"What did Weisbach say when you told him?"

"He said he thought we better give it to Homicide, but to ask you first."

Thank God! Personnel conflict avoided.

"Write this down, Jason. The true sign of another man's intelligence is the degree to which he agrees with you."

Washington laughed.

"I'll be in touch," he said, and hung up.

"Who was that?" Amy asked.

"Jason Washington."

"I thought so. How did he know you were here? What did you do, put an ad in the *Bulletin*? Who else knows where you spent the night?"

"There is a very short list of people who have to know where I am all the time. The tour lieutenant knows where to find me. Since only Matt and Jason called, to answer your question two people have reason to suspect I spent the night here."

"God!"

"There is a solution to the problem," Peter said. "I could make an honest woman of you."

"Surely you jest," she said after a moment's pause.

"I don't know if I am or not," Peter said. "You better not consider that a firm offer."

She stood up. "Now I'm sorry I fixed your face," she said, and walked toward the bathroom.

"Nice ass," he called after her.

She gave him the finger without turning and went into the bathroom, closing the door.

Jesus, where did that "make an honest woman of you" crack come from?

He stood up and started looking for his clothing.

Lieutenant Foster H. Lewis, Sr., of the Ninth District, a very tall, well-muscled man, was sitting in a wicker arm-chair on the enclosed porch of his home reading the *Philadelphia Bulletin* when Officer Foster H. Lewis, Jr., of Special Operations, pushed the door open and walked in.

Tiny, who knew his father was working the midnight-out tour, was surprised to see him. It was his father's custom, when he came off the midnight-out tour,z to take a shower and go to bed and get his eight hours' sleep. And here he was, in an obviously fresh white shirt, immaculately shaven, looking as if he was about to go on duty.

"I thought you were working the midnight-out," Tiny said.

"Good morning, son. How are you? I am fine, thank you for asking," Lieutenant Lewis said dryly.

"Sorry."

"I was supposed to fill in for Lieutenant Prater, who was ill," Lieutenant Lewis said. "When I got to the office, he had experienced a miraculous recovery. And *I* thought *you* were working days."

"I'm working," Tiny said, and gestured toward the car parked in the drive.

"How can you be working and here?"

"My orders, Lieutenant, sir, are to stay close to the radio, in case I'm needed."

"You needn't be sarcastic, Foster, it was a reasonable question."

"Inspector Wohl told me to give Matt Payne some company," Tiny said. "I wasn't needed."

"What a tragedy!" Lieutenant Lewis said.

"I thought I'd come see Mom," Tiny said.

"Since I would not be here, you mean?"

"Pop, every time I see you, you jump all over me."

"I wasn't aware of that."

"Just now," Tiny said. "The implication that I'm screwing off being here."

"I didn't say that."

"That's what you meant."

"You are driving a departmental vehicle, presumably on duty, visiting your family."

"I'm doing what I'm ordered to do. Pop, I'm a pretty good cop! Inspector Wohl expects me to be available if he needs me. I don't think he expected me to just sit in the car and wait for the radio to go off."

"You believe that, don't you?"

"Believe what?"

"That you're a pretty good cop."

"I'm not as good a cop as you are, but yeah, I'm a pretty good cop."

"I'm sure you will take offense when I say this, but you don't know what being a police officer really means."

"You mean, I never worked in a district?"

"Exactly."

"Come on, Pop. If Inspector Wohl thought I would learn anything riding around in a car, walking a beat, that's what he'd have me doing."

"That sort of thing is beneath you, right?"

"I think we better stop this before either one of us says something we'll be sorry for," Tiny said.

Lieutenant Lewis looked at his son for a moment before replying.

"I'm not saying that what you're doing is not important, or that you don't do it well."

"It is important—we're going to put a dirty captain and a dirty lieutenant away—and I helped. Wohl and Washington wouldn't have let me get close to that job if they didn't think I could handle it."

"All I'm saying, Foster," Lieutenant Lewis said, "is that I am concerned that you have no experience as a police officer on the street. You don't even have any friends who are common, ordinary policemen, do you?"

"I guess not," Tiny said.

"Would you indulge me if I asked you to do something?"

"Within reason."

It came out more sarcastically, more disrespectfully than Tiny intended, and there was frost for a moment in his father's eyes. But then apparently he decided to let it pass.

"Did I understand you to say that, so long as you keep yourself available, you're free to move about the city?"

"That's right."

"Go inside, say hello to your mother, tell her you're coming to dinner tonight, and that we're going for a ride. Police business."

"A ride? What police business?"

"We're going to the Thirty-ninth District. I have a friend there, a common ordinary policeman, who I want you to meet. You might even learn something from him."

Police Officer Woodrow Wilson Bailey, Sr., badge number 2554 of the Thirty-ninth District, who had twenty-four years on the job, twenty-two of it in the Thirty-ninth District, wanted only one thing from the Philadelphia Police Department. He wanted to make it to retirement, tell them where to mail his retirement checks, and go back home to Hartsville, South Carolina.

Having done that, it was his devout hope that he would never have to put on a uniform, look at a gun, or see

Philadelphia, Pennsylvania, ever again so long as the Good Lord saw fit to let him live.

He thought of it as going back to Hartsville, although in fact he could never remember living there. He had been brought to Philadelphia from Hartsville at the age of three by his father, who had decided that as bad as things might be up north, with the depression and all, they couldn't be any worse than being a sharecropper with a wife and child to feed on a hardscrabble farm in South Carolina.

The first memory of a home that Officer Bailey had was of an attic room in a row house on Sydenham in North Philadelphia. There was a table in it, and two beds, one for Mamma Dear and Daddy, and one for him, and then when Charles David came along, for him and Charles David. There was an electric hot plate, and a galvanized bucket for water. The bathroom was one floor down, and shared with the three families who occupied the five rooms on the second floor.

The room was provided to them by the charity of the Third Abyssinian Baptist Church, to which Officer Bailey and his family still belonged.

He had vague memories of Daddy leaving the apartment in the morning to seek work as a laborer, and much more clear memories of Daddy leaving the room (and later the two-room apartment on the second floor of another row house) carrying his shoe-shine box to walk downtown to station himself at the Market Street Station of the Pennsylvania Railroad to shine the shoes of the rich white folks who rode the train in from places with funny-sounding names like Bala Cynwyd and Glen Riddle.

And he had memories of Hartsville from those times, too. Of going to see Granny Bailey and Granny Smythe back in Hartsville. Mamma Dear and Daddy had believed with the other members of the Third Abyssinian Baptist Church that if it was in the Bible, that was all there was to it, you did what it said, and you spent eternity with the Good Lord, or you didn't, and you spent eternity in the fiery fires of Hell.

It said in the Good Book that you were supposed to Honor
Thy Mother and Thy Father, and that meant you went to see
your mother and your father at least at Christmas, and more
often if you could afford it, and affording it meant saving up
to buy the bus tickets, and for a few little presents to take
with you, even if that meant you didn't get to drink Coca-
Cola or go to the movies.

Bailey had liked Hartsville even then, even if he now recognized that Granny Smythe's "farm" was nothing more
than a weathered shack without inside plumbing that sat on
three acres she had been given in the will of old Mr.
Smythe—probably because it wasn't worth the powder to
blow it away—whose father had bought Granny Smythe's
father at a slave auction in Beaufort.

There were chickens on Granny Smythe's farm, and a
couple of dogs, and almost always a couple of pigs, and the
whole place had seemed a much nicer place to live than in a
row house in North Philadelphia.

He had asked several times why they had to live in
Philadelphia, and Daddy had told him that he didn't expect
him to understand, but that Philadelphia was a place where
you could better yourself, get a good education, and make
something of yourself.

Bailey remembered being dropped off with Charles
David at the Third Abyssinian Baptist Church by Mamma
Dear, wearing a crisp white maid's uniform, so he and
Charles David could be cared for, and she could work and
make some money and realize her and Daddy's dream of
buying a house that would be theirs, instead of paying rent.

He remembered the beating Daddy had given him with a
leather belt when he was in the fifth grade at the Dunbar Elementary School and the teacher had come by the house
they were then renting and reported that he had not only
been cutting school, but giving her talk-back in class, and
running around with the wrong crowd.

Charles David, who was now a welder at the Navy Ship-
yard, still told that story, said that he got through high school

because he had been there when Daddy had taken a strap to Woodrow for cutting school and sassing the teacher at Dunbar, and he was smart enough to learn by vicarious experience.

Woodrow had graduated from Dunbar Elementary School and gone on to graduate from William Penn High School. By then, Daddy had gone from shining shoes inside the Market Street Station to shining them in a barbershop on South Ninth Street, and finally to shining them in the gents' room of the Rittenhouse Club on Rittenhouse Square. He was on salary then, paid to be in the gents' room from just before lunch until maybe nine o'clock at night, shining anybody who climbed up on the chair's shoes for free. It was part of what you got being a member of the Rittenhouse Club, getting your shoes shined for free.

The members weren't supposed to pay the shoe-shine boy, but, Daddy had told him, maybe about one in four would hand him a quarter or fifty cents anyway, and at Christmas, about three or four of the members whose shoes he had shined all year would wish him "Merry Christmas" and slip him some folding money. Usually it was ten or twenty dollars, but sometimes more. The first one-hundred-dollar bill Woodrow had ever seen in his life one of the Rittenhouse gentlemen had given to his father at Christmas.

That hundred dollars, and just about everything else Daddy and Mamma Dear could scrape together (what was left, in other words, after they'd given the Good Lord's Tithe to the Third Abyssinian Baptist Church, and after they'd put money away to go home to Hartsville at Christmas and maybe to go home for a funeral or a wedding or something like that), had gone into coming up with the money for the down payment on the house, and then paying the house off.

The house was another reason Woodrow really hated Philadelphia. Daddy and Mamma Dear had worked their hearts out, done without, to pay for the thing, and they had just about paid it off when the neighborhood had started to go to hell.

Woodrow did not like to curse, but *hell* was the only word that fit, and he knew the Good Lord would not think he was being blasphemous.

Trash moved in. Black trash and white trash. Drinkers and adulterers and blasphemers, people who took no pride in the neighborhood or themselves.

It had been bad when Woodrow had finished William Penn High School and was looking for work, it was worse when, at twenty-two, he'd applied for a job on the cops, and it had grown worse ever since. He spent his first two years in the Twenty-second District, learning how to be a cop, and then they had transferred him—they'd asked him first how he would feel about it, to give the devil his due—to the Thirty-ninth District which was then about thirty percent black (they said "Negro" in those days, but it meant the same thing as 'nigger' and everybody knew it) and getting blacker.

"You live there, Woodrow," Lieutenant Grogarty, a red-faced Irishman, had asked him. "How would you feel about working there, with your people?"

At the time, truth to tell, Woodrow had thought it would be a pretty good idea. He had still thought then—he was only two years out of the Academy and didn't know better—that a police officer could be a force for good, that a good Christian man could help people.

He thought that one of the problems was that most cops were white men, and colored folks naturally resented that. He thought that maybe it would be different if a colored police officer were handling things.

He'd been wrong about that. His being colored hadn't made a bit of difference. The people he had to deal with didn't care if he was black or yellow or green. He was The Man. He was the badge. He was the guy who was going to put them in jail. They hated him. Worse, he hadn't been able to help anyone that he could tell. Unless arresting some punk *after* he'd hit some old lady in the back of her head, and stolen her groceries and rent money and spent it on

loose women, whiskey, or worse could be considered helping.

He had been bitter when he'd finally faced the truth about
this, even considered quitting the cops, finding some other
job. He didn't know what other kind of job he could get—
all he'd ever done after high school before he came on the
cops was work unskilled labor jobs—but he thought there
had to be something.

He had had a long talk about it with the Pastor Emeritus
of the Third Abyssinian Baptist Church, Rev. Dr. Joshua
Steele—that fine old gentleman and servant of the Good
Lord was still alive then, eat up with cancer but not willing
to quit—and Dr. Steele had told him that all the Bible said
was that if you prayed, the Good Lord would point out a
Christian man's path to him. Nothing was said about that
path being easy.

"You ask the Good Lord, Woodrow, if He has other plans
for you, and if so, what. If He wants you to do something
else, Woodrow, He'll let you know. You'll *know*, boy. In
your heart, you'll know."

Woodrow, after prayerful consideration, had decided that
if the Good Lord wanted him to do something else, he would
have let him know. And since he didn't get a sign or anything, it was logical to conclude that the Lord was perfectly
happy having him do what he was doing.

Which wasn't so strange, he came to decide. While he
wasn't able to change things much, or help a lot of people,
every once in a while he was able to do something for somebody.

And maybe locking up punks who were beating up and
robbing old people was really helping. If they were in jail,
they at least weren't robbing and beating up on people.

Three months later, Woodrow met Joellen, who had come
up from Georgia right after she finished high school. He
never told her—she might have laughed at him—but he took
meeting her as a sign from the Good Lord that he had done
the right thing. Joellen was like a present from the Good

Lord. And so was Woodrow Wilson Bailey, Jr., when he come along twenty months later.

The Lord giveth and the Lord taketh away. Woodrow didn't know if he could have handled Mamma Dear and Daddy being taken into heaven within four months of each other if it hadn't been for Joellen, and with her already starting to show what the Good Lord was giving them: Woodrow Wilson, Junior.

That meant two more trips back home to Hartsville. Mamma Dear had told Daddy in the hospital that she had been paying all along for a burial policy, sixty-five cents a week for twenty years and more, that he didn't know about, and that she wanted him to spend the money to send her back to Hartsville and bury her beside her Mamma, Granny Smythe. She didn't want to be buried in Philadelphia, Pennsylvania, beside strangers.

Four months after they buried Mamma Dear, Woodrow buried Daddy beside her. That was really when Woodrow decided he was going to come home to Hartsville, and when he told Joellen what he had decided, she said that was fine with her, she didn't like living up north anyhow.

There was no work he could get in Hartsville that paid anything like what he was making on the cops, and they didn't even know what a pension for colored people was in Hartsville, so that meant he had to stay on the cops, put in his time, and then retire to Hartsville.

That had been a long time ago, and at the time he'd thought he could sell the house that Mamma Dear and Daddy had sacrificed so much for, and maybe buy a little farm in Hartsville. Let somebody else work it on shares, not work it himself.

That hadn't turned out. With the trash moving into the neighborhood, you couldn't sell the place at hardly any price today. But he and Joellen had been able to save some money, and with his police pension, it was going to be all right when they went home to Hartsville.

Several times in the last couple of years, he had been offered different jobs in the Thirty-ninth District. Once the Captain had asked him if he wanted to help the Corporal, be what they called a "trainee" (which sounded like some kid, but wasn't) with the administration, but he told him no thank you, I'd just as soon just work my beat than be inside all day. Another time, another *two* times, they'd asked him did he want to do something called "Community Relations."

"We want people to start thinking about the police as being their friends, Woodrow," a lieutenant had told him, a *colored* lieutenant. "And with your position in the community, your being a deacon at Third Abyssinian Baptist Church, for example, we think you're just the man to help us."

He told the Lieutenant, "Thank you, sir, for thinking about me, but I'm not interested in anything like that, I don't think I'd be any good at it."

What Woodrow thought he was good at was what he did, what he wanted to do until he got his time in and could go home to Hartsville, South Carolina. He worked his beat. He protected old people from getting hit in the head and having their grocery money stolen by some punk. He looked for new faces standing around on corners and talked to them, and told them he didn't like funny cigarettes or worse sold on his beat and that he had a good memory for faces.

The punks on the street corner could call him Old Oreo, or Uncle Tom, or whatever they liked, and it didn't bother him much, because he knew he was straight with the Good Lord and that was all that mattered. The Bible said all there was to say about bearing false witness against your neighbor. And also because he knew what else the punks who called him names told the new punks: "Don't cross that mean old nigger, he'll catch you alone when there's nobody around and slap you up aside of the head with his club or his gun and knock you into the middle of next week."

He liked to walk his beat. You could see much more of what was going on just ambling down the street than you could from inside an RPC. A lot of police officers hated to get out of their cars, but Woodrow was just the opposite. He liked to walk, say hello to people, be seen, see things he wouldn't have been able to see driving a car.

Officer Bailey was not surprised to get the call telling him to meet the Sergeant, but when he got there, he was surprised to see Lieutenant Foster H. Lewis, Sr., standing by the car, talking to the Sergeant.

He and Lewis went back together a long time. He was a good man, in Bailey's opinion. God-fearing, honest, hard-working. But Bailey was a little worried when he saw him. Lewis was assigned to the Ninth District.

What's he doing here?

Maybe he's been sent to talk me into taking one of those special jobs in Community Relations the Lieutenant had talked to me about and I turned down.

When the Sergeant saw Bailey coming, he shook Lieutenant Lewis's hand, got back in his car, and drove off. Lieutenant Lewis stood in the middle of the street and waited for Bailey to drive up.

"How are you, Woodrow?" Lieutenant Lewis said, offering his hand.

"Pretty good, Lieutenant. How's yourself?"

"We were riding around—" Lieutenant Lewis said, interrupting himself to point at the new car parked at the curb. Woodrow saw that it was an unmarked car, the kind inspectors and the like got, and that a black man was behind the wheel.

"—and we had some time, and I thought maybe we could have a cup of coffee or something."

"I can always find time to take a cup of coffee with you," Woodrow said. "Right over there's as good a place as any. At least it's clean."

"The Sergeant said it would be all right if you put yourself out of service for half an hour."

"I'll park this," Woodrow said.

When he came back from parking the car, he recognized the man driving the car.

"This your boy, isn't it, Foster? He wasn't nearly so big the last time I saw him."

"How do you do, sir?" Tiny said politely.

"Well, I'll be. I recognized him from his picture in the paper. When they arrested those dirty cops."

They went in the small neighborhood restaurant. An obese woman brought coffee to the table for all of them.

"Miss Kathy, this is Lieutenant Foster, and his boy," Woodrow said. "We go back a long way."

"Way back," Lieutenant Lewis agreed. "When I graduated from the Academy Officer Bailey sort of took me under his wing."

"Is that so?" the woman said, and walked away.

"When Foster here finished the Academy, they sent him right to Special Operations, put him in plain clothes, and gave him a car," Lieutenant Lewis said. "Things have changed, eh, Woodrow?"

"You like what you're doing, boy?"

"Yes, sir."

"I was thinking the other day that if I had to do it all over again, I wouldn't," Bailey said.

Lieutenant Lewis laughed.

"You don't mean that, Woodrow," he said.

"Yes, I do mean it. Don't take this the wrong way, boy, but I'm glad I'm not starting out. I don't think I could take another twenty-some years walking this beat."

"I was telling Foster that walking a beat is what the police are all about," Lieutenant Lewis said.

"Well, then, the country's in trouble," Bailey said. "Because we're losing, Foster, and you know it. Things get a little worse every day, and there doesn't seem to be anything that anybody can do about it."

"What I was trying to get across to Foster was that there's no substitute for the experience an officer like yourself gets," Lieutenant Lewis said.

"Well, maybe you're right, but the only thing my experience does is make me tired. Time was, I used to think I could clean up a place. Now I know better. All I'm doing is slowing down how fast it's getting worse. And I only get to slow it down a little on good days."

Lieutenant Lewis laughed politely.

"I was thinking, Woodrow," he said, "that since Foster hasn't had any experience on the streets, that maybe you'd be good enough to let him ride around with you once in a while. You know, show him the tricks of the trade."

"Good Lord," Officer Bailey laughed, "why would he want to do that?"

Lieutenant Lewis glanced at his son. He saw that it was only with a great effort that Officer Foster H. Lewis, Jr., was able to keep his face straight, not let it show what he was thinking.

"My father is right, Mr. Bailey," Tiny said. "I could probably learn a lot from you."

That response surprised and then delighted Lieutenant Lewis, but the delight was short-lived:

"The only thing you could learn by riding around with me," Officer Bailey said, "is that Satan's having his way, and if you have half the brains you were born with, you already know that."

Officer Lewis looked at his watch.

"Is there a phone around here, Mr. Bailey? I've got to check in."

"There's a pay phone outside," Bailey said. "But most likely somebody ripped the handset off for the fun of it. You go see Miss Kathy, and tell her I said to let you use hers."

"Thank you," Tiny said.

When he was out of earshot, Officer Bailey nodded approvingly.

"Nice boy, Foster," he said. "You should be proud of him."

"I am," Lieutenant Lewis said.

•　　•　　•

Men in light blue uniforms, suggesting State Police uniforms, with shoulder patches reading "Nesfoods International Security," stood at the gates of the Detweiler estate. They were armed, Matt noticed, with chrome-plated Smith & Wesson .357 caliber revolvers, and their Sam Browne belts held rows of shining cartridges.

"Anyone trying to shoot their way in here's going to have his hands full," Matt said softly as he slowed and lowered the window of Amy's station wagon.

"You really have a strange sense of humor," Amy said, and leaned over him to speak to the security man.

"I'm Dr. Payne," Amy said, "and this is my brother."

One of the two men consulted a clipboard.

"Yes, Ma'am, you're on the list," the security man said, and the left of the tall wrought-iron gates began to open inward.

Matt raised the window.

"And you're back on Peter's list, too, I see," Matt said.

"Matt, I understand that you're under a terrible strain," Amy said tolerantly, either the understanding psychiatrist or the sympathetic older sister, or both, "but please try to control your mouth. Things are going to be difficult enough in here."

"I wonder how long it's going to be before Mother Detweiler decides that if I had only been reasonable, reasonable defined as resigning from the Police Department and taking my rightful position in society, Penny wouldn't have stuck that needle in her arm, and that this whole thing is my fault."

"That's to be expected," Amy said. "The important thing is that you don't accept that line of reasoning."

"In other words, she's already started down that road?"

"What did you expect?" Amy said. "She, and Uncle Dick, have to find someone to blame."

"Give me a straight answer, Doc. I don't feel I'm responsible. What does that make me?"

"Is that your emotional reaction, as opposed to a logical conclusion you've come to?"

"How about both?"

"Straight answer: You're probably still in emotional shock. Have you wept?"

"I haven't had time to," Matt said. "I didn't get to bed until about three."

"More people showed up at your apartment?" Amy said, annoyance in her voice.

"No, I went to the bar where the Homicide detectives hang out with Jason Washington. He was trying to make me palatable to them."

"What does that mean?"

"When I go back on the job, I'm going to spend some time in Homicide."

"What's all that about?"

"It's a long story. What I will ostensibly be doing is working on the Inferno job."

"What's the 'Inferno job'?"

"Washington and I walked up on a double homicide on Market Street, in a gin mill called the Inferno Lounge."

"The bar owner? They killed his wife? I heard something on the radio."

"The wife and business partner had their brains blown out. The husband suffered a .32 flesh wound to the leg."

"Is there something significant in that?" Amy asked.

"Let us say the version of the incident related by the not-so-bereaved husband is not regarded as being wholly true," Matt said.

"But why are you going to Homicide?" Amy asked.

She didn't get an answer.

"Jesus Christ, what's this?" Matt exclaimed. "It looks like a used-car lot."

Amy looked out the windshield. The wide cobblestone drive in front of the Detweiler mansion and the last fifty yards of the road leading to it were crowded with cars, a substantial percentage of them Cadillacs and Lincolns. There were five or six limousines, including two Rolls Royces.

"Dad said family and intimate friends," Amy said. "It's apparently gotten out of hand."

"Intimate friends, or the morbidly curious?" Matt asked. "With a *soupçon* of social climbers thrown in for good measure?"

"Matt, have those acidulous thoughts if they make you feel better, but for the sake of Uncle Dick and Aunt Grace—and Mother and Dad—please have the decency to keep them to yourself."

"Sorry," he said, sounding contrite.

"What were they supposed to say when someone called, or simply showed up? 'Sorry, you're not welcome'?"

"Oh, shit, there's Chad," Matt said. "And the very pregnant Daffy and friend."

"Why are you surprised, and why 'oh, shit'?"

"I would just as soon not see them just now."

Mr. Chadwick Thomas Nesbitt IV glanced down the drive as the station wagon drove up, recognized the occupants, and touched the arm of his wife. Mrs. Nesbitt in turn touched the arm of Miss Amanda Chase Spencer, a strikingly beautiful blonde who was wearing a black silk suit with a hat and veil nearly identical to Mrs. Nesbitt's. All three stopped and waited on the lower of the shallow steps leading to the flagstone patio before the mansion's front door.

"How are you holding up, buddy?" Chad asked, grasping Matt's arm.

"Oh, Matt," Daffy said. "Poor Matt!"

She embraced him, which caused her swollen belly to push against him.

"Hello, Matt," Amanda said. "I'm so very sorry."

"Thank you," Matt said, reaching around Daffy to take the gloved hand she extended.

"I still can't believe it," Daffy said as she finally released Matt.

"I'm Amelia Payne," Amy said to Amanda.

"How do you do?"

"I thought this was supposed to be family and immediate friends only," Matt said, gesturing at all the cars.

"Matt, I can't believe you said that!" Daffy said, horrified.

Matt looked at her without comprehension.

"Amanda's been staying with us, for Martha Peebles's engagement party," Chad said coldly.

"Oh, Christ, I wasn't talking about you, Amanda," Matt said, finally realizing how what he had said had been interpreted.

"I know you weren't," Amanda said.

"I didn't see you out there," Matt said.

"I didn't want you to," Amanda said simply.

"Penny and Amanda were very close," Daffy said.

"No, we weren't," Amanda corrected her. "We knew each other at Bennington. That's all."

Good for you, Matt thought. *Cut the bullshit.*

Chad Nesbitt gave her a strange look.

"Shall we go in?" he said, taking his wife's arm.

Baxley, the Detweiler butler, opened the door to them. He was a man in his fifties, and wearing a morning coat with a horizontally striped vest.

"Mr. Detweiler's been expecting you, Doctor," he said.

The translation of which is that Mother D is about to lose control. Or has already lost it, Matt thought.

"I'll go up," Amy said. "Thank you, Baxley."

"Coffee has been laid in the library," Baxley said. "Miss Penny is in the sitting room."

"Thank you, Baxley," Chad Nesbitt said. He put his hand on Matt's arm.

"Take care of him, Chad," Amy said. "I'll go see Aunt Grace."

"I will," Chad said. "Coffee first, Matt?"

"Yeah."

As they walked across the foyer, Matt glanced through the open door of the sitting room. He could see the foot of a glistening mahogany casket, surrounded by flowers.

Shit, I didn't even think about flowers.

Mother certainly sent some in my name, knowing that I wouldn't do it myself.

Heads turned as the four of them went into the library. There were perhaps twenty-five people in the room, most of whom Matt knew by sight. A long table had been set with silver coffee services and trays of pastry. A man in a gray jacket and two maids stood behind the table. A small table behind them held bottles of whiskey and cognac.

Chad propelled Matt to the table.

"I need a little liquid courage myself to face up to going in there," Chad said, indicating to the manservant to produce a bottle of cognac. "Straight up, Matt? Or do you want something to cut it with?"

I don't want any at all, strangely enough. I don't need any liquid courage to go in there and look at Penny's body. For one thing, it's not Penny. Just a body. And I'm used to bodies. Just the other day, I saw two of them, both with their brains blown all over the room. If that didn't bother me, this certainly won't. I am not anywhere close to the near-state of emotional collapse that everyone seems to think I'm in.

"It's a little early for me, Chad," Matt said. "Maybe later."

"Suit yourself," Chad said, taking the cognac bottle from the man behind the table, pouring half an inch of it into a snifter, and tossing it down.

"I wish I could have one of those," Daffy said.

"Baby, you can't," Chad said sympathetically.

"If it's a girl, I want to name her Penelope," Daffy said.

Matt saw this idea didn't please the prospective father, but that he was wise enough not to argue with his wife here.

"You're not having anything?" Amanda asked, at Matt's elbow.

"Probably later," he said.

"Let's get it over with," Chad said.

"That's a terrible thing . . ." Daffy protested.

"Unless you want to go in alone first, Matt?" Chad asked solicitously.

Anything to get away from these three. Go in there alone, stay what seems to be an appropriate period for profound introspection and grief, and then get the hell out.

"Thank you," Matt said softly.

"Thank you," the hypocrite said, with what he judged to be what his audience expected in grief-stricken tone and facial demeanor.

He smiled wanly at Chad, Daffy, and Amanda and walked away from them, out of the library, across the foyer and into the sitting room. There was a line of people, maybe half a dozen, waiting for their last look at the mortal remains of Miss Penelope Detweiler. He took his place with them, and slowly made his way to the casket, looking for, and finally finding, behind the casket, a floral display bearing a card reading "Matthew Mark Payne" and then noticing the strange mingled smells of expensive perfume on the woman in front of him and from the flowers, and comparing it with what he had smelled in the office of the Inferno Lounge, the last time he'd looked at mortal remains. There it had been the sick sweet smell of the pools of blood under the bodies, mingled with the foul odors of feces and urine released in death.

And then it was his turn to look down at Penny in her coffin.

She looks as if she's asleep, he thought, *which is the effect the cosmetic technologist at the undertaker's was struggling to achieve.*

And then, like a wall falling on him, and without warning, his chest contracted painfully, a wailing moan saying "Oh, shit!" in a voice he recognized as his own came out of it, and his chest began to heave with sobs.

He next became aware that someone was pulling him away from the casket, where his right hand was caressing the cool, unmoving flesh of Penny's cheeks, and then that the someone was Chad, gently saying, "Come on, ol' buddy. Just come along with us," and then that Daffy's swollen belly was pressing against him as they led him out of the sit-

ting room past those next in line, and that, when he looked
at her, tears were running down her cheeks, cutting courses
through her pancake makeup.

"Inspector Wohl," Peter answered his telephone.
"The funeral's over," Amy said.
"I was hoping you'd call. How did it go?"
"Matt has a way with words. When we got here, he said
it was 'intimate friends, and the morbidly curious, with a
soupçon of social climbers thrown in for good measure.'"
"How did he handle it?"
"He broke down when he saw her in the casket. Really
broke down. Chad Nesbitt and his very pregnant wife had to
practically carry him out of the room."
There was a moment's silence before Wohl said: ~
"You said last night you expected something like that to
happen."
"That was a clinical opinion; professionally, I'm relieved.
It's the first step, acceptance, in managing grief. Personally,
he's my little brother. It was awful. I felt so damned sorry for
him."
"How's he now? Where is he now?"
"Oh, now he's got his stiff upper lip back in place. He and
Chad are into the booze. There's quite a post-interment party
going on out here."
"You want me to send someone out there and get him? I
sent Tiny Lewis to sit on him, but . . ."
"I know," Amy said. "What I was hoping to hear was you
volunteering to come out here and get the both of us."
"It was bad for you?"
"As we were coming back here from the cemetery—I
thought Grace Detweiler might need me, so I rode with
them—I caught her looking at me as if she had just realized
that if I had done my job, Penny would still be here."
"That could be an overactive imagination."
"I don't think so. I got the same look here in the house
when I was getting a tranquilizer out of my purse for her.

She's decided—seeing how Matt collapsed completely probably had a lot to do with it—that he's still an irresponsible boy, who can't be blamed. She needs somebody to blame. I make a fine candidate to be the real villain, because I really didn't help Penny at all."

There was a moment's silence, and then Wohl said, "I'm on my way, Amy," and the line went dead in her ear.

"It's a good thing I know you're a doctor," Inspector Peter Wohl said to Dr. Amelia Payne as they came off the elevator into the lobby of the Delaware Valley Cancer Society Building on Rittenhouse Square.

"Meaning what?"

"The folklore among us laypersons is don't mix booze and pills."

"That's a good general rule of thumb," Amy said. "What I gave Matt is what we doctor persons prescribe as a sedative when the patient person has been soaking up cognac like a sponge. It is my professional opinion that that patient person will be out like a light for the next twelve to eighteen hours without side effects. Any other questions, layperson?"

Wohl smiled at her.

"How about dinner tonight?"

"Absolutely not."

"I guess that makes breakfast tomorrow out of the question."

"I didn't say that," Amy said. "I said no dinner. I have to make my rounds, and then there's a very sick young woman I want to spend some time with. But I didn't say anything about breakfast, or, for that matter, a midnight supper with candles and wine, being out of any question."

"My place or yours, doctor person?"

She didn't reply directly.

"We left my car at the Detweilers's."

"Give me the keys. I'll have someone run me out there, and I'll drop it by—where? The hospital? Your place?"

"Wouldn't it be easier if you took it to your place? When

I leave the hospital, I'll catch a cab out there. It'll probably be after eleven."

"Done," he said, putting his hand out for the keys.

"You're headed for the hospital now?" he asked. She nodded. "You want a ride?"

"Where are you going?"

"Wherever you need to go is right on my way."

"I'll catch a cab," she said.

"You're sure?"

She nodded.

Their eyes met, and held. Somewhat hesitantly, Wohl moved his face closer to hers.

"Don't push me, Peter," Amy said, and then moved her face closer to his and kissed him on the lips.

Then she quickly walked away from him, out the door and onto Rittenhouse Square. He started to follow her, then changed his mind.

He went to the receptionist's desk and asked to use her telephone.

"Of course," she said with a smile that suggested she did not find him unattractive.

He smiled at her and dialed a number from memory.

"Inspector Wohl," he said as he watched Amy get into a cab. "Anything for me?"

"Chief Lowenstein's been trying to reach you all afternoon, sir," the tour lieutenant reported.

"Anything else?"

"No, sir."

"I'll call Chief Lowenstein and get back to you."

"Yes, sir."

Wohl broke the connection with his finger and dialed Chief Lowenstein's private number.

"Lowenstein."

"Peter Wohl, Chief."

"Where are you, Peter?"

"Center City. Rittenhouse Square."

"With Matt Payne?"

"I just left him."

"How is he?"

"His sister gave him a pill she said will knock him out until tomorrow."

"I really feel sorry for him," Lowenstein said, and then immediately added: "I need to talk to you, Peter."

"I'm available for you anytime, Chief."

"Why don't you let me buy you a drink at the bar in the Warwick?"

"Yes, sir."

"Ten minutes, Peter," Lowenstein said. "Thank you."

FIFTEEN

Chief Inspector of Detectives Matthew Lowenstein was sitting, with an eight-inch black cigar in his mouth, on a stool at the street end of the bar in the Warwick Hotel when Inspector Peter Wohl got there.

"Sorry to keep you waiting, Chief."

"What will you have, Peter?" Lowenstein asked, ignoring the apology.

"I would like a triple scotch, but what I'd better have is a beer," Wohl said.

"Bad day for you?" Lowenstein asked, chuckling, and got the bartender's attention. "Give this nice young man one of these. A single."

"Thank you," Peter said.

"I turned in my papers this morning," he said. "You hear about that?"

Wohl nodded.

"Carlucci came out to the house and made me a deal to stay."

Wohl's face was as devoid of expression as he could make it.

"The deal," Lowenstein said, "is that I have his word that you will bring me in on anything interesting his personal detective squad, now called Ethical Affairs Unit, comes up with, and I get to define the term 'interesting.' You have any problem with that, Peter?"

"I had a problem with keeping you out of the Cazerra investigation. That wasn't my idea, Chief."

"So Carlucci told me. I asked you, do you have any problems with the new arrangement?"

"None at all."

"Tell me what interesting things you have heard today, Peter."

"How about yesterday, Chief?"

"Start with yesterday."

"I had lunch with Armando C. Giacomo, Esquire, at the Rittenhouse Club. Weisbach and I did. Mr. Paulo Cassandro really doesn't want to go to jail. As a public-spirited citizen, he is willing to testify against Cazerra in exchange for immunity from prosecution."

Lowenstein snorted.

"Giacomo is pissing in the wind. He knows he has nothing to deal with. And if he did, he would have gone to the District Attorney with it. Why you?"

"I thought that was interesting. Weisbach told him that, offhand, the only thing he could think of that we were interested in was the Inferno doer, or doers. And/or the Kellog doer."

"And how did the dapper little dago react to that?"

"He didn't say no."

"You think either one was a mob hit, Peter?"

"I didn't until Giacomo didn't say no."

"Interesting."

"I thought so. And then Jason Washington called me this

morning. One of his informants said that the Inferno was a mob hit, and gave him a name. Frank—Frankie—Foley."

There was a just-perceptible pause as Lowenstein searched his memory.

"Never heard of him."

"Neither has Washington. Or Harris. Or me. Or Intelligence or Organized Crime."

"Who's the informant?"

"Washington said that what this guy has given him in the past—which wasn't much—was reliable. I think he would have said something if there was a mob connection."

"Huh!" Lowenstein snorted.

"Going back even further than yesterday, the day Kellog was shot, that night, his widow showed up at Washington's apartment. Did you hear about that?"

"Tell me about it," Lowenstein said.

Which means either that you did hear about it or didn't hear about it, but if you did, you want to hear my version of it anyway.

"She told Washington (a) her husband was dirty, (b) the entire Narcotics Five Squad is dirty, and (c) that they did her husband."

"What did Washington think about it?"

"He said he believes she thinks she's telling the truth."

"So what are you going to do with this? All of this?"

"I told Washington to give the Frankie Foley name to Homicide. By now, they probably have it."

"And the Five Squad allegations?"

"Before Ethical Affairs popped up, I was going to have a quiet word with a staff inspector I know pretty well, and ask him to please keep me out of it."

Lowenstein chuckled. "A staff inspector named Weisbach?"

"Yeah."

"And now?"

"This is the first time I've really thought hard about it. It seems to me the lines of authority are fuzzy. Dirty cops on the Narcotics Five Squad would seem to be Ethical Affairs' business. Somebody on the Narcotics Five Squad doing Officer Kellog would seem to belong to Homicide."

"Are you asking me?"

"Yes."

"What's Washington's role going to be in Ethical Affairs?"

"I have been ordered to give Weisbach whatever support he needs. So far as I'm concerned, that means he gets the Special Operations Investigation Section, which means he gets Washington."

"Why don't you leave it that way? Let Washington run that down independently of Homicide? If he's investigating corruption, and comes across something that looks like the Kellog homicide, he can pass it along."

"That's fine with me."

"And I will have a word with Henry Quaire and suggest that he have Wally Milham run down this—what was the name?—Frankie Foley lead. Assisted by Detective Payne."

"Can I ask why?"

"I think there may be something to it. Gut feeling."

"Really? Why?"

"I just told you: gut feeling. Write this down, Peter: When you don't have a clue, go with your gut feeling."

"Thank you, Chief," Wohl said, smiling.

"And I would like Milham to come up with something, to prove to Carlucci that a detective can have a very active sex life and still be a good detective."

"I've known that all along," Wohl said.

"I'll bet you have." Lowenstein laughed. "I think that when we finally get the true story of Mr. Atchison's recent tragedy, it will turn out that money was involved. Insurance on the wife, maybe. Business problems with the partner. If that's so, that means he would not have the dough to hire a professional hit man. And the mob only does that sort of thing for adequate compensation. And I don't think they'd be interested in doing a contract hit for somebody like Atchison in the first place."

Wohl nodded his head in agreement.

"And following that lead will be instructional for Payne," Lowenstein went on. "He will learn that most homicides are solved wearing out shoe leather, not by brilliant reasoning. Or, in this case, by an anonymous tip that takes a hell of a lot of legwork to come up with what's necessary to make it stand up in court."

"Who do you think did Officer Kellog?"

"If I had to bet, I'd bet on Washington's gut feeling. He thinks the widow's telling the truth. I hope to hell the Narcotics Five Squad is not involved, but I wouldn't be at all surprised if there was a Narcotics connection."

"Either would I," Wohl said, somewhat sadly.

He looked at his drink. It was empty. He idly moved the glass so that ice cubes spun inside.

"Another, Peter?" Lowenstein asked.

"I shouldn't, but I will," Wohl said, and held up the glass to attract the bartender.

When he was to think about it afterward, with more than a little chagrin, Matt Payne realized that if he hadn't been three quarters of the way into the bag, he never would have gone to Homicide at all that night.

At the time, he hadn't been thinking too clearly. The only thing he had been sure about was that he hadn't wanted one of Amy's pills. Pretending to swallow it while she watched was easier than arguing with her about it.

What he would do, he originally thought, was have a couple of drinks, enough to make him sleepy, and then fall in bed.

But by the third Famous Grouse, he thought that maybe it would be a good idea to go to the Fraternal Order of Police bar. By the fifth drink, it seemed to be a splendid idea. So he went down and got in the Porsche.

By the time he got to Broad and Market, going to the FOP

bar seemed less a splendid idea. Everybody in the place would have heard about Penny; everybody he knew would be offering sympathy, and he didn't want that.

He drove around City Hall, and headed down South Broad Street, headed for Charley McFadden's house. Charley was working days, he would get him out of bed, and they would have a couple of drinks someplace.

Five blocks down South Broad, he realized that would also be a bad idea, an imposition. Charley would, out of pity, get out of bed and be a good guy. Not fair to Charley.

Dropping in on Peter Wohl was similarly a bad idea. For one thing, Peter lived way the hell out in Chestnut Hill. More importantly, he might have—probably did have—company, spelled A-m-y, and not only would he be an unwelcome guest, but they would correctly surmise that he had not swallowed Amy's pill.

And then he thought of Wally Milham. Milham was working midnight to eight. And Milham's personal life was nearly as fucked up as his own. The Mayor had gotten up on a moral high horse at Martha Peebles' party because Milham had gotten involved with his wife's sister, and, worse, was using this as a basis to suspect that Milham was somehow involved in the Kellog shooting.

Milham, Matt reasoned, would not only be up and awake, but might welcome some company.

Matt made an illegal U-turn on South Broad Street and headed for the Roundhouse.

Matt had been to Homicide often enough to know how to get past the wooden barrier. There was a little button on the inside of the barrier, which activated the solenoid that opened the gate.

There were half a dozen detectives in the room, one of whom looked up, registering surprise, when he saw Matt. And then he gestured with his finger across the room to where Wally Milham sat at a desk before a typewriter.

Matt walked over to him. It was a moment before Milham became aware that he was standing there.

"Well, I expected you, but not so soon," Wally Milham said.
"Excuse me?"
Milham pushed a memorandum across his desk. Matt picked it up.

CITY OF PHILADELPHIA

MEMORANDUM

TO: SERGEANT ZACHARY HOBBS

FROM: COMMANDING OFFICER, HOMICIDE UNIT

SUBJECT: INFORMANT'S TIP

1. We have an informant's tip on the Inferno job concerning an individual named Frank, or Frankie, Foley. The informant, whose information in the past has been reliable, identifies this subject as a "mob-connected hit man."

2. Neither Records, Intelligence or Organized Crime has anything on him.

3. Assign Detective Milham to investigate this lead, instructing him to continue his investigation, making daily reports to you, until such time as further information is developed, or until he is convinced there is nothing to it.

Detective Payne, of Special Operations, will be working in the Homicide Unit for an indefinite period. When he reports for duty, assign him to assist Detective Milham.

Henry C. Quaire
Henry C. Quaire
Captain

cc: Chief Inspector Lowenstein
82-S-1AE (Rev. 3/59) RESPONSE TO THIS MEMORANDUM MAY BE MADE HEREON IN LONGHAND

"I didn't expect you for a couple of days," Milham said. "I heard about . . . I thought the funeral was today."

"It was," Matt said.

Milham looked at Matt intently for a moment, then suddenly stood up. He took his coat from the back of the chair he had been sitting on and shrugged into it.

"Come on, Payne," he said.

"Where are we going?"

"Out," Milham said, and gestured toward the door.

"You drive over here?" Milham asked when they came out of the back door of the Roundhouse.

"Yeah."

"Where'd you park?" Milham asked.

Matt pointed at the Porsche.

"Nice wheels," Milham said. "Leave it, we'll pick it up later."

"Whatever you say," Matt replied.

They got in Milham's unmarked three-year-old Ford, left the parking lot, went south on Eighth Street, crossed Market and turned right on Walnut Street to South Broad, and then left.

"How much have you had to drink?" Milham asked.

"I had a couple."

"More than a couple, to judge from the smell," Milham said. "That wasn't really smart, Payne."

"I couldn't sleep."

"I mean coming into Homicide shitfaced," Milham said. "Lucky for you, Hobbs and Natali went out on a job—a stabbing, two Schwartzers fighting over a tootsie in the East Falls project—and Logan, who was on the desk, either didn't smell you or didn't want to. It could have gone the other way. If it had, Lowenstein would have heard first thing in the morning that you showed up drunk. I get the feeling he would love to tell that to the Mayor."

"Oh, shit!" Matt said.

"I think you were lucky, so forget it. But don't do it again."

"Sorry," Matt said.

"We're going to a bar called Meagan's," Milham said, changing the subject somewhat, "where you are going to have either coffee or a Coke."

Milham handed Matt a clipboard, then turned on the large, specially installed light mounted on the headliner. Matt saw that the clipboard held a pad of lined paper and a Xerox of a page from the telephone book. On closer examination, there were two Xerox pages. There was also a pencil-written list of what looked like bars.

"There are ninety-seven Foleys in the phone book," Milham said. "We may have to check every one of them out. Just because there's no Frank or Francis listed doesn't mean there's nobody at that address named Frank or Francis. In the morning, I'll check driver's licenses in Harrisburg, and see if they have a Frank or Francis matching one of these addresses. Right now, I'm working on a hunch."

"What kind of a hunch?"

"A hunch hunch. There are eleven Foleys in the phone book in a six-block area in South Philly. There are twelve bars in that six-block area. A couple of them will probably still be open. One—Meagan's—I know stays open late. We will ask, 'Is this the place where Ol' Frankie Foley drinks?' "

"What about this tip? Where did it come from? Is it any good?"

"We are probably on a wild-goose chase, but you never know until you know. As to where it came from, I don't know. Not from someone inside Homicide. Who knows? Lowenstein thinks it's worth checking out, that's all that matters."

Meagan's Bar, on Jackson Street, turned out to be an ordinary neighborhood bar. There were half a dozen customers, two of them middle-aged women, sitting at the bar, each with a beer in front of them. There was a jukebox, but no one had fed it coins. A television, with a flickering picture, was showing a man and a peroxide blonde in an apron demonstrating a kitchen device guaranteed to make life in the kitchen a genuine joy.

The bartender, a heavyset man in his fifties, hoisted himself with visible reluctance from his stool by the cash register and walked to them, putting both hands on the bar and wordlessly asking for their order.

"Ortleib's," Milham ordered.

"I think I better have coffee," Matt said.

"No coffee," the bartender said.

"One more, and then I'll drive you home," Milham said.

"What the hell," Matt said. "Why not?"

When the bartender served the beer, Milham laid a five-dollar bill on the bar.

"Where are we?" he asked the bartender.

"What do you mean, where are you? This place is called Meagan's."

"I mean where, where. What is this, Jackson Street?"

"Jackson and Mole streets."

"Doesn't Frank Foley live around here?"

"Frank who?"

"Frankie Foley. My cousin. I thought he lived right around here, on South Mole Street."

"Short fat guy? Works for Strawbridge's?"

"No. Ordinary-sized. Maybe a little bigger. And I thought he worked for Wanamaker's."

"Right. Yeah. He comes in here every once in a while."

"He been in tonight?"

"Haven't seen him in a while."

"Yeah, well, what the hell. Listen, if he does come in, tell him his cousin Marty, from Conshohocken, said hi, will you?"

"Yeah, if I see him, I'll do that."

"I'd be obliged."

"You're a long way from Conshohocken."

"Went to a wake. Jack O'Neill. May he rest in peace."

"Didn't know him."

"He retired from Budd Company."

"Didn't know him," the bartender said, made change, and went back to his stool.

Milham looked at Matt and raised his beer glass.

"Good ol' Jack," he said.

"May he rest in peace," Matt said.

"I think he made me," Milham said when they were back in his car. "He was being cute with that 'short fat guy?' line. And I got lucky when I said Wanamaker's. I'll bet when we finally find Mr. Foley, he will work in Wanamaker's, and now we know he lives around here. It may not be our Frankie, but you never can tell. Sometimes you get lucky."

"If he made you," Matt said, "and was cute, he's going to tell this guy somebody, a cop, was looking for him."

"Good. If it is our Frankie, it will make him nervous. Unless he's got a cousin from Conshohocken. Give me the clipboard."

Milham switched on the light, consulted the Xerox pages of the telephone book, and drew a circle around the name "Foley, Mary" of 2320 South Eighteenth Street.

"Maybe he lives with his mother," Milham said, handing the clipboard back to Matt. He switched off the overhead light and started the engine.

They drove to South Eighteenth Street, and drove slowly by 2320. It was a typical row house, in the center of the block. There were no lights on.

They visited three more bars. Two of them had coffee. None of their bartenders had ever heard of Frank, or Frankie, Foley.

"I don't know what to do with you," Milham said. "On one hand, you still smell like a brewery. On the other hand, so do I. You want to take a chance on going back to the Roundhouse with me, to see what everybody else has come up with?"

"Whatever you think is best," Matt said, chagrined.

"What the hell, we have to get your car anyway," Milham said. "Just try not to breathe on anybody."

●   ●   ●

"Sergeant, this is Detective Payne," Milham said. "Payne, this is Sergeant Zachary Hobbs."

Hobbs offered his hand, and looked at Matt closely.

"We didn't expect you for a couple of days," he said.

"You weren't here," Milham replied for him, "when he came in. Your memo was in my box, so I took him with me."

"You find this Foley guy?"

"I think we know where he lives, and that he works for Wanamaker's."

"The bartender at the Inferno says there was a guy named Foley in there that night," Hobbs said. "That's in your box, too."

Milham nodded.

"Payne, Captain Quaire knows about your, uh, personal problem. You don't have to come to work, is what I'm saying, until you feel up to it," Hobbs said.

"I think I'd rather work than not," Matt said. "But thank you."

"You need anything, you let me know. Did Wally show you the memo?"

"Yes, he did."

"OK. You work with Wally."

Matt nodded.

"I think you'd better see Lieutenant Natali," Hobbs said. "Let him know you're here." He gestured across the room. Matt saw Lieutenant Natali in a small office.

Jesus, I hope he's got a cold or something, and can't smell the booze.

He had met Lieutenant Natali once before. The circumstances flooded his mind.

He had been escorting Miss Amanda Spencer to a prewedding dinner honoring Miss Daphne Soames Brown and Mr. Chadwick Thomas Nesbitt IV, at the Union League Club.

No wonder Amanda said I hadn't seen her at Martha Peebles's party; she hadn't wanted me to. I'm trouble, dangerous. If I were her, I wouldn't have wanted to see me either.

When he had pulled the Porsche onto the top floor of the

Penn Center Parking Garage, there had been a body lying in a pool of blood, that of a second-rate gangster named Tony the Zee Dezito, who had been taken out with a shotgun blast in what was almost certainly a contract hit by party or parties unknown for reasons unknown.

Nearby was Miss Penelope Detweiler, a lifelong acquaintance, also lying in a pool of blood. Matt's original conclusion that Penny, like him and Amanda en route to Daffy and Chad's party, was an innocent bystander was soon corrected by the facts. She had been in the parking garage to meet Tony the Zee, with whom she was having an affair.

And almost certainly, I know now, to get something from him to stick in her arm, or sniff up her nose. It was that goddamn Dezito who gave Penny her habit.

Narcotics had had a tail on Tony the Zee, and when Matt had gone to Homicide to give them a statement, a Narcotics sergeant, an asshole named Dolan, and another Narcotics asshole had been waiting for him there. They had taken him into the interview room, sat him down in the steel captain's chair with the handcuffs, and as much as accused him of being involved with either Tony the Zee or Narcotics, or both. And then taken him to Narcotics, if not under arrest, then the next thing to it, to continue the interrogation and to search the Porsche.

Lieutenant Natali had been the tour lieutenant in Homicide that night, hadn't liked what he had seen, and had called Peter Wohl. Wohl had come to Narcotics like the Cavalry to the rescue and gotten him out.

Natali had bent, if not regulations, then departmental protocol, and thus stuck his neck out, by calling Peter Wohl. He was therefore, by definition, a proven good guy.

Matt walked to the office and stood in the door until Natali looked up and waved him inside. He stood up and put out his hand.

"I didn't expect to see you so soon, Payne," he said. "I, uh, heard what happened. I'm sorry."

"Thank you," Matt said.

It was evident on Natali's face that he, too, was recalling the circumstances of their first meeting.

"I thought I would rather work than sit around."

That's not true. I'm here because I got shitfaced and didn't want to go to bed. I'm a goddamned hypocrite and a liar.

"Yeah," Natali said. "I understand." He paused and then went on. "Payne, some of the people here are going to resent you being here."

"I thought they would."

"But they know—Captain Quaire passed the word—that you had nothing to do with it. So I don't think it will be a problem. If there is one, you come to me with it."

"Thank you."

"You'll be working with Wally Milham. There's a memo . . ."

"I saw it."

"OK. I don't think you'll have any trouble with Milham. And he's a good Homicide detective. You can learn a lot from him. Homicide works differently. I don't know how much experience you had at East Detectives . . ."

"Not much," Matt said. "Most of it on recovered stolen vehicles."

Natali smiled understandingly.

"I did a few of those myself, when I made detective," he said. "We don't get as many jobs here," Natali went on. "And when one comes in, everybody goes to work on it. There's an assigned detective, of course. Milham, in the case of the Inferno Lounge job. But everybody works on it."

"I understand. Or I think I do."

"You'll catch on in a hurry," Natali said. "If you have any problems, come see me."

"Thank you, sir."

When he went to Wally Milham's desk, Milham was working his way through a thick stack of paper forms. He read one of the forms, and then placed it facedown beside the unread stack.

"You better take a look at these," Milham said, tapping

the facedown stack without raising his eyes from the document he was reading.

Matt pulled up a chair and slid the facedown stack to him.

Matt turned over the stack. They were all carbon copies of 75-49s, the standard Police Department Detective Division Investigation Report.

He started to read the first one:

INVESTIGATION REPORT   PHILADELPHIA POLICE DEPARTMENT

Yr	C.C.#	DIST	COMPL.#		INITIAL(49)		DIST/UNIT	
REPORT DATE		SUPPLEMENTAL				PREPARING	
CLASSIFICATION		CODE	CONTINUATION			Homicide/9th Dist.	

PREVIOUS CLASSIFICATION   CODE | DATE AND TIME | PLACE OF OCCURRENCE

| COMPLAINANT | AGE | RACE | ADDRESS | | PHONE | | TYPE OF PREMISES |
| Alicia Atchison | 25 | W | 320 Wilson Avenue. Media, PA | | | |

DATE AND TIME REPORTED | REPORTED BY | ADDRESS

FOUNDED ☐ YES ☐ NO   ARREST ☐ CLEARED   ☐ EXCEPTIONALLY CLEARED

STOLEN | ☐ CURRENCY, BONDS, ETC. ☐ FURS   ☐. AUTOS | RECOVERED VALUE
PROPERTY | ☐ JEWELRY, PRECIOUS METALS ☐ CLOTHING   ☐ MISC |
INSURED   ☐ YES ☐ NO

DETAILS

    AUTOPSY: Alicia Atchison

       1. Pronouncement: Saturday, May 20, 1975 at 5:39 a.m., at 1908 Market Street, the scene, by Dr. Howard D. Mitchell, Medical Examiners Office.

       2. Transporting of Body: From the scene to the Medical Examiners Office in Morgue Wagon #61538, manned by Lewis Martin.

       3. Post: Saturday, May 20, 1975 at 9:30 a.m., Medical Examiners Office by Dr. Howard D. Mitchell.

       4. Findings: Gunshot wounds (4) of head. Craniocerebral Injuries. Manner of Death: Homicide.

INVESTIGATOR (Type and Sign Name) | SERGEANT | LIEUTENANT

Alonzo Kramer | *Zachary Hobbs* |
Alonzo Kramer #967 | Zachary Hobbs # 396

75–49 (Rev 3/63)   DETECTIVE DIVISION

The telephone on the desk rang. Without taking his eyes from the 75-49s before him, Milham reached for it.

"Homicide, Milham," he said.

Matt looked up in natural curiosity.

"Hello, honey," Milham said, his voice changing.

The Widow Kellog, Matt decided, *and that makes it none of my business.*

He turned his attention to the second 75-49:

INVESTIGATION REPORT PHILADELPHIA POLICE DEPARTMENT

Yr	C.C.#	DIST	COMPL.#	INITIAL(49)	DIST/UNIT
REPORT DATE		SUPPLEMENTAL			PREPARING
CLASSIFICATION			CODE	CONTINUATION	Homicide/9th Dist.

PREVIOUS CLASSIFICATION CODE | DATE AND TIME | PLACE OF OCCURRENCE

COMPLAINANT	AGE	RACE	ADDRESS	PHONE	TYPE OF PREMISES
Anthony J. Marcuzzi	52	W.	6105 Palter Avenue		

DATE AND TIME REPORTED | REPORTED BY | ADDRESS

FOUNDED ☐ YES ☐ NO   ARREST ☐ CLEARED   ☐ EXCEPTIONALLY CLEARED

STOLEN | ☐ CURRENCY, BONDS, ETC. ☐ FURS   ☐. AUTOS | RECOVERED VALUE
PROPERTY | ☐ JEWELRY, PRECIOUS METALS ☐ CLOTHING ☐ MISC
INSURED   ☐ YES ☐ NO

DETAILS

AUTOPSY: Anthony J. Marcuzzi.

1. Pronouncement: Saturday, May 20, 1975 at 5:39 a.m., at 1908 Market Street, the scene, by Dr. Howard D. Mitchell, Medical Examiners Office.

2. Transporting of Body: From the scene to the Medical Examiners Office in Morgue Wagon #61538, manned by Lewis Martin.

3. Post: Saturday, May 20, 1975 at 9:30 a.m., Medical Examiners Office by Dr. Howard D. Mitchell.

4. Findings: Gunshot wounds (3) of head. Craniocerebral Injuries. Manner of Death: Homicide.

INVESTIGATOR (Type and Sign Name) | SERGEANT | LIEUTENANT

Alonzo Kramer | *Zachary Hobbs* |
Alonzo Kramer #967 | Zachary Hobbs # 396

75–49 (Rev 3/63)   DETECTIVE DIVISION

"Jesus Christ!" Milham said, softly but with such intensity that Matt's noble intention to mind his own business was overwhelmed by curiosity.

"Baby," Milham said. "You stay there. Stay inside. I'll be right there!"

I wonder what the hell that's all about.

Milham hung the telephone up and looked at Matt.

"Something's come up," he said. "I gotta go."

Matt nodded.

"Tell you what, Payne," Milham said, obviously having thought over what he was about to say. "Take that stack with you and go home. You all right to drive?"

"I'm all right."

"I'll call you about ten tomorrow morning. You read that, see if you come up with something."

"Right."

"OK. You'll find some manila envelopes over there," Milham said, pointing. "I really got to go."

"Anything I can do?"

"Yeah, if anybody asks where I went, all you know is I told you to go home."

"OK."

"Ten tomorrow, I'll call you at ten tomorrow," Milham said, and went to retrieve his pistol from a filing cabinet.

SIXTEEN

Matt left the Police Administration Building and found his car. The interior lights were on. Because, he saw, the door was ajar.

Christ, was I so plastered when I came here that I not only didn't lock the car, but didn't even close the damned door? No wonder Milham was worried if I was all right to drive.

Or did somebody use a Car Thief's Friend and open the door? Did I leave anything inside worth stealing?

He pulled the door fully open and stuck his head inside.

There was no sign of damage; the glove compartment showed no sign that anyone had tried to force it open.

I deduce that no attempt at Vehicular Burglary has occurred. I am forced to conclude that I was shitfaced when I drove in here. Shit!

There was a white tissue on the floor under the steering wheel.

Penny's Kleenex. With her lipstick on it.

He picked it up and looked at it.

What the hell do I do with it? Throw it away? I don't want to do that. Keep it, as a Sacred Relic? I don't want to do that, either.

He patted his pocket and found a book of matches.

He unfolded the Kleenex, struck a match, and set the Kleenex on fire. He held it in his fingers until that became painful, and then let what was left float to the ground. He watched until it was consumed and the embers died.

Then he got in the Porsche and drove out of the Roundhouse parking lot.

His stomach hurt, and he decided that was because he still hadn't had anything to eat. He drove over to the 1400 block of Race Street where he remembered a restaurant was open all night. He ordered two hamburgers, changed his mind to three hamburgers, a cup of coffee, a large french fries, and two containers of milk, all to go.

Then he got back in the Porsche and drove home.

The red light was blinking on his answering machine. He was tempted to ignore it, but finally pushed the Play Messages button.

Predictably, there was a call from his mother, asking if he was all right. And one from his father, same question. And there were seven No Message blurps; someone had called, and elected not to leave a message.

He opened the paper bag from the St. George Restaurant and started to unwrap a hamburger.

The telephone rang.

He debated answering it, but finally ran and grabbed it just before the fifth ring, which would turn on the answering machine.

"Hello?"

There was no reply, but someone was on the line.

"If you're going to talk dirty to me, please start now," Matt said.

There was a click and the line went dead.

"Fuck you, pal," Matt said, hung the telephone up, and went back to the hamburger.

The telephone rang again.

"Goddamn it!"

He snatched the phone from the wall and remembered at the last moment that the caller, this time, might be his mother, and one did not scream obscenities at one's mother.

"Hello?"

And again there was no reply.

"Oh, goddamn it!"

"Were you asleep?" It was a female voice.

Jesus Christ! Amanda?

"Amanda?"

"I was worried about you," Amanda said.

"I'm all right."

"I knew this was going to be a bad idea. I told myself you would be all right."

"I'm glad you called," he said. "What was going to be a bad idea? Jesus, it's quarter after three. Was that you on the machine? You called and didn't leave a message?"

There was no reply, which told him it had indeed been Amanda who had called and elected not to leave a message.

"How long have you been trying to reach me?"

"I got here about eleven," she said, very softly.

"Where's here? Home?"

"No."

"Where are you?"

"In the Warwick Hotel."

"The Warwick? I thought you were staying with Chad?"

"I was. They put me on the train at seven."

"I don't understand."

"What happened is that I kicked myself most of the way to Newark for being afraid what Chad and Daffy would think if I told him I was worried about you and wanted to see you. So I got off in Newark and came back. At the time, it seemed like a reasonable idea."

"Jesus, that was nice of you," he said.

"I haven't had anything to eat," she said. "Damn you. Where were you?"

"On the job. Working."

"I should have guessed that," she said. "I thought maybe you were out getting sloshed."

"I started to," he said. "And then I decided I'd better go to work."

There was a long pause, and then she said:

"This is your town. Is there someplace I can get something to eat this time of the morning?"

"How about a lukewarm hamburger and some limp french fries?"

There was another long pause.

"You mean at your place?"

"I stopped off at a restaurant on my way home," he said.

"I'm so hungry I'm tempted to accept," Amanda said. "But knowing you, you'd get the wrong idea."

"Oh, hell, I wouldn't—Jesus, Amanda!"

"All I want to be is your friend, Matt, OK? I thought you could use one."

"Absolutely. I understand. Nothing else ever entered my mind."

"OK. As long as you understand that."

"I do. Perfectly. Look, you want me to bring the hamburger there?"

"No," she said, after a just-perceptible pause. "I know where you live. Give me ten, fifteen minutes. I have to get dressed again. The last call was going to be the last call."

"I'll come get you."

"I'll be there in ten minutes," Amanda said, and hung up.

"I will be damned," Matt thought aloud. "That was really very nice of her."

He went back to the table, took knives and forks and salt and pepper and plates from cabinets, and laid them on the table. Then he got a pot from under the sink and poured the coffee into it.

At least I can offer her hot coffee!

Then he went into the living room and sat down in his chair. *While I wait, I'll take a look at this stuff:*

INVESTIGATION REPORT			PHILADELPHIA POLICE DEPARTMENT		

Yr | C.C.# | DIST | COMPL.# | INITIAL(49) | | DIST/UNIT |
REPORT DATE   SUPPLEMENTAL | PREPARING
CLASSIFICATION |CODE |CONTINUATION   Homicide/9th Dist.

PREVIOUS CLASSIFICATION   CODE | DATE AND TIME |PLACE OF OCCURRENCE

COMPLAINANT	AGE	RACE	ADDRESS	PHONE	TYPE OF PREMISES
Alicia Atchison	25	W	320 Wilson Avenue, Media, PA		

DATE AND TIME REPORTED |REPORTED BY |ADDRESS

FOUNDED ☐ YES ☐ NO   ARREST ☐ CLEARED   ☐ EXCEPTIONALLY CLEARED

STOLEN |☐CURRENCY, BONDS, ETC. ☐ FURS   ☐. AUTOS | RECOVERED VALUE
PROPERTY |☐ JEWELRY, PRECIOUS METALS ☐CLOTHING ☐ MISC |
INSURED   ☐YES ☐NO

DETAILS

A. ORIGIN:

On Saturday, May 20, 1975 at 4:20 a.m., Sergeant Jason Washington, Special Operations Division, notified Sergeant Edward McCarthy #380 via Police Radio, that two persons—Alicia Atchison, 25 years, White, 320 Wilson Ave, Media, Penna., and Anthony J. Marcuzzi, 52 years, White, 6105 Palter Ave. had been shot and killed and that Gerald N. Atchison had been shot in the leg. That this shooting occurred inside The Inferno Lounge Bar & Restaurant, 1908 Market Street.

B. ASSIGNMENT:

1. Homicide: At 4:30 a.m., Detective Wallace H. Milham #626 was assigned by Sergeant Zachary Hobbs #396 and he immediately proceeded to the scene.

2. Division: Detective Edgar Hayes #680 assigned by Sergeant Thomas Spiers #336 of Central Detective Division.

3. Crime Lab: Technicians William Walters and Doyle Cohan were assigned by Sergeant Zachary Hobbs of the Homicide Unit.

4. Other Units:

Major Theft: Detectives Salvatore Domenico #734 and Ellis Davison #927 were assigned on May 20, 1975 at 9:00 A.M.

INVESTIGATOR (Type and Sign Name) | SERGEANT |LIEUTENANT

Alonzo Kramer | *Zachary Hobbs* |
Alonzo Kramer   #967 | Zachary Hobbs # 396

75–49 (Rev 3/63)   DETECTIVE DIVISION

INVESTIGATION REPORT   PHILADELPHIA POLICE DEPARTMENT

Yr	C.C.#	DIST	COMPL.#		INITIAL(49)		DIST/UNIT	
REPORT DATE		SUPPLEMENTAL				PREPARING		
CLASSIFICATION			CODE	CONTINUATION		Homicide/9th Dist.		

PREVIOUS CLASSIFICATION   CODE | DATE AND TIME | PLACE OF OCCURRENCE

COMPLAINANT	AGE	RACE	ADDRESS	PHONE	TYPE OF PREMISES
Alicia Atchison	25	W	320 Wilson Avenue, Media, PA		

DATE AND TIME REPORTED | REPORTED BY | ADDRESS

FOUNDED ☐ YES ☐ NO   ARREST ☐ CLEARED   ☐ EXCEPTIONALLY CLEARED

STOLEN | ☐ CURRENCY, BONDS, ETC. ☐ FURS   ☐. AUTOS | RECOVERED VALUE
PROPERTY | ☐ JEWELRY, PRECIOUS METALS ☐ CLOTHING ☐ MISC |
INSURED ☐ YES ☐ NO

DETAILS

C. SCENE:

       Intelligence Unit: Detectives Arthur Mason #908 and Robert McGrory #746 were assigned on May 20, 1975 at 10:00 a.m.

     1. Arrival: Sergeant Zachary Hobbs #396 and Detective Wallace H. Milham #626 arrived at the scene at 5:05 a.m., Saturday, May 20, 1975.

     2. Present: Chief Inspector Matthew Lowenstein Detective Bureau.
                 Staff Inspector Michael Weisbach
                 Captain Henry C. Quaire #42, Homicide Unit.
                 "   "   Thomas Curran #31, Central DD.
                 "   "   Alexander Smith #17, 9th District.
                 Lieutenant Louis Natali #233, Homicide Unit.
                 Sergeant Zachary Hobbs #396, Homicide Unit.
                 "   "   James Thom #498, Central DD.
                 "   "   Jason Washington #342, Special Operations
                 "   "   Edward McCarthy #380, Homicide Unit.
                 "   "   Gerald Kennedy #576, 9th District.
                 Detective James Whatley #607, Central DD.
                 "   "   Adolphus Fowler #792, Central DD.
                 "   "   Wallace H. Milham #626, Homicide Unit.
                 "   "   David Rocco #615, Central DD.
                 "   "   John Hanson #931, Major Theft.
                 "   "   Wilfred Malone #772, Intelligence Unit.
                 "   "   Edgar Hayes #680, Central DD.

INVESTIGATOR (Type and Sign Name) | SERGEANT | LIEUTENANT

Alonzo Kramer | *Zachary Hobbs* |
Alonzo Kramer   #967 | Zachary Hobbs # 396

75–49 (Rev 3/63)   DETECTIVE DIVISION

| INVESTIGATION REPORT | PHILADELPHIA POLICE DEPARTMENT |

Yr	C.C.#		DIST	COMPL.#		INITIAL(49)		DIST/UNIT	
REPORT DATE	SUPPLEMENTAL			PREPARING
CLASSIFICATION		CODE	CONTINUATION	Homicide/9th Dist.

| PREVIOUS CLASSIFICATION | CODE | DATE AND TIME | | PLACE OF OCCURRENCE |

| COMPLAINANT | | AGE | RACE | ADDRESS | | PHONE | | TYPE OF PREMISES |
| Alicia Atchison | | 25 | W | | 320 Wilson Avenue, Media, PA |

| DATE AND TIME REPORTED | | REPORTED BY | | ADDRESS |

| FOUNDED ◻ YES ◻ NO   ARREST ◻ CLEARED   ◻ EXCEPTIONALLY CLEARED |

| STOLEN | ◻CURRENCY, BONDS, ETC. ◻ FURS   ◻.AUTOS | RECOVERED VALUE |
| PROPERTY | ◻ JEWELRY, PRECIOUS METALS ◻CLOTHING   ◻ MISC | |
| INSURED   ◻YES ◻NO |

DETAILS

   c. SCENE: (Continued)

              Detective James Wood #816, Homicide Unit.
                " "   Matthew Payne #701, Special Operations.
              Policeman Charles Shagren #3243, 9th District.
                " "   Frederick Marchese #4188, 9th District.
                " "   Thomas Daniels #4553, 9th District.
                " "   David Fowler #3665, 9th District.
                " "   Edward Schirmer #2559, 9th District
                " "   Lewis Roberts #3775, 9th District.
                " "   Frederick E. Rogers #4998, 9th District.
                " "   Robert Peters #3784, 9th District.
               Policeman Joseph Hart #2539, 9th District.
                " "   John McDonough #4178, 9th District.
                " "   Paul Kummerling #4228, 9th District.
              Technician Corsey Coy, Crime Lab.
                " "   Wilfred Doyle, Crime Lab.
                " "   David Dennison, Crime Lab.
                " "   Harry Withjack, Crime Lab.
              Dr. Howard D. Mitchell, Medical Examiners Office.
              Photographer Jose Aquila, Medical Examiners Office.

   3. Outside Description:

      1908 Market Street is a one story brick building housing
Inferno Lounge & Restaurant. It is located on the south side of
Market Street and is between multi-story buildings. On the west side

| INVESTIGATOR (Type and Sign Name) | SERGEANT | | LIEUTENANT |

Alonzo Kramer | *Zachary Hobbs* | |
Alonzo Kramer   #967 | | Zachary Hobbs # 396 |

INVESTIGATION REPORT				PHILADELPHIA POLICE DEPARTMENT	
Yr	C.C.#	DIST	COMPL.#	INITIAL(49) DIST/UNIT	
REPORT DATE		SUPPLEMENTAL			PREPARING
CLASSIFICATION		CODE	CONTINUATION		Homicide/9th Dist.

PREVIOUS CLASSIFICATION	CODE	DATE AND TIME	PLACE OF OCCURRENCE

COMPLAINANT	AGE	RACE	ADDRESS	PHONE	TYPE OF PREMISES
Alicia Atchison	25	W	320 Wilson Avenue, Media, PA		

DATE AND TIME REPORTED	REPORTED BY	ADDRESS

FOUNDED ☐ YES ☐ NO   **ARREST** ☐ **CLEARED**   ☐ **EXCEPTIONALLY CLEARED**

STOLEN ☐ CURRENCY, BONDS, ETC. ☐ FURS   ☐. AUTOS **RECOVERED VALUE**
PROPERTY ☐ JEWELRY, PRECIOUS METALS ☐ CLOTHING   ☐ MISC
INSURED ☐ YES ☐ NO

DETAILS

C. SCENE: (Continued)

of 1908 is a former office building which is now unoccupied. On the east side is a four story commercial building occupied by various businesses. Inferno Lounge & Restaurant runs from Market Street to Ludlow Street. Ranstead Street is located to the south of Market. Entrance to 1908 can be gained from either Market or an alley off Ludlow Street. Market is a one way eastbound street. Parking is restricted to certain hours and when permitted, is on the north side.

Ludlow Street can be entered from 18th or 19th Streets. A parking lot runs from Market to Ludlow Street west of the unoccupied office building.

The rear entrance of The Inferno is on an alley off Ludlow Street. On the west end of the building is a concrete stairway having 6 steps to the door which leads into the hallway. There are two large windows in the wall about 7 feet from the ground which are protected by a heavy wire screen with a metal frame. These windows are in the kitchen. Above the 2nd step of this concrete stairway there is a boarded up window. At the bottom of the stairs there were 2 metal trash cans and a carton of trash containing broken whiskey bottles. Flush with the pavement there was a solid metal door which opened in the middle for entrance into the basement. Underneath this metal door is a well about 4 feet deep. Above this metal door is a heavy metal wire door. These protect the inner wooden door which leads into the basement. The weather was clear and warm.

INVESTIGATOR (Type and Sign Name)	SERGEANT	LIEUTENANT
Alonzo Kramer	*Zachary Hobbs*	
Alonzo Kramer #967	Zachary Hobbs # 396	

75–49 (Rev 3/63)   DETECTIVE DIVISION

| INVESTIGATION REPORT | PHILADELPHIA POLICE DEPARTMENT |

INVESTIGATION REPORT   PHILADELPHIA POLICE DEPARTMENT

Yr | C.C.# | DIST | COMPL.# | INITIAL(49) | | DIST/UNIT |
REPORT DATE   SUPPLEMENTAL | PREPARING
CLASSIFICATION |CODE |CONTINUATION   Homicide/9th Dist.

PREVIOUS CLASSIFICATION   CODE | DATE AND TIME |PLACE OF OCCURRENCE

COMPLAINANT |AGE |RACE |ADDRESS |PHONE |TYPE OF PREMISES
Alicia Atchison | 25 | W | 320 Wilson Avenue, Media, PA

DATE AND TIME REPORTED |REPORTED BY |ADDRESS

FOUNDED ☐ YES ☐ NO   ARREST ☐ CLEARED   ☐ EXCEPTIONALLY CLEARED

STOLEN |☐CURRENCY, BONDS, ETC. ☐ FURS   ☐. AUTOS |RECOVERED VALUE
PROPERTY |☐ JEWELRY, PRECIOUS METALS ☐CLOTHING ☐ MISC |
INSURED   ☐YES ☐NO

DETAILS

    C. SCENE: (Continued)

     4. Inside Description:

      Entrance to 1908 Market Street is made through a large glass door which opens out north to west and once inside, about 3 feet south, is a large lattice work which makes you turn to the right-east. This is the bar area and the bar is set off to the right. The bar is approximately 22 feet long north to south and 7 feet wide east to west. The building at this point is 14 feet wide east to west and 28 feet in length north to south.

      The bar has bar chairs around it and against the west wall, starting from the lattice work, is a cigarette machine, a juke box and two booths with tables that seat two, each.

      North of the bar area is a dining room at which point the building is only 12 feet wide east to west and 47 feet in length north to south. Along the west wall of this dining room are six booths with tables, which seat 4 people each. North of the last booth is a piano.

      Along the east wall is a seating area made by a bench placed on angles so that four tables can be placed in front of the bench, to make each table a separate party. Each table has two chairs.

INVESTIGATOR (Type and Sign Name) | SERGEANT |LIEUTENANT

Alonzo Kramer | *Zachary Hobbs* |
Alonzo Kramer   #967 | Zachary Hobbs # 396

75–49 (Rev 3/63)   DETECTIVE DIVISION

INVESTIGATION REPORT	PHILADELPHIA POLICE DEPARTMENT		

Yr | C.C.#   **| DIST |COMPL.#**   **|INITIAL(49) | |DIST/UNIT |**
REPORT DATE   **SUPPLEMENTAL**   **| PREPARING**
CLASSIFICATION   **|CODE |CONTINUATION**   Homicide/9th Dist.

PREVIOUS CLASSIFICATION CODE | DATE AND TIME   **|PLACE OF OCCURRENCE**

COMPLAINANT   **|AGE |RACE |ADDRESS**   **|PHONE**   **|TYPE OF PREMISES**
Alicia Atchison | 25 | W | 320 Wilson Avenue, Media, PA

DATE AND TIME REPORTED   **|REPORTED BY**   **|ADDRESS**

FOUNDED ☐ YES ☐ NO   ARREST ☐ CLEARED   ☐ EXCEPTIONALLY CLEARED

STOLEN   **|☐CURRENCY, BONDS, ETC. ☐ FURS**   **☐. AUTOS |RECOVERED VALUE**
PROPERTY |☐ JEWELRY, PRECIOUS METALS ☐CLOTHING   ☐ MISC |
INSURED ☐YES ☐NO

DETAILS

C. SCENE: (Continued)

    4. Inside Description: (Continued)
        West of this bench is a service table, then a large potted artificial flower arrangement, then a stairway having six steps that lead to another dining room. This stairway is 4 feet wide. There is an iron railing that runs along the western edge of the stairway. At the top of the stairway the iron railing is extended until it reaches the western wall. There is a lattice work in front of the iron railing and extends up to the ceiling. This takes the place of a wall and it has an opening at the top of the stairway which permits entrance into the rear dining room.

        In the rear dining room, starting from the stairway, along the east wall going south to north, is a radiator, a clothes rack and a large air conditioner which is built into the wall. Next there are two tables each seating four. North of the tables is a partition that is built out of the east wall about 4 feet, then turns at a 90° angle going north for about another 4 feet. This is the entrance to the rest rooms. The building at this point extends about 4 feet further to the east. In this extension the ladies room is to the south and the mens room is to the north.

        North of the lattice work that separates the rear dining room from the lower dining room were two open hutches which contained glasses, dishes, linens, etc. In the corner there was a table that had a coffee warmer. Against the west wall going south to north were five tables with chairs, each table seating four. Then one table that seats two. The first table north of the lattice work

INVESTIGATOR (Type and Sign Name) | SERGEANT   **|LIEUTENANT**

Alonzo Kramer | *Zachary Hobbs* |
Alonzo Kramer   #967 | Zachary Hobbs # 396

75–49 (Rev 3/63)   **DETECTIVE DIVISION**

INVESTIGATION REPORT			PHILADELPHIA POLICE DEPARTMENT		

Yr | C.C.# | DIST | COMPL.# | INITIAL(49) | | DIST/UNIT |
REPORT DATE   SUPPLEMENTAL | PREPARING
CLASSIFICATION |CODE |CONTINUATION   Homicide/9th Dist.

PREVIOUS CLASSIFICATION   CODE | DATE AND TIME |PLACE OF OCCURRENCE

COMPLAINANT |AGE |RACE |ADDRESS | PHONE |TYPE OF PREMISES
Alicia Atchison | 25 | W | 320 Wilson Avenue, Media, PA

DATE AND TIME REPORTED |REPORTED BY |ADDRESS

FOUNDED ☐ YES ☐ NO   ARREST ☐ CLEARED   ☐ EXCEPTIONALLY CLEARED

STOLEN |☐CURRENCY, BONDS, ETC. ☐ FURS   ☐.AUTOS |RECOVERED VALUE
PROPERTY |☐ JEWELRY, PRECIOUS METALS ☐CLOTHING ☐ MISC |
INSURED   ☐YES ☐NO

DETAILS

C. SCENE: (Continued)

contained two plastic containers which held dirty dishes, glasses, etc. All the other tables were covered with white tablecloths and on the floor was what appeared to be a new green rug. About 6 feet north of the last table there was an entrance to a hallway about 3 feet wide. This hallway leads to the rear exit of the building. The overall length of this hallway is approximately 40 feet long and about 4 feet wide. There was an entrance into the kitchen through a doorway that is about 25 feet from the rear door.

The rear entrance is guarded by two doors. The inner door, which is wooden, opens inwardly from right to left. It has a sliding bolt at the top and bottom, but they were not bolted. The outer door is made of a heavy wire with a metal frame. This door opens outwardly right to left and had two padlocks which were in an open position. These were inserted in the hasp, top and bottom of the door frame.

Going south into the kitchen from the rear service area of the rear dining room is a large double entrance. Going south about 15 feet is a wall to the west that has four shelves on it. At the end of this wall and west about 3 feet is an entrance to the hall for the rear exit. The wall continues west to Ludlow Street. The basement steps are located between the hall wall and the kitchen wall that has the shelves on it.

INVESTIGATOR (Type and Sign Name) | SERGEANT |LIEUTENANT

Alonzo Kramer | *Zachary Hobbs* |
Alonzo Kramer   #967 | Zachary Hobbs # 396

75-49 (Rev 3/63)   DETECTIVE DIVISION

INVESTIGATION REPORT				PHILADELPHIA POLICE DEPARTMENT	
Yr | C.C.#	| DIST	|COMPL.#		|INITIAL(49)	| |DIST/UNIT
REPORT DATE		SUPPLEMENTAL		|	PREPARING
CLASSIFICATION		|CODE	|CONTINUATION		Homicide/9th Dist.

PREVIOUS CLASSIFICATION	CODE | DATE AND TIME	|PLACE OF OCCURRENCE

COMPLAINANT	|AGE	|RACE	|ADDRESS	|PHONE	|TYPE OF PREMISES
Alicia Atchison	| 25	| W	| 320 Wilson Avenue, Media, PA		

DATE AND TIME REPORTED	|REPORTED BY	|ADDRESS

FOUNDED ☐ YES ☐ NO   ARREST ☐ CLEARED   ☐ EXCEPTIONALLY CLEARED

STOLEN   \|☐CURRENCY, BONDS, ETC. ☐ FURS   ☐. AUTOS \|RECOVERED VALUE
PROPERTY \|☐ JEWELRY, PRECIOUS METALS ☐CLOTHING   ☐ MISC   \|
INSURED   ☐YES ☐NO

DETAILS

C. SCENE: (Continued)

    4. Inside Description: (Continued)

       On the east section of the kitchen is a washing section separated by a small wall and then starts the food and preparation area. The stoves are located against the north wall at the rear of the building.

       There is a flight of 14 steps from the kitchen to the basement running north to south and a door at the kitchen that opens into the cellar from left to right.

       In the north wall of the basement near the east corner is a wooden door that leads to a well under the pavement on the alley off Ludlow Street. This door and well are used for putting the trash out onto the alley. This well is about 4 feet deep, 4 feet wide and 4 feet long. The well is covered over with 2 metal doors that are flush with the sidewalk.

       These metal doors open up from the well from the center. They are locked by a metal sliding bolt that is located under the west metal door. This metal sliding bolt was found to be in an open position.

       Also covering the rear cellar door is a heavy metal wire door that protects the top portion of the wooden inner door. This metal door is kept locked by a hasp and padlock which were found to be in a locked position.

INVESTIGATOR (Type and Sign Name)	| SERGEANT	|LIEUTENANT
Alonzo Kramer	| *Zachary Hobbs*	|
Alonzo Kramer #967	| Zachary Hobbs # 396	

75–49 (Rev 3/63)	DETECTIVE DIVISION

INVESTIGATION REPORT	PHILADELPHIA POLICE DEPARTMENT

Yr	C.C.#	DIST	COMPL.#		INITIAL(49)		DIST/UNIT	
REPORT DATE	SUPPLEMENTAL			PREPARING
CLASSIFICATION	CODE	CONTINUATION	Homicide/9th Dist.

PREVIOUS CLASSIFICATION	CODE	DATE AND TIME	PLACE OF OCCURRENCE

COMPLAINANT	AGE	RACE	ADDRESS	PHONE	TYPE OF PREMISES
Alicia Atchison	25	W	320 Wilson Avenue, Media, PA

DATE AND TIME REPORTED	REPORTED BY	ADDRESS

FOUNDED ☐ YES ☐ NO   ARREST ☐ CLEARED   ☐ EXCEPTIONALLY CLEARED

STOLEN	☐ CURRENCY, BONDS, ETC. ☐ FURS ☐. AUTOS	RECOVERED VALUE
PROPERTY	☐ JEWELRY, PRECIOUS METALS ☐ CLOTHING ☐ MISC	
INSURED	☐ YES ☐ NO

DETAILS

C. SCENE: (Continued)
   4. Inside Description: (Continued)

The wooden door opens into the basement from left to
right. This door is locked with a latch lock. It was observed
that this lock was slightly sprung and can not be securely
locked.

It was observed that a 2 x 4 piece of wood, approximately
3 feet long was against the north wall west of the wooden door.
This 2 x 4 is used to place under the doorknob of the wooden door
to help secure the door from being opened from the outside.

From the north wall going south are a number of boxes and
debris. The last step of the stairway that leads into the cellar
is 25 feet 5 inches south of the north wall. From the north basement wall to the north wall of the office is 33 feet 8 inches.

Along the outside north wall of the office are racks for
storage. South of the steps, along the west wall, is a refrigerator, then an open storage area, an ice machine and then a store-
room that is used by the employees for changing their clothing.

The office in the basement is built alongside the east
wall and has exposed studding on the outside and is enclosed from
the inside with sheetrock. The north wall of the office is 7 feet
1 inch wide east to west and the south wall is 9 feet 6 inches
wide east to west. The office is 18 feet 8 inches in length north to
south and the west wall is offset so that it is wider at the south end.

INVESTIGATOR (Type and Sign Name)	SERGEANT	LIEUTENANT
Alonzo Kramer	*Zachary Hobbs*	
Alonzo Kramer #967	Zachary Hobbs # 396	

75–49 (Rev 3/63)   DETECTIVE DIVISION

INVESTIGATION REPORT		PHILADELPHIA POLICE DEPARTMENT	

| Yr | C.C.# | DIST | COMPL.# | INITIAL(49) | DIST/UNIT |
REPORT DATE   SUPPLEMENTAL   PREPARING
CLASSIFICATION   CODE | CONTINUATION   Homicide/9th Dist.

PREVIOUS CLASSIFICATION   CODE | DATE AND TIME | PLACE OF OCCURRENCE

| COMPLAINANT | AGE | RACE | ADDRESS | PHONE | TYPE OF PREMISES |
| Alicia Atchison | 25 | W | 320 Wilson Avenue, Media, PA | | |

DATE AND TIME REPORTED | REPORTED BY | ADDRESS

FOUNDED ☐ YES ☐ NO   ARREST ☐ CLEARED   ☐ EXCEPTIONALLY CLEARED

STOLEN | ☐ CURRENCY, BONDS, ETC. ☐ FURS   ☐. AUTOS | RECOVERED VALUE
PROPERTY | ☐ JEWELRY, PRECIOUS METALS ☐ CLOTHING   ☐ MISC
INSURED   ☐ YES ☐ NO

DETAILS

C. SCENE: (Continued)

4. Inside Description: (Continued)

Entrance can be gained to the office by a doorway that is 5 feet 5 inches south of the north wall. The door opens in to the office from right to left. Inside the office along the west wall going south, were two boxes behind the open door. Past the south of the entranceway where the west is extended out were liquor shelves divided into two sections, with bottles of assorted liquors and wines on them. Next is a four drawer file, a box, then a chair with a cardboard carton on it, in the southwest corner. Under the first rack of shelves at the entryway is an open safe.

Along the north wall was a coat rack and in the northeast corner was a round board on a milk carton, which is used as a table. Along the east wall, going south, was a sofa and a chair and then a desk. On the wall behind the chair was a large area with what appeared to be blood. On the east wall in the southeast corner was a pay phone. The south wall had an air space knocked out at the top acting as a window. Between the south wall and the desk was a desk chair.

The safe was found open with the door opening from the left to the right. Inside the safe were several rolls of coins, assorted papers and an empty box for a Colt Cobra revolver. In front of the safe, on the floor, was a metal container which contained money and papers. At the base of this metal container were marks that appeared

INVESTIGATOR (Type and Sign Name) | SERGEANT | LIEUTENANT

Alonzo Kramer | *Zachary Hobbs*
Alonzo Kramer   #967 | Zachary Hobbs # 396

75–49 (Rev 3/63)   DETECTIVE DIVISION

INVESTIGATION REPORT			PHILADELPHIA POLICE DEPARTMENT			
Yr I C.C.#	I DIST	ICOMPL.#		INITIAL(49) I	IDIST/UNIT I	
REPORT DATE		SUPPLEMENTAL		I	PREPARING	
CLASSIFICATION		ICODE ICONTINUATION			Homicide/9th Dist.	

PREVIOUS CLASSIFICATION	CODE I DATE AND TIME	IPLACE OF OCCURRENCE

COMPLAINANT	IAGE	IRACE IADDRESS	I PHONE	ITYPE OF PREMISES
Alicia Atchison	I 25 I W	I 320 Wilson Avenue, Media, PA		

DATE AND TIME REPORTED	IREPORTED BY	IADDRESS

FOUNDED ❐ YES ❐ NO   ARREST ❐ CLEARED   ❐ EXCEPTIONALLY CLEARED

STOLEN   I❐CURRENCY, BONDS, ETC. ❐ FURS   ❐.AUTOS IRECOVERED VALUE
PROPERTY I❐JEWELRY, PRECIOUS METALS ❐CLOTHING   ❐ MISC   I
INSURED   ❐YES❐NO

DETAILS

C. SCENE: (Continued)

to be blood. Alongside this metal container was a empty paper
box and then a lid that is turned up. In front of the metal container and paper box, about 1 1/2 feet east, was an area of
splatter blood.

5. Body:

     Alicia Atchison - Found victim to be stretched out in the
chair on the east wall between the desk and sofa. She was
stretched out with her body and legs facing west and her head in
an easterly direction tilted back facing up. Her face was completely covered with blood, both of her arms hanging down. She
was wearing a white sweater that was open, a dark blue dress,
stockings with no shoe on her right foot. A white shoe was on
her left foot and under the left foot was a white shoe, which
was apparently from this victim. Her clothing, arms, legs and
shoes all had blood on them. Directly under her, on the floor,
was an extremely large pool of blood.

     Anthony J. Marcuzzi - Found victim lying on the floor on
his left side, his legs in a northwest direction and his head in
a southeast direction facing west. His back was leaning up
against the sofa and his head was directly under the body of
Alicia Atchison. He was lying in an extremely large pool of
blood. There was blood on the right side of his face around the
temple area and right ear, blood from his nose and mouth which
ran down the left side of his face.

INVESTIGATOR (Type and Sign Name) | SERGEANT   ILIEUTENANT

Alonzo Kramer | *Zachary Hobbs*   I
Alonzo Kramer   #967 | Zachary Hobbs # 396

75–49 (Rev 3/63)   DETECTIVE DIVISION

INVESTIGATION REPORT

PHILADELPHIA POLICE DEPARTMENT

| Yr | C.C.# | | DIST | COMPL.# | | INITIAL(49) | | DIST/UNIT | |

REPORT DATE   SUPPLEMENTAL | PREPARING

CLASSIFICATION |CODE |CONTINUATION   Homicide/9th Dist.

PREVIOUS CLASSIFICATION   CODE | DATE AND TIME |PLACE OF OCCURRENCE

| COMPLAINANT | |AGE | RACE |ADDRESS | | PHONE | |TYPE OF PREMISES |

Alicia Atchison | 25 | W | 320 Wilson Avenue, Media, PA

DATE AND TIME REPORTED |REPORTED BY |ADDRESS

FOUNDED ☐ YES ☐ NO   ARREST ☐ CLEARED   ☐ EXCEPTIONALLY CLEARED

STOLEN |☐CURRENCY, BONDS, ETC. ☐ FURS   ☐. AUTOS |RECOVERED VALUE

PROPERTY |☐ JEWELRY, PRECIOUS METALS ☐CLOTHING   ☐ MISC |

INSURED   ☐YES ☐NO

DETAILS

C. <u>SCENE:</u> (Continued)

      His left arm was extended out from under his body in a northwest direction and his right arm was folded across his chest. He was wearing a brown suit, white shirt, brown tie and shoes and socks.

      6. <u>Crime Lab:</u>

      (a) <u>Direction:</u> On Saturday, May 20, 1975, Technicians Corsey Coy and Wilfred Doyle were directed at the crime scene by Sergeant Zachary Hobbs, to take a total of 47 photographs, also to make a sketch of the scene, search same for latent fingerprints and preserve evidence found at scene and submit same.

      (b) <u>Latent Prints:</u> Technician Corsey Coy lifted over-laps and partial prints from the safe and a Seagrams V-O bottle that was on the desk, both being inside the office.

      Latent Prints were developed from the stem of a glass that was on top of the desk inside the office and from a plain glass that was found on the bar. These prints were checked by Corsey Coy and David Dennison with positive results, both latent prints being of Anthony J. Marcuzzi.

      (c) <u>Direction:</u> On Saturday, May 20, 1975, Technicians Harry Withjack and David Dennison were directed to the scene to assist in making a sketch and search of the scene.

INVESTIGATOR (Type and Sign Name) | SERGEANT |LIEUTENANT

Alonzo Kramer | *Zachary Hobbs* |

Alonzo Kramer   #967 | Zachary Hobbs # 396

75–49 (Rev 3/63)   DETECTIVE DIVISION

• • •

When Detective Wally Milham pushed open the door of the Red Robin Diner at Frankford and Levick it was nearly empty, and for at least fifteen seconds, which seemed like much longer, he couldn't find Helene Kellog. But then he saw her, in a booth halfway down the counter, staring into a coffee cup on the table.

She had a kerchief around her head, and was wearing a cotton raincoat.

He walked quickly to the booth and slid onto the seat facing her.

"Hi," he said.

She looked up at him and smiled wanly, but didn't speak, and when he touched her hand, she pulled it away.

"Tell me exactly what happened," he said.

"My mother came into my room. I hadn't heard the phone ring, it's downstairs in the hall. And she told me I had a call—"

"When was this?"

"Just before I called you."

"You were in bed?"

"Of course I was in bed. It was . . . God, I don't know. Late. Of course I was in bed. Everybody was in bed. My mother had to get out of bed to answer the phone . . ."

"Take it easy, honey," Milham said gently.

"I'm frightened, Wally."

"Tell me exactly what happened."

"He said, he said, 'Keep your . . .' Wally, he said, 'Keep your fucking mouth closed, bitch, or you'll get the same thing your fucking husband did.'"

"Sonofabitch," Milham said. "Did you recognize the voice?"

Helene shook her head.

"Honey, do you know something about—what your husband was doing, something dirty, that you haven't told me?"

"No. But, Wally, they must know I went to see Sergeant Washington."

"You did what?"

"Oh, God, I didn't tell you, did I?"

"Didn't tell me what?"

"That I went to see Sergeant Washington."

"No, you didn't," Milham said. "What exactly did you tell Washington?"

"I told him that the Narcotics Five Squad is all dirty, that Jerry was dirty, and that they probably are the ones who killed him."

"Jesus!"

"I didn't tell you because I didn't want to involve you," Helene said.

"Honey, I'm involved," Wally said, and added, "You're probably right. Somebody knows you talked to Washington. What did you do, call him up?"

"I went to see him."

"Well, somebody from Five Squad was at Special Operations, and recognized you, or somebody at Special Operations told somebody at Five Squad . . ."

"I went to his house," Helene said. "I didn't go to Special Operations. Which means that if Five Squad knows, he told them."

Milham considered that for two seconds.

"No. Not Washington. He's a straight arrow. He didn't tell anybody, except maybe somebody at Internal Affairs."

"What's the difference? They know."

"What are they afraid you'll tell somebody?"

Helene shrugged helplessly. "I don't know. I don't know what they're doing dirty, just that they are."

"Your husband never told you where the money came from?"

Helene shook her head.

"Wally, I don't want them to do anything to my mother and father."

"They won't. The dumbest thing they could do is try to do something to you. Or them. The whole Police Department would come down on them."

"Huh!" she snorted. "They don't want to go to jail; there's no telling what they'll do."

"They're just trying to scare you, is all. Christ, I wish you had told me about this. I could have got to Washington and nobody would ever have known."

"I told you, I didn't want to involve you."

"And I told you, I'm involved in whatever you do," Milham said. He reached out for her hand again, and this time she did not move it away.

When he looked at her face, tears were running down her cheeks.

"Honey, don't do that. I can't stand to see you cry."

"Wally, what am I going to do?"

"The question is what are we going to do. You understand?"

"OK. We," Helene said, and tried to smile.

"OK. So you're not going back to your mother's. That's one thing."

"What is she going to say? What do I say to her?"

"What did you say when you left the house?"

"I told her I had to go somewhere, and that I would call. She didn't like it at all."

"OK. So you call her again, and tell her you have to go away for a couple of days, and that you'll call her."

"She won't like it."

"Honey, for Christ's sake! They called you there because they knew you were there."

She nodded a grudging acceptance of that.

"So where do I go?"

"My place," he suggested without much conviction in his voice.

"I can't do that, and you know it," Helene said.

"OK. We'll talk about that later. Tonight we'll go to a motel."

"Not we, Wally. I'm not up to anything like that."

"OK. We get you in a motel. You go to bed. Get your rest. I'll think of something."

"Something what?"

"I don't know. Something," Milham said. "One thing at a time."

She looked at him and squeezed his hand.

"Helene," Wally said. "Everything's going to be all right. You're not alone." She squeezed his hand. "I love you," Wally said.

She squeezed his hand again.

He stood up.

"Come on, let's get out of here."

"You think maybe they followed me here?"

"Of course not," he said.

But when they went to his car, he looked up and down the street to make sure there was nothing suspicious, and as they drove to the Sheraton Hotel, on Roosevelt Boulevard and Grant Avenue, he made three or four turns to be absolutely sure no one was following them.

He didn't like the idea of leaving her alone, but he understood why she didn't want him to stay with her, and he knew that he couldn't press her about that; she would think that all he wanted to do was get in bed with her.

He got the key from the desk clerk, who sort of smirked at him, making it clear he thought that what they were up to was a little quickie.

He stood outside the motel door.

"Get the room number off the phone, and I'll call you in the morning," Wally said.

"OK," she said, "wait here."

She came back with the number written inside a matchbook, and handed it to him.

"I'll call you in the morning," he said.

"Yes."

She looked at him, and leaned forward and kissed him on the cheek.

"Thank you, Wally," she said.

"Aaaah. I'll call you in the morning. Just lock the door and get some sleep."

"Right."

"Good night, Helene. I'll call you in the morning."

"Right."

He had taken a dozen steps toward his car when she called his name.

"Wally?"

"Yeah?"

He walked back to her.

"Wally, I love you, too," Helene said.

"I know," he said. "But thank you for saying it."

"I don't want you to go," Helene said.

She took his hand and pulled him into the motel room.

Matt's door buzzer sounded.

He pushed the button that opened the door and went to the top of the stairs to wait for Amanda.

The doorway was filled with a rent-a-cop, a huge one Matt did not know.

"Sorry to bother you, Mr. Payne, but there's a young lady here says you expect her."

"Of course," Matt said, and ran down the stairs.

"Thanks a lot," Matt said to the rent-a cop.

"Hello," Amanda said softly, and walked quickly past him and up the stairs. She was wearing a suit with a white blouse. He could smell soap.

He closed the door in the face of the rent-a-cop and went after Amanda, carefully averting his eyes so that she wouldn't have any reason at all to suspect he was looking up her skirt as she went up the stairs.

She waited for him at the top of the stairs.

"You know what he thought, don't you?" Amanda asked.

"No. What did he think?"

"He thought I was a call girl."

"Don't be silly."

"I'm not being silly. He as much as accused me in the elevator. And why not? Who else would be going to a bachelor apartment at this hour?"

"A friend," Matt said.

"God, I'm sorry I ever got started on this!"

"I'm not."

"I meant it, Matt, when I said I'm here as a friend."

"Absolutely. I know that."

She met his eyes, and then quickly averted hers.

"Do you know how to warm up a hamburger?" Matt asked. "I put the coffee in a pot, and we can heat that. But the hamburgers are cold."

"You put the meat patty in a frying pan," Amanda said. "You have a frying pan?" He nodded. "And—you said french fries?" Matt nodded again. "You put french fries in the oven."

"I've got one of those, too," Matt said.

"Good," she said. "Show me."

"I'm glad you came," Matt said. "Thank you."

"Just as long as you understand why I came," she said. "OK?"

"Absolutely. I told you that."

She went in the kitchen. He turned the oven on and handed her a frying pan.

When she bent over to put the french fries in the oven, he looked down her blouse and told himself he was really a sonofabitch.

When she stood up, he could tell by the look in her eyes that she knew he had looked down her blouse.

He backed two steps away from her and smiled uneasily.

"If anybody finds out I came here," Amanda said, "they wouldn't understand."

"Nobody will ever find out," Matt said. He held up three fingers in the Boy Scout salute. "Scout's Honor."

"Oh, God," Amanda groaned.

"Bad joke," he said. "Sorry."

"And they would, of course, be right," Amanda said. "Oh, hell! 'In for a penny'—*oh, God!*—'in for a pound.'"

"Excuse me?"

"You know what my reaction was when I heard Penny was dead?"

"What?"

"Thank God. She was going to suck Matt dry and ruin his life." She looked intently at his face, then moaned. "Oh, God, I shouldn't have told you!"

"Isn't that why you came here, to tell me that? Amanda, that's really—decent—of you. And it really took balls."

"Balls?" she parroted, gently mocking.

"It took courage," he corrected himself. "But you're not the only one who felt that way. Penny . . . Penny apparently did not enjoy the universal approval of my friends. Half a dozen people told me exactly, or paraphrased, what you just did."

"That's not why I came," Amanda said. "I wanted to be with you."

"You're a good friend," Matt said.

She met his eyes, then looked away, and then met them again.

"Maybe that, too," Amanda said softly.

"Jesus, Amanda."

"Does that come as such a surprise? Am I making as much of a fool of myself as I think I am?"

He reached out and touched her cheek with his fingers.

She moved her head away and looked to the side.

"For God's sake, don't feel sorry for me," she said.

"What I'm doing is wondering what would happen if I tried to put my arms around you."

She turned her face to look at him. She looked into his eyes for a long moment.

"Why don't you try it and find out?" Amanda asked.

SEVENTEEN

Matt Payne rolled over in bed, grabbed the telephone on the bedside table, and snarled, "Hello."

"Good morning," Amanda Spencer said, a chuckle in her voice. "Somehow I thought you'd be in a better mood than you sound like."

Still half asleep, Matt turned and looked in confusion at where he expected Amanda to be, lying beside him. He was obviously alone in his bed.

"Where are you?"

"Thirtieth Street Station," she said.

"Why?"

"You have to come here to get on a train."

"Jesus H. Christ!"

"I have a job, Matt."

"Call in and tell them you were run over by a truck."

"It was something like that, wasn't it? How do you feel this morning?"

"Right now, desolate."

She chuckled again.

"Don't call me, Matt. I'll call you."

"Did I do something wrong?"

"This is what I think they call the cold, cruel light of day," Amanda said. "I need some time to think."

"Second thoughts, you mean? Morning-after regrets?"

"I said I need some time to think. But no regrets."

"Me either," he said.

He was now fully awake. He picked his watch up from the bedside table. It was ten past eight.

"You could have said something," he said, somewhat petulantly.

"I'm saying it now," Amanda said. "I have a job, I have to go to work, and I need some time to think."

"Damn!"

"If it makes you feel any better, I didn't really want to leave. But it was the sensible thing to do."

"Screw sensible."

"Have you got any morning-after regrets?"

"I'm still in shock, but no regrets."

"We both got a little carried away last night."

"Anything wrong with that?"

"That's what I want to think about," Amanda said. "I'll call you, Matt. Don't call me."

The phone went dead in his ear.

"Damn!"

"Push the damned button, Matt," Inspector Peter Wohl said into the microphone beside Detective Payne's doorbell. "The Wachenhut guy told me he knows you're up there."

A moment later the solenoid buzzed, and Wohl pushed the door open and started up the narrow flight of stairs.

"I didn't know who it was," Matt said from the head of the stairs. He was wearing khaki trousers, a gray, battered

University of Pennsylvania sweatshirt, and was obviously fresh from the shower.

He looks more than a little sleepy, Peter thought. *Probably still feeling the pill Amy gave him.*

"How are you doing?"

"I was just about to go out and get some breakfast."

"Not necessary," Wohl said, handing him a large kraft paper bag. "Never let it be said that I do not take care of my underlings."

Matt sniffed it.

"Smells great. What is it?"

"Western omelet, bagels, orange juice, and coffee."

"Thank you, Peter," Matt said.

"I expected to find you still in bed," Wohl said.

"Huh?"

"Amy said that the pill she gave you . . ." Wohl stopped. He had followed Matt into the kitchen and seen the stack of Forms 75-49. "What's this?"

"75-49s on the Inferno job," Matt said. "Milham told me to read them."

"When did you see Milham?"

"Last night. Early this morning. I went over there—"

"You didn't take Amy's pill?" Wohl asked, but it was a statement rather than a question.

"No, I didn't," Matt confessed. "I had a couple of drinks here, decided going to the FOP was a good idea, started out for there, changed my mind, and went to Homicide."

"Why?" Wohl asked, a tone of exasperation in his voice.

"At the time it seemed like a good idea," Matt said.

Wohl reached into his jacket pocket and came out with an interoffice memorandum. He handed it to Matt.

"One of the reasons I came here was to show you this. I guess you've seen it."

Matt glanced at it.

"Yeah. Milham had a copy."

"Lowenstein sent me one," Wohl said, taking the memorandum back and then crumpling it in his fist. He looked around, remembered the garbage can was under the sink, and went to it and dropped the memorandum in it.

"For some reason, I'm not sore at you," Wohl said. "I think I should be."

"I didn't want that damned pill," Matt said.

"That, I understand. But you shouldn't have gone to Homicide until I sent you."

"Sorry," Matt said.

"Oh, hell, I'd have probably done the same thing myself," Wohl said. "Unwrap the omelets."

"Lieutenant Natali was very nice to me," Matt said.

"Natali's a nice fellow," Wohl said. "Where's your cups? I hate coffee in a paper cup."

"In the cabinet."

"Are you really all right? Amy thinks you're still in what she calls a condition called 'grief shock.'"

"Amy's a nice girl," Matt said, gently mocking. "But what I'm in is a condition called 'Oh, what a sonofabitch you are, Matt Payne.'"

"I told you, what Penny did to herself wasn't your fault."

"Somebody came to see me last night," Matt said. "To comfort me in my condition of grief shock."

"Somebody, I gather from the tone of your voice, female. And?"

"She comforted me," Matt said.

Wohl looked at him to make sure he had correctly interpreted what he had said.

"Who?"

"I don't think I want to tell you."

"Nice kind of girl, or the other?"

"Very nice kind of girl."

"Good for you," Wohl said. "But I don't think I'd tell Amy."

"I've been trying to wallow in guilt, but I don't seem to be able to."

"What's in it for the girl?"

"I just think she was being nice. Maybe a little more."

"The one from New York? Amanda, something like that?"

"Jesus Christ!"

"I saw her looking at you at Martha Peebles's."

"I didn't see her at Martha Peebles's."

"I repeat, good for you, Matt. Don't wallow in guilt."

The door buzzer sounded.

Matt looked surprised.

"Detective McFadden, I'll bet," Wohl said. "Here to comfort you in your condition of grief shock, with firm orders to keep you off the sauce."

"You really do take care of me, don't you?" Matt asked.

"Somebody has to, or the first thing you know, you're crawling around on a ledge like an orangutan."

"Thank you, Peter," Matt said, pushing the button to open the door, and walked to the head of the stairs.

It was, instead of Detective McFadden, Detective Milham.

"You're up, I hope?" Milham asked. "I know I said ten . . ."

"Having breakfast. Come on up."

"I've got somebody with me. Is that all right?"

"Sure."

Milham took a step backward and a woman Matt had never seen before, but who he intuited was the Widow Kellog, appeared in the doorway and started up the stairs.

"I know we're intruding," she said as she reached Matt.

"Not at all."

"I'm Helene Kellog," she said.

"Matt Payne," Matt said. "How do you do? Come on in."

He led her to the kitchen.

"Mrs. Kellog, this is Inspector Wohl."

"Oh, God," Helene said.

"How do you do, Mrs. Kellog?" Wohl said politely, standing up.

Milham appeared.

It's a toss-up, Matt thought, *which of them looks unhappier at finding Wohl up here.*

"Hello, Wally," Wohl said. "How are you?"

"Wally, we should leave," Helene said.

"Not on my account, I hope," Wohl said.

"Inspector—" Milham began, and then stopped. Wohl looked at him curiously. "Inspector, Mrs. Kellog got a death threat last night."

"Damn you, Wally," Helene said.

"Did you really?" Wohl asked. "Please sit down, Mrs. Kellog. Let me get you a cup of coffee."

"I don't mean to be rude, but . . ."

"Helene, honey, we just can't pretend it didn't happen."

"Please, sit down," Wohl repeated.

She reluctantly did so.

"Mrs. Kellog, you're with friends," Wohl said.

The door buzzer sounded again. Helene glanced toward the stairway with fright in her eyes.

"That has to be McFadden," Wohl said. "You want to let him in, Matt?"

It was McFadden, laden with a kraft paper bag.

"I stopped by McDonald's and got some Egg Mc-Muffins," he said, handing Matt the bag as he reached the top of the stairs. "I thought maybe you hadn't eaten."

"I really want to go," Helene said, getting up from the table.

"Who's that?" McFadden asked.

"Charley, this is Mrs. Helene Kellog," Wohl said. "Mrs. Kellog, this is Detective McFadden."

"Please, Wally," Helene said.

"I'm going to have to be firm about this," Wohl said. "If you've had a death threat, I want to know about it. If you won't tell me about it, Mrs. Kellog, Wally will have to."

"I knew we shouldn't have come here," Helene said, but, with resignation, she sat back down.

"At least we have enough food," Wohl said. "Have you had any breakfast, Mrs. Kellog?"

"No," she said softly.

"Have an Egg McMuffin and a cup of coffee," Wohl said.

"Wally will tell me what's happened, and then you can fill in any blanks."

Milham looked as if he was torn between regret that he had to tell Wohl and relief.

"Helene called me at the Roundhouse last night," he said. "She told me there had been a telephone call."

"Where was she?"

"At my mother's," Helene said. "I mean, I got the call at my mother's. I called Wally from the Red Robin Diner."

"And what exactly did your caller say?"

"He told me that unless I kept my mouth shut, I'd get the same thing that happened to Jerry," Helene said.

"In just about those exact words?"

"He used dirty words," she said.

"You didn't happen to recognize the voice?" Wohl asked.

She shook her head.

"I can certainly understand why you're upset," Wohl said.

"Upset? I'm scared to death. Not only for me. I'm afraid for my mother and father."

"Well, I was about to say, you're safe now. We're friends, Mrs. Kellog. You think this call came from somebody on the Narcotics Five Squad?"

"Of course it did," Helene snapped. "Who else? What I'd like to know . . ."

Wohl waited a moment for her to continue, and when she did not, he asked, gently: "What would you like to know?"

"Nothing, forget it."

"She'd like to know how that damned Five Squad heard she'd talked to Washington," Wally Milham said. "And so would I."

"And so would I," Wohl said. "We'll find out. And until we do, until we get to the bottom of this, you won't be alone, Mrs. Kellog. You're living with your mother for the time being?"

"I was. Not now. I don't want them involved in this."

"So where will you be staying?"

"Helene stayed in a motel last night," Milham said.

"That can get kind of expensive," Wohl thought aloud. "Isn't there some place you can stay?"

Helene and Wally looked at each other helplessly.

"She could stay here," Matt heard himself say. The others looked at him in what was more confusion than surprise. "My mother's been on my back for me to stay with her for a couple of days."

"I couldn't do that," Helene said.

"I know it's not much," Matt said. "But if anybody was looking for you, they wouldn't look for you here. And there's a rent-a-cop downstairs twenty-four hours a day. And it's just going to sit here, empty."

"Jesus, Payne," Milham said. "That's very nice of you, but . . ."

"Why not?" Matt said. "I mean, really, why not?"

"I told you you were among friends, Mrs. Kellog," Wohl said. "I think it's a good idea."

"I just don't know," she said, and started to sniffle.

"I think you should, honey," Milham said.

"OK. It's settled," Matt said.

"Thank you very much," Helene said, formally. "Just for a few days."

"Wally, you take her to get her things, and then come back here," Wohl ordered.

"Right," Milham said, and then, quickly, as if he was afraid she would change her mind, "Come on, honey. Let's go."

"If I'm not here when you get back, I'll leave a key with the rent-a-cop," Matt said.

Helene looked at him.

"Wally was right," she said. "He said you were a very nice guy."

When they had gone down the stairs, and heard the door close after them, Wohl said, "That was nice of you, Matt."

"Christ, they can't afford living in a motel," Matt said.

"And won't your mother be pleasantly surprised to have you at home?" Wohl asked drolly. He stood up and went to the telephone and dialed a number.

"Inspector Wohl for the Chief," he said a moment later, and then: "Chief, I promised to let you know if anything interesting happened. The Widow Kellog got a death threat—specifically, 'Keep your mouth shut, or you'll get the same thing as your husband,' or words to that effect embroidered with obscenity—last night."

The outraged, familiar voice of Chief Inspector Lowenstein could be heard all over the kitchen: "I'll be goddamned! Where is she?"

"With Detective Milham. He took her to fetch some clothing. Matt Payne offered her his apartment to stay in."

"That really burns me up," Lowenstein said, unnecessarily adding, "what happened to her. That was nice of Payne. What are you going to do about it?"

"I'm going, first of all, to have someone sit on her. Discreetly."

"Your people?"

"My people, and since we're going to have to do this around the clock, I'd like to borrow one of yours for as long as this lasts."

"Who?"

"McFadden. He was here, at Payne's apartment, when this came up."

"Northwest Detectives? That McFadden? The one who took down Dutch Moffitt's murderer?"

"That McFadden."

"OK. He's yours. I'll call Northwest Detectives."

"Thank you. And then I'm going to give this to Weisbach and Washington. What I would like to know is who told Narcotics Five Squad that she'd talked to Washington."

"You don't know for sure that they know that," Lowenstein said.

"No. But it strikes me as highly probable."

Lowenstein grunted, and then said: "Peter, if you need anything else, let me know. Keep me posted. And thank you for the call."

"Yes, sir. Thank you."

He hung up the telephone, then leaned against the wall.

"It's time, I think," he said thoughtfully, "that we practice a little psychology. That woman is frightened. I think she knows more about what's going on dirty with that Five Squad than she's told anybody, including Milham, and right now, he's the only cop she really trusts. She trusts Matt a little, because Milham likes him, and because he offered the apartment. And she thinks that Washington is straight, otherwise she would never have gone to him. So we'll try to build a little trust by association."

He turned back to the telephone and dialed a number.

"Jason, is Weisbach there?" he asked, and when the reply was that he wasn't, added: "Put out the arm for him, please, and ask him to meet me at Payne's apartment right away. I want you here, too, Jason. Right away."

They could not hear what Washington replied.

"The Widow Kellog got a death threat telephone call this morning, telling her to keep her mouth shut or get the same thing that happened to her husband. Matt offered his apartment as a place for her to stay. Milham just took her to pick up some clothes. When they come back here, I want her to feel she's surrounded by cops she can trust."

And again, Washington made a reply they couldn't hear.

"Oh, sure, we're going to sit on her. I'm taking that threat very seriously. Be prepared, when you get here, to assign, in her hearing, everybody but Tiny a duty schedule to sit on her. I borrowed McFadden from Lowenstein. If you can find Martinez and Tiny, I'd like them here, too. Once she sees that she's surrounded by cops, I want to leave her alone with you and Weisbach. Maybe you can get her to talk now."

Washington made another inaudible reply, to which Wohl responded, "Yeah."

Then: "Jason, switch me to Captain Pekach, will you?"

"David? Are you in uniform?"

Now Matt and Charley McFadden could hear Pekach's reply: "Yes, I am."

"OK. Good. I want you, in a Highway car, to be parked

on the sidewalk in front of Matt Payne's apartment in twenty minutes. You come up. And I think it would be a good idea to have another Highway car parked with you. Tell them to get out of the car and be standing conspicuously on the sidewalk. I'll explain it all to you when you get here."

He hung up and turned to face Matt and McFadden again.

"In her presence, I will order the Commanding Officer of Highway to have a Highway car pass her parents' home not less than once each half hour," he said, "and to check on any car, or person, who looks halfway suspicious."

"You're really taking that threat seriously, aren't you?" Matt asked.

"Somebody shot her husband," Wohl said. "If they're willing to do that once . . ."

"If somebody is watching her parents' house, they'll probably make the Highway drive-bys."

"Good, let's make them nervous," Wohl said. He paused, almost visibly having another thought. "If I was wondering what Mrs. Kellog told Washington, I think I'd also be worrying what she told Milham. So I think you'd better stick with him, Matt, instead of sitting on her."

"OK."

"I think it would also make her feel better to know he's not walking around alone. Question: Should Milham be here when she talks to Washington or not?"

"She seems to listen to him," McFadden said.

"Yeah," Matt said.

"OK. So you pack your bag, Matt, and be ready to get out when I tell you. Take McFadden with you. Go to Homicide and let him read the 75-49s on Kellog. I'll call Quaire and fix it with him. If anything has come up that looks like it has a connection with this, call me."

"Right."

When Matt returned to the kitchen after getting dressed, and carrying a small suitcase into which he had put his toilet kit and a spare pair of shoes, Charley McFadden was at the

kitchen table, reading the 75-49s on the Inferno job. Wohl
was in the living room, studiously writing in his notebook.

"Interesting," Charley said. "I've never seen Homicide
75-49s before."

"That's because God doesn't love you," Matt said piously.

McFadden looked at him curiously.

"How are you doing?" he asked.

"Fine," Matt said, cheerfully and immediately, and then,
chagrined, remembered he was supposed to be grief-
stricken.

"Yeah?" Charley asked suspiciously. "Are you on something? Wohl . . ." He quickly corrected himself, remembering that *Inspector* Wohl was ten feet away: ". . . Inspector
Wohl said your sister gave you a pill."

Matt didn't want to get into the subject of the pill, and he
didn't want to lie to McFadden. He avoided a direct reply.

"I'm OK, Charley," he said, and leaned over McFadden's
shoulder hoping he could find something in the 75-49s that
would allow him to change the subject.

He found something, on the page Charley was just about
to turn facedown.

"Bingo!"

McFadden looked up at him.

"What the hell does that mean?"

"Look here," Matt said, and pointed toward the bottom of
the page. "We had a tip that the doer was somebody named
Frankie. Milham and I, starting from zilch, were out looking
for him early this morning. We think we found him, on 2320
South Eighteenth Street. And here's a Frankie who was in
the Inferno, and there's a description."

"I know that neighborhood," McFadden said, and then
was interrupted when the door buzzer sounded.

"This is Captain Pekach," a metallic voice announced.

"Push the button, Charley," Matt said. "I'll stack this stuff
together."

He read again the page Charley had been reading:

INVESTIGATION REPORT	PHILADELPHIA POLICE DEPARTMENT

Yr | C.C.#	| DIST	| COMPL.#	| INITIAL(49)	| | DIST/UNIT	|
REPORT DATE		SUPPLEMENTAL	|	PREPARING	
CLASSIFICATION		| CODE | CONTINUATION		Homicide/9th Dist.	

PREVIOUS CLASSIFICATION   CODE I DATE AND TIME   I PLACE OF OCCURRENCE

COMPLAINANT	I AGE	I RACE	I ADDRESS	I PHONE	I TYPE OF PREMISES
Alicia Atchison	I 25	I W	I 320 Wilson Avenue, Media, PA		

DATE AND TIME REPORTED   I REPORTED BY   I ADDRESS

FOUNDED ❐ YES ❐ NO   ARREST ❐ CLEARED   ❐ EXCEPTIONALLY CLEARED

STOLEN   I ❐ CURRENCY, BONDS, ETC. ❐ FURS   ❐. AUTOS I RECOVERED VALUE
PROPERTY I ❐ JEWELRY, PRECIOUS METALS ❐ CLOTHING   ❐ MISC   I
INSURED   ❐ YES ❐ NO

DETAILS

    D. INTERVIEWS: (Continued)

    Informative Witnesses: (Continued)

        12. Pontalle, Henriette, 37-W, 220 N. 15th Street,
interviewed by Detective Rocco Andretti #743, on May 20, 1975 at
10:05 a.m., inside Homicide Unit Hdqts.

        Stated - That she is a waitress at the Inferno Lounge &
Restaurant, and that she worked on May 19, 1975 from 12:00 a.m.
until 10:00 p.m. She said business was slow all day. She saw
nothing out of the ordinary during her work. The last time she
saw Mrs. Atchison was about (9:00 p.m. when she had dinner with
her husband and Marcuzzi. She left the Inferno with Marcuzzi on
some sort of business. Atchison was in the Inferno when she went
off duty. Stated that as far as she knew, there was no trouble
between Atchison and his wife, or between Atchison and Marcuzzi.

        13. Melrose, Thomas, 20-W, 2733 N. Portman Street, inter-
viewed by Detective Rocco Andretti #743, on May 20, 1975 at
10:45 a.m., inside Homicide Unit Hdqts.

        Stated - That he is a bartender at the Inferno
Lounge & Restaurant, and that he was working on the night
of May 19, 1975. He went to work at 3:00 p.m. and quit work
shortly after eleven. He said business was slow. He saw
nothing out of the ordinary during the night. Around eleven
p.m., Atchison asked him to stay a couple of minutes more,
as he had business to transact with a customer named

INVESTIGATOR (Type and Sign Name) | SERGEANT   I LIEUTENANT

Rocco Andretti | *Zachary Hobbs*   I
Rocco Andretti   #743 | Zachary Hobbs # 396

75–49 (Rev 3/63)   DETECTIVE DIVISION

INVESTIGATION REPORT	PHILADELPHIA POLICE DEPARTMENT

Yr | C.C.# | DIST |COMPL.# | INITIAL(49) | |DIST/UNIT |
REPORT DATE   SUPPLEMENTAL | PREPARING
CLASSIFICATION |CODE |CONTINUATION   Homicide/9th Dist.

PREVIOUS CLASSIFICATION   CODE | DATE AND TIME |PLACE OF OCCURRENCE

COMPLAINANT |AGE |RACE |ADDRESS |PHONE |TYPE OF PREMISES
Alicia Atchison | 25 | W | 320 Wilson Avenue, Media, PA

DATE AND TIME REPORTED |REPORTED BY   · |ADDRESS

FOUNDED ☐ YES ☐ NO   ARREST ☐ CLEARED   ☐ EXCEPTIONALLY CLEARED

STOLEN |☐CURRENCY, BONDS, ETC. ☐ FURS   ☐. AUTOS |RECOVERED VALUE
PROPERTY |☐ JEWELRY, PRECIOUS METALS ☐CLOTHING ☐ MISC |
INSURED   ☐YES ☐NO

DETAILS

D. INTERVIEWS: (Continued)

   Informative Witnesses: (Continued)

"Frankie" in the office. "Frankie" is a white male approx. 25 years old, and sometimes comes into the Inferno. Stated he does not know what was the nature of the business, but that Atchison sometimes made loans. Atchison and "Frankie" returned to the bar from the office a few minutes at 11 p.m. "Frankie" left the Inferno. Atchison took over the bar. Neither Mrs. Atchison or Marcuzzi were in the bar when he left. Stated that as far as he knew, there was no trouble between Atchison and his wife, or between Atchison and Marcuzzi.

INVESTIGATOR (Type and Sign Name) | SERGEANT |LIEUTENANT

Rocco Andretti | *Zachary Hobbs* |
Rocco Andretti #743 | Zachary Hobbs #396

75–49 (Rev 3/63)   DETECTIVE DIVISION

"Well, what do we do now? Go back to your place?" Detective McFadden inquired of Detective Payne as they came out of the Detective Bureau in the Roundhouse and waited for the elevator.

There had been nothing in the 75-49s on the Kellog job that Matt thought Wohl would be interested in, and nothing much new on the Inferno job that Matt found in Milham's box.

"I don't think so," Matt said. "I think he'll get on the radio when whatever is going to happen at the apartment has happened."

"So where shall we go in that spanking-new unmarked car? You all have cars like that?"

"God loves us."

"Knock that shit off, will you, Matt? It's blasphemous."

"Sorry," Matt said, meaning it. He had trouble remembering that Charley was almost, if not quite, as devoutly Roman Catholic as Mother Moffitt, his grandmother, and took sincere offense at what he had not thought of as anything approaching blasphemy.

"What are you going to do about that name you picked up on in the 75-49?"

"Frankie, you mean?"

"Yeah."

"Wait for Milham, I guess."

"That's my neighborhood, Matt. And I think I know a guy who could probably give us a good line on him. Or are you afraid of spooking him?"

Matt remembered what Milham had said when they had come out of the bar after Milham had told the bartender he was Frankie's cousin from Conshohocken, that he hoped the bartender would tell Frankie a cop had been looking for him, that it would make Frankie nervous.

"No. I get the feeling that Milham would like it if Frankie got a little nervous."

"OK. Let's do that."

"Who are we going to see?"

"Sonny Boyle, we went to St. Monica's at Sixteenth and Porter."

Timothy Francis "Sonny" Boyle, who was twenty-seven years of age, weighed 195 pounds, and stood six feet one inch tall, had not known for the past year or so what to think about Charles Thomas McFadden.

Sonny had decided early on that the world was populated by two kinds of people: those that had to work hard for a living because they weren't too smart, and a small group of the other kind, who didn't have to work hard because they used their heads.

He had been in maybe the second year at Bishop Neuman High School when he had decided he was a member of the small group of the other kind, the kind who lived well by their wits, figuring out the system, and putting it to work for them.

He had known Charley since the second grade at St. Monica's, and liked him, really liked him. But that hadn't stopped him from concluding that Charley was just one more none-too-bright Irish Catholic guy from South Philly who would spend his life doing what other people told him to do, and doing it for peanuts.

He had not been surprised when Charley had gone on the cops. For people like Charley, it was either going into the service, or going on the cops, or becoming a fireman, or maybe in Charley's case, since his father worked in the sewers, getting on with U.G.I., the gas company.

Charley, Sonny had decided when he had heard that Charley had gone on the cops, would spend his life riding around in a prowl car, or standing in the middle of the street up to his ass in snow and carbon monoxide, directing traffic. With a little bit of luck, and the proper connections, he might make sergeant by the time he retired. And in the meantime, he would do what other people told him to do, and for peanuts.

Charley, Sonny had decided, wasn't smart enough to figure out how to make a little extra money as a cop, and if he tried to be smart, he wouldn't be smart enough and would get caught at it.

He had really been surprised to hear that Charley had become a detective. It took him a lot of thought to realize that what it probably was was dumb luck. As asshole named Gerry Gallagher had got himself hooked on drugs, desperately needed money, and had tried to stick up the Waikiki Diner on Roosevelt Boulevard in Northeast Philly.

Tough luck for the both of them, the Commanding Officer of the Highway Patrol, a big mean sonofabitch named Captain "Dutch" Moffitt, had been having his dinner in the Waikiki. He tried to be a hero, and Gallagher was dumb enough to shoot him for trying. Killed him. With a little fucking .22-caliber pistol.

Now the one thing you don't want to do, ever, is shoot a cop, any cop. And Moffitt was a captain, and the Commanding Officer of Highway Patrol. There were eight-thousand-plus cops in Philadelphia, and every last fucking one of them had a hard-on for Gallagher.

If you were white and between sixteen and forty and looked anything like the description the cops put out on the radio, you could count on being stopped by a cop and asked could you prove you weren't at the Waikiki Diner when the Highway Captain got himself shot.

Every cop in Philly was looking for Gallagher. Charley McFadden and his partner, a little Spic named Gonzales or Martinez or one of them Spic names like that, had caught him. They chased him down the subway tracks, near the Frankford-Pratt Station in Northeast Philly where the train is elevated. The dumb sonofabitch slipped and got himself cut in little pieces by a train that had come-along at the wrong time.

Now the cops certainly knew, Sonny had reasoned at the time, that McFadden wasn't Sherlock Holmes, and if he had found Gallagher it had to be dumb luck. That didn't matter.

Charley was a fucking hero. He was the cop who got the guy who shot Captain Dutch Moffitt. Got his picture in the newspapers with Mayor Carlucci and everything.

The next thing Sonny heard was that Charley was now a Highway Patrolman. Highway Patrolmen, everybody knew, were the sharp cops. They *could* find their asses with only one hand. What the hell, Sonny had reasoned, it was a payback. Even if Charley wasn't too smart, he had done what he did, and Highway would make an exception for the guy who had caught the guy who shot the Highway commander.

The next thing Sonny heard about Charley after that was that he was now a detective. That was surprising. Sonny knew that you had to take a test to be a detective, and unless Charley had changed a whole hell of a lot since Bishop Neuman High School, taking tests was not his strong point.

Then Sonny figured that out, too. Charley hadn't been able to cut it as a Highway Patrolman. You couldn't be a dummy and be a Highway Patrolman, and Highway had probably found out about Charley in two or three days.

So what to do with him? Make him a detective. It sounded good, and despite what you saw on the TV and in the movies, all detectives weren't out solving murders and catching big-money drug dealers. A lot of them did things that didn't take too much brains, like looking for stolen cars, and checking pawnshops with a list of what had been heisted lately, things like that.

And then Sonny had heard that there were some Police Department big shots, chief inspectors and the like, who got to have a chauffeur for their cars and to answer their phones, and that sometimes these gofers were detectives.

That's what Charley McFadden was probably doing, Sonny Boyle reasoned. It fit. The Police Department figured they owed him for catching Gallagher, and there was nothing wrong with being a detective, and he could be useful doing something, like driving some big shot around, that other cops would rather not do themselves.

All of this ran through Timothy Francis Boyle's mind when he saw Charles Thomas McFadden walk into Lou's Crab House àt Eleventh and Moyaminsing.

What surprised him now was how Charley was dressed. He looked nice. Not as classy as the young guy with him— the other guy was not a cop; you don't buy threads like he's wearing on what they pay cops—but nice. Nice jacket, nice white shirt, nice slacks, even a nice necktie.

And he was also surprised when McFadden headed for the booth where Sonny was waiting for his runners to bring the cash and numbers to him.

Did he just spot me? Or was he looking for me?

"Well, aren't we in luck?" Charley McFadden said as he slid into the booth beside Sonny. "Timothy Francis Boyle himself, in the flesh!"

"How are you, Charley?" Sonny asked, and smilingly offered his hand. "Nice threads."

"Thanks," Charley said. "Sonny, say hello to my friend Matt Payne."

"Pleased to meet you," Sonny said. He gave the other guy his hand, and was surprised that he wasn't able to give it a real squeeze the way he wanted to. This Payne guy was stronger than he looked like.

"How do you do, Mr. Boyle?" Matt said.

Main Line, Sonny decided. *If he talks like that—like he keeps his teeth together when he talks—and dresses like that, he's from some place like Merion or Bala Cynwyd. I wonder what the fuck he's doing with McFadden.*

"Long time no see," Sonny said. "What brings you down this way?"

Charley put two fingers in his mouth, causing a shrill whistle which attracted the waitress's attention. "Two coffees, darling," he called out. "Put them on Sonny's bill."

"On my bill, my ass," Sonny said.

"For old times' sake, Sonny, right? Besides, I've told Matt you're a successful businessman."

"You did?"

"I told him you are one of the neighborhood's most successful numbers runners and part-time bookies."

"Jesus Christ, Charley, that's not funny."

"Don't be bashful," McFadden said. "He's always been a little bashful, Matt."

"Has he really?" Matt said.

"Yeah. What do you expect, with a name like Francis? That's a girl's name."

"When it's a girl, they spell it with an *e*," Sonny said. "Damn it, you know that." He looked at Matt Payne. "Charley and me go back a long ways. He's always pulling my leg."

Who the fuck is this guy? What the hell is this all about?

One of Sonny's runners—Pat O'Hallihan, a bright, red-headed eighteen-year-old who worked hard, was honest, and for whom Sonny saw a bright future—came into Lou's Crab House, carrying a small canvas zipper bag with his morning's receipts. He stopped when he saw that Sonny was not alone in the booth. Sonny made what he hoped was a discreet gesture telling him to cool it.

It was not discreet enough.

"Turn around, Matthew," McFadden said. "The kid in the red hair? Three to five he's one of Sonny's runners."

Matt turned and looked.

"Is he really?" he asked.

"Charley, you are not funny," Sonny said.

"Who's trying to be funny?" McFadden said. "I was just filling Detective Payne in on the local scumbags."

"Detective" Payne? Is he telling me this Main Line asshole in the three-hundred-fifty-dollar jacket and the fifty-dollar tie is a cop?

"You're a cop?" Sonny's mouth ran away with him.

"Show him your badge, Matthew," McFadden said.

"Sonny—I suppose in his line of work, it's natural—don't trust anybody."

The Main Line asshole reached into the inside breast pocket of his three-hundred-fifty-dollar Harris tweed jacket with leather patches on the elbows and came out with a small folder. He opened it and extended it to Sonny, which afforded Sonny the opportunity to see a Philadelphia Police Department detective's badge and accompanying photo identification.

"You don't look like a cop," Sonny said.

"Don't I really?" Matt asked.

"Detective Payne is with Special Operations," Charley said. "You familiar with Special Operations, Sonny?"

"Sure."

What the fuck is Special Operations? Oh, yeah. That new hotshot outfit. They're over Highway Patrol.

"You know what Detective Payne said when I told him what line of work you're in, Sonny?"

"I don't know what you're talking about."

"Detective Payne said, 'Bookmaking and numbers running is a violation of the law. I think we should find your friend and throw his ass in jail.' Isn't that what you said, Matt?"

"Hmmmm," Matt said thoughtfully. "Yes, that is essentially what I said."

"You're kidding, right?"

"No," Matt said. "I was not speaking in jest."

"I'm getting out of here," Sonny said. "And just for the hell of it, wiseass, you can't search me without a reason, and even if you did, you wouldn't find a thing on me."

"You're not going anywhere, Sonny," McFadden said, and his voice was no longer pleasant. "Until I tell you you can."

"I'll bet, Charles," Matt said, "that if I was to show that young man with the red hair my badge, and ask if he would be kind enough to open his bag for me . . ." He interrupted himself, jumped to his feet, and walked quickly to the red-head.

"I want you to put that bag on that table," he said, showing him his badge. "In sight. And I want you to sit in that booth with your hands flat on the table until I tell you to move. You understand me?"

The redhead followed Matt's pointing, to the last booth in the line.

"Am I busted?" the redhead asked, very nervously.

"If you mean 'arrested,' not yet. And perhaps that can be avoided. It depends on Mr. Boyle."

He waited until the redhead had done what he had ordered him to do, then walked back to the booth and sat down.

"Excuse me, Detective McFadden," he said politely. "Please continue."

"So you bust him, so what?" Sonny said.

"I hope that won't be necessary," Matt said. "But in that unhappy happenstance, you would lose the morning's receipts. That would provide sufficient justification, I would think, Mr. Boyle, for Special Operations to assign whatever police personnel proved to be necessary to save the innocent citizens of this area from gambling czars such as yourself. And I think there is a good possibility that after we have his mother and his parish priest talk to that young man in Central Lockup, he might be willing, to save his soul from eternal damnation, ninety days in prison, and the first entry on his criminal record, to tell us who had given him his present employment, and precisely where and with whom he plied his trade."

"Speaking of which," Charley McFadden said. "The minute the word gets out that the cops have your receipts, you're going to have a lot of winners, Sonny. They're not too smart, but they're smart enough to know if they claim they won, you're either going to have to have a receipt proving they didn't, or pay off. That could be very expensive, Sonny."

"Interesting thought, Detective McFadden," Matt said.

"Thank you, Detective Payne."

Sonny, now visibly nervous, looked between Matt and Charley.

"OK, McFadden," Sonny said. "What do you want?"

"Now that we have you in the right frame of mind, Mr. Boyle," Matt said, "Detective McFadden wishes to probe your presumably extensive knowledge of Philadelphia's criminal community."

"Huh?"

"Tell us about Frankie Foley, Sonny," Charley said.

Oh, shit! I didn't even think about him. What the fuck has Foley done now? Christ, did he hit the Narcotics cop?

"Never heard of him," Sonny said.

"Think hard," Charley said.

Sonny shrugged helplessly.

"Never heard of him, Charley," Sonny said. "I swear to God!"

"You were apparently wrong, Charles," Matt said. "Mr. Boyle will not be cooperative. Mr. Boyle, you are under arrest for violating the laws of the City of Philadelphia and the Commonwealth of Pennsylvania vis-à-vis gambling and participating in an organized gambling enterprise. You have the right to an attorney . . ."

"Jesus Christ, Charley!" Sonny said. "Now wait a minute."

"Remember who he is now, Sonny?" Charley asked.

". . . and if you cannot afford an attorney," Matt went on, "one will be appointed for you." He paused. "I don't seem to have my handcuffs, Charles. Might I borrow yours?"

"Charley, can we talk? Private?" Sonny asked.

"I have other things on my agenda, Mr. Boyle. I don't have time to waste on you," Matt said.

"Matt, Sonny and I go back a long way," Charley said. "Be a good guy. Give me a minute alone with him."

Matt gave this some thought. He looked impatiently at his wristwatch.

"Very well," Matt said. "I will have a word with his accomplice."

He got up and walked to the booth where Pat O'Hallihan sat with his hands obediently on the table.

"I don't like your friend, Charley," Sonny said.

"I don't think he likes you, either. Too bad for you. He's a mean sonofabitch sometimes. You don't know who he is?"

Sonny shook his head.

"He's the guy who popped the Northwest Serial Rapist in the head. Blew his brains out."

"No shit, that's him?"

"That's him."

"Charley, you're going to get me killed," Sonny said. "I'm not shitting you."

"How am I going to get you killed?"

"Frankie Foley's a hit man for the mob. If he finds out I've been talking to you, I'm a dead man."

"An *Irish* hit man for the mob? Come on, Sonny."

"I'm telling you. He does hits they don't want to do themselves."

Sonny looked over at Pat O'Hallihan. Matt Payne had the zipper bag open and was searching through its contents.

"How do you know?" Charley asked.

"I know. I know. Trust me."

"'How do you know?' I asked."

"He . . . uh, Jesus, Charley, you're going to get me killed."

"Think about it, Sonny," Charley said. "When the word gets out that two cops were in here asking you about Frankie Foley, and then hauled you off, Frankie's going to think you told on him anyway."

Sonny Boyle felt sick to his stomach.

"He's come to me a couple times and told me he needed alibis. Usually right after *somebody* hit one of the Guineas."

"Lately?"

"I ain't seen him, I swear to God, in a month."

"Where does he usually hang out?"

"Meagan's Bar."

"He's in the deep shit now, Sonny."

"You think he hit the narc?"

"You tell me, Sonny."

"I ain't heard nothing, Charley, I swear to God."

"Payne wants to lock you up, Sonny. You're going to have to do better than that."

"Christ, I don't know any more than I told you. And that's enough to get me killed. Those Dagos don't fuck around."

"You're going to have to do better than that," Charley repeated.

"I can ask around," Sonny said. "I hear things sometimes."

"I'll bet you do," Charley said.

"I swear to God, if I hear anything, I'll call you."

"I believe you, Sonny," Charley said. "But I don't know about Payne. He wants this guy. He'll do anything to get him."

"You lock me up, all you get is what I already told you," Sonny argued. "Let me ask around, Charley. It makes sense."

Charley considered that for a moment.

"I'll try, Sonny," he said. "I don't know . . ."

"Talk to him, Charley. I'll make it worth your while."

Charley shrugged and walked over to the booth where Matt was now counting thick, rubber-band-bound stacks of one-dollar bills.

Matt got up and walked with Charley to a corner of the room. Charley began to talk to him. Sonny did not think Payne looked at all happy with what Charley was saying.

But finally, after flashing Sonny Boyle a look of utter contempt, he shrugged and walked out of the restaurant. Charley went back to Boyle's booth.

"That took some doing," he said. "My ass is now on the line. Don't fuck with me about this, Sonny. If that mean sonofabitch comes down on me, I'll really come down on you. You understand?"

"Charley, I understand. The first thing I hear—"

"And you better hear something, and soon," Charley interrupted. He laid a calling card on the table, took out a pen, and wrote another number on it. "My home phone is on there. The one I wrote is Special Operations. Call me there, not at Northwest Detectives."

"You're in Special Operations now?"

"I expect to hear from you soon, Sonny," Charley said, and walked out of the restaurant.

Sonny looked out the window and watched him get into a new Ford unmarked car and drive away.

He walked over to where Pat O'Hallihan sat.

"Jesus Christ, what was that all about?" Pat asked.

"Don't worry about it," Sonny said. "Charley McFadden and I are old pals. We were in the same class at Bishop Neuman High School."

"What about the one with me?"

"You were in pretty fancy company. That was Payne. You remember when a detective shot that sicko in the Northwest who was carving up women?"

"That was him?"

"That was him."

"What was this all about?"

"Nothing. Don't worry about it. Everything's under control. Now, order me a cup of coffee. I got to make a telephone call."

"Right."

Sonny Boyle went to the pay phone by the door to the men's room and called Frankie Foley's house. Frankie's mother said he was at work, and gave him the number of the warehouse at Wanamaker's where Frankie worked.

It took some time to get Frankie on the phone—his boss obviously didn't like him getting personal calls at work—but finally he came on the line and Sonny told him that two Special Operations detectives were asking questions about him, that one of the detectives was a real hotshot, the cop that shot the Northwest Serial Rapist in the head, and that they seemed to think Frankie had something to do with the Narcotics cop who got himself hit.

He assured Frankie that of course he hadn't told them a fucking thing.

EIGHTEEN

The radio went off as Matt Payne and Charley McFadden headed north on South Broad Street.

"William Fourteen."

"That's me," Matt said.

Charley looked around, found the microphone on its hook under the dash, and picked it up.

"Fourteen," he said.

"What's your location?"

"South Broad, near City Hall."

"Meet the Inspector at the schoolhouse."

"En route," Charley said, and replaced the microphone. "Well, at least we know where to go," he said.

"I hope we did the right thing," Matt said. "I'll bet your ol' buddy was on the phone before we turned the corner, telling Foley we were asking about him."

"Hey," Charley said, his tone making it clear he thought

it was a naive observation. "What's the difference? Bad guys think there's a cop behind every tree."

Fifteen minutes later, he gave Matt a smug glance when the same question and answer was paraphrased by Inspector Wohl and Sergeant Washington.

"Is this going to cause a problem?" Wohl asked. "Foley will know now we're interested in him."

"Malefactors," Washington intoned solemnly, "in my experience, see the menacing forces of exposure and punishment lurking behind every bush. Often this causes them to do foolish things."

Wohl chuckled.

"I do see a jurisdictional problem," Washington went on. "On one hand, we are interested in Mr. Foley's possible involvement with the Inferno job, which would put him in Wally Milham's basket. On the other, Mr. Boyle suggested Mr. Foley has something to do with Officer Kellog's murder, which would fall into Joe D'Amata's zone of interest. Or possibly mine, if I am to follow allegations of corruption in the Narcotics Five Squad."

Wohl smiled again.

"Going along with your 'menacing forces of exposure and punishment' theory, Jason, it seems to me that you are the most menacing of all."

"I will interpret that as a compliment," Washington said.

"You and Matt were in on the Inferno job from the beginning. So why don't you two go see Mr. Atchison first? Right now, McFadden can go see Joe D'Amata and tell him what Mr. Boyle has had to say, and that I suggest it might be helpful if you were there when he speaks with Mr. Foley."

Washington nodded.

"And then McFadden can go to see Milham at Matt's apartment—"

"Where I devoutly hope he is having at least a modicum of success in trying to convince the Widow Kellog that she should *not* regard me as menacing," Washington interrupted. "And tell me what she knows about Five Squad."

"—and tell him what McFadden's friend has told us about Mr. Foley," Wohl continued. "That will also place Charley at Matt's apartment, where he can work out the sitting-on-Mrs. Kellog schedule with Martinez and Tiny Lewis."

"A masterful display of organizational genius," Washington said.

"And meanwhile, I'll bring Inspector Weisbach in on all this. Any questions?"

McFadden held up his hand.

"How do I get from here to Matt's place, Inspector?"

"Take the car Matt's driving."

"If I went with him, and met Jason . . . where are we going to see Atchison?"

"In the beast's lair," Washington said. "At his home."

"I could pick up my car at the apartment, if I went with Charley."

"Meet me at the Media police station," Washington said. "Where I will be stroking the locals."

"I'll call out there if you like, Jason," Wohl offered.

"Thank you, no. Lieutenant Swann and I are old friends," Washington said. He got to his feet. "I am reluctant to say this, aware as I am of your already monumental egos, but you two done good."

McFadden actually blushed.

"I ally myself with the comments of Sergeant Washington," Wohl said. "Especially the part about your already monumental egos."

Detective Matthew Payne had been inside the Media Police Headquarters before, the circumstances of which came to mind as he pulled the Porsche into a visitors' parking slot outside the redbrick, vaguely Colonial-appearing building in the Philadelphia suburb.

It had been during his last year at Episcopal Academy. He had been in the company of Mr. Chadwick Thomas Nesbitt IV and two females, all of them bound for the Rose Tree Hunt Club. One of the females had been Daffy Browne, he remembered, but he could not recall either the name or the face of the one he'd been with in the backseat of Mr. Chadwick Thomas Nesbitt III's Rolls-Royce Silver Shadow.

He remembered only that he had finally managed to disengage the fastening of her brassiere only moments before a howling siren and flashing lights had announced the presence of the Media Police Department.

Chad was charged with going sixty-eight miles per hour in a forty-mile-per-hour zone; with operating a motor vehicle under the influence of alcohol; with operating a motor vehicle without a valid driver's license in his possession; and operating a motor vehicle without the necessary registration documents therefore.

Chad didn't have a driver's license in his possession because it had been confiscated by his father to make the point that failing two of four Major Curriculum subjects in Mid-Year Examinations was not socially acceptable behavior. He didn't have the registration for the Rolls because he was absolutely forbidden to get behind the wheel of the Rolls under any circumstances, not only while undergoing durance vile. He was driving the Rolls because his parents were spending the weekend in the Bahamas, and he thought they would never know.

Everyone in the Rolls had been charged with unlawful possession of alcoholic beverages by minors. The Rolls was parked on the side of the Baltimore Pike, and all four miscreants (the females sniffling in shame and humiliation) were hauled off to Media Police Headquarters and placed in a holding cell.

It had been necessary to telephone Brewster Cortland Payne II at five minutes to two in the morning. Mr. Payne had arrived at the police station a half hour later, arranged the appropriate bail for the females, and taken them home, leaving a greatly surprised Matt and Chad looking out from behind the holding cell bars.

Brewster Cortland Payne II had a day or two later informed Matt that he had decided spending the night in jail would have a more efficacious effect on Matt (and Chad) than anything he could think of to say at the time.

Matt got out of the Porsche and walked into Police Headquarters.

"Help you?" the sergeant behind the desk asked.

"I'm Detective Payne," Matt said. "I'm supposed to meet Sergeant Washington in Lieutenant Swann's office?"

"Down the corridor, third door on the right."

Washington and Lieutenant Swann, a tall, thin man in his forties, were drinking coffee.

"How are you, Payne?" Lieutenant Swann said after Washington made the introduction. "I know your dad, I think. Providence Road, in Wallingford?"

"Yes, sir," Matt said.

"Known him for years," Lieutenant Swann said.

Is he laughing at me behind that straight face?

"Lieutenant Swann's been telling me that Mr. Atchison is a model citizen," Washington said. "An officer in the National Guard, among other things."

"When we heard about what happened, we thought it was the way it was reported in the papers," Swann said. "This is very interesting."

"Strange things happen," Washington said. "It may have been just the way it was reported in the papers."

"But you don't think so, do you, Jason?"

"I am not wholly convinced of his absolute innocence," Washington said.

"You want me to go over there with you, Jason?"

"I'd rather keep this low-key, if you'll go along," Jason said. "Just drop in to ask him about Mr. Foley."

"Whatever you want, Jason. I owe you a couple."

"The reverse is true, Johnny," Washington said. "I add this to a long list of courtesies to be repaid."

Lieutenant Swann stood up and put out his hand.

"Anytime, Jason. Nice to see you—again—Payne."

Goddamn it, he does remember.

"It was much nicer to come in the front door all by myself," Matt said.

"Well, what the hell," Lieutenant Swann said, laughing. "We all stub our toes once in a while. You seem to be on the straight and narrow now."

"I don't know what that was all about," Washington said, "but appearances, Johnny, can be deceiving."

320 Wilson Avenue, Media, Pennsylvania, was a two-story brick Colonial house sitting in a well-kept lawn on a tree-lined street. A cast-iron jockey on the lawn held a sign reading "320 Wilson, Atchison." There was a black mourning wreath hanging on the door. Decalcomania on the small windows of the white door announced that the occupants had contributed to the Red Cross, United Way, Boy Scouts, and the Girl Scout Cookie Program. When Washington pushed the doorbell, they could hear chimes playing, "Be It Ever So Humble, There's No Place Like Home."

A young black maid in a gray dress answered the door.

"Mr. Atchison, please," Jason said. "My name is Washington."

"Mr. Atchison's not at home," the maid said. The obvious lie made her obviously nervous.

"Please tell Mr. Atchison that Sergeant Washington of the Philadelphia Police Department would be grateful for a few minutes of his time."

She closed the door in their faces. What seemed like a long time later, it reopened. Gerald North Atchison, wearing a crisp white shirt, no tie, slacks, and leaning on a cane, stood there.

"Good afternoon, Mr. Atchison," Washington said cordially. "Do you remember me?"

"Yeah, sure."

"How's the leg?" Washington asked.

For answer, Atchison raised the cane and waved it.

"You remember Detective Payne?"

"Yeah, sure. How are you, Payne?"

"Mr. Atchison."

"We really hate to disturb you at home, Mr. Atchison," Washington said. "But we have a few questions." .

"I was hoping you were here to tell me you got the bastards who did . . ."

"We're getting closer, Mr. Atchison. It's getting to be a process of elimination. We think you can probably help us, if you can spare us a minute or two."

"Christ, I don't know. My lawyer told me I wasn't to answer any more questions if he wasn't there."

"Sidney Margolis is protecting your interests, as he should. But we're trying to keep this as informal as possible. To keep you from having to go to Mr. Margolis's office, or ours."

"Yeah, I know. But . . ."

"Let me suggest this, Mr. Atchison, to save us both time and inconvenience. I give you my word that if you find any of my questions are in any way inconvenient, if you have any doubt whatever that you shouldn't answer them without Mr. Margolis's advice, you simply say 'Pass,' and I will drop that question and any similar to it."

"Well, Sergeant, you put me on a spot. You know I want to cooperate, but Margolis said . . ."

"The decision, of course, is yours. And I will understand no matter what you decide."

Atchison hesitated a moment and then swung the door open.

"What the hell," he said. "I want to be as helpful as I can. I want whoever did what they did to my wife and Tony Marcuzzi caught and fried."

"Thank you very much," Washington said. "There's just a few things that we'd like to ask your opinion about."

"Whatever I can do to help," Atchison said. "Can I have the girl get you some coffee? Or something stronger?"

"I don't know about Matt here, but the detective in me tells me it's very likely that a restaurateur would have some drinkable coffee in his house."

"I have some special from Brazil," Atchison said. "*Bean* coffee. Dark roast. I grind it just before I brew it."

"I accept your kind invitation," Washington said.

"And so do I," Matt said.

"Let me show it to you," Atchison said.

They followed him into the kitchen and watched his coffee-brewing ritual.

Washington, Matt thought, looked genuinely interested.

Finally they returned to the living room.

"Sit down," Atchison said. "Let me know how I can help."

Washington sipped his coffee.

"*Very* nice!"

"I'm glad you like it," Atchison said.

"Mr. Atchison," Washington began. "As a general rule of thumb, in cases like this, we've found that usually robbers will observe a place of business carefully before they act. And we're working on the premise that whoever did this were professional criminals."

"They certainly seemed to know what they were doing," Atchison agreed.

"So it would therefore follow that they did, in fact, more than likely, decide to rob your place of business some time, days, weeks, before they actually committed the crime. That they (a) decided that your establishment was worth their time and the risk involved to rob; and (b) planned their robbery carefully."

"I can see what you mean," Atchison said.

"Would you say that it was common knowledge that you sometimes had large amounts of cash on the premises?"

"I think most bars and restaurants do," Atchison said. "They have to. A good customer wants to cash a check for a couple of hundred, even a thousand, you look foolish if you can't accommodate him."

"I thought it would be something like that," Washington said. "That's helpful."

"And I never keep the cash in the register, either, I always keep it downstairs in the safe. You know that neighborhood, Sergeant, I don't have to tell you. Sometimes, when there's a busy night, I even take large amounts of cash out of the register and take it down and put it in the safe."

"In other words, you would say you take the precautions a prudent businessman would take under the circumstances."

"I think you could say that, yes."

"We've found, over the years—and I certainly hope you won't take offense over the question—that in some cases, employees have a connection with robberies of this nature."

"I guess that would happen."

"Would you mind giving me your opinion of Thomas Melrose?" Washington asked. "He was, I believe, the bartender on duty that night?"

"Tommy went off duty before those men came in," Atchison replied, and then hesitated a moment before continuing: "I just can't believe Tommy Melrose would be involved in anything like this."

"But he was aware that you frequently kept large amounts of cash in your office."

"Yes, I guess he was," Atchison said reluctantly.

"How long has Mr. Melrose been working for you?" Washington asked.

"About nine months," Atchison replied, after thinking about it.

"He came well recommended?"

"Oh, absolutely. You have to be very careful about hiring bartenders. An open cash drawer is quite a temptation."

"Do you think you still have his references? I presume you checked them."

"Oh, I checked them, all right. And I suppose they're in a filing cabinet someplace."

"When you feel a little better, Mr. Atchison, do you think we could have a look at them?"

"Certainly."

"Mr. Melrose said that business was slow the night of this incident."

"Yes, it was."

"He said there was, just before he went off duty, only one customer in the place; and that when that last customer left, you took over for him tending bar."

"That's right. I did. You have to stay open in a bar like mine. Even if there's no customers. There might be customers coming in after you closed, and the next time they wanted a late-evening drink, they'd remember you were closed and go someplace else."

"I understand."

"The one customer who left just before you took over from Mr. Melrose: Do you remember him? I mean, was there anything about him? You don't happen to remember his name?"

Atchison appeared to be searching his memory. He shook his head and said, "Sorry."

Washington stood up. "Well, I hate to leave good company, and especially such fine coffee, but that's all I have. Thank you for your time, Mr. Atchison."

"Have another before you go," Atchison said. "One for the road."

"Thank you, no," Washington said. "I think Mr. Melrose said the customer was named Frankie. Does that ring a bell, Mr. Atchison?"

Atchison shook his head again. "No. Sorry."

"Probably not important," Washington said. "I would have been surprised if you had remembered him, Mr. Atchison. Thank you again for your time."

He put his hand out.

"Anything I can do to help, Sergeant," Atchison said.

"Cool customer," Jason Washington said with neither condemnation nor admiration in his voice, making it a simple professional judgment.

"You gave him two chances to remember Frankie Foley," Matt said.

"It will be interesting to see if Mr. Foley remembers Mr. Atchison," Washington said, and then changed the subject: "Did your father really leave you in durance vile overnight?"

"Swann told you, did he?"

"Your father's wisdom made quite an impression on Lieutenant Swann," Washington said. "And you haven't been behind bars since, have you?"

"No," Matt said, and then thought aloud: "Unless you want to count the time those Narcotics assholes hauled me off the night Tony the Zee got himself hit."

"I'm not sure you have considered the possibility that the Narcotics officers were simply doing their job."

"Taking great pleasure in what they were doing."

"Well, the tables have turned, haven't they? They thought they had a dirty cop. And now you're going to see if it can be proved that they are dirty."

"Am I going to work on that?"

"You and everybody else. Compared to coming up with something on the Narcotics Five Squad that will result in indictments, bringing Atchison before a grand jury will be fairly easy."

"How come?"

"We have a crime scene on the Inferno job, and other evidence. We have two good suspects. I think we can get a motive without a great deal of effort. A good deal of shoe leather may be required, but it isn't a question of *if* we will get Atchison, but *when*. So far as the Narcotics Five Squad is concerned, we don't know what they have done, only that they have done it, and we don't know what 'it' is, except the Widow Kellog's definition of 'it' as dirty."

"You can't get any specifics out of her?"

"Not a one," Washington replied. "But I believe she believes she is telling the truth that the whole squad is dirty. And to support that, they do own, without a mortgage, a condominium at the shore, and a boat. Their combined, honestly acquired, income is not enough to pay for those sorts of luxuries. And then we have the threatening telephone call."

"How do you think Five Squad heard she had talked to you?"

"There's no way that they could have. I think the simple explanation for that is that someone on Five Squad knew that Homicide would be talking to her, and they didn't want her volunteering any information."

"And you think that's why Kellog was killed?"

"It looks to me as if there are two possibilities, one of which no one seems to have considered very much. That he was killed in connection with his honest labor as a Narcotics officer. He knew something—where are the tapes from his tape recorder?—and had to be silenced. And of course it is entirely possible that he was killed by someone on the Five Squad for the same reason. His wife had left him. He might have wanted her back bad enough . . ."

"Milham and Mrs. Kellog seem pretty tight; I don't think she was going to go back to her husband."

"I noticed that," Washington said. "But neither of us have any way of knowing what Kellog was thinking, perhaps irrationally. Losing your wife to another man is traumatic. If she left him because of what he was doing, or, more to the point, because of what it was doing to him, and thus to their relationship, it's entirely possible that he thought by *stopping* what he was doing he might be able to get her back. Whatever was on those tapes that we can't find might have been his insurance."

"Excuse me?" Matt interrupted. He was having trouble following Washington's reasoning; the introduction of the missing tapes left him wholly confused.

"I'm quitting, I'm through," Washington said. "I'm not going to squeal, but just to keep anyone from getting any clever ideas, I have tapes of whatever that will wind up in the hands of Internal Affairs if anything happens to me."

"This is starting to sound like a cops show on television," Matt said. "A very convoluted plot."

"Yes," Washington said thoughtfully. "It does. And that bothers me." He was silent for a moment, then changed the subject. "For a number of reasons, including not wanting Wally Milham to think I'm pushing him out of the way, I am not going with you when you chat with Mr. Foley."

"OK," Matt said. "You going to tell me the other reasons?"

"I'll take you back to the Media police station," Washington said, ignoring the question. "We will get Wally Milham on the telephone and decide where you are to meet. Then you can get in your car and meet him. Relay to him in appropriate detail the essence and the ambience of our conversation with Mr. Atchison."

"OK."

Officer Paul Thomas O'Mara, Inspector Wohl's administrative assistant, knocked on Wohl's office door, and then, without waiting for a reply, pushed it open.

"Mr. Giacomo for Inspector Weisbach on Four," he announced.

Staff Inspector Michael Weisbach was sitting slumped on Wohl's couch, his legs stretched out in front of him, balancing a cup of coffee on his chest.

Wohl, behind his desk, picked up one of the telephones and punched a button.

"Peter Wohl, Armando," he said. "How are you? How odd that you should call. Mike and I were just talking about you. Here he is."

Weisbach smiled as he walked behind Wohl's desk and took the telephone. They had not been talking about Giacomo. They had been discussing the time-consuming difficulty they would have in investigating the personal finances of the Narcotics Five Squad, and the inevitability that their interest would soon become known.

"Hello, Armando," Weisbach said. "What can I do for you?"

He moved the receiver off his ear so that Wohl could hear the conversation.

"I wanted you to know I haven't forgotten our conversation at luncheon, Mike, and that I have already begun to accumulate some information—nothing yet that I'd feel comfortable about passing on to you—but I am beginning to hear some interesting things. I need some time, you'll understand, to make certain that what I pass on to you is reliable."

"My heart is always warmed, Armando, when citizens such as yourself go out of their way to assist the police."

Wohl chuckled.

"I consider it my civic duty," Giacomo said.

"Armando, perhaps I could save you some time, keep you from chasing a cat, so to speak, that's already nearly in the bag. In our own plodding way, we have come up with a name. What I'm getting at, Armando, is that it would bother me if you came up with a name we already have, and you would still figure we owed you."

"What's the name?"

"Frankie Foley," Weisbach said.

"He wasn't, between us, one of the names I heard. Frankie Foley?"

"Frankie Foley."

"How interesting."

"Nice to talk to you, Armando," Weisbach said. "I appreciate the call."

He hung up.

"Why did you give him Foley's name?" Wohl asked. "A question, not a criticism."

"By now, Foley probably knows we're looking at him. If he told Giacomo, or the mob found out some other way, Italian blood being stronger than Irish water, they may have decided to give him to us to keep Cassandro out of jail."

"Michael, you are devious. I say that as a compliment."

"So maybe, with Foley taken off the table, Giacomo may come up with another name."

Frankie Foley waited impatiently, time card in hand, for his turn to punch out. He really hated Wanamaker's, having to spend all day busting open crates, breaking his hump shoving furniture around, and for fucking peanuts.

It would, he consoled himself, soon be over. He could tell Stan Wisznecki, his crew chief, to shove his job up his ass. He would go to work in the Inferno, get himself some decent threads with the money Atchison owed him, and wait for the next business opportunity to come along. And he wasn't going to do the next hit for a lousy five thousand dollars. He'd ask for ten, maybe even more, depending on who he had to hit.

Frankie had been a little disappointed with the attention, or lack of it, paid to the Inferno hit by the newspapers and TV. There had been almost nothing on the TV, and only a couple of stories in the newspapers.

He had, the day after he'd made the Inferno hit, clipped out Michael J. O'Hara's story about it from the *Bulletin* with the idea of keeping it, a souvenir, like of his first professional job.

But after he'd cut it out he realized that might not be too smart. If the cops got his name somehow, and got a search warrant or something, and found it, it would be awkward explaining what he was doing with it.

Not incriminating. What the fuck could they prove just because he'd cut a story out of the newspaper? He could tell them he'd cut it out because he drank in the Inferno. Shit, if they pressed him, he could say he cut it out because he had fucked Alicia Atchison.

But it was smarter not to have it, so he had first crumpled up the clipping and tossed it in the toilet, and then, when he thought that the front page now had a hole in it where the story had been, tore off the whole front page and sliced it up with scissors and flushed the whole damn thing down the toilet. He really hated to throw the story away, but knew that it was the smart thing to do.

And anyway, the word would get out who'd done the hit among the people who mattered. That was what mattered.

He knew he'd done the right thing, not keeping the clipping, when Tim McCarthy, who ran Meagan's Bar for his father-in-law, called him up and told him that a couple of cops had been in the bar, asking about him, and giving Tim some bullshit that one of them was a cousin from Conshohocken.

What that meant, Frankie decided professionally, was that his name had come up somehow. That was to be expected. He drank at the Inferno, and he had been in there the night he'd made the hit. The cops probably had a list of two hundred people who drank in the Inferno. They probably got his name from the bartender. Which was the point. He was only one more name they would check out. And the bartender, if he had given the cops his name, would also have told them that he had left the Inferno long before the hit.

The cops didn't have a fucking thing to connect him with the hit, except Atchison, of course, and Atchison couldn't say a fucking word. It would make him an accessible, or whatever the fuck they called it.

He hadn't been too upset, either, when Sonny Boyle had called him to tell him two detectives had been to see him about him. He had been sort of flattered to learn who they were. One of them was the cop that had caught up with the guy who shot the Highway Patrol captain, and the other detective was the guy who had shot the pervert in Northwest Philly who was cutting the teats off women. What that was, Frankie decided professionally, was that the ordinary cops and detectives was having trouble finding him. He didn't have no record, for one thing, and the phone was in his mother's name. So when the ordinary cops couldn't find him, the hotshots had started looking for him.

Well, fuck the hotshots too. They would eventually find him—it would be kind of interesting to see how long finding him took—and they would ask him questions. *Yeah, I was in the Inferno that night. I go in there all the time. I been talking to Mr. Atchison about maybe becoming his headwaiter. Where was I at midnight? I was home in bed. Ask my mother. No, I don't have no idea who might have shot them two. Sorry.*

The dinge ahead of him in line finally figured out how to get his time card punched and Frankie stepped to the time clock, punched out, put the card in the rack, and walked out of the building.

He had gone maybe thirty feet down the street when there was a guy walking on each side of him. The one on his right had a mustache, one of the thin kind you probably have to trim every day. The other one was much younger. He didn't look much like a cop, more like a college kid.

"Frank Foley?" the one with the mustache asked.

"Who wants to know?"

"We're police officers," the guy with the mustache said.

"No shit? What do you want with me?"

"You are Frank Foley?"

"Yeah, I'm Frank Foley. You got a badge or something?"

The guy with the mustache produced a badge.

"I'm Detective Milham," he said. "And this is Detective Payne."

Frankie took a second look at the kid.

"You the guy who shot that pervert in North Philly? The one who was cutting up all them women?"

"That's him," Milham said.

"I'll be goddamned," Frankie said, putting out his hand. "I thought you'd be older. Let me shake your hand. It's a real pleasure to meet you."

The kid looked uncomfortable.

Modesty, Frankie decided.

Frankie was genuinely pleased to meet Detective Payne.

This guy is a real fucking detective, Frankie decided, *somebody who had also shot somebody. Professionally. When you think about it, what it is is that we're both professionals. We just work the other side of the street, is all.*

"Detective Payne," Milham said, "was also involved in

the gun battle with the Islamic Liberation Army. Do you remember that?"

Payne looked at Milham with mingled surprise and annoyance.

"The dinges that robbed Goldblatt's?" Frankie asked.
"That was you, too?"

"That was him," Milham said.

"Mr. Foley, we're investigating the shooting at the Inferno Lounge," Matt said.

"Wasn't that a bitch?" Frankie replied. "Jesus, you don't
think I had anything to do with that, do you?"

"We just have a few questions we'd like to ask," Matt said.

"Such as?"

"Mr. Foley," Wally Milham said, "would you be willing to
come to Police Administration with us to make a statement?"

"A statement about what?"

"We've learned that you were in the Inferno Lounge that
night."

"Yeah, I was. I stop in there from time to time. I guess I
was there maybe an hour before what happened happened."

"Well, maybe you could help us. Would you be willing to
come with us?" Wally asked.

"How long would it take?"

"Not long. We'd just like to get on record what you might
have seen when you were there. It might help us to find the
people who did it."

*The smart thing for me to do is look like I'm willing to
help. And what the fuck choice do I have?*

"Yeah, I guess I could go with you," Frankie said.

"We've got a car right over there, Mr. Foley," Matt said.
"And when we're finished, we'll see that you get wherever
you want to go."

Frankie got in the backseat of the car and saw for himself
that the story that went around that once you got in the backseat of a cop car, you couldn't get out until they let you; that
there was no handles in the backseat was bullshit. This was
like a regular car; the handles worked.

He got a little nervous when he saw the two detectives having a little talk before they got in themselves. They had their backs to him, and talked softly, and he didn't hear what Detective Milham said to Detective Payne:

"This asshole thinks you're hot shit, Matt. Sometimes that means they'll run off at the mouth. When we get to the Roundhouse, you interview the sonofabitch. Charm the bastard."

"You think he did it?"

"This fucker is crazy. Let's see what he has to say."

STATEMENT OF: John Francis "Frankie" Foley

DATE AND TIME: 5:40 p.m. May 22, 1975

PLACE: Homicide Division, Police Admin. Bldg. Room A.

CONCERNING: Robbery/Homicide at Inferno Lounge

IN PRESENCE OF: Det. Wallace J. Milham, Badge 626

INTERROGATED BY: Det. Matthew M. Payne, Badge 701

RECORDED BY: Mrs. Jo-Ellen Garcia-Romez, Clerk/typist

I AM Detective Payne. This is Mrs. Garcia-Romez, who will be recording everything we say on the typewriter.

We are questioning you concerning the murder homicide at the Inferno Lounge.

We have a duty to explain to you and to warn you that you have the following legal rights:

A. You have the right to remain silent and do not have to say anything at all.

B. Anything you say can and will be used against you in Court.

75-331D(Rev.7/70)   Page 1

C. You have a right to talk to a lawyer of your own choice before we ask you any questions, and also to have a lawyer here with you while we ask questions.

D. If you cannot afford to hire a lawyer, and you want one, we will see that you have a lawyer provided to you, free of charge, before we ask you any questions.

E. If you are willing to give us a statement, you have a right to stop anytime you wish.

1. Q. Do you understand that you have a right to keep quiet and do not have to say anything at all?
A. Yeah. I understand.

2. Q. Do you understand that anything you say can and will be used against you?
A. Did I miss something? Am I arrested or something?

3. Q. Do you want to remain silent?
A. No.

4. Q. Do you understand you have a right to talk to a lawyer before we ask you any questions?
A. Yeah, but what you guys said was just that you wanted to talk to me.

5. Q. Do you understand that if you cannot afford to hire a lawyer, and you want one, we will not ask you any questions until a lawyer is appointed for you free of charge?
A. Yes, I do.

6. Q. Do you want to talk to a lawyer at this time, or to have a lawyer with you while we ask you questions?
A. I don't have nothing to hide.

7. Q. Are you willing to answer questions of your own free will, without force or fear, and without any threats and promises having been made to you?
A. Yeah, yeah, get on with it.

(Det. Milham) Frankie, to clear things up in your
mind. That's what they call the Miranda questions.
Everybody we talk to gets the same questions.

A: Am I arrested, for Christ's sake, or not?

(Det. Milham) You are not under arrest.

A: You had me worried there for a minute.

8. Q. For the record, Mr. Foley, state your name,
city of residence, and employment.
    A. Frank Foley, Philadelphia. Right now, I work
for Wanamaker's.

9. Q. Mr. Foley, were you in the Inferno Lounge the
night there was a double murder there?
    A. Yeah, I was. Just before midnight.

10. Q. What were you doing there?
    A. I stopped in for a drink. I drink there every
once in a while.

11. Q. That's all? Just for a drink?
    A. I been talking with Atchison, the guy who
owns it, about maybe going to work there as the
headwaiter.

12. Q. Does the Inferno have a headwaiter?
    A. Well, you know what I mean. I'd sort of keep
an eye on things. That's a pretty rough neighborhood, you know what I mean.

13. Q. Oh, you mean sort of be the bouncer?
    A. They don't like to use that word. But yeah,
sort of a bouncer.

14. Q. You have experience doing that sort of thing?
    A. Not really. But I was a Marine. I can take
care of myself. Handle things. You know.

15. Q. When you were in Inferno, the night of the
shooting, did you talk to Mr. Atchison about your
going to work for him?
    A. I guess we talked about it. When I came in,
we went to his office for a drink. I don't remember
exactly what we talked about, but maybe we did. We
been talking about it all along.

16. Q. You went to his office? You didn't drink at
the bar?
    A. Mr. Atchison don't like to buy people drinks
at the bar. You know. So we went downstairs to his
office.

17. Q. Was Mrs. Atchison in the Inferno when you
were there?
   A. No. He said she and Marcuzzi went somewheres.

18. Q. You knew Mrs. Atchison?
   A. Yeah, you could put it that way. Nice-looking
broad. Had a roving eye, you know what I mean?

19. Q. You knew her pretty well, then?
   A. Not as well as I would have liked to.

20. Q. Tell us exactly what you did when you went to
the Inferno?
   A. Well, I went in, and had a drink at the bar,
and then Atchison came over, and asked me to go to
the office, and we had a drink down there. And then
I left.

21. Q. How long would you say you were in the Inferno?
   A. Thirty minutes, tops. Ten minutes, maybe, in
the bar and then fifteen, twenty minutes down in his
office.

22. Q. We've heard that Mr. Atchison used to keep a
lot of money in the office. That he used to make
loans. You ever hear that?
   A. Yeah, sure. He did that. That was one of the
reasons we was talking about me working for him.
People sometimes don't pay when they're supposed to.

23. Q. And you were going to help him collect his
bad debts.
   A. Not only that. Just be around the place. Keep
the peace. You know.

24. Q. When you were in the Inferno, did you notice
anything out of the ordinary?
   A. No. If you're asking did I see anybody in
there who looked like they might be thinking of
sticking the place up, hell no. If I'd have seen
anything like that, I would have stuck around.

25. Q. You said Mrs. Atchison had a roving eye. Do you think that what happened there had anything to do with that? Was she playing around on the side, do you think?

A. Well, she may have been. Like I said, she seemed to like men. But I don't know nothing for sure.

26. Q. When you left the Inferno, where did you go?

A. Home. It was late.

27. Q. Have you got any idea who might have robbed the Inferno and killed those two people?

A. There's a lot of people in Philadelphia who do that sort of thing for a living. Have I got a name? No.

28. Q. That's about all I have. Unless Detective Milham...?

A. (Det. Milham) No. I think that's everything. Thank you, Mr. Foley.

29. Q. (Mr. Foley) Could I ask a question?

(Det. Payne) Certainly.

(Mr. Foley) When you shot that nutcase who was cutting up the women, what did you use?

(Det. Payne) My .38 snub-nose.

(Mr. Foley) And on the dinge who did the Goldblatt job? Same gun?

(Det. Payne) Yes.

(Mr. Foley) You got more balls than I do. If my life was on the line, I'd carry a .45 at least. You ever see what a .45'll do to you?

(Det. Payne) Yes, I have. But we can carry only weapons that are authorized by the Department.

(Mr. Foley) That's bullshit.

(Det. Payne) Off the record, I agree with you.

(Mr. Foley) Sometime maybe, I'll see you around, we'll have a beer or something, and we can talk about guns. I was in the Marine Corps. They teach you about guns.

(Det. Payne) I'd like to do that.

(Det. Milham) I think that's all, Mr. Foley. Thank you for your time and cooperation.

(Mr. Foley) That's all? I'm through?

(Det. Milham) That's all. Thank you very much.

NINETEEN

"Frankie's in love with Matt," Wally Milham said. "He wants to buy him a drink and tell him about guns."

"Jesus Christ!" Matt said.

Jason Washington raised his hand somewhat imperiously and made a circling motion with his extended index finger, as a signal to the waitress that he wanted another cup of espresso.

They were in Café Elana, a new (and rather pretentious, Matt thought) Italian coffeehouse in Society Hill.

"That sometimes happens," Washington said, returning his attention to the table. "I think it has more to do with Matt representing authority than his charming personality. You might find it interesting, Matthew, to discuss the phenomenon with your sister."

"In this case, it's because Matt shoots people," Milham said. "Frankie found that fascinating."

"Frankie found a kindred soul, in other words?" Washington asked, nodding. "Let's think about that."

"There's something wrong with that guy," Matt said.

"There's something wrong, as you put it, with most people who commit homicide," Washington said. "Or did you have something special in mind?"

"He seems detached from reality," Matt said. "The only time he seemed at all concerned with having been picked up and taken to a Homicide interview room was when I went through the Miranda business; that made him worry that he had been arrested. But even that didn't seem to bother him very much. As soon as Wally told him he wasn't under arrest . . ."

"Matthew, you realize, I hope, that the moment he was told that he wasn't under arrest, all the ramifications of his being informed of his Miranda rights became moot."

"I thought going through the routine might unnerve him," Matt said. "And I didn't get anywhere close to asking him about his involvement in either the robberies or the murders. I just asked him if he was in the Inferno, what he was doing there, and if he saw anything out of the ordinary."

"No harm done in this case," Washington said, "but you were close to the edge of the precipice."

"Matt asked me before he gave him the Miranda." Wally came to Matt's defense. "It made sense to me. He's right, there is something wrong with this guy. I agreed that it might shake him up, and I told him not to get into the murder itself. Either the Inferno murders, or Kellog's."

"Then, Wallace," Washington pronounced, "the two of you were teetering on the precipice, in grave risk of providing a defense counsel six weeks out of law school with an issue that would cloud the minds of the jurors."

Washington let the criticism sink in for a moment, then went on: "Having said that, it was not a bad idea. Professor Washington just wanted to make the point in his Homicide 101 Tutorial for Detective Payne that there are enormous risks in dancing around Miranda. In my experience, the more heinous the crime alleged, the greater the concern from the bench about the rights of the accused."

"I didn't turn Matt loose, Jason," Milham said, his annoyance at the lecture visible and growing as he spoke. "And he wasn't a loose cannon. I was prepared to shut him off if he was getting into something he shouldn't have. I didn't have to."

"I intended no offense, Wallace," Washington said. "Nevertheless, my observations were in order. It would offend me if, because of some procedural error, Mr. Foley and Mr. Atchison got away with what they did."

"OK," Milham said.

"I have the feeling that neither of you feel Foley was involved with Officer Kellog's murder. Is that—"

"He's tied to the Inferno," Milham said. "Atchison says he doesn't know Frankie, and Frankie tells us he's going to work there as a bouncer."

"Unless, of course, he is in fact a contract killer," Washington said. "While I was waiting for you two to show up, I considered the anomaly of a nice Irish boy being so employed by the mob. Unusual, of course, but not impossible. I read the 75-49s on the Kellog job. There was nothing of great value stolen from the house. The only thing Mrs. Kellog reported as missing were her wedding and engagement rings. She left them there when she left Officer Kellog. Some other minor items are missing: a silver frame, holding their wedding picture; a portable television; and a silver coffee service. The street value of everything would not exceed two or three hundred dollars. And, of course, the tapes from the telephone recording device. Not enough for a burglar to kill over. The manner, the professional manner, so to speak, in which Officer Kellog was shot suggests assassination, rather than anything else. Perhaps the tapes were what his murderer was after."

"Narcotics Five Squad?" Milham said doubtfully. "Jason, I have trouble thinking . . ."

"As do I. Unless what was on those tapes was so incriminating that desperate measures were required. Or . . ."

"Or what?"

"What was on those tapes was incriminating vis-à-vis the mob. The decision was made to eliminate Officer Kellog and get the tapes. And to put distance between the mob and any Narcotics involvement, or involvement between the mob and the Narcotics Five Squad, an outside contract killer was employed. Perhaps Matt's admirer. I don't think we should conclude that Mr. Foley was not involved with Officer Kellog's murder."

"If this character is a hit man, and I have trouble with that—he's not that smart—why the hell is he working at Wanamaker's?" Milham said.

"Interesting question," Washington said. "There are all sorts of possible explanations. For example, let us suppose that Mr. Foley has been engaged, by the mob, as a loan shark among the Wanamaker's warehouse labor force. He secured the repayment of a loan under such violent conditions that it came to the attention of the mob that here was a young man of reliability and ambition, perhaps suited for more important things."

"Hell, why not?" Milham said.

"Letting my imagination run free," Washington said, "I tried to come up with a credible scenario as to why Mr. Atchison lied to us about Mr. Foley. He is no fool, and he must have known that we would learn from the bartender that Mr. Foley was in there that night. Let us suppose that Mr. Atchison knows, or suspects, that Mr. Foley has a mob connection. Let us suppose further that Mr. Atchison has been having difficulty of some sort with the mob. Or Mr. Marcuzzi was in some sort of difficulty with them. Mr. Marcuzzi was hit, with Mrs. Atchison as an innocent bystander, so to speak. Mr. Atchison was spared, with a warning, explicit or implied, to keep his mouth shut. Knowing or suspecting that Mr. Foley has a mob connection, he was reluctant to point a finger at him. I was taken with his lack of concern for Mr. Marcuzzi. It is possible that he knew what Marcuzzi had been up to and decided that he had gotten his just deserts."

"You mean, you don't think Frankie did the Inferno job?" Matt asked.

"I didn't say that," Washington said. "What I'm saying is that we have yet to come up with a motive for Mr. Atchison being involved in the deaths of his wife and partner. No large amount of recently acquired insurance, et cetera, et cetera."

"And if we confront Atchison with lying about Foley, he confesses to running a loan-shark operation with Foley as the enforcer," Matt said.

"Precisely," Washington said. "And we have little physical evidence, except for the bullets removed from the bodies of Mrs. Atchison and Mr. Marcuzzi. That's useless unless we have the guns and can tie them to Foley or somebody else. Maybe there were two robbers."

"Well, we could send Matt to have a drink with Frankie and talk about guns," Milham said jokingly.

"He might not be too sharp, but he's shrewd," Matt said. "I don't think I'd get anything from him."

"Neither do I, but let's think that through," Washington said.

"Jesus!" Matt said. "Can I let my imagination run free?"

"Certainly."

"Foley likes to talk. Boast. I have the feeling that working in Wanamaker's embarrasses him."

"So?"

"So maybe he would boast to somebody else."

"I don't follow you, Matthew," Washington said. There was a tone of impatience in his voice.

"A guy comes up to him in a bar. Tells him he's heard that Frankie has connections. Maybe tells him he wants to buy a gun."

"That's stretching, Payne," Milham said. "You don't

think he's going to sell the guns he used at the Inferno, do
you? They're probably at the bottom of the river."

Matt met Washington's eyes.

"Hay-zuz," he said. "Wearing all his gold chains."

It was a full thirty seconds before Washington spoke.

"I think Matthew may have something."

"Hay-zus?" Milham asked.

"Detective Jesus Martinez," Washington said. "Let me
run this past Lieutenant Natali, maybe Captain Quaire, too.
It would help if I could say the assigned detective had no objections."

"Anything that works," Milham said.

"I would suggest to you, Matthew, that while Mr. Foley
presented a picture of complete composure in the Roundhouse, he may start to worry when he has had time to think
things over. It is also possible that he may communicate
with Mr. Atchison, or vice versa, which may make Mr.
Atchison less confident than he was when we left him. In
any event, there is nothing else that I can see that any of us
can do today. I suggest we hang it up for the night."

"I'll see if I can get anything out of Helene," Milham
said. "And I'll check with Homicide and see if anything new
has come up."

Every evening except Sunday, between 8:00 and 8:15 P.M.
an automobile, most often a new Buick, stopped near the
middle of the 1200 block of Ritner Street in South Philadelphia. A man carrying a small zipper bag would get out of the
passenger seat, walk to the door of the residence occupied
by Mr. and Mrs. Timothy Francis "Sonny" Boyle, and ring
the bell.

The door would be opened, the man would enter, and the
door would be closed. Usually less than a minute later, the
door would reopen, and the man, still carrying what appeared to be the same small zipper bag, would appear, de-
scend the stairs, and get back in the car, which would then
drive off.

There were, in fact, two bags. The bag the man carried into the house would more often than not be empty. The bag the man carried from the house would contain the records of Mr. Boyle's business transactions of that day, and the cash proceeds therefrom, less Mr. Boyle's commission.

Mr. Boyle was in the numbers business. His clientele would "buy a number," that is select a number between 000 and 999. The standard purchase price was one dollar. If the number selected "came up," that is, corresponded to the second comma-separated trio of numbers of activity on the New York Stock Exchange for that day, the lucky number holder received $500. For example, if 340,676,000 shares were traded on the stock exchange on one particular day, the winning number would be 676, and anyone who had purchased number 676 could exchange his receipt for his purchase for $500.

The operation of Mr. Boyle's business was quite simple. Most of the sales were conducted through small retail businesses, candy stores, grocery stores, newspaper stands, and the like. Individual customers would buy a number and be given a receipt. The storekeeper would turn over his carbon copy of the number selected, and his cash receipts (less a ten percent commission for his trouble), to one of Mr. Boyle's runners. The numbers runner would in turn pass the carbons and the receipts to Mr. Boyle, for which service he was paid five percent of total receipts. Mr. Boyle would prepare a list of numbers purchased from the carbons, and put the carbons and the cash, less ten percent for his commission, into the zipper bag for collection by the gentleman who called at his home each evening.

Sale of numbers was closed off at half past two in the afternoon. The New York Stock Exchange closed at three. By three-fifteen, the day's transactions had been reported on radio and television, and Mr. Boyle was made aware which number had hit, if any. Or, far more commonly, that no number had been hit. Or, far less commonly, that two or three individuals had purchased numbers that had hit. Only once in

Mr. Boyle's experience (and he had been a runner before becoming a "numbers man" himself) had five individuals bought a number that had hit. He considered it far more probable that he would be struck by lightning than for it to happen that six individuals would select the same winning number.

But in any event, the laws of probability were not Mr. Boyle's concern. All winning numbers were paid by his employers and did not come out of his pocket. When a number did hit, Mr. Boyle almost always had sufficient funds from that day's receipts to pay it. If winnings exceeded receipts, a rare happenstance, he would make a telephone call and there would be enough cash in the zipper bag brought to his door to make payment, which was religiously made the next business day.

At 7:15 P.M. Mr. Boyle was sitting in his shirtsleeves at his kitchen table concluding the administration of the day's business when he heard the doorbell ring.

He was idly curious, but did not allow it to disturb his concentration. His work was important, and he took pride in both his accuracy, his absolute honesty, both to his clients and to his employers, and his timeliness. He had failed only twice to be ready when the man with the bag appeared at his door. His wife, Helen, moreover, had strict orders that he was not to be disturbed when he was working unless the house was on fire.

The kitchen table was covered with carbons of numbers selected that day, which would be forwarded, and with stacks of money, folded in half, and kept together with rubber bands. The folded stacks of money—the day's receipts—were predominantly dollar bills, but with the odd five-, ten-, and twenty-dollar bills assembled in their own stack. There were also three stacks of tens, crisp new bills, bound by paper strips bearing the logotype of the Philadelphia Savings Fund Society, and marked "$500."

These crisp new ten-dollar bills would be used to pay yesterday's winners, those whose number had come up. This, Mr. Boyle believed, had a certain public relations aspect.

He could have, of course, paid the winners from the day's receipts. There were a lot of people who would say money is money, it doesn't matter where it comes from, so long as it can be spent. But Sonny believed that winners were happier to receive a stack of crisp new bills than they would be had he paid them with battered old currency, no telling where the hell it's been. It made them feel better, and if they felt better, they would not only keep picking numbers, but would flash the wad of new bills around, very likely encouraging their friends and neighbors to put a buck, or a couple of bucks, on the numbers.

The swinging door from the dining room opened.

"Honey," Helen said, to get his attention.

Sonny looked up at her with annoyance. She knew the rules.

"What?" he asked, less than politely.

"Mr. D'Angelo is here," Helen said.

Marco D'Angelo was Mr. Boyle's immediate supervisor. He normally drove the Buick which appeared ritualistically between 8:00 and 8:15 P.M., looking up and down the street as his assistant went into the Boyles' residence.

As Sonny understood the hierarchy, Mr. D'Angelo worked directly for Mr. Pietro Cassandro. Mr. Pietro Cassandro was the younger brother of Mr. Paulo Cassandro, who was, as Sonny understood it, a made man, and who reported directly to Mr. Vincenzo Savarese, who was, so to speak, the Chairman of the Board.

Sonny didn't *know* this. But it was what was said. And he had not considered it polite to ask specific questions.

Sonny glanced at his watch. Marco D'Angelo was not due for another forty-five minutes.

"He's here? Now? What time is it?"

Mr. D'Angelo appeared in the kitchen.

"Whaddaya say, Sonny?" he said. "Sorry to barge in here like this."

"Anytime, Marco," Sonny replied. "Can I get you something?"

"Thank you, no," Mr. D'Angelo said. "Sonny, Mr. Cassandro would like a word with you. Would that be all right?"

"I'm doing the day's business," Sonny said, gesturing at the table.

"This won't take long," Mr. D'Angelo said. "Just leave that. So we'll be a little late, so what, it's not the end of the world. Finish up when you come back."

"Whatever you say, Marco," Sonny said. "Let me get my coat."

Mr. Boyle was not uncomfortable. He had seen Mr. Pietro Cassandro on several occasions but did not *know* him. He searched his memory desperately for something, anything, that he had done that might possibly have been misunderstood. He could think of nothing. If there was something, it had been a mistake, an honest mistake.

The problem, obviously, was to convince Pietro Cassandro of that, to assure him that he had consciously done nothing that would in any way endanger the reputation he had built over the years for reliability and honesty.

Sonny did not recognize the man standing by Marco D'Angelo's black Buick four-door. He was a large man, with a massive neck showing in an open-collared sports shirt spread over his sports-jacket collar. He did not smile at Sonny.

"You wanna get in the back, Sonny?" Mr. D'Angelo ordered. "Big as I am, there ain't room for all of me back there."

"No problem at all," Sonny said.

He got in the backseat. Mr. D'Angelo slammed the door on him and got in the passenger seat.

They drove to La Portabella's Restaurant, at 1200 South Front Street, which Sonny had heard was one of Mr. Paulo Cassandro's business interests. The parking lot looked full, but a man in a business suit, looking like a brother to the man driving Marco D'Angelo's Buick, appeared and waved them to a parking space near the kitchen.

They entered the building through the kitchen. Marco D'Angelo led Sonny past the stoves and food-preparation tables, and the man with the thick neck followed them.

Marco D'Angelo knocked at a closed door.

"Marco, Mr. Cassandro."

"Yeah," a voice replied.

D'Angelo pushed the door open and waved Sonny in ahead of him.

It was an office. But a place had been set on the desk, at which sat another large Italian gentleman, a napkin tucked in his collar. He stood up as Sonny entered the room.

The large Italian gentleman was, Sonny realized with a sinking heart, Mr. Paulo Cassandro, Pietro's brother. He had just had his picture in the newspaper when he had been arrested for something. The Inquirer had referred to him as a "reputed mobster."

"Sonny Boyle, right?" Mr. Cassandro asked, smiling and offering his hand.

"That's me," Sonny said.

"Pleased to meet you. Marco's been telling me good things about you."

"He has?"

"I appreciate your coming here like this."

"My pleasure."

"Get him a glass," Paulo Cassandro ordered. "You hungry, Sonny? I get you up from your dinner?"

"No. A glass of wine would be fine. Thank you."

"You're sure you don't want something to eat?"

"No, thank you."

"Well, maybe after we talk. I figure I owe you for getting you here like this. After we talk, you'll have something. It's the least I can do."

"Thank you very much."

"Marco tells me you're pretty well connected in your neighborhood. Know a lot of people. That true?"

"Well, I live in the house my mother was born in, Mr. Cassandro."

"The name Frank Foley mean anything to you, Sonny?"

Sonofabitch! I didn't even think of that!

"I know who he is," Sonny said.

"Me asking looks like it made you nervous," Paulo said. "Did it make you nervous?"

"No. No. Why should it?"

"You tell me. You looked nervous."

Sonny shrugged and waved his hands helplessly.

"Tell me about this guy," Paulo said.

"I don't know much about him," Sonny said.

"Tell me what you do know."

"Well, he's from the neighborhood. I see him around."

"I get the feeling you don't want to talk about him."

"Mr. Cassandro, can I say something?"

"That's what I'm waiting for, Sonny."

"I sort of thought you knew all about him, is what I mean."

"I don't know nothing about him; that's why I'm asking. Why would you think I know all about him?"

"I got the idea somehow that you knew each other, that he was a business associate, is what I meant."

"Where would you get an idea like that?"

"That's what people say," Sonny said. "I got that idea from him. I thought I did. I probably misunderstood him. Got the wrong idea."

"Sonny, I never laid eyes on this guy. I wouldn't know him if he walked in that door right this minute," Paulo said.

"Well, I'm sorry I had the wrong idea."

"Why should you be sorry? We all make mistakes. Tell me, what sort of business associate of mine did you think he was?"

"Nothing specific. I just thought he worked for you."

"You don't know where he works?"

"He works at Wanamaker's."

"Doing what?"

"I don't know. In the warehouse, I think."

"Just between you and me, did you really think I would have somebody working for me who works in the Wanamaker's warehouse?"

"No disrespect intended, Mr. Cassandro."

"I know that, Sonny. Like I told you, Marco's been saying good things about you. Look, I know you were mistaken, and I understand. But when you were mistaken, what did you think this guy did for me?"

Sonny did not immediately reply.

"Hey, you're among friends. What's said in this room stays in this room, OK?"

"I feel like a goddamned fool for not knowing it was bullshit when I heard it," Sonny said. "I should have known better."

"Known better than what, Sonny?" Paulo Cassandro said, and now there was an unmistakable tone of impatience in his voice.

"He sort of hinted that he was a hit man for you," Sonny said, very reluctantly.

"You're right, Sonny," Paulo said. "You should have known it was bullshit when you heard it. You know why?"

Inspiration came, miraculously, to Sonny Boyle. He suddenly knew the right answer to give.

"Because you're a legitimate businessman," he said.

"Right. All that bullshit in the movies about a mob, and hit men, all that bullshit is nothing but bullshit. And you should have known that, Sonny. I'm a little disappointed in you."

"I'm embarrassed. I just didn't think this through."

"Right. You didn't think. That can get a fella in trouble, Sonny."

"I know."

"Ah, well, what the hell. You're among friends. Marco says good things about you. Let's just forget the whole thing."

"Thank you."

"You know what I mean about forgetting the whole thing?"

"I'm not exactly sure."

"You know what you did tonight, Sonny?"

"No."

"You wanted to be nice to the wife. You wanted to surprise her. You know a guy who works in the kitchen out there. You come to the back door and told him to make you two dinners to go. He did."

"Right, Mr. Cassandro."

"That it was on the house is nobody's business but yours and mine, right? And you didn't see nobody but your friend, right?"

"Absolutely, Mr. Cassandro."

"Marco," Paulo Cassandro said. "Get them to make up a takeout. Antipasto, some veal, some pasta, some fish, spumoni, the works, a couple bottles of wine. And then take Sonny here home."

"Yes, Mr. Cassandro."

Paulo Cassandro extended his hand.

"I would say that it was nice to see you, Sonny, but we didn't, right? Keep up the good work. It's appreciated."

"Thank you, Mr. Cassandro."

"You see anybody here by that name, Marco?"

"I don't," Marco D'Angelo said.

"Sorry," Sonny said.

"Ah, get out of here. Enjoy your dinner," Paulo Cassandro said.

Impulsively, when he reached the Media Inn, at the intersection of the Baltimore Pike and Providence Road, Matt continued straight on into Media, instead of turning left onto Providence Road toward the home in Wallingford in which he had grown up.

Except for a lantern-style fixture by the front door, there were no lights on in the brick Colonial house at 320 Wilson Avenue; Mr. Gerald North Atchison, restaurateur and almost certain conspirator in a double murder, was apparently out for the evening.

There was time for Matt to consider, as he slowly approached and rolled past the house, that driving by wasn't the smartest thing he had done lately.

What if he had been home? So what? What did I expect to find?

He pressed harder on the Porsche's accelerator and dropped his hand to the gearshift.

To hell with it. I'll go home, and hope I can look—what did Wohl say Amy said? A condition of "grief shock"?—sufficiently grief-shocked to convince my mother that I am not the sonofabitch I have proven myself to be.

Jesus! What if Amanda calls the apartment and Milham's girlfriend answers the phone? Amanda will decide that I am letting some other kind female soul console me in my grief shock! And be justifiably pissed. Worse than pissed, hurt. I'll have to call her.

And that's not so bad. She said not to call her. But this gives me an excuse. Jesus, I'm glad I thought about that!

There was a sudden light in the rear of the house at 320 Wilson, growing in intensity. Matt looked over his shoulder—it was difficult in the small interior of the Porsche—and saw that the left door of the double garage was going up.

He pulled quickly to the curb, stopped, and turned his lights off. A moment later, a Cadillac Coupe de Ville backed out of the driveway onto the street, turned its tail toward Matt, and drove off in the other direction.

With his lights still off, Matt made a U-turn, swore when his front wheel bounced over the curb he could not see, then set off in pursuit.

Why the hell am I doing this?

Because I think I'm Sherlock Holmes? Or because I really don't want to go home and have Mother comfort me in my grief shock?

Or maybe, just maybe, because I'm a cop, and I'm after that bastard?

Not without difficulty—the traffic on the Baltimore Pike through Clifton Heights and Lansdowne toward Philadelphia was heavy, and there were a number of stoplights, two of which left him stopped as the Cadillac went ahead—he kept Atchison in sight.

Atchison drove to the Yock's Diner at Fifty-seventh and Chestnut, just inside the city limits. Matt drove past the parking lot, saw Atchison get out of his car and walk toward the diner, and then circled the block and entered the parking lot.

Atchison knew him, of course, so he couldn't go in the diner. He walked toward the diner, deciding he would try to look in the windows. He passed a car and idly looked inside. There was a radio mounted below the dash, and when he looked closer, he could see the after-market light mounted on the headliner. An unmarked car.

The occupants of which will see me stalking around out here, rush out, blow whistles, shine flashlights, and accuse me of auto burglary.

There was a three-foot-wide area between the parked unmarked car and the diner itself, planted with some sort of hardy perennial bushes which were thick and had thorns. He scratched both legs painfully, and a grandfather of a thorn ripped a three-inch slash in his jacket.

He found a footing and hoisted himself up to look in the window.

There will be a maiden lady at this table, two maiden ladies, who will see the face in the window, scream, and cause whoever's in the unmarked car to rush to protect society.

The table was unoccupied. Matt twisted his head—clinging to the stainless-steel panels of the diner wall made this difficult—and looked right and then left.

Mr. Gerald North Atchison was sitting at a banquette, alone, studying the menu.

Jesus, why not? What did I expect? People have to eat. Going to a diner is what hungry people do.

He dropped off the wall and turned to fight his way back through the jungle.

You are a goddamn fool, Matthew Payne. The price of your Sherlock Holmes foolishness is your ripped jacket. Be grateful that the guys in the unmarked car didn't see you.

But, Jesus, why did he come all the way here? He could have eaten a hell of a lot closer to his house than this—the Media Inn, for example.

He stood motionless for a second, then turned back to the diner and climbed up again.

Mr. Gerald North Atchison, smiling, was giving his order to a waitress whose hair was piled on top of her head.

What are you doing here, you sonofabitch?

He looked around the diner again.

Frankie Foley was sitting at the diner's counter, the remnants of his meal pushed aside, drinking a cup of coffee, holding the cup in both hands.

"You want to climb down from there, sir, and tell us what you're doing?"

Matt quickly looked over his shoulder. Too quickly. His right foot slipped and he fell backward onto one of the larger perennial thornbushes.

"Shit!" Matt said.

"Jesus!" one of the detectives said, his tone indicating that the strange behavior of civilians still amazed him.

"I'm a Three Six Nine," Matt said.

Both detectives, if that's what they were, entered the thornbush jungle far enough to put their hands on Matt's arm and shoulders and push him up out of the thornbush.

"I'm Detective Payne, of Special Operations," Matt said. "Let me get out of here, and I'll show you my identification."

The two eyed him warily as he reached into his jacket for his identification.

The larger of the two took the leather folder, examined it and Matt critically, and finally handed it back.

"What the hell are you doing?" he asked.

"Right now, I need some help," Matt said.

"It sure looks like you do," the second of them said.

"There's a man in there named Gerald North Atchison," Matt said. "You hear about the double homicide at the Inferno?"

"I heard about it," the larger one said.

"It was his wife and partner who were killed," Matt said. "And there is another man in there, Frankie Foley, who we think is involved."

"I thought you said you was Special Operations," the larger detective said. "Isn't that Homicide's business?"

"I'm working the job," Matt said. "I followed Atchison here from his house. I think he's here to meet Foley. That would put a lot of things together."

"What kind of help?" the larger one asked.

"I can't go in there. They both know my face."

"What are you looking for?"

"I don't know," Matt said, aware of how stupid that made him sound. "See if they talk together. Anything. I don't think it's a coincidence that they're both here together."

"If they've got enough brains to pour piss out of a boot," the larger one said, "they'd transact their business out here in the parking lot, where nobody would see them."

It was a valid comment, and Matt could think of no reply to make.

"Harry," the smaller one said, "I could drink another cup of coffee."

"I'd appreciate it," Matt said.

"If you need some help, why don't you get on the radio?" the larger one said.

"I'm driving my own car."

"Where are these guys?"

"Atchison, five eight or nine, a hundred ninety pounds, forty-something, in a suit, is in the second banquette from the kitchen door. Foley, twenty-five, six one, maybe two hundred pounds, is in a two-tone sports coat, third or fourth seat from the far end of the counter."

"We'll have a look," the larger one said. "I'm Harry Cronin, Payne, South Detectives. This is Bob Chesley."

Chesley waved a hand in greeting; Cronin offered his hand.

"You tore the shit out of your jacket, I guess you know," he said, then signaled for Chesley to go into the diner ahead of him.

A minute after that, Cronin followed Chesley into the diner. Matt walked away from the diner, stationing himself behind the second line of cars in the parking lot.

Five minutes later, he saw Foley come out of the diner. Matt ducked behind a car and watched Foley through the windows. Foley went to a battered, somewhat gaudily re-painted Oldsmobile two-door and got in. The door closed, and a moment later the interior lights went on.

Matt couldn't see what he was doing at first, but then Foley tapped a stack of money on the dashboard. The door opened wider, and he could see an envelope flutter to the ground. The door closed, the engine cranked, the lights came on, and Foley drove out of the parking lot.

"That one," Detective Cronin reported as he approached Matt, "went into the crapper carrying a package. A heavy package. He came out a minute or two later without it. Then the fat guy went in the crapper, and when he came out, he had the package."

Matt ran over and retrieved the envelope. It was blank, but Matt remembered a lecture at the Police Academy—and it had been a question on the detective's exam—where the technique of lifting fingerprints from paper using nihydrous oxide had been discussed. An envelope with Foley's and Atchison's prints on it would be valuable.

"I'd love to know what's in that package," Matt said when he went back to where Cronin waited.

"It was heavy and tied with string," Cronin said. "It could be a gun. Guns. More than one."

"Shit," Matt said.

"Guns don't help?"

"In the last couple of days, I've had several lectures about not giving defense attorneys an edge," Matt said. "I'm afraid we'd get into an unlawful search-and-seizure, and lose the guns as evidence."

"If they are guns," Cronin said. "That's just a maybe."

"Shit," Matt said.

"I could bump into the fat guy, and maybe the package would fall to the ground and rip open . . ."

"And maybe it wouldn't."

"You call it, Payne."

"I think I had better be very careful," Matt said.

"Whatever. Anything else?"

"I'm going to follow him. I don't suppose you could tag along?"

"I don't know. I'd have to check in."

"Fuck it," Matt thought aloud. "I started this myself, I'll do it myself. Anyway, he might catch on if two cars followed him."

"You know that he hasn't caught on to you already?"

"No, I don't."

They waited in silence for another ten minutes.

"If you saw a gun barrel or something sticking out of a ripped package, that would be sufficient cause for you to ask for a permit, right?" asked Matt.

"Absolutely. A wrapped-up gun is a concealed weapon."

"He's got a permit to carry concealed, but you could get the serial numbers."

"I'll go bump the sonofabitch," Cronin said.

Five minutes after that, Gerald North Atchison came out the Yock's Diner. Detective Cronin stepped from between two parked cars and bumped into him, hard enough to make Atchison stagger. But he didn't drop the package, and he held on to it firmly while Cronin profusely apologized for not watching where he was going, and tried to straighten Atchison's clothing.

Detective Cronin, still apologizing, went into the diner. Atchison watched him, then turned and walked quickly to his car. Matt trotted to his Porsche and followed him out of the parking lot.

Atchison drove back toward Media. Just making the light, he turned left on Providence Road. The line of traffic was such that Matt could not run the stoplight. He fumed impatiently until it finally gave him a green left-turn signal, and then took out after Atchison's Cadillac.

It was nowhere in sight. There weren't even any red taillights glowing in the distance.

Matt put his foot to the floor. When he passed the residence of Mr. and Mrs. Brewster Cortland Payne II, he was going seventy-five miles an hour. There were lights on in the kitchen, and he had a mental picture of his mother and father at the kitchen table.

Just beyond the bridge over the railroad tracks near the Wallingford Station, he was able to pick out the peculiar taillight assembly of a Cadillac. He gradually closed the distance between them.

Atchison drove into and through Chester, to the river, then through a run-down area of former shipyards and no-longer-functioning oil refineries, weaving slowly between enormous potholes and junk strewn on the roadway.

Matt turned off his headlights, which kept, he felt, Atchison from noticing that he was being followed but which also denied him a clear view of the road. He struck several potholes hard enough to worry about blowing a tire, and making a trip to enrich the alignment technicians at the Porsche dealership a certainty.

And then he ran over something metallic, which lodged itself somewhere under the Porsche, set up a terrifying howl of torn metal, and gave off a shower of sparks.

He slammed on the brakes, wondering if he had done so because he was afraid Atchison would hear the screeching or see the sparks, or because it hurt to consider what damage was being done to the Porsche.

He jumped out, looking in frustration at Atchison's disappearing Cadillac. And then the brake lights came on and the Cadillac stopped.

Christ, he saw me!

What do I do now?

There was a sudden light as the Cadillac's door opened. Atchison got out, looked around, seemed fascinated with the Porsche, and then slammed the car door shut.

It took Matt's eyes some time to adjust to the now pitch darkness, but when they did he saw Atchison—nothing more than a silhouette—walking away from the car.

He ran after him. When he got close he saw that they were next to the river, and that Atchison was on a pier extending into it.

He saw Atchison make a move like a basketball player. A shadow of something arced up into the sky, fell, and in a moment, Matt could faintly hear a splash.

Atchison now walked quickly back to the Cadillac, fired it up, and started to turn around. As the headlights swept the area, Matt dropped to the ground. His hands touched something wet and sticky. He put his fingers to his nose. It smelled as foul as it felt.

Atchison's Cadillac rolled past him. It stopped at the Porsche. Atchison got half out of the car, looked around, then got all the way out. It looked for a moment as if he was going to try the door, but then he stumbled over something.

Then he got back in the car and drove rapidly away.

Matt got to his feet, rubbed his hands against his jacket to cleanse them of whatever the hell it was on his hands—the jacket was ruined anyway—and walked back to his car.

He saw what Atchison had stumbled over. A curved automobile bumper.

That which caused that unholy screech and the shower of sparks. With a little bit of luck, Atchison will think that's why the Porsche is here, and not that I ran over the goddamn thing when I was tailing him.

The Cadillac's taillights were no longer visible.

What the hell, he's probably going home anyway.

Matt opened the car door with two fingers, got the keys from the ignition, then opened the hood and took out the jack. It took him fifteen minutes to dislodge the bumper from the car's underpinnings.

TWENTY

Inspector Peter Wohl was visibly disturbed when he opened the door to his apartment and found Detective Payne standing there.

"What the hell do you want? Are you drunk, or what?"

"Atchison threw something I'll bet is guns in the river," Matt said.

"What the hell are you talking about?"

"In Chester," Matt said. "I followed him."

"You did what? What the hell gave you the idea you had that authority?"

"He met Frankie, Frankie gave him a package, and Atchison threw it in the river in Chester."

"I'll want to hear all about this, Detective Payne, but not here, and not when you're obviously shitfaced. I'll see you in my office at eight o'clock."

The door slammed in Detective Payne's face. He waited

a moment and then started down the stairs. He was halfway down when light told him the door had reopened. He looked over his shoulder.

Amelia Payne, Ph.D., M.D., attired in a terry-cloth bathrobe, stood at the head of the stairs.

"Matt, what happened to you?"

You may be his lady love, but first of all, you are my big sister, who takes care of her little brother.

"Are you drunk?" Amy asked, more in sympathy than moral outrage.

"Not yet."

"Well, come in here," Amy said. "What does 'not yet' mean?"

"I mean that getting drunk right now seems like a splendid idea, one that I will pursue with enthusiasm, once I have a bath."

"What is that stuff on you?" Wohl demanded, in curiosity, not sympathy.

"I don't think I want to find out."

"Come up here," Amy ordered.

She is now in her healer-of-mankind role.

Matt climbed the stairs.

"It's all over you!" Amy announced.

"I've noticed."

She wiped a finger, professionally, across his forehead.

"There's irritation. It's a caustic of some sort. You need a long hot bath."

"If he's coming in here," Inspector Wohl said, resigned to the inevitable, "he's going to take his clothes off first."

Fifteen minutes later, attired in the robe Amy had been wearing when she appeared at the top of the steps, Detective Payne entered Inspector Wohl's living room. Inspector Wohl and Dr. Payne were now fully clothed.

"I am under instructions to apologize for accusing you of being drunk," Wohl said. "You want a beer?"

"I'd love a beer," Matt said.

Wohl walked into his kitchen, returned with a bottle of Ortleib's, and handed it to Matt.

"I am under further instructions to question you kindly, having been reminded that you are undoubtedly in a condition of grief shock," Wohl said. "So why don't we start at the beginning?"

"I don't like your sarcasm, Peter," Amy said. "Look at his face and hands! He's been burned! Have you got any sort of an antiseptic lotion?"

"Listerine?" Wohl asked. "Where did you get that stuff on you, anyway?"

"No, not Listerine, stupid!"

"On a pier, or near a pier, near the old refineries in Chester," Matt said.

"Where you had followed, you said, Mr. Atchison?"

"That will have to wait until I do something about his face and hands," Amy said. "I probably should take him to an emergency room."

"I'm all right," Matt said.

"You must have something around here," Amy said to Peter Wohl.

"Look in the medicine cabinet," Wohl said. "You were telling me you followed Atchison? And I was asking you where the hell you got the idea—"

"Stop it, Peter," Amy ordered. "For God's sake, what's the matter with you?"

She glowered at him, then marched into the bedroom. Thirty seconds later she was back, triumphantly displaying a tube of medicine.

"This will do," she said. "Why didn't you tell me you had it?"

"I don't even know what it is," Wohl said.

Amy daubed the ointment on Matt's face, then rubbed it in on his hands.

"Give me that, I've got a nasty scratch on my leg," Matt said.

Wohl looked.

"I'm just dying to learn where you've been besides on a pier in Chester," he said sweetly.

"I got these in the bushes outside the Yock's Diner on Fifty-Seventh and Chestnut. That's where I saw Atchison and Foley."

"You *have* been a busy little junior Sherlock Holmes, haven't you?"

"Peter, for Christ's sake, at least hear me out!"

Wohl glared at him.

"OK. Fair enough. We're back at square one. Start at the beginning."

Ten minutes later, Wohl dialed a number from memory.

"Tony, I hate to call you at this hour, but this is important. Go out to South Detectives. I'll call out there and tell them you're coming. I want you to get a statement from two detectives. One of them is named Cronin, and the other's name is Chesley. The first thing you say to them is to keep their mouths shut about what happened tonight at the Yock's Diner on Fifty-Seventh and Chestnut. If they spread the story around the squad room, it'll be public knowledge in the morning. Then I want you to question them, separately, about what went on at the Yock's Diner. Payne was there, he followed Atchison there. Frankie Foley was there. Frankie arrived with a package. Atchison left with the package. Payne thinks Atchison gave Foley an envelope, and he thinks there was money in the envelope. Atchison then went to the riverfront in Chester and threw a package in the river. Payne suspects the package contained guns. What I want from the detectives are the facts, not what they think or surmise, something they can testify to in court without getting blown out of the witness chair by Atchison's lawyer."

Detective Tony Harris asked a question, during which Inspector Wohl glanced at Detective Payne. Detective Payne's face bore, in addition to a glistening layer of medicated ointment, a look of smug vindication. Inspector Wohl, tempering the gesture with a smile, extended his right hand toward

Detective Payne, the palm upward, all but the center finger folded inward.

Detective Payne was not cowed.

"When you're right, you're right," he said.

Inspector Wohl returned his attention to the telephone.

"I know a couple of people in the Chester Police Department," he said. "I'm going to call them, and then Payne and I are coming out there. Payne says he can find the pier; he marked the site with an old bumper. I'm going to ask the Chester cops to guard the site until we can get our divers out there at first light. What I'm hoping, Tony, is that Sherlock Holmes, Junior, got lucky again. I think he may have. Call me when you're finished. I don't care what time it is."

He put the phone back in the cradle.

"What we have, hotshot," he said, turning to Matt, "is a lot of ifs. *If* the package does contain firearms. *If* those firearms can be ballistically connected with the weapons used in the Inferno. *If* we can tie the guns to either Atchison or Foley."

"If all else fails, we can shake the two of them up," Matt argued. "What were they doing together in the Yock's Diner? What did the package Foley gave him contain?"

Wohl could think of no counterargument.

"And when we find your pier, I will drop you off at your family's home in Wallingford," he said.

"He can't go to Wallingford at this hour, looking like that," Amy announced. "Mother and Dad have gone through enough in the last couple of days without him showing up looking like that."

"And you can't go to your apartment, either, can you, with Milham's girlfriend there? That leaves here, doesn't it?" Wohl asked.

"I could go to a hotel."

"No he—" Amy began. Wohl held up his hand to interrupt her. To Matt's surprise, she stopped.

"If this thing works out, I may have to forgive you for a

large assortment of sins, but I will not forgive you, Matt, for this."

He gestured around the apartment. Amy took his meaning, and blushed.

Detective Payne smiled.

"Chastity, goodness, and mercy shall follow you all the days of your lives," he paraphrased piously.

"Why, you little sonofabitch!" Amelia Payne, Ph.D., M.D., said.

The Philadelphia Marine Police Unit occupies part of a municipal pier on the Delaware River just south of the Benjamin Franklin Bridge.

When Detective Payne arrived at ten minutes to seven, at the wheel of his Porsche, which shuddered alarmingly whenever he exceeded thirty miles per hour, and looking both as if he had fallen asleep on the beach and was suffering from terminal sunburn, and as if his clothing had shrunken (he was wearing a complete ensemble borrowed from Inspector Peter Wohl, who was two inches shorter and twenty-five pounds lighter than he was, there having been no time for him to get his own clothing), the parking lot was crowded with personal and official vehicles.

There were two Mobile Crime Laboratory vans, and a similar-size van bearing the insignia of the Marine Police Unit; two radio patrol cars; two unmarked cars (one of which he recognized as belonging to Wally Milham); a green Oldsmobile 98 coupe (which he knew to be the personal automobile of Chief Inspector Dennis V. Coughlin); a police car bearing the insignia of the Chester Police Department; and an assortment of personal automobiles.

That Denny Coughlin was driving his own car, rather than being in his official car chauffeured by Sergeant Francis Holloran, made it clear to Matt that he was present in his role of Loving Uncle in Fact, rather than as a senior member of the Philadelphia police hierarchy.

Chief Coughlin and Detective Milham were standing on the pier. Coughlin waved him over.

"What the hell did you do to your face, Matty?" he asked, his gruffness not quite masking his concern.

"It's not as bad as it looks," Matt said.

"Amy said it'll be gone in a couple of days," Coughlin said, his tone making it clear that he had serious doubts about the accuracy of the diagnosis.

"They're ready for us," Milham said, and gestured over the side of the pier. Matt looked down. There was a forty-foot boat down there, festooned with flood- and spotlights, a collection of radio antennae, a radar antenna, and what looked like a standard RPC bubble gum machine.

The rear deck was crowded with diving equipment and people, including a neatly uniformed sergeant of the Chester Police Department. His dapper appearance contrasted strongly with the appearance of officers of the Marine Police Unit, who had reported for duty prepared to go to work, which meant that their badges were pinned to work clothing.

There was a lieutenant (presumably the Marine Police Unit commander) standing by the wheel, and a sergeant actually at the boat's controls.

Matt followed Milham down a flight of stairs onto a floating pier and then jumped aboard the boat after him.

"Chief," the Inspector called up to Coughlin. "Would you like to ride along with us, sir?"

It was a pro forma question, asked because lieutenants generally recognize the wisdom of being very courteous under any circumstances to chief inspectors. The expected response would normally have been, "No, thank you. But thank you for asking."

Chief Coughlin looked at his watch, looked thoughtful, then said, "What the hell, there's nothing on my desk that won't wait a couple of hours."

He then quickly came down the flight of stairs onto the floating pier and jumped onto the boat.

"Don't let me get in your way, Lieutenant," he called,

then went to the Chester police sergeant. "I'm Chief Coughlin," he said, offering his hand. "We appreciate your courtesy, and especially you coming in here like this."

"Anything we can do to help," the Sergeant said. "I thought I might make it easier to find the site."

"We appreciate it," Coughlin said.

The diesel engines roared, and the boat moved away from the pier and headed downstream. To his left, Matt could see the Nesfoods International complex on the Camden shore, and to his right, on Society Hill, he thought he could make out the apartment of Mr. and Mrs. Chadwick T. Nesbitt IV.

I wonder what Vice President Nesbitt is doing at this hour of the morning? Trying to come up with some clever way to sell another ten billion cans of chicken soup?

Matt watched as Denny Coughlin made his way among the other police officers and technicians. Matt was impressed, but not particularly surprised, that Coughlin knew most of their names. Somewhat unkindly, knowing that it would offend Coughlin if he knew what he was thinking, Matt thought he was working the crowd of cops just about as effectively as Jerry Carlucci worked a crowd of voters.

Then the Sergeant from the Chester Police Department embarrassed him.

"You're Detective Payne, right?"

"Right," Matt said, shaking the Sergeant's hand. "Nice to meet you."

"I don't mean to put down what you did. It was good work," the Sergeant said. "But you know what I was just thinking?"

Matt smiled and shook his head.

"I was thinking it must be nice to work for a police department where there's enough money to surveil somebody like this guy Atchison. We just don't have the dough to pay for twenty-four-hour surveillance, even on a murder job. How many officers did you have on the detail?"

"I really don't know," Matt said.

That is far from the truth. I know precisely how many.

Zero. And the surveillance of Mr. Atchison will cost the Philadelphia Police Department zero dollars, because it was not only not authorized, but as Peter pointed out with some emphasis, another manifestation of what's wrong with me; that I am an undisciplined hotshot who goes charging off in all directions without thinking.

The cost of whatever it's going to cost to fix the Porsche, and I don't like to think how much that's going to be, plus the cost of a new jacket, shirts, pants, necktie, and loafers, is going to be borne personally by Detective Matt Payne. I don't even dare to put in for overtime.

It didn't take as long to reach the pier along the Chester waterfront as Matt expected it would.

And finding the pier was easy. There was a Chester police car sitting on it, and it could be seen a half-mile away.

Thirty minutes after the Marine Police Unit boat tied up to the pier, a police diver, wearing a diving helmet, bobbed to the surface with a package. It was a white plastic garbage bag, wrapped in duct tape.

"That it, Matty?" Denny Coughlin asked.

"That looks like what I saw Atchison carry out of the Yock's Diner."

"Good job, Matty."

Unless, of course, it contains something like the records of the loan-shark operation Atchison was operating, and not guns.

A police photographer recorded the diver in the water, the package on the deck, and then as a laboratory technician carefully cut the duct tape away. Inside the plastic garbage bag was a paper bag. Inside the paper bag, wrapped in mechanic's wiping cloths, were three guns. A large revolver, which a ballistics technician identified for another technician to write down as a .44-40 single-action six-shot revolver, of Spanish manufacture, a .38 Special Caliber six-shot Colt revolver, and a Savage .32 ACP semiautomatic pistol.

● ● ●

Officer Woodrow Wilson Bailey, Sr., woke to the smell of brewing coffee and fried ham. It pleased him. He didn't complain or feel sorry for himself most days that he didn't get to eat breakfast with Joellen and Woodrow Junior. Policing was a twenty-four-hour-a-day job, and everybody had to take their fair turn working the four-to-midnight tours, and the midnight-to-eight-in-the-morning tours. And truth to tell, he sort of liked the last-out tour; there was something he liked about cruising around the deserted streets, say, at half past three or four, when all the punks had finally decided to go to bed.

But it was nice when he was working the day shift, and could sit down at the kitchen table and have breakfast with Joellen and Woodrow Junior. Having breakfast like that every day was one of the things Woodrow looked forward to, when he got his time in and went home to Hartsville.

He got out of bed and took a quick shower and a careful shave, then put on his terry-cloth bathrobe and went down to the kitchen. He really hated it when he dribbled coffee or egg or redeye gravy or something on a clean uniform shirt and had to change it, so he ate in his bathrobe. All you had to do if you made a pig of yourself on your bathrobe was throw it in the washing machine. Joellen knew he took pride in the way he looked in his uniform, and always had one clean and pressed waiting for him. That was a lot of work, and Woodrow knew it, and made a genuine effort not to get his uniform dirty, so that what Joellen did for him would not be wasted.

"I was about to come see if you were going to take breakfast with us," Joellen said when he walked in the kitchen.

"I could smell that cooking," Woodrow said. "It would wake a dead man."

Joellen smiled and kissed him.

"Good morning, son."

"Good morning, sir," Woodrow Junior said. He was wearing a white shirt and a blue sweater and a necktie. He was a junior at Cardinal Dougherty High School, and they had a dress code there. More important, they taught Christian morals, even if they weren't Protestant Christians. It would have been nicer if Third Abyssinian had a church-run school that Woodrow Junior could have gone to, but they didn't.

And he certainly couldn't have sent Woodrow Junior to a public high school. The corridors of the public schools, Woodrow sometimes thought, were not a bit better than the corners of the neighborhood. You could buy anything in there, and it was no place to send your child unless you didn't care what was going to happen to him, what he would see, what punks would give him trouble.

Woodrow thought it was a truly Christian act on the part of the Catholics to let Protestant Baptist boys like Woodrow into their schools. And there were a lot of them. There was a charge, of course, but in Woodrow's case it was reduced because Joellen went over there every day and helped out in the cafeteria for free.

Woodrow sat down at the kitchen table. Woodrow Junior bent his head, and standing behind her husband, Joellen closed her eyes and bent her head.

"Dear Lord, we thank You for Your bounty which we are now about to receive, and for Thy many other blessings. We ask You to watch over us. Through Thy Son, our Lord and Saviour, Jesus Christ."

Joellen and Woodrow Junior said, "Amen," and Joellen put breakfast on the table: sunny-side-up eggs and ham, red-eye gravy and grits, and the biscuits Mamma Dear had taught Joellen to make before the Good Lord took her into heaven.

Then Woodrow went upstairs and put on his uniform, and started to get his gun out of the drawer. He glanced down at his shoes and almost swore. There was a scratch across the toe of the left one, and the toe of the right one was smudged. He wondered when that had happened. He closed the drawer in the dresser where he kept his gun, and went back down to the kitchen.

Joellen watched as he put on a pair of rubber gloves and very carefully polished his shoes.

"Woodrow Junior would have done that if you'd have told him," Joellen said.

"I messed them up, I'll make them right," he said.

Then he went back upstairs, got his gun from the drawer, went back downstairs, kissed Joellen good-bye. He got his uniform cap and his nightstick from the hall clothes hanger and left the house.

It was seven blocks to the District Headquarters at Twenty-second and Hunting Park Avenue.

Woodrow walked briskly, looking to see what he could see, thinking that when roll call was over and he went on patrol he'd cruise the alleys. He'd been off for seventy hours, and there was no telling what might have happened in that time.

It was a morning like any other. There was absolutely nothing different about it that would have made him suspect that before the day was over, he would be in the office of the Northwest Police Division Inspector, getting his hand shook, and having his picture made with the Mayor of the City of Philadelphia.

Having decided *First things first*, Matt limped to Imported Motor Cars, Ltd., Inc., from the Marine Police Unit pier. There the Senior Maintenance Advisor, a somewhat epicene young man in a blazer and bow tie and three maintenance technicians in spotless white thigh-length coats which made them look more, Matt thought, like gynecologists waiting for a patient than automobile mechanics, confirmed his worst fears about the Porsche.

"Whatever did you do to it?" the Senior Maintenance Advisor asked, in what Matt thought was mingled horror and joy as he calculated the size of the repair bill.

Well, I was chasing a murder suspect down by the refineries in Chester, and I had to turn the headlights off so that he wouldn't know he was being followed.

"I ran over a bumper," Matt said.

"I'll say you did!"

"You should have left it where you did it," one of the maintenance technicians volunteered, his tone suggesting Matt deserved a prize for Idiot of the Year. "Called a wrecker. No telling how much damage to the suspension you did driving it in."

Imported Motor Cars, Ltd., Inc., evidently felt such enormous sympathy for him, or figured they could make up the cost when they presented him with the bill, that they gave him a loaner. A new 911 Demonstrator. Matt suspected that sometime in the next day or two he would receive a call from Imported Motor Cars, Ltd., Inc., asking him, taking into consideration what the repair bill for repairing the damage he had done to his old car would be, would he be interested in a very special deal on the car he was now driving?

He then went to his apartment. There was no one there. Helene Kellog had apparently gone off with Wally Milham someplace—Wally had said that it would be three o'clock, maybe later, before the lab was finished testing the guns taken from the river—or possibly had calmed down enough to go to work.

There was evidence of her presence in the apartment—a can of hair spray, a mascara brush, and a jar of deodorant on the sink in his bathroom—when he stripped out of Wohl's clothes and went to take a shower.

That reminded him that he had not telephoned Amanda on the pretense that she should not be concerned if she called the apartment and a woman answered.

The hot water of the shower exacerbated whatever the hell he had been rolling around in on the Chester pier had done to his face and hands. When he wiped the condensation off the mirror to shave, he looked like a lobster. A lobster with a three-square-inch albino white spot on the right cheek, which served to make the rest of his face look even redder.

And shaving hurt, even with an electric razor.

He had just about finished dressing when the telephone rang.

That's obviously Inspector Wohl, calling to apologize for having spoken harshly to me, and to express the gratitude and admiration of the entire Police Department for my brilliant detecting.

Or the President of the United States, (b) being quite as likely as (a).

Jesus, maybe it's Amanda!

"Hello."

"You're a hard man to find, Matt," the familiar voice of Mrs. Irene Craig, his father's secretary, said. "Hold on." Faintly, he could hear her add, presumably over the intercom to his father, "Triumph! Perseverance pays!"

"Matt? Good morning."

"Good morning, Dad."

"I've been concerned about you, and not only because we rather expected to see you at home last night and no one seems to know where you are."

"Sorry, I was working."

"Are you working now?"

"No. I just got out of the shower."

."I don't suppose you would have time to come by the office for a few minutes?"

"Yes, sir, I could."

"Fine, I'll see you shortly," his father said, and hung up.

He did that, Matt hypothesized, correctly, *so that I wouldn't have time to come up with an excuse not to go to his office. I wonder what he wants.*

"What in the world happened to your face?" Brewster Cortland Payne II greeted him twenty minutes later.

"I don't suppose you would believe I fell asleep under a sunlamp?"

"I wouldn't," said Irene Craig. "You'll have to do better than that. Would you like some coffee, Matt?"

"Very much, thank you. Black, please."

His father waved him into one of two green leather–upholstered chairs facing his desk.

"Two, Irene, please, and then hold my calls," his father said.

He waited until Mrs. Craig had served the coffee, left, and closed the door behind her.

"What did happen to your face?"

"I fell into something that, according to Amy, was some kind of caustic."

"Amy's had a look at you?"

Matt nodded.

"How did it happen?"

"I was working."

"That's what I told your mother, that you were probably working. First, when you didn't show up for dinner as promised, and again when you didn't show up by bedtime, and a third time when Amanda Spencer called at midnight."

"Amanda called out there?"

"She was concerned for you," Matt's father said. "Apparently, she called the apartment several times. A woman answered one time, and then she called back and there was a man, who either didn't know where you are or wouldn't tell her."

"God!"

"Your mother said it must have been very difficult for Amanda to call us."

"Oh, boy!"

"I wasn't aware that you and Amanda were close," Matt's father said, carefully.

Matt met his eyes.

"That's been a very recent development," Matt said after a moment. "I don't suppose it makes me any less of a son-ofabitch, but . . . there was nothing between us before Penny killed herself."

"I didn't think there had been," his father said. "You've never been duplicitous. Your mother, however, told me that she saw Amanda looking at you, quote, 'in a certain way,' unquote, at Martha Peebles's party."

"Jesus, that's the second time I heard that. I hope the Detweilers didn't see it."

"So do I," his father said. He came around from behind his desk and handed Matt a small sheet of notepaper.

"Your mother told Amanda that she would have you call her as soon as we found you," he said. "The first number is her office number, the second her apartment. I think you'd better call her; she's quite upset."

"What does Mother think of me?"

"I think she's happy for you, Matt," Brewster Cortland Payne II said, and walked toward his door. "I am."

He left the office and closed the door behind him.

Matt reached for the telephone.

TWENTY-ONE

There are a number of City Ordinances dealing with the disposition of garbage and an equally large number of City Ordinances dealing with the setting of open fires within the City. A good deal of legal thought has gone into their preparation, and the means by which they were to be enforced.

In theory, citizens were encouraged to place that which they wished to discard in suitable covered containers of prescribed sizes and construction. The containers were to be placed according to a published schedule in designated places in such a manner that garbage-collection personnel could easily empty the containers' contents into the rear collection area of garbage trucks.

The ordinances spelled out in some detail what was "ordinary, acceptable" garbage and what was "special types of refuse" and proscribed, for example, the placing of toxic material or explosive material or liquids in ordinary containers.

448

The setting of open fires within the City was prohibited under most conditions, with a few exceptions provided, such as the burning of leaves at certain times of the year under carefully delineated conditions.

Violation of most provisions was considered a Summary Offense, the least serious of the three classifications of crimes against the Peace and Dignity of the City and County of Philadelphia and the Commonwealth of Pennsylvania. The other, more serious, classifications were Misdemeanors (for example, simple assault and theft of property worth less than $2000) and Felonies (for example, Murder, Rape, and Armed Robbery).

It was spelled out in some detail what malefactors could expect to receive in the way of punishment for littering the streets with garbage, for example, with small fines growing to potentially large fines, and growing periods of imprisonment for second, third, and subsequent offenses.

Similarly, there were pages of small type outlining the myriad punishments which could be assessed against malefactors who were found guilty of setting open fires in violation of various applicable sections of the ordinances, likewise growing in severity depending on the size and type of fire set, the type material set ablaze, under what circumstances, and the number of times the accused had been previously convicted of offending the Peace and Dignity of the City, County, and Commonwealth by so doing.

As a general rule of thumb, the residents of Officer Woodrow Wilson Bailey's beat were not cognizant of the effort that had been made by their government to carefully balance the rights of the individual against the overall peace and dignity of the community insofar as garbage and setting fires were concerned. Or if they were aware of the applicable ordinances in these regards, they decided that their chances of having to face the stern bar of justice for violating them was at best remote.

If they had a garbage can, or a cardboard box, or some other container that could be used as a substitute, and if they

remembered what day the garbageman came, they often—
but by no means always, or even routinely—put their
garbage on the curb for pickup.

It had been Officer Woodrow Wilson Bailey's experience
that a substantial, and growing, number of the trash—white,
brown, and black—who had moved into the neighborhood had
decided the least difficult means of disposing of their trash was
to either carry it into (or throw it out the window into) their
back-yards and alleys when the garbage cans inside their
houses filled to overflowing, or the smell became unbearable.

There was little he could do about this. The criminal justice system of Philadelphia was no longer able to cope with
many Summary Offenses, and issuing a citation for littering
was nothing more than a waste of his time and the taxpayers' money. He would show up in court, the accused would
not, and the magistrates were reluctant to issue a bench warrant for someone accused of littering a back street in North
Philadelphia. The police had more important things to do
with their time.

He privately thought that if the trash wanted to live in
their own filth, so be it.

At a certain point in time, however, backyards became filled
to overflowing with refuse. Just about as frequently, the piles
of garbage became rat-infested. When either or both of these
circumstances occurred, the trash's solution to an immediate
problem was to set the garbage on fire. This both chased the
rats away and reduced the height of the garbage piles.

It was at this point that Officer Woodrow Wilson Bailey
drew the line. This was a violation of the law that presented
a clear and present danger to innocent persons.

Even trash had rights. It was not fair or just that they get
somebody else's rats. And not all the people on Woodrow's
beat were trash. There were a lot of folks who reminded
Woodrow of Mamma Dear and Daddy, hardworking, Christian people who had worked all their lives to buy their own
home, and when they'd finally finished, about the time they
went on retirement, they found that the neighborhood's hav-

ing gone to hell meant they couldn't sell their house for beans, and were stuck in the neighborhood with the trash.

It was, in Woodrow's mind, a sin that trash should set fires that could burn down the houses next door, taking all the poor old folks had left in the world.

Woodrow did not think of it, as some people concerned with social justice certainly would, as taking the law into his own hands. He thought of it first as something that had to be done, and rationalized that he was providing a genuine service to the people he had sworn to protect.

He dealt with people who set fires in his own way, without getting the overworked criminal justice system involved. And over the last couple of years, the word had gone out on his beat that burning garbage was socially unacceptable conduct, and that doing so brought swift punishment.

Officer Bailey was thus surprised and angry when through the open window of RPC 3913, as he rode slowly down an alley behind Shedwick Street, his nostrils detected the peculiar smell of burning garbage.

He stopped the car, put his head out the window and sniffed, and then backed the car up.

There was smoke rising above the wooden fence separating the backyard of a row house from the alley.

He was less surprised when he searched his memory and came up with the identity of the occupant of the house. White trash, and a junkie. White trash born right here in Philadelphia. His name, Woodrow recalled, was James Howard Leslie. White Male, twenty-six, 150 pounds, five feet nine. He had been in and out of some kind of confinement since he was twelve. Lived with some brown-trash Puerto Rican woman. Not married to her. Three kids; none of them looked like they ever had a decent meal.

Now he had a mental image of him. Junkie type. Long, dirty hair, looked like he hadn't had a bath—and probably hadn't—in two weeks. Had a little scraggly beard on the point of his chin. Called himself "Speed."

Officer Bailey got out of his car, taking his stick with him.

There was a gate in the fence, held shut with a chain and a rusty lock. Woodrow put his stick in the chain and twisted. The chain and rusty lock held; the rotten wood of the fence crushed under the pressure and gave way.

Woodrow pulled the gate open and entered the backyard. His anger grew. The fire was coming from a pile of garbage against the fence. The fire would almost certainly set the fence on fire. He saw a rat scurry out from the pile.

Flames flickered on the garbage pile. There was an old tire on the pile. Once a tire caught fire, you could hardly put it out. Tires burned hot and hard and gave off thick smoke.

First things first; get the fire out.

There was a grease can with a Texaco sign on it. Woodrow picked it up. It was empty, but there was the smell of gasoline.

"Trash!" Woodrow muttered in angry contempt.

Speed had used gasoline to start the fire. That was dangerous.

Moving quickly, Woodrow went to a water spigot. He knew where to find it, even behind the trash. All these houses were alike, like they were stamped out with a cookie cutter.

He rinsed out the Texaco grease bucket twice, then filled it up with water.

It took six buckets of water to put the fire out, and Woodrow threw a seventh one on the garbage, to be sure. As he looked for a hint of smoke, he glanced at his shoes. The shoes he had shined with such care just two hours before were now covered with filth.

Then he went to the rear door of the residence and knocked on it. There was no response. Woodrow knocked again, and again there was no response. Woodrow gave the door a couple of good licks with his stick.

"Who the fuck is that?" a voice demanded in indignation.

"Speed, get your trashy ass out here!"

James Howard Leslie appeared behind the dirty glass of his kitchen door, and then opened it.

He did not seem particularly happy to see Officer Bailey,

but neither did he seem at all concerned. He was wearing dirty blue jeans, a bead necklace, and nothing else.

"What's happening?" Mr. Leslie inquired.

Officer Bailey lost his temper. He caught Mr. Leslie's wrist and twisted it behind his back. Then he marched Mr. Leslie off his porch and to the smoldering pile of garbage, and manipulated Mr. Leslie's body so that his nose was perhaps six inches from the garbage.

"That's what's happening, Speed," Officer Bailey said.

"Man, you're hurting me! What the fuck!"

"You trying to burn the neighborhood down, Speed? What's the matter with you? You lost the sense you were born with?"

"What the fuck is the big deal? So I burned some garbage! So what the fuck?"

At this point in similar situations, it was normally Officer Bailey's practice to first hurt the trash a little, either with a slap in the face or by jabbing them in the abdomen with his stick to get their attention. To further get their attention, he would then put handcuffs about their wrists and search them for weapons and illegal substances. Very often he encountered the latter, if only a few specks of spilled marijuana in their pockets.

Then he would explain in some detail what crimes they had committed, with special emphasis on the punishments provided by law. If he had found illegal substances on their persons, so much the better.

By then, the malefactor would be contrite. He did not want to go through the inconvenience he knew would be associated with an arrest: detention in the Thirty-ninth District, followed by transportation way the hell downtown to Central Lockup. And then several hours in Central Lockup before being arraigned before a magistrate.

The malefactors knew that the magistrate would probably release them on their own recognizance, and that if they actually got to trial they would walk, but it was a fucking pain in the ass to go through all that bullshit.

Officer Bailey would at some point shortly thereafter inform the trash there was a way to avoid all the inconvenience. They could make their backyard so clean they could eat off it. Get rid of all the garbage, right down to where there once had been grass. Get it all in plastic bags or something, and put it out on the street so the garbageman could take it off.

And keep it that way from now on, or Officer Bailey, who was going to check, would come down on their trashy asses like a ton of bricks, they could believe that.

Far more often than not, the malefactors would agree to this alternate solution of the problem at hand.

Mr. Leslie had, indeed, heard stories about the old black cop who had a hair up his ass about burning garbage, and had heard stories that if he caught you, he'd make you clean up the whole goddamned place or throw your ass in jail.

He was debating—*Jesus Christ, I'm tired*—whether it would be better to let the cop lock him up, or clean up the yard. It would take fucking forever to get all this shit out of here.

Mr. Leslie was not given the opportunity to make a choice.

Officer Bailey just spun him around and, guiding him with one hand on his arm and the other on his shoulder, led him to the cop car. He opened the door and guided Mr. Leslie to a seat in the rear.

Then he returned to the backyard, and the pile of garbage. He took a mechanical pencil from his pocket, squatted beside the garbage, and began to shove things aside. The first item he uncovered was a wedding picture.

He looked at it carefully.

"Lord almighty!" he said wonderingly.

He stirred the garbage a bit more. He was looking for the frame it was logical to assume would be with a photograph of what was supposed to be the happiest moment of a man's life. He could not find one.

He stopped stirring, and, still squatting, was motionless in thought for about thirty seconds.

Then he stood up and walked to Leslie's house. He rapped on the door with his nightstick until the brown-trash Puerto Rican woman appeared.

She stared at him with contempt.

"Teléfono?" Officer Bailey inquired.

The brown-trash woman just looked at him.

He looked over her shoulder, saw a telephone sitting on top of the refrigerator, pointed to it and repeated, *"Teléfono."*

Her expression didn't change, but she shrugged, which Officer Bailey decided could be interpreted to mean that she had given him permission to enter her home.

And now the phone won't work. They won't have paid that bill either.

There was a dial tone.

"Homicide, Detective Kramer."

"Detective, this is Officer Woodrow W. Bailey, of the Thirty-ninth District."

"What can I do for you, Bailey?"

"I'd like to talk to somebody working the job of that police officer, Kellog, who was murdered."

"What have you got, Bailey?"

"You working the job, Detective?"

"The assigned detective's not here. But I'm working it."

"What I got may not be anything, but I thought it was worth telling you."

"What have you got, Bailey?"

"A fellow named James Howard Leslie—he's a junkie, done some time for burglary—was burning garbage in his backyard."

"And?" Detective Kramer asked, somewhat impatiently.

"I put the fire out, and then I got a good look at what he was burning. I don't know . . ."

"What, Bailey?"

"There was a photograph of Officer Kellog and his wife, on their wedding day, in his garbage."

There was a moment's silence, and then Detective

Kramer asked, very carefully: "How do you know it was Officer Kellog?"

"There's a sign on the wall behind him. 'Good Luck Officer Kellog From the Seventeenth District.' And I remembered his picture in the newspapers."

"Where's the picture now?"

"I left it there."

"Where's the guy . . . Leslie, you said?"

"In my car. I arrested him for setting an unlawful fire."

"Where are you?"

"Behind his house. In the alley. The 1900 block of Sedgwick Street."

"I'll be there in ten minutes. Don't let him out of your sight, don't let anybody near where you found the picture, and don't touch nothing you don't have to."

Bailey hung up the telephone, then called the Thirty-ninth District and asked for a supervisor to meet him at the scene.

"What have you got, Bailey?" the Corporal inquired.

"A garbage burner," Bailey said, and hung up.

He nodded at Leslie's Puerto Rican woman, then walked back through the yard to his car and got behind the wheel.

"Hey, Officer, what's happening?" Mr. Leslie inquired, sliding forward with some difficulty on the seat to get closer to the fucking cop.

"You under arrest, Speed," Officer Bailey replied. "For setting a fire in your backyard."

"Oh, Jesus Christ, man! For burning some fucking garbage?"

"If I was you, I'd just sit there and close my mouth," Officer Bailey replied.

As a general rule of thumb, unless the visitor to the Mayor's office was someone really important ("really important" being defined as someone of the ilk of a United States Senator, the Governor of the State of Pennsylvania, or the Cardinal Archbishop of the Diocese of Philadelphia) Mrs. Annette Cossino, the Mayor's secretary, would escort the visitor to the door of the Mayor's office, push it open, and say, "The Mayor will see you now."

The visitor would then be able to see the Mayor deep in concentration, dealing with some document of great importance laid out on his massive desk. After a moment or two, the Mayor would glance toward the door, look surprised and apologetic, and rise to his feet.

"Please excuse me," he would say. "Sometimes . . ."

Visitors would rarely fail to be impressed with the fact that the Mayor was tearing himself from Something Important to receive them.

This afternoon, however, on learning that Chief Inspector Matt Lowenstein had asked for an appointment for himself and Inspector Peter Wohl, His Honor had decided to deviate from the normal routine.

While he could not be fairly accused of being paranoid, the threatened resignation of Chief Lowenstein had caused the Mayor to consider that he really had few friends, people he could really trust, and that Matt Lowenstein was just about at the head of that short list.

"When he comes in, Annette," the Mayor ordered, "you let me know he's here, and I'll come out and get him."

Such a gesture would, the Mayor believed, permit Chief Lowenstein to understand the high personal regard in which he was held. And Peter Wohl would certainly report the manner in which Lowenstein had been welcomed to the Mayor's office to his father. The Mayor was perfectly willing to admit—at least to himself—that his rise through every rank to Commissioner of the Philadelphia Police Department—which, of course, had led to his seeking the mayoralty—would not have been possible had not Chief Inspector Augustus Wohl covered his ass in at least half a dozen really bad situations.

And when he thought about that, he realized that Inspector Peter Wohl was no longer a nice young cop, but getting to be a power in his own right. And that he could safely add him to the short list of people he could trust.

He was pleased with his decision to greet Lowenstein and Wohl in a special manner.

And was thus somewhat annoyed when he pulled the door to his office open, a warm smile on his face, his hand extended, and found that Chief Lowenstein was at Annette's desk talking on the telephone.

Finally, Chief Lowenstein hung up and turned around.

"Sorry," Lowenstein said.

"What the hell was that?" Carlucci asked, somewhat sharply.

"Henry Quaire," Lowenstein said. "There may be a break in the Kellog murder."

"What?" the Mayor asked.

He's not being charming, Peter Wohl thought. *When Lowenstein told him that, he went right back on the job. He's a cop, and if there is one thing a cop hates worse than a murdered cop it's a murdered cop with no doers in sight.*

"A uniform in the Thirty-ninth working his beat came across a critter, junkie, petty criminal with a record six feet long, including burglaries, burning garbage in his backyard. In the garbage was Officer Kellog's wedding picture. The uniform called Homicide."

"There was mention of a wedding picture in the 49s," Carlucci said. "In a silver frame."

"Right," Lowenstein said.

"Where else would he get a picture of Kellog?" Carlucci asked, thoughtfully rhetoric. "Have you got the frame?"

"Yeah. That's why Quaire called me. We got a search warrant. They found not only a silver frame, but a dozen—thirteen, actually—tape cassettes. They were in the fire, but maybe Forensics can do something with them. If Mrs. Kellog can identify the frame, or there's something on the tapes . . ."

"Where's the critter?"

"Right now, he's on his way from the Thirty-ninth to Homicide," Lowenstein said.

"Who's going to interview him?"

Lowenstein shrugged. "Detective D'Amata is the assigned detective."

"Peter, do you have Jason Washington doing anything he can't put off for a couple of hours?" the Mayor asked, innocently.

That is, Wohl noted mentally, *the first time the Mayor has acknowledged my presence.*

"You want to take it away from D'Amata?" Lowenstein asked.

"I'd like an arrest in that case," Carlucci said. "If you think it would be a good idea to have Washington talk to this critter, Matt, I'd go along with that."

"Shit," Lowenstein said. "You find Washington, Peter," he ordered. "I'll call Quaire."

"Yes, sir," Peter said.

"Only if you think it's a good idea, Matt," the Mayor said. "It was only a suggestion."

"Yeah, right," Lowenstein said, and walked back to Mrs. Annette Cossino's desk and reached for one of the telephones.

"D'Amata will understand, Peter," the Mayor said.

"Yes, sir," Peter said. "I'm sure he will."

"Annette," the Mayor called. "Call the Thirty-ninth. Tell the Commanding Officer I want him and this uniform standing by to come here if I need them."

"Yes, Mr. Mayor," Mrs. Cossino said.

"Henry," Lowenstein said into the telephone. "When they bring in the critter from the Thirty-ninth, handcuff him to a chair in an interview room and leave him there until Washington shows up. Wohl's putting the arm out for him now. I think that's the way to handle the interview, and the Mayor agrees."

He hung the phone up and turned to face Carlucci.

"Are you pissed at me, Matt?" Carlucci, sounding genuinely concerned, asked.

"When am I not pissed at you?" Lowenstein said. "It goes with the territory."

"You don't think it was a good idea?"

"That's the trouble. I think it was a very good idea," Lowenstein said.

"Sergeant Washington is en route to the Roundhouse, Mr. Mayor," Wohl repeated.

"Great!" Carlucci said enthusiastically. Then he smiled broadly. "Let's do this all over."

"What?" Lowenstein asked in confusion.

"Well, Chief Lowenstein," Carlucci said, and grabbed Lowenstein's hand and pumped it. "And Inspector Wohl! How good of you both to come see me! It's always a pleasure to see two of the most valuable members of the Police Department here in my office. Come in and have a cup of coffee and tell me how I may be of assistance!"

Lowenstein shook his head in resignation.

"Jesus Christ!"

"What *can* I do for you, Chief?"

"Stop the bullshit, Jerry," Lowenstein said, chuckling.

"OK," Carlucci said agreeably. "What's up?"

"Last night, a couple of South detectives saw one John Francis Foley pass a package to one Gerald North Atchison. Shortly thereafter, Detective Payne of Special Operations saw Mr. Atchison throw said package off a pier in Chester—"

"How did South detectives get involved in this?" Carlucci asked, and Wohl saw that he had slipped back into being a cop.

"Payne was surveilling Atchison. He ran into the South detectives and asked for their assistance."

"OK," Carlucci said thoughtfully. "Go on."

"The package was retrieved early this morning by a police diver. The lab just came up with a positive ballistics match to the murder weapons."

"Fingerprints?"

Lowenstein shook his head. "Weapons were cleaned. I thought I'd show it to you before I sent someone over to Tom Callis's office with it."

"Let me see," Carlucci said, holding out his hand. Lowenstein handed the Mayor an envelope. Carlucci made a "come in" gesture with his hand, walked ahead of them into his office, sat down at his desk, and opened the envelope.

FORENSICS LABORATORY REPORT		PHILADELPHIA POLICE DEPARTMENT
REPORT DATE	SUPPLEMENTAL	
CLASSIFICATION		
DATE AND TIME REPORTED	PREPARED BY	Tech. Harry Withjack
DETAILS:		

The Forensics Laboratory conducted the following examinations of evidence submitted, with results as follows:

(1) Projectiles:

(A) Three (3) bullets taken from the head of Anthony J. Marcuzzi (In envelope marked Case #2397.)

(B) Four (4) bullets taken from the head of Alicia Atchison. (In envelope marked Case #2398.)

(C) One (1) bullet taken from the leg of Gerald N. Atchison. (In envelope marked Case #2399.)

(D) Three (3) .38 Special Caliber bullets fired from Colt Revolver Serial #286955 in the Police Laboratory.

(E) Three (3) .44-40 caliber bullets fired from six-shot single-action revolver (No Manufacturer's Name) probably of Spanish Manufacture, Serial #9133 in the Police Laboratory.

(F) Three (3) .32 ACP bullets fired from Savage semiautomatic pistol Serial #44078 in the Police Laboratory.

Bullets described in (A) and (B) above were removed by Dr. Howard D. Mitchell, Medical Examiners Office, during the course of autopsies performed on the decedents, on Saturday, May 20, 1975 and turned over to Detective Wallace J. Milham. Submitted to Ballistics Lab by Detective Milham on property receipt #201308 on May 20, 1975.

Bullet described in (C) above was taken from the leg of Gerald N. Atchison by K. Lewis Hailey, MD, at Hahnemann Hospital on May 20, 1975, and turned over to Detective Wallace J. Milham. Submitted to Ballistics Lab by Detective Milham on property receipt #201322 on May 20, 1975.

Bullets described in (D), (E), and (F) above were fired by the undersigned under test conditions witnessed by Lieutenant Thomas P. McNamara.

APPROVED: (Type and Sign Name)	SERGEANT	LIEUTENANT

Thomas P. McNamara

Thomas P. McNamara, Officer In Charge

75–91 (Rev 3/70)

462 ▪ W.E.B. Griffin

FORENSICS LABORATORY REPORT		PHILADELPHIA POLICE DEPARTMENT
REPORT DATE	SUPPLEMENTAL|	
CLASSIFICATION|		
DATE AND TIME REPORTED	|PREPARED BY	Tech. Harry Withjack |
DETAILS:		

(2) Analysis:

(A) Ballistic Laboratory Report #640742: (From the head of Anthony J. Marcuzzi):

1. One (1) BULLET SPECIMEN, marked 640742X1 on base area for identification purposes, uncoated lead, caliber .44, bearing one knurled cannelure, weight 198.5 grains, fired from a smokeless powder cartridge, considerably mutilated and distorted, with large piece of bone and flesh tissue adhered. General rifling characteristics: Indeterminable.

2. One (1) BULLET SPECIMEN, marked 640742X2 on base area for identification purposes, uncoated lead, caliber .44, bearing one knurled cannelure, weight 205.8 grains, fired from a smokeless powder cartridge, considerably distorted. General rifling characteristics: five lands and five grooves with a right hand direction of twist.

3. One (1) BULLET SPECIMEN, marked 640742X3 on base area for identification purposes, uncoated lead, caliber .44, bearing one knurled cannelure, weight 215.7 grains, fired from a smokeless powder cartridge, considerably distorted. General rifling characteristics: five lands and five grooves with a right hand direction of twist.

(B) Ballistic Laboratory Report #640743: (From the head of Alicia Atchison):

1. One (1) BULLET SPECIMEN and two bullet fragments, bullet specimen marked 640743X1 on flattened surface and fragments marked x1 for identification purposes, uncoated lead, caliber .38 Special, bearing one knurled cannelure, total weight 142.87 grains, fired from a smokeless powder cartridge, considerably flattened and distorted. General rifling characteristics: five lands and five grooves with a right hand direction of twist.

APPROVED: (Type and Sign Name)	|SERGEANT	|LIEUTENANT
	Thomas P. McNamara	
	||Thomas P. McNamara,	Officer In Charge

75–91 (Rev 3/70)

FORENSICS LABORATORY REPORT	PHILADELPHIA POLICE DEPARTMENT
REPORT DATE	SUPPLEMENTAL|
CLASSIFICATION|	
DATE AND TIME REPORTED |PREPARED BY Tech. Harry Withjack	

DETAILS:

(2) Analysis: (Continued)

2. One (1) BULLET SPECIMEN, marked 640743X2 on base area for identification purposes, uncoated lead, caliber .38 Special, bearing one knurled cannelure, weight 137.37 grains, fired from a smokeless powder cartridge, considerably mutilated and distorted. General rifling characteristics: five lands and five grooves with a right hand direction of twist.

3. One (1) BULLET SPECIMEN, marked 640743X3 on base area for identification purposes, uncoated lead, caliber .38 Special, bearing one knurled cannelure, weight 127.3 grains, fired from a smokeless powder cartridge, considerably mutilated and distorted. General rifling characteristics: five lands and five grooves with a right hand direction of twist.

4. One (1) BULLET SPECIMEN, marked 640743X4 on base area for identification purposes, uncoated lead, caliber .44, bearing one knurled cannelure, weight 205.5 grains, fired from a smokeless powder cartridge, considerably mutilated and distorted, with large piece of bone and flesh tissue adhered. General rifling characteristics: Indeterminable.

(C) Ballistic Laboratory Report #640744: (From the leg of Gerald N. Atchison):

One (1) BULLET SPECIMEN, marked 640744X1 on base area for identification purposes, uncoated lead, caliber .32, bearing one knurled cannelure, weight 80.25 grains, fired from a smokeless powder cartridge, slightly distorted. General rifling characteristics: six lands and six grooves with a left hand direction of twist.

(3) Determinations:

(A) Microscopic comparative examination of .44 caliber bullets removed from the heads of Anthony J. Marcuzzi and Alicia

APPROVED: (Type and Sign Name)	|SERGEANT	|LIEUTENANT
Thomas P. McNamara		
|Thomas P. McNamara, Officer In Charge		

75–91 (Rev 3/70)

464 ■ W.E.B. Griffin

FORENSICS LABORATORY REPORT		PHILADELPHIA POLICE DEPARTMENT
REPORT DATE	SUPPLEMENTAL|	
CLASSIFICATION|		
DATE AND TIME REPORTED	|PREPARED BY	Tech. Harry Withjack	

DETAILS:

(3) Determinations: (Continued)

Atchison shows that all bullets were fired from the same revolver, Microscopic comparative examination of bullets fired from .44-40 Caliber Revolver Serial #9133 in the Police Laboratory with bullets removed from Marcuzzi and Atchison's heads shows identical markings, indicating the .44-40 Revolver #9133 fired all tested bullets. (B) Microscopic comparative examination of .38 Special caliber bullets removed from the head of Alicia Atchison shows that all bullets were fired from the same revolver. Microscopic comparative examination of bullets fired from .38 Special Caliber Colt Revolver Serial #286955 in the Police Laboratory with bullets removed from Atchison's head shows identical markings, indicating the .38 Special Colt Revolver #286955 fired all tested bullets.

(C) Microscopic comparative examination of .32 ACP bullets removed from the leg of Gerald N. Atchison with bullets fired from Savage .32 ACP semiautomatic pistol, Serial #44078 in the Police Laboratory shows identical markings, indicating the .32 ACP caliber Savage pistol #44078 fired all tested bullets.

APPROVED: (Type and Sign Name)	|SERGEANT	|LIEUTENANT

Thomas P. McNamara

||Thomas P. McNamara, Officer In Charge

75–91 (Rev 3/70)

Carlucci carefully stuffed the report back into its envelope, then looked at Lowenstein.

"It may be enough," Carlucci said. "It is for an arrest, anyway."

"I thought so," Lowenstein said. "I'll have it sent to Callis within the hour."

"What the hell, Matt," Carlucci said. "I mean, you're right here in the neighborhood, right? Why don't you, both of you, take this to Tom? See if he has any problems with it? Give him my very best regards when you do."

James Howard Leslie had been sitting in the steel captain's chair in the Homicide Unit interview room, handcuffed to its seat, for almost an hour when the door opened and a very large, important-looking black man walked in.

No one had spoken to him during that time, nor had anyone so much as opened the door to look at him. He suspected that he was being watched through the somewhat fuzzy mirror on the wall, but he couldn't be sure.

"James Howard Leslie?" the black man asked.

Leslie didn't reply.

"Good afternoon," Jason Washington said. "If you'd like, I can remove the handcuff."

"I don't give a fuck one way or the other."

Washington unlocked the handcuff and stood back. Leslie rubbed his wrist.

"I don't even know what the fuck's going on," Leslie said.

"You've been in here some time, I understand." Washington said. "Is there anything I can get for you? Would you like a Coca-Cola, a cup of coffee, a sandwich?"

"What I would like is to know what the hell is going on. All I did was try to burn some garbage."

"I understand. That's why I'm here, to explain to you what's going on. And while we're talking, would you like a Coca-Cola, or a cigarette?"

"I could drink a Coke."

Washington opened the door. "Sergeant," he ordered sternly, "would you please get a Coca-Cola for Mr. Leslie?"

Leslie heard someone reply.

"Fuck him! Let the fucking cop killer drink water!"

"I said get him a Coca-Cola."

"Whose side are you on, anyway?" the voice said.

"That wasn't a suggestion, it was an order," Washington said sharply.

Two minutes later, a slight, dapper man with a pencil-thin mustache entered the interview room with a Coca-Cola, thrust it into Leslie's hand with such violence that liquid erupted from the neck of the bottle and spilled on Leslie's shirt and trousers.

The slight, dapper man then left the interview room. Just before the door slammed shut, Leslie heard the man say, "Fuck Special Operations, too."

Washington handed Leslie a crisp white handkerchief to clean his shirt and trousers.

"He and Officer Kellog were friends," Washington said, in explanation.

"What?"

"It doesn't matter," Washington said. He leaned on the wall by the door, waited until Leslie had finished mopping at himself and started to return the handkerchief.

"Keep it," Washington said. "You may need it again."

"Thanks," Leslie said.

"As I understand what's happened here," Washington said conversationally, "Officer Bailey of the Thirty-ninth District extinguished a fire in your backyard. In doing so, he found a photograph of Officer Kellog on his wedding day."

"I don't know what the fuck you're talking about. Officer who?"

"The finding of the photograph was, in the opinion of the Honorable Francis X. McGrory, Judge of the Superior Court, sufficient cause for him to issue a search warrant for your home."

"I told you, I don't know what the fuck you're talking about."

"A search of your home was then conducted by detectives of the Homicide Bureau. A silver frame was discovered. It has since been positively identified by Mrs. Helene Kellog as her property. Mrs. Kellog previously reported the framed photograph to have been stolen from her home."

"So what?"

"Mrs. Kellog's husband, Police Officer Jerome H. Kellog, was found dead in his home. Shot to death. Inasmuch as his silver-framed wedding photograph was known to be present in his home prior to the robbery, and missing from his home immediately after the robbery, it is presumed that the framed photograph was stolen during the robbery."

"So what?"

"During the search authorized by Judge McGrory, Homicide detectives found other items among those things you were attempting to burn known to be the property of Police Officer Kellog. Specifically, thirteen recording tapes. And some other items."

"I keep telling you, I don't know what the fuck you're talking about."

"Mr. Leslie, you are presently being held for setting an unlawful fire," Washington said. "And, I believe, for maintaining an unsanitary nuisance."

"Then what the fuck am I doing here?"

"Very shortly, I think you can count on a Homicide detective coming in here and arresting you for the murder of Officer Kellog. I came here to see if I could explain your situation to you."

"What the hell does that mean?"

"If you are arrested for the murder of Officer Kellog, you will receive the required Miranda warning. I understand you have been arrested before, and know what that means. You will be advised of your rights, and provided with an attorney."

"Who the hell are you?"

"I'm a police officer, an investigator for the Special Operations Division: We are sometimes asked, in cases like this, to see if we can't get through a situation like this as smoothly as possible. To save everyone concerned time and money."

"I don't know what the hell you're talking about."

"I'll try to explain it to you. In my judgment, from what the Homicide Bureau Commanding Officer has shown and told me, what Homicide has here is a pretty strong case of circumstantial evidence against you. What I mean by that is that no one actually saw you shoot Officer Kellog. There were no witnesses. That means, when your case comes to trial, the District Attorney—I think I should explain that to you, too."

"Explain what?"

"The District Attorney, Mr. Thomas Callis, rarely goes into court himself. *Assistant* district attorneys actually do the prosecuting. The exception to that rule is when a police officer has been killed. Mr. Callis himself prosecutes such cases. He was a police officer himself when he was a young man. So I think you can expect, when your case comes to trial, that you will be prosecuted by him personally. Do you understand that?"

"I guess so."

"Fine. Well, what Mr. Callis will have to do in your trial will be to convince the jury that although no one actually saw you shoot Officer Kellog—"

"I didn't shoot anybody! I don't know what the fuck this is all about!"

"In that case, you—through your attorney, and I suppose you know that if you can't afford to hire an attorney, one will be assigned to you from the Office of the Public Defender. And I must admit that some of those young men and women are really quite competent. They're young and dedicated, fresh from law school, and really try hard."

"I don't have any fucking money," Leslie said.

"Yes, we know," Washington said. "As I was saying, if

you say you are innocent, your defense counsel will enter a plea of not guilty on your behalf. Then it will be up to Mr. Callis to convince the jury that, although no one actually saw you shoot Officer Kellog, the circumstances surrounding the incident prove that you and only you could have done it.

"Mr. Callis will try to convince the jury that the only way you could have come into possession of the silver frame the Homicide detectives found in your home, and tapes they found in your home, and the photograph of Officer Kellog Officer Bailey found in the fire you set—"

"I don't know anything about no fucking photograph!"

"You will be given the chance to explain how tapes made by Officer Kellog, tapes of his voice and telephone calls, came into your possession."

"I don't know nothing about no fucking tapes, either!"

"Your public defender will try to prove that," Washington said. "Mr. Callis will be given the opportunity to try to convince the jury that you stole the framed photograph and the tapes and the other things from Officer Kellog's home, and that in the conduct of that robbery, Officer Kellog came home and you shot him."

"I didn't do nothing like that."

"And then it will be your attorney's turn to convince the jury that it wasn't you. If you can find someone, someone the jury would believe, who will go into court and swear that you were with them during the time of the robbery, that might help. Or if you could explain how the photograph of Officer Kellog and the silver frame and tapes and the other things came into your possession, that would help your case."

"People are always throwing shit over the fence," Leslie said.

"That might explain the photograph," Washington said, reasonably, "but not the frame, which was found inside your house."

Leslie looked uncomfortable.

"Your defense counsel could also have as witnesses people who know you, and would testify to your character, to try to make the point that you're not the sort of fellow who would do something like this," Washington said. "But if he did that, under the law Mr. Callis could introduce evidence to the contrary. You've been arrested, I understand, for burglary on several occasions."

"So what? That doesn't mean I did the cop."

"There is an alternative," Washington said.

"What?"

The door opened and another detective, this one a huge white man wearing cowboy boots, stepped inside.

"Excuse me, Mr. Washington, District Attorney Callis is on the telephone for you."

"I was afraid of that," Washington said. "I don't know how long this will take, Mr. Leslie, but I'll try to come back."

He left the interview room.

"Who the fuck uncuffed you?" the large detective asked rhetorically, walked quickly to Leslie, grabbed his right arm, clamped the handcuff on his wrist, muttered, "Fucking Special Operations hotshot!" under his breath, and stormed out of the interview room, slamming the door closed and leaving Mr. Leslie alone again.

Outside the room, he walked directly to Sergeant Washington, who was sitting on a desk holding a mug of coffee in his hands.

"That's my mug, Jason."

"I won't say I'm sorry, because I am not."

The large detective laughed.

"I didn't think you would be. You think this is going to work?"

"I think we have established in his mind that (a) you don't like him; (b) that shooting a policeman is not socially acceptable conduct; and (c) that he can't beat this unless the nice black man comes up with some solution. The test of these assumptions will come when I go back in."

"You want me to go back in there and accidentally bump him around a little?"

"I think that would be counterproductive. As frightening as you are, Arthur, I think his imagination should be allowed to run free."

"Your call. Changing the subject: There's a story going around that your pal Payne climbed out on a thirteenth-floor ledge of the Bellvue-Stratford to fix a wire?"

"All too true, I'm afraid. I have remonstrated with him."

"What's with him, Jason?"

"He's young. Aside from that, he's a damned good cop."

"I meant, if he's got all the dough everybody thinks he has, why is he a cop?"

"He has all the dough everybody thinks he has," Washington said. "Did you ever think, Arthur, that some people are, so to speak, born to be policemen?"

"You, for example?"

"It's possible. You and me. I can't imagine doing anything else."

"Shit, neither can I. What would I do? Sell used cars?"

"Some of it is the challenge, I think. That explains people like you and me. And probably Payne. But what about people like Officer Bailey? I talked to him before I came here. The reason Leslie is in there is because Bailey, after years on the job, still takes personal pride and satisfaction in protecting people from critters like Leslie. He knows he can't personally clean up the Thirty-ninth District, but 'You don't burn your garbage on my beat.' "

Arthur grunted.

"How long are you going to let the critter's imagination run free?"

"I think fifteen minutes should suffice," Washington said. He looked at his watch. "Another five and a half minutes, to be specific."

"That big guy cuffed me again," Leslie said in some indignation, raising his shackled wrist to demonstrate.

Washington made no move to unlock the handcuff.

"I just came in to tell you I have to leave. I have to go to see Mr. Callis. The decision is yours, Mr. Leslie, and now is when you're going to have to make it."

"What decision?"

"Whether you wish to insist on your innocence, or—"

"Or what?"

"Be cooperative."

"Like what?"

"How serious is your narcotics addiction, Mr. Leslie?"

"I ain't no addict, if that's what you're saying."

"I can't possibly help you, Mr. Leslie, if you don't tell me the truth. Your records show that you have undergone a drug-rehabilitation program. Why lie about it?"

"I got it under control."

"Then you were not under the influence of narcotics when you burglarized Officer Kellog's home? Your defense counsel might be able to introduce that at your trial. 'Diminished capacity' is the term used."

"I don't know what that means."

"It means that if you weren't aware of what you were doing, because of 'diminished capacity' because you were on drugs, you really didn't know what you were doing, and should be judged accordingly."

"Which means what?"

"Let me explain this to you as best I can. If you are not cooperative, they're going to take you to court and ask for the death penalty. In my judgment, they have enough circumstantial evidence to get a conviction."

"And if I'm cooperative, what?"

"You probably would not get the death penalty. It's possible that the District Attorney would be agreeable to having evidence of your drug addiction given to the court, and that the court would take it into consideration when considering your sentence."

"Shit."

"I'm not a lawyer, Mr. Leslie. You should discuss this with a lawyer."

"When do I get a lawyer?"

"When Homicide arrests you for murder, and your Miranda rights come into play. That's going to happen. What you have to decide, *before* you are arrested for murder, is whether you want to cooperate or not."

"I could plead, what did you say, 'diminished capacity'?"

"What I said was that you can either tell the truth, and make it easier on yourself and Homicide, or lie, and make it harder on yourself and Homicide."

"You're not going to be around for this?"

"No. But I've talked to Lieutenant Natali, and explained to him the situation here, and I think the two of you would be able to work something out that would be in everybody's best interests."

"Jesus, I don't know," Leslie said.

"I've got to go. I'll ask Lieutenant Natali to come here and talk to you."

"Jesus, I wish you could stick around."

"I could come to talk some more, later, if you'd like."

"Yeah."

Washington put out his hand. Leslie's right arm was handcuffed to the chair, so he had to shake Washington's hand with his left hand.

"Good luck, Mr. Leslie," Washington said.

"Jesus Christ, I don't know what to do."

"Talk it over with Lieutenant Natali," Washington said. He walked to the door and pulled it open, then closed it.

"Just between us, Mr. Leslie, to satisfy my curiosity. Why did you think you had to shoot Officer Kellog?"

"Well, shit," Leslie said. "I had to. He seen my face. He was a cop. I knew he'd find me sooner or later."

"Yes," Washington said. "Of course, I understand."

"I'm going to hold you to what you said about coming to talk to me," Leslie said.

"I will," Washington said. "I said I would, and I will."

He left the interview room.

Lieutenant Natali and Detective D'Amata came out of the adjacent room. They had been watching through a one-way mirror.

Natali quoted, "I had to. He seen my face. He was a cop."

"Christ!" D'Amata said in mingled disgust and horror.

"What's really sad," Washington said, "is that he doesn't acknowledge, or even understand, the enormity of what he's done. The only thing he thinks he did wrong is to get caught doing it."

"You don't want to stick around, Jason?" D'Amata said. "I'll probably need your help."

Washington looked at Lieutenant Natali.

"Does Joe know who Mrs. Kellog believed was responsible for her husband's death?"

"You mean Narcotics Five Squad?" D'Amata asked.

"I thought he should know," Natali said. "I told him to keep it under his hat."

"That's what I was doing, Joe, when they sent me here. But to coin a phrase, 'Duty calls.' Or how about, 'It's a dirty job but somebody has to do it'? Do I have to tell you I'd much rather stay here?"

Both Natali and D'Amata shook their heads. Natali touched Washington's arm, and then Washington walked out of Homicide.

The Honorable Thomas J. "Tony" Callis, the District Attorney of the County of Philadelphia, had decided he would personally deal with the case of Messrs. Francis Foley and Gerald North Atchison rather than entrust it to one of the Assistant District Attorneys subordinate to him.

This was less because of his judgment of the professional skill levels involved (although Mr. Callis, like most lawyers, in his heart of hearts, believed he was as competent an attorney as he had ever met) than because of the political implications involved.

He was very much aware that the Hon. Jerry Carlucci,

Mayor of the City of Philadelphia, was taking a personal interest in this case, a personal interest heavily flavored with political implications. The *Ledger*, which was after Carlucci's scalp, had been running scathing editorials bringing to the public's attention the Police Department's inability to arrest whoever had blown Atchison's wife and partner away. (Alternating the "Outrageous Massacre of Center City Restaurateur's Wife and Partner" editorials, Tony Callis had noted, with equally scathing editorials bringing to the public's attention that a cop had been brutally murdered in his kitchen, and the cops didn't seem to know anything about that, either.)

Mr. Callis, a large, silver-haired, ruddy-faced, well-tailored man in his early fifties, had a somewhat tenuous political alliance with Mayor Carlucci. It was understood between the parties that either would abandon the other the moment it appeared that the alliance threatened the reelection chances of either.

As a politician possessed of skills approaching the political skills of the Mayor, the District Attorney had considered the possibility that Mayor Carlucci would be happy to drop the ball, the Inferno ball, into his lap. That he would, in other words, be able to get the *Ledger* off his back by making an arrest in the case on information that might not hold up either before a grand jury or in court.

"My Police Department," the Mayor might well say, "with its usual brilliance, nabbed those villains. If they walked out of court free men, that speaks to the competence of Mr. Callis."

Proof—not that any was needed—that this case had heavy political ramifications came when the police officers sent to the District Attorney's office to present their evidence gathered turned out to be Chief Inspector of Detectives Matthew Lowenstein and Inspector Peter Wohl, Commanding Officer of the Special Operations Division. Mr. Callis—who normally disagreed with anything written in the *Ledger*, which had opposed him in the last election—

was forced to admit that there was indeed more than a grain of truth in the *Ledger*'s editorial assertion that the Special Operations Division had become Carlucci's private police force.

And with Chief Lowenstein's opening comment, when he was shown into Callis's office:

"Mr. District Attorney, I bring you the best regards of our mayor, whose office Inspector Wohl and I just left."

"How gracious of our beloved mayor! Please be so kind, Chief Inspector, to pass on my warmest regards to His Honor when you next see him, which no doubt will be shortly after we conclude our little chat."

"It will be my pleasure, Mr. District Attorney."

"How the hell are you, Matt?" Callis asked, chuckling. "We don't see enough of each other these days."

"Can't complain, Tom. How's the wife?"

"Compared to what? How are you, Peter?"

"Mr. Callis," Wohl said.

"You're a big boy now, Peter. A full inspector. You don't have to call me 'Mister.'"

Wohl smiled and shrugged, and raised his hands in a gesture of helplessness.

"My saintly father always told me, when you're with a lawyer, be respectful and keep one hand on your wallet," Wohl said.

Callis chuckled. "Give my regards to the saintly old gentleman, Peter. And your mother."

"Thank you, I will."

"OK. Now what have we got?"

"We have the guns used in the Inferno murders. We have—" Lowenstein began.

"Tell me about the guns, Matt," Callis interrupted.

Lowenstein opened his briefcase. He took a sheaf of Xerox copies from it and laid it on Callis's desk.

"The lab reports, Tom," he said. "They're pretty conclusive."

"Would you mind if I asked Harry Hormel to come in

here?" Callis asked. "If I can't find the time to prosecute, it'll almost certainly be Harry."

"By all means," Lowenstein said smoothly. "I'd like to get Harry's opinion."

District Attorney Callis punched his intercom button and very politely asked his secretary to see if she could determine if Mr. Hormel was in the building, and if so, if he could spare a few minutes to come to his office.

A faint smile flickered across Peter Wohl's face. He was perfectly sure that Hormel had been ordered, probably far less courteously, to make himself available.

"Harry," Callis had almost certainly said, "don't leave the office until you check with me. Lowenstein and Wohl are coming over with something on the Inferno murders. I'll need you."

Or words to that effect: Mr. Harrison J. Hormel was an assistant district attorney. He had come to the District Attorney's Office right after passing the bar examination twenty-odd years before and had stayed.

Only a small number of bright young lawyers fresh from law school stayed on. Many of those who did were those who felt the need of a steady paycheck and were not at all sure they could earn a living in private practice. Hormel, in Peter's opinion, was the exception to that rule of thumb. He was a very good lawyer, and a splendid courtroom performer. Juries trusted him. He could have had a far more lucrative legal career as a defense counsel.

Peter had decided, years before, that Hormel had stayed on, rising to be (at least de facto) the best prosecutor in the DA's Office because he took pride and satisfaction in putting evil people where they could do no more harm.

And Peter knew that whether District Attorney Callis or Assistant District Attorney Hormel prosecuted Foley and Atchison would not be based on professional qualifications—Callis was not a fool, and was honest enough to admit that Hormel was the better prosecutor—but on Callis's weighing of the odds on whether the case could be won or lost. If conviction looked certain, he would prosecute, and take the glory. If there was some doubt, Hormel would be assigned. It was to be hoped that his superior skill would triumph. If Foley and/or Atchison walked, the embarrassment would be Hormel's, not Callis's.

Callis took his glasses, which, suspended around his neck on an elastic cord, had been resting on his chest, and adjusted them on his nose. Then he leaned forward on his desk and began to read, carefully, the report Lowenstein had given him.

Assistant District Attorney Hormel entered Callis's office while Callis was reading the report. He quietly greeted Lowenstein and Wohl, then stretched himself out in a leather armchair to the side of Callis's desk.

Wordlessly, Callis handed him the report, page by page, as he finished reading it. When he himself had finished reading it, he looked at Chief Inspector Lowenstein and made a gesture clearly indicating he was not awed by the report.

Lowenstein handed him another sheaf of Xerox copies.

"The 75-49s on the recovery of the murder weapons," he said.

Callis again placed his glasses on his nose and read the 75-49s carefully, again handing the pages as he finished them to Assistant District Attorney Hormel.

As he read page four, he said: "Denny Coughlin was a witness to the recovery? What was he doing there?"

"Chief Coughlin did not see fit to inform me of his reasons," Lowenstein said. "Inspector Wohl suspects that he thought it would be nice to go yachting at that hour of the morning."

"Oh, shit, Matt." Callis laughed.

Callis finished reading the 75-49s, and then everybody waited for Hormel to finish.

"There are some problems with this," Hormel said.

"Such as?"

"What was this Special Operations detective doing surveilling Mr. Atchison?"

"At the direction of the Commissioner, Detective Payne was detailed to Homicide to assist in the investigation," Lowenstein said.

"I'd love to know what that was all about," Callis said, looking at Lowenstein. "Was that before or after you threatened to retire?"

"Gossip does get around, doesn't it?" Lowenstein said. "I didn't *threaten* to retire. I *considered* retiring. I changed my mind. If you're suggesting I in any way was unhappy with the detail of Detective Payne to Homicide, I was not. He is a very bright young man, as those 75-49s indicate."

"He was assigned to surveil Atchison?"

"He was ordered to assist the assigned detective in whatever way the assigned detective felt would be helpful," Lowenstein replied.

"Presumably," Hormel said, "there was coordination with the Media Police Department?"

"That same afternoon, Detective Payne accompanied Sergeant Washington to interview Mr. Atchison at his home. That was coordinated with the Media Police Department."

"Jason's back working Homicide? I hadn't heard that," Callis said.

"Sergeant Washington and Detective Payne were the first police officers on the scene of the Inferno Lounge murders," Lowenstein said. "Inspector Wohl was kind enough to make them both available to me to assist in the conduct of Homicide's investigation of the murders."

Callis snorted.

"'Detective Payne,'" Hormel said, obviously playing the role of a defense attorney, "'you look like a very young man. How long have you been a police officer? How long have you been a detective?'"

"'How long have you been assigned to Homicide?'" Callis picked up on Hormel's role playing. "'Oh, you're not assigned to Homicide? Then you really had no previous experience in conducting a surveillance of a murder suspect? Is that what you're telling me?'"

"And then we get to re-direct," Wohl said. "Our distinguished Assistant District Attorney—or perhaps the District Attorney himself—approaches the boy detective on the stand and asks, 'Detective Payne, were you in any way involved in the apprehension of the so-called Northwest Serial Rapist? Oh, was that you who was forced to use deadly force to rescue Mrs. Naomi Schneider from the deadly clutches of that fiend?'"

Callis chuckled.

"Very good, Peter."

"'And were you involved in any way, Detective Payne, in the apprehension of the persons subsequently convicted in the murders at Goldblatt's Furniture Store? Oh, was that you who was in the deadly gun battle with one of the murderers? Mr. Atchison was not, then, the first murderer with whom you have dealt?'"

"That could be turned against you. It could make him look like a cowboy," Callis said.

"The dark and stormy night is what bothers me," Hormel said. "We have to convince the jury that the package Denny Coughlin saw them take from the river was the same package Atchison tossed in there. That's a tenuous connection."

"The two South detectives saw the package being passed from Foley to Atchison," Lowenstein said.

"No, they didn't," Hormel argued. "There's room for reasonable doubt about that. And it was a dark and stormy night. 'How can you testify under oath, Detective Payne, that the package taken from the river by police divers was the package you saw Mr. Atchison carry out of Yock's Diner? How can you testify under oath that, if the night was as dark as you have testified it was, and you were as far from Mr. Atchison as you say you were, that what he threw, if indeed he threw anything, into the river was that package? You couldn't really see him, could you? You're testifying to what you may honestly believe happened, but, honestly, you didn't really see anything, did you?'"

"Ah, come on, Harry!" Lowenstein protested.

"I'm inclined to go with Harry," Callis said. "This is weak."

Lowenstein stood up.

"Always a pleasure to see you, Tom," he said. "And you, too, Harry."

"Where are you going?"

"To carry out my orders," Lowenstein said. "I was instructed to show you what we have. Then I was instructed to arrest the sonsofbitches. Come on, Peter."

Wohl stood up and offered his hand to Harry Hormel.

"Now, wait a minute," Callis said. "I didn't say it was no good. I said it was weak."

"It is," Hormel agreed.

"Harry," the District Attorney said. "You've gone into court with less then this, and won. Peter made a good point. All you have to do is convince the jury that these two were pursued by one of the brightest detectives on the force. A certified hero. If you handle that angle right, you can go for the death penalty and get it."

"It's weak," Harry Hormel repeated.

"Let Harry know when you have them, Matt," Callis said. "I'm sure he would like to be there when you confront them with the guns."

TWENTY-TWO

For Frankie Foley, there had been a certain satisfying finality about his meeting with Gerry Atchison in the Yock's Diner the previous night. He had received his final payment for the hit, and he'd gotten rid of the guns. The job was done.

He presumed that Atchison would safely dispose of the weapons somewhere, probably throw them in the Delaware, or bury them in the woods when he was out playing weekend warrior with the National Guard. It didn't matter.

Frankie knew that once Atchison had taken the guns, and once he'd gotten out of the diner without anyone seeing them together, everything was going to be fine.

Frankie personally thought that the bullshit Atchison insisted on going through, making him leave the guns in the garbage can in the toilet of the Yock's Diner, and coming out, and then Atchison going in to get them, was some really

482

silly bullshit. Atchison must have been watching spy movies on the TV or something.

It would have made much more sense for them just to have met someplace, even in the parking lot of the Yock's Diner, for Christ's sake, swapped the dough for the guns, and gotten in their cars and driven away.

On the other hand, which was why Frankie had gone along with the swapping-in-the-crapper bullshit, doing it that way had been safer than meeting him in a dark parking lot someplace.

Frankie didn't trust Atchison. He hadn't trusted him in the Inferno when he'd done the job, and had taken steps to make sure that Atchison hadn't hit him after he'd hit the wife and the partner, which would have been smart, which would have made it look like the dead guy on the floor had robbed the place and killed the partner and the wife, and Atchison was the fucking hero who had killed him.

That "dead men tell no tales" wasn't no bullshit. He was the only guy who could pin the job on Atchison, and Atchison knew it. If he was dead, Atchison could relax. The cops would look for-fucking-ever—or at least until something else came along—for the two robbers Atchison had made up and told the cops about.

Frankie had considered that the reverse was also true, that if Atchison was dead, Atchison couldn't get weak knees or something and tell the cops, "Frankie Foley is the guy who murdered my wife." He considered hitting Atchison. It would be no trouble at all. He could have been waiting for him in the parking lot at the Yock's Diner, put a couple of bullets into his head, and driven off and that would have been the end of it.

Except that maybe it wouldn't have really been the end of it. The cops would look like even bigger assholes if Atchison got hit and they couldn't catch who had done him, either. The *Ledger* was already giving the cops a hard time about that. The cops would get all excited all over again, and maybe they'd get lucky.

Frankie didn't think Atchison would have the balls to try to kill him himself, otherwise he would have killed his wife and the partner by himself, right? And Atchison didn't know no other professional hit men, or else he would have hired one of them to do the job, right?

So the smart thing to do—the professional thing—was just stop right where he was. He had been paid to do a job, and he had done it, and got paid for it, and that should be the end of it. Go on to other things, right?

If he did it that way, in a couple of weeks he could go to work in the Inferno, and tell Wanamaker's what they could do with their fucking warehouse. The word would get out that he had done the job for Atchison, and sooner or later other jobs would come along.

What he would have liked to have done was maybe catch an airplane and go to Las Vegas and see if he would have any luck gambling. Frankie had never been to Vegas, but he had heard there was a lot of pussy that hung around the tables, and that if they thought you were a high roller, they even sent pussy to your room. That would really be nice, go out there, win a lot of money at the crap tables, and get some pussy thrown in for good measure. But that would not have been professional. What he had to do, for a little while anyway, was play it cool.

The cops might be watching him, and they might wonder how come he could afford to quit fucking Wanamaker's, not to mention where he got the money to go to Vegas. In a couple of weeks, about the time he would go see Atchison and remind him about the maître d' job, the cops would lose interest in the Inferno job, and in him. There would be other things for the cops to do.

Neither was he, Frankie decided, going to start to spend the five grand he got right away, get a better car or something, or even some clothes. That would attract attention. When he was working at the Inferno, it would be different. If he turned up with some dough, he could explain it saying he'd won it gambling. Everybody knew that maître d's were right in the middle of the action.

Having decided all this, Frankie then concluded that there would be no real harm in going by Meagan's Bar and having a couple of drinks, and maybe letting Tim McCarthy see that he was walking around with a couple, three, hundred-dollar bills snuggled up in his wallet. Not to mention letting Tim see that he was walking around not giving a tiny fuck that detectives were asking questions about him.

And who knows, there just might be some bored wife in there looking for a little action from some real man. Tim, and if not Tim, then ol' diarrhea mouth himself, Sonny Boyle, were talking about him to people, telling people not to let it get around, but that cops was asking about Frankie Foley. Tim and Sonny would be passing that word around, that was for damn sure, you could bet on it.

Women like dangerous men. Frankie had read that someplace. He thought it was probably true.

Frankie got home from Wanamaker's warehouse a couple of minutes after six. He grabbed a quick shower, put on the two-tone jacket and a clean sports shirt, told his mother he'd catch supper some other place, he had business to do, and walked into Meagan's Bar at ten minutes to seven.

He really would have liked to have had a couple of shooters, maybe a jigger glass of Seagram's-7 dropped into a draft Ortleib's, but he thought better of it and ordered just the beer.

Not that he was afraid of running off at the mouth or something, but rather that there maybe just might be some bored wife in there looking for a little action—you never could tell, he thought maybe he was on a roll—and if that happened, he didn't want to be half shitfaced and ruin the opportunity.

He paid for the Ortleib's with one of the three hundred-dollar bills he'd put in his wallet, told Tim to have a little something with him, and when Tim made him his change, just left it there on the bar, like he didn't give a shit about it, there was more where that come from.

He was just about finished with the Ortleib's, and looking for Tim to order another, when somebody yelled at Tim:

"Hey, Tim, we need a couple of drinks down here. And give Frankie another of whatever he's having."

At the end of the bar, where it right-angled to the wall by the door, were two guys. Guineas, they looked like, wearing shirts and ties and suits. That was strange, you didn't see guineas that often in Meagan's. The guineas had their bars and the Irish had theirs.

But these guys had apparently been in here before. They knew Tim's name, and Tim called back, "Johnnie Walker, right?" which meant he knew them well enough to remember what they drank.

"Johnnie Black, if you got it," one of the guineas called back. "And, what the hell, give Frankie one, too."

What the hell is this all about? Frankie wondered. *What the hell, a couple of guineas playing big shot. They're always doing that kind of shit. Something in their blood, maybe.*

Tim served the drinks, first to the guineas, and then carried another Ortleib's and the bottle of Johnnie Walker and a shot glass to where Frankie sat.

"You want a chaser with that, or what?" Tim asked as he filled the shot glass with scotch.

"The beer's fine," Frankie said.

He raised the shot glass to his lips and took a sip and looked at the guineas and waved his hand.

One of the guineas came down the bar.

"How are you, Frankie?" he said, putting out his hand. "The scotch all right? I didn't think to ask did you like scotch."

"Fine. Thanks. Do I know you?"

"I dunno. Do you? My name is Joey Fatalgio."

"Don't think I've had the pleasure," Frankie said.

They shook hands.

"I know who you are, of course," Joey Fatalgio said, and winked.

What the fuck is with the wink? This guy don't look like no fag.

"I come in here every once in a while," Frankie said.

"And maybe I seen you at the Inferno," Fatalgio said. "Me and my brother—Dominic—that's him down there, we go in there from time to time."

"Yeah, maybe I seen you in the Inferno," Frankie said. "I hang out there sometimes. And I'm thinking of going to work there."

"Hey, Dominic!" Joey Fatalgio called to his brother. "Bring your glass down here and say hello to Frankie Foley."

Dominic hoisted himself off his stool and made his way down the bar.

"Frankie, Dominic," Joey made the introductions, "Dominic, Frankie."

"How the hell are you, Frankie?" Dominic said. "A pleasure to meet you."

"Likewise," Frankie said.

"Frankie was just telling me he's thinking of going to work at the Inferno," Joey said.

"Going to work? The way I heard it, he already did the job at the Inferno," Dominic said, and he winked at Frankie.

Frankie felt a little nervous.

There were guineas on the cops. Are these two cops?

"Shut the fuck up, for Christ's sake, Dominic," Joey Fatalgio said. "What the fuck's wrong with you?" He turned to Frankie. "You should excuse him, Frankie. Sometimes he gets stupid."

"Fuck you, Joey," Dominic said.

"There are places you talk about certain things, asshole," Joey said, "and places you don't, and this is one of the places you don't. Right, Frankie?"

"Right," Frankie agreed.

"No offense, Frankie," Dominic said.

"Ah, don't worry about it," Frankie said.

"He don't mean no harm, but sometimes he's stupid," Joey said.

"Fuck you, Joey, who do you think you are, Einstein or somebody?"

"Where do you guys work?" Frankie said, both to change the subject—Dominic looked like he was getting pissed at the way his brother was talking to him—and to see what they would say. He didn't think they were cops, but you never really could tell.

"We're drivers," Joey said.

"Truck drivers?"

"I'm a people driver," Joey said. "Asshole here is a stiff driver."

"Huh?"

Joey reached in his wallet and produced a business card, and gave it to Frankie. It was for some company called Classic Livery, Inc., with an address in South Philly, and "Joseph T. Fatalgio, Jr." printed on the bottom.

"What's a livery?" Frankie asked.

"It goes back to horses," Joey explained. "Remember in the cowboy movies where Roy Rogers would park his horse in the livery stables?"

"Yeah," Frankie said, remembering. "I do."

"I think it used to mean 'horses for hire' or something like that," Dominic said. "Now it means limousines."

"Limousines?"

"Yeah. Limousines. Mostly for funerals, but if you want a limousine to get married in, we got white ones. We even got a white Rolls-Royce."

"No shit?"

"Costs a fucking fortune, but you'd be surprised how often it gets rented," Dominic went on.

"Most of our business is funeral homes," Joey said. "Only the bride, usually, gets a limousine ride for a wedding. But if you don't get to follow the casket to the cemetery in a limousine for a funeral, people will think you're the family black sheep."

"I guess that's so," Frankie agreed, and then started to hand the Classic Livery business card back to Joey.

Joey held up his hand to stop him.

"Keep it," he said. "You may need a limousine someday."

"Yeah," Dominic said. "And they'll probably give you a professional discount."

Joey laughed in delight.

"I told you shut up, asshole," he said.

"A professional discount for what?" Frankie asked, overwhelmed by curiosity.

"Shit, you know what for. Increasing business," Dominic said.

Joey laughed.

"I don't know what you're talking about," Frankie said.

"Right," Joey said, and laughed, and winked.

"Yeah, right," Dominic said.

"Actually, Frankie, that's sort of the reason we're here."

"What is?" Frankie asked.

"What you don't know we're talking about," Joey said softly, moving so close to Frankie that Frankie could smell his cologne. "Frankie, there's a fellow we know wants to talk to you."

"Talk to me about what?"

Joey winked at Frankie.

"I don't know," Joey said. "But what I do know about this fellow is that he admires a job well done."

"He's done a job or two himself," Dominic said. "If you know what I mean."

"He already told you he don't know what you're talking about, asshole," Joey said.

"Right," Dominic said.

"What this fellow we know wants to talk to you about, Frankie," Joey said, "is a job."

"What kind of a job?"

"Let's say a job where you could make in an hour about

ten times what you make in a month pushing furniture around the Wanamaker's warehouse."

"Yeah?"

"Let's say this fellow we know has a sort of professional admiration for the way you did your last job, and we both know I'm not talking about throwing furniture on the back of some truck."

"Who is this guy?"

"He's like you, Frankie, he likes to sort of maintain a low profile, you know what I mean. Have a sort of public job, and then have another job, like a part-time job, every once in a while, a job that not a hell of a lot of other people can do, you know what I mean."

"Why does he want to talk to me?" Frankie asked.

"Sometimes, what I understand, with his full-time job, he can handle a part-time job, too, when one comes along. But sometimes, you know what I mean, more than one part-time job comes along. Actually, in this case, what I understand is that there's three, four part-time jobs come along, and this fellow can't handle all of them himself. I mean, you'd have to keep your mouth shut—you can keep your mouth shut, can't you, Frankie?"

"Like a fucking clam," Frankie said.

"I figured you could, a fellow in the part-time job business like you would have to keep his mouth shut. What I'm saying here, Frankie, is that you would be like a subcontractor. I mean, you come to some financial understanding with this fellow, you do the job, and the whole thing would be between you two. I mean, the people who hired him for the particular part-time job I think this fellow has in mind wouldn't ever find out that this fellow subcontracted it. They might not like that. I mean, they pay this fellow the kind of money they pay, they expect him to do the job himself, not subcontract it. But what they don't know can't hurt them, right?"

"Right," Frankie said.

"So maybe you would be willing to talk to this fellow,

Frankie?" Dominic asked. "I mean, he'd appreciate it. And if you can't come to some sort of mutually satisfactory arrangement, then you walk away, right? No hard feelings. You'd lose nothing, and it might be in your mutual interest to get to know this fellow. You never know what will happen next week."

"What the hell," Frankie said. "Why not?"

Frankie had never seen so many Cadillacs in one place in his life as there were lined up in the garage of Classic Livery, Inc.

He thought there must be maybe a hundred of them, most of them black limousines. There were also a dozen Cadillac hearses, and that many or more flower cars. Plus a whole line of regular Cadillacs and Lincolns, and he saw the white Rolls-Royce Dominic had told him they had.

The floor of the garage was all wet. Frankie decided that they washed the limousines every day, and had probably just finished washing the cars that had been used.

He had never really thought about where the limousines at weddings and funerals had come from, but now he could understand that it must be a pretty good business to be in.

I wonder what they charge for a limousine at a funeral. Probably at least a hundred dollars. And they could probably use the same limousine for more than one funeral in a day. Maybe even more than two. Say a funeral at nine o'clock, and another at eleven, and then at say half past one, and one at say four o'clock.

That's four hundred bucks a day per limousine!

Jesus Christ, somebody around here must be getting rich, even if they had to pay whatever the fuck it costs, thirty thousand bucks or whatever for a limousine. Four hundred bucks a day times five days is two fucking grand a fucking week! After fifteen weeks, you got your money for the limousine back, and all you have to do after that is pay the driver and the gas. How long will a limousine last? Two, three years at least . . .

Joey Fatalgio stopped the regular Cadillac he had parked around the corner from Meagan's Bar, and pointed out the window.

"Through that door, Frankie, the one what says 'No Admittance.' You'll understand that this fellow wants to talk to you alone."

"Yeah, sure," Frankie said.

"I'll go park this and get a cup of coffee or something, and when you're finished, I'll take you back to Meagan's. OK?"

"Fine," Frankie said.

He got out of the car and walked to the door and knocked on it.

"Come in!" a voice said.

Frankie opened the door.

A large, olive-skinned man in a really classy suit was inside, leaning up against what looked like the garage manager's desk.

He looked at Frankie, looked good, up and down, for a good fifteen seconds.

"No names, right?" he said. "You're Mr. Smith and I'm Mr. Jones, right?"

"Right, Mr. Jones," Frankie said.

Jones, my ass. This is Paulo Cassandro. I seen his picture in the papers just a couple of days ago. The cops arrested him for running some big-time whore ring, and bribing some fucking cop captain.

"Thank you for coming to see me, Mr. Smith," Cassandro said.

"Don't mention it, Mr. Jones."

"Look, you'll understand, Mr. Smith, that what you hear about something isn't always what really happened," Cassandro said. "I mean, I understand that you would be reluctant to talk about a job. But on the other hand, for one thing, nobody's going to hear a thing that's said in here but you and me, and from what I hear we're in the same line of business, and for another, you'll understand that, with what I've got riding on this, I have to be damned sure I'm not dealing with no amateur."

"I know what you mean, Mr. Jones," Frankie said.

"You want to check me, or the room, for a wire, I'll understand, Mr. Smith. I'll take no offense."

Jesus Christ, I didn't even think about some sonofabitch recording this!

"No need to do that," Frankie said, feeling quite sophisticated about it. "I trust you."

"That's good. I appreciate that trust. In our line of work, trust is important. You know what I mean."

"Yeah."

"So tell me about the job you did on Atchison and Marcuzzi."

And Frankie Foley did, in great detail. From time to time, Mr. Cassandro asked a question to clarify a point, but most of the time during Frankie's recitation he just nodded his head in what Frankie chose to think was professional approval.

"In other words, you think it was a good, clean job, with no problems?"

"Yeah, I'd say that, Mr. Jones."

"You wouldn't take offense if I pointed out a couple of things to you? A couple of mistakes I think you made?"

"Not at all," Frankie said.

"Well, the first mistake you made, you fucking slimeball, was thinking you're a tough guy," Paulo Cassandro said.

He pushed himself off the desk and walked to the door and opened it.

Joey and Dominic Fatalgio came into the office.

"Break the fingers on his left hand," Paulo Cassandro ordered.

"What?" Frankie asked.

Joey wrapped his arms around Frankie, pinning his arms to his sides. Dominic pulled the fingers of Joey's left hand back. Frankie screamed, and then a moment later screamed much louder as the joints and knuckles were either separated from their joints or the finger bones broken or both.

"Oh, please, Mr. Cassandro," Frankie howled. "For Christ's sake!"

"That was another mistake," Paulo said, and punched Frankie in the face while holding a heavy cast-metal stapler in his hand.

"You never seen me in your life, you understand that, ass-hole?" Mr. Cassandro said.

Frankie now had his left hand under his right arm. When he opened his mouth to reply, he spit out two teeth. His whole arm seemed to be on fire. He wondered if he was going to faint.

"Yes, sir," he said.

"One of the mistakes you made, you pasty-faced Irish cocksucker, was going around saying untrue things, letting people think, *telling* people, that you were working for some Italian mob. For one thing, there is no mob, and if there was, there wouldn't be no stupid fucking Irish shit-asses in it. The Italians in Philadelphia are law-abiding businessmen like me. You insulted me. Worse, you insulted my mother and my father when you started spreading bullshit like that around. You understand that, you fucking Mick?"

Frankie nodded his head to indicate that he was willing to grant the point Mr. Cassandro had just made.

Mr. Cassandro struck Mr. Foley again with the heavy cast-metal stapler, this time higher on the face, so that the skin above Mr. Foley's eye was cut open, and he could no longer see out of his left eye.

"Say 'Yes, sir,' you fucking Mick scumbag!"

"Yes, sir," Mr. Foley said.

Mr. Cassandro, with surprising grace of movement, then kicked Mr. Foley in the genital area.

Mr. Foley fell to the floor screaming faintly, but in obvious agony.

Mr. Cassandro watched him contemptuously for a full minute.

"Stop whining, you Irish motherfucker," he said conversationally, "and stand up, or I'll really give you something to cry about."

With some difficulty, Mr. Foley regained his feet. He had great difficulty becoming erect, because of the pain in his groin, and because his entire right side now seemed to be shuddering with pain.

"Now I'm going to tell you something, and I want you to listen carefully, because I don't want to have to repeat myself. You don't even know shit about the law, so I'm going to educate you. You know what happens when you plead guilty to murder?"

Mr. Foley looked at Mr. Cassandro in utter confusion.

"Nine times out of ten, it don't mean shit," Mr. Cassandro said, "when you confess and plead guilty, which is what you're going to do."

That penetrated Mr. Foley's wall of pain.

"Confess?" he asked.

"Right. Confess. What happens is your lawyer can usually come up with something that will make the jury feel sorry for you, so they won't vote for the death penalty. Even if he can't do that, the judge usually knocks down the chair to life without parole, and what that means is that you have to do maybe twenty years."

"Why?" Mr. Foley asked, somewhat piteously.

"I told you. You dishonored the Italian people of Philadelphia. And if there was a mob, you would have dishonored them too. How would it be if it got around that a stupid Mick asshole like you was associated with the mob? If there was a mob."

"I didn't say any—" Mr. Foley began, only to be interrupted again by Mr. Cassandro striking him a third time in the face with the heavy cast-metal stapler. This blow caught him in the corner of the mouth, causing some rupture of mucous membrane and skin tissue and a certain amount of bleeding.

"You know what's worse than going to the slammer for

twenty years, Frankie?" Mr. Cassandro asked conversationally after Mr. Foley had again regained his feet. "Even worse, if you think about it, than getting the chair?"

Frankie shook his head no and then muttered something from his swollen and distorted mouth that might have been "No, sir."

"Dying a little bit at a time, is what would be worse," Mr. Cassandro said. "You know what I mean by that?"

Again there came a sound from Mr. Foley and a shake of the head that Mr. Cassandro interpreted to mean that Mr. Foley needed an explanation.

"Show him," Mr. Cassandro said.

Mr. Joey Fatalgio went to Mr. Foley, this time grabbing his left hand, which Mr. Foley was holding against his body with his upper right arm, and twisted it behind his back. Then he grabbed Mr. Foley's right wrist, and forced Mr. Foley to place his right hand, so far undamaged, on the desk at which Mr. Cassandro had been standing.

Mr. Cassandro moved away from the desk. Mr. Dominic Fatalgio then appeared at the desk, holding a red fire ax in his hand, high up by the blade itself. He flattened Mr. Foley's hand on the desk, and struck it with the ax, which served to sever Mr. Foley's little finger between the largest and next largest of its joints.

Mr. Foley screamed again, looked at his bleeding hand, and the severed little finger, and fainted.

Mr. Cassandro looked down at him.

"We don't want him dead," he said conversationally. "Wake him up, wrap a rag or something around his hand, and make sure he understands that if I hear anything at all I don't want to hear, I will cut the rest of his fucking fingers off."

Mr. Dominic Fatalgio nodded his understanding of the orders he had received and began to nudge Mr. Foley with the toe of his shoe.

Mr. Cassandro left the office, and then returned.

"Make sure you clean this place up," he said. "I don't

want Mrs. Lucca coming in here in the morning and finding that finger. She'd shit a brick."

Both Mr. Dominic and Mr. Joey Fatalgio laughed. Mr. Cassandro then left again, carefully closing the door behind him.

There were a number of problems connected with the arrests of Mr. Atchison and Mr. Foley for the murders of Mrs. Atchison and Mr. Marcuzzi.

The first problem came up when Chief Inspector Matthew Lowenstein telephoned the Hon. Jerry Carlucci, Mayor of the City of Philadelphia, on his unlisted private line in Chestnut Hill to tell him that the Honorable Thomas Callis, District Attorney of Philadelphia County, had been his usual chickenshit self, but had come around when he had told him that he was going to arrest the two of them whether or not Callis thought there was sufficient evidence.

"He already called me, Matt," the Mayor said. "To let me know what a big favor he was doing me."

"That figures," Lowenstein said.

"Would it cause any problems for you," the Mayor began, which Chief Lowenstein correctly translated to mean, *This is what I want done, you figure out how to do it,* "to bring Mickey O'Hara along when you arrest Atchison and the shooter, preferably both?"

Chief Lowenstein hesitated, trying to find the words to tactfully suggest this might not be such an all-around splendid idea as the Mayor obviously thought it to be.

"When I had Officer Bailey in here this afternoon, to personally congratulate him for his good work in catching that scumbag who shot Officer Kellog, I had the idea Mickey was a little pissed."

"Why should Mickey be pissed?"

"All the other press people were here, too," the Mayor said. "Now, I'm not saying he did anything wrong, there was no way he could have known I figure I owe O'Hara," the Mayor said, "but when Captain Quaire put out the word to the press that we had solved the Officer Kellog job, I think Mickey got the idea I wasn't living up to my word. I'd like to convince him that I take care of my friends."

"No problem. I'll put the arm out for Mickey," Lowenstein said. "He'll have that story all to himself."

"I was thinking maybe both arrests," the Mayor said. "You mind if I ask how you plan to handle them?"

And if I said, "Yeah, Jerry, now that you mention it, I do," then what?

"We're going to pick up Foley first thing in the morning," Lowenstein said. "He's not too smart, and I wouldn't be at all surprised if we could get him to confess before we arrest Atchison."

"At his house?"

"As soon as he walks out the door. I don't like taking doors, and we found out when he goes to work. We'll be waiting."

"Who's we?"

"We is Lieutenant Natali and Detective Milham, backed up by a couple of district uniforms in case we need them. I don't think we will."

"And Atchison?"

"I thought—actually Peter Wohl thought, and I agree with him—that it would avoid all sorts of jurisdictional problems if we could get him into Philadelphia, rather than arresting him at his house in Media. So Jason Washington called his lawyer—"

"Who's his lawyer?"

"Sid Margolis."

The Mayor snorted. "That figures."

"And Washington said he has a couple of questions for him, and he thought Margolis might want to be there when he asked him, and could he ask him at Margolis's office. Margolis called back and set it up for twelve o'clock."

"Good thinking. You open to a couple of suggestions?"

"Of course."

"Well, I think Tom Callis would like to get his picture in

the newspapers too, and if I could tell him I had set it up for him and O'Hara to be there when you arrest Atchison . . ."

"No problem. You want to call him, or do you want me to?"

"I'll call him," the Mayor said. "And tell him to call you. And I think it would be a nice gesture if you allowed Detective Payne to go to both arrests. It would show the cooperation between Homicide and Special Operations. And what the hell, the kid deserves a little pat on the back. He did work overtime to catch Atchison with the guns."

"He'll be there. I'll call Peter Wohl and set it up."

"And then, so the rest of the press isn't pissed because Mickey got the exclusive on the arrests, I thought I'd have a little photo opportunity in my office, like the one this afternoon when I congratulated Officer Bailey, and personally thank everybody, everybody including you and Peter, of course."

"And including Detective Milham?"

"Of course including Detective Milham. He's a fine police officer and an outstanding detective who did first-class work on this job."

They call that elective memory, Chief Lowenstein thought. *Our beloved mayor has* elected *not to recall that the last time we discussed Detective Milham, he was my Homicide detective who can't keep his pecker in his pocket.*

"Good idea," Lowenstein said.

"I'll have Czernich set it up," the Mayor said. "Thanks for the call, Matt, and keep me posted."

"Yes, sir," Chief Lowenstein said.

It was necessary for Chief Lowenstein to telephone Mayor Carlucci at his office at ten-thirty the next morning to report that a small glitch had developed in the well-laid plans to effect the arrest of Mr. John Francis Foley.

His whereabouts, the Chief was forced to inform the Mayor, were unknown. When he had not come out of his

house to go to work when he was supposed to, Detectives
Milham and Payne had gone to his door and rung the bell.

His mother had told him that she was worried about John
Francis. He had gone out the night before and not returned.
He rarely did that. If he decided to spend the night with a
friend, Mrs. Foley reported, he always telephoned his
mother to tell her. John Francis was a good boy, his mother
said.

"You're telling me you don't know where this scumbag
is?" the Mayor asked.

"Well, we know he's not at the Wanamaker's warehouse," Lowenstein, more than a little embarrassed, reported. "We're working on known associates."

"Speaking of known associates, you do have an idea
where Mr. Atchison is right now, don't you?"

"The Media police are watching his house. He's there."

"Find Foley, Matt," the Mayor ordered. "Soon."

"Yes, sir."

"Why don't you call the police?" the Mayor said, his sar-
casm having been ignited. "Maybe he got himself arrested.
Or check the hospitals. Maybe he got run over with a truck.
Just find him, Matt!"

"Yes, sir."

Chief Lowenstein replaced the pay telephone in Meagan's
Bar into its cradle. He looked thoughtful for a moment, and
then asked himself a question, aloud.

"Why the hell not?"

He dropped another coin in the slot, dialed a number, and
told the lieutenant who answered to call the hospitals and
see if they had a patient, maybe an auto accident or something, named John Francis Foley. And while he was at it,
check the districts and see if anybody by that name had been
arrested.

INVESTIGATION REPORT
PHILADELPHIA POLICE DEPARTMENT

Yr	C.C.#		DIST	COMPL.#		INITIAL(49)		DIST/UNIT	

REPORT DATE   SUPPLEMENTAL | PREPARING

CLASSIFICATION |CODE |CONTINUATION   Homicide/9th Dist.

PREVIOUS CLASSIFICATION   CODE | DATE AND TIME |PLACE OF OCCURRENCE

COMPLAINANT	|AGE	|RACE	|ADDRESS		PHONE	|TYPE OF PREMISES

Alicia Atchison | 25 | W | 320 Wilson Avenue, Media, PA

DATE AND TIME REPORTED |REPORTED BY |ADDRESS

FOUNDED ❐ YES ❐ NO · ARREST ❐ CLEARED   ❐ EXCEPTIONALLY CLEARED

STOLEN |❐CURRENCY, BONDS, ETC. ❐ FURS   ❐.AUTOS |RECOVERED VALUE
PROPERTY |❐ JEWELRY, PRECIOUS METALS ❐CLOTHING   ❐ MISC |
INSURED   ❐YES ❐NO

DETAILS

E.   Arrests

    1. Defendant #1 Foley, John Francis, 25 years, white, 2320
South 18th Street. PP#375783, two previous arrests. Occupation:
Laborer (Wanamaker's). Born: 2/5/50. On Thursday, May 25, 1975 at
9:55 a.m., taken into custody at Memorial Hospital by Lieutenant
Louis Natali #233; Sergeant Zachary Hobbs #396; Detective Wallace
J. Milham #626 and Detective Matthew M. Payne #701.

    Description

    Foley, John Francis, is a white male, 6'1", 189 lbs., light
brown hair, light blue eyes, wearing a hospital gown. He had been
taken to the Emergency Room of Memorial Hospital by a Sixth District
van after having been found in a semi-conscious state at Chestnut
and S. 9th Streets. He was treated by Emergency Room personnel
supervised by M.C. Chobenzy, MD, for various injuries and admitted
to Memorial Hospital for further treatment and observation.

    His left hand had been placed in a cast applied under Dr.
Chobenzy's supervision. Finger bones and joints were fractured.
His right hand had been placed in a cast and bandaged under Dr.
Chobenzy's supervision. The little finger had been recently ampu-
tated, it is not known how. He also had a swollen right eye, cut
upper lip, lacerations on back of his head, a laceration on the
left side of his face at the eye line, and various other bruises
and contusions of the face and body.

INVESTIGATOR (Type and Sign Name) | SERGEANT |LIEUTENANT

Wallace J. Milham | *Zachary Hobbs* |
Wallace J. Milham #626 | Zachary Hobbs # 396

75–49 (Rev 3/63)   DETECTIVE DIVISION

INVESTIGATION REPORT				PHILADELPHIA POLICE DEPARTMENT	

Yr | C.C.# | DIST | COMPL.# | INITIAL(49) | | DIST/UNIT |

REPORT DATE   **SUPPLEMENTAL**   **PREPARING**

CLASSIFICATION |CODE |CONTINUATION   Homicide/9th Dist.

PREVIOUS CLASSIFICATION   **CODE | DATE AND TIME** |**PLACE OF OCCURRENCE**

COMPLAINANT |AGE |RACE |ADDRESS | PHONE |TYPE OF PREMISES

Alicia Atchison | 25 | W | 320 Wilson Avenue, Media, PA

DATE AND TIME REPORTED |REPORTED BY |ADDRESS

FOUNDED ☐ YES ☐ NO   ARREST ☐ CLEARED   ☐ EXCEPTIONALLY CLEARED

STOLEN |☐CURRENCY, BONDS, ETC. ☐ FURS   ☐.AUTOS | RECOVERED VALUE

PROPERTY |☐ JEWELRY, PRECIOUS METALS ☐CLOTHING ☐ MISC |

INSURED   ☐YES ☐NO

DETAILS

E. ARRESTS (Continued)

    Defendant #1 John Francis Foley (Continued)

    Description (Continued)

   It was determined by Long Tay Hu, MD, that his physical condition was such that no further hospitalization was required, and he was discharged from the hospital into police custody.

The clothing he had been wearing at the time of his admission to the hospital was returned to him at that time. There was apparent dried blood on his shirt, trousers, and jacket, and evidence of bloody fecal matter on his under pants.

    He appeared to be sober.

Defendant #1 was taken to the Homicide Division, Police Department Headquarters, Franklin Square for interview.

   2. Defendant #2 Atchison, Gerald North, 42-W, 320 Wilson Avenue, Media, PA, no previous record. Occupation: Bar Owner. Born: 12/25/32. On Thursday, May 25, 1975 at 12:01 p.m., taken into custody at the law offices of Sidney Margolis, Esq., PSFS Building, Phila. by Lieutenant Louis Natali #233, Sergeant Zachary Hobbs #396, Detective Wallace J. Milham #626, and Detective Matthew M. Payne #701, as directed by District Attorney Thomas Callis. Defendant was taken to Room 759,

---

INVESTIGATOR (Type and Sign Name) | SERGEANT |LIEUTENANT

Wallace J. Milham | *Zachary Hobbs* |

Wallace J. Milham #626 | Zachary Hobbs # 396

75–49 (Rev 3/63)   **DETECTIVE DIVISION**

INVESTIGATION REPORT PHILADELPHIA POLICE DEPARTMENT

Yr	C.C.#	DIST	COMPL.#	INITIAL(49)	DIST/UNIT
REPORT DATE		SUPPLEMENTAL			PREPARING
CLASSIFICATION			CODE	CONTINUATION	Homicide/9th Dist.

PREVIOUS CLASSIFICATION   CODE DATE AND TIME   PLACE OF OCCURRENCE

COMPLAINANT	AGE	RACE	ADDRESS	PHONE	TYPE OF PREMISES
Alicia Atchison	25	W	320 Wilson Avenue, Media, PA		

DATE AND TIME REPORTED   REPORTED BY   ADDRESS

FOUNDED ☐ YES ☐ NO   ARREST ☐ CLEARED   ☐ EXCEPTIONALLY CLEARED

STOLEN   ☐ CURRENCY, BONDS, ETC. ☐ FURS   ☐. AUTOS RECOVERED VALUE
PROPERTY ☐ JEWELRY, PRECIOUS METALS ☐ CLOTHING ☐ MISC
INSURED   ☐ YES ☐ NO

DETAILS

E. ARRESTS (Continued)

　　Defendant #2 Gerald North Atchison (Continued)

City Hall, Sheriff's Cellroom and then transported to the Police
Detention Center, Police Department Headquarters, Franklin Square.

　　Description

　　Defendant #2 is a white male, 5'8", 187 lbs., brown hair,
brown eyes, wearing a gray suit, white shirt, black tie, black
shoes. He was on crutches at the time. He did not appear to be
under the influence of alcohol or drugs.

F. INTERVIEWS

　　1. Defendant John Francis Foley

Stated - During the winter of 1974 he went into The Inferno
to meet a friend and was introduced to Gerald Atchison. Gerald said that he heard that he was a killer and that he wanted to have somebody killed. The deal was supposed to be for
Gerald's wife. Then Marcuzzi came into the picture and Gerald
decided that he wanted him killed too. Gerald decided that
Alicia and Marcuzzi would be done together in The Inferno.

On Monday, May 15, 1975, he saw Gerald and Gerald gave him
a Savage .32, a Spanish .44 and a Colt .38. Gerald didn't want to

---

INVESTIGATOR (Type and Sign Name) | SERGEANT | LIEUTENANT

Wallace J. Milham | *Zachary Hobbs* |
Wallace J. Milham #626 | Zachary Hobbs # 396

75–49 (Rev 3/63)   DETECTIVE DIVISION

INVESTIGATION REPORT

PHILADELPHIA POLICE DEPARTMENT

| Yr | C.C.# | | DIST | COMPL.# | | INITIAL(49) | | DIST/UNIT | |

REPORT DATE   SUPPLEMENTAL | PREPARING

CLASSIFICATION |CODE |CONTINUATION   Homicide/9th Dist.

PREVIOUS CLASSIFICATION   CODE | DATE AND TIME |PLACE OF OCCURRENCE

| COMPLAINANT | |AGE | RACE |ADDRESS | | PHONE | |TYPE OF PREMISES |
| Alicia Atchison | | 25 | W | | 320 Wilson Avenue, Media, PA | |

DATE AND TIME REPORTED |REPORTED BY |ADDRESS

FOUNDED ☐ YES ☐ NO   ARREST ☐ CLEARED   ☐ EXCEPTIONALLY CLEARED

STOLEN |☐CURRENCY, BONDS, ETC. ☐ FURS   ☐. AUTOS | RECOVERED VALUE

PROPERTY |☐ JEWELRY, PRECIOUS METALS ☐CLOTHING ☐ MISC |

INSURED   ☐YES ☐NO

DETAILS

F. INTERVIEWS (Continued)

    Defendant #1 John Francis Foley (Continued)

get hit with a big gun. Gerald wanted to get hit with something
light. He told Gerald that the best place would be the restaurant
and that they would work out the details together as to how it
would be done.

Gerald said that he would send Alicia downstairs telling her to
pretend to read a book and to watch Anthony Marcuzzi with the
receipts. He would tell Alicia that he thought that Anthony was
cheating him. Gerald would get rid of the bartender, so he would
have an excuse not to go with Alicia.

Foley was to go down into the cellar and wait for Alicia and
Anthony to get into the office together and Gerald would give the
signal with the juke box that it was all clear upstairs. He would
then be able to go in and do the killing. Then he was supposed to
go upstairs, shoot Gerald, and leave the place.

On Friday, May 19, 1975, sometime around 10:00 pm, he met Gerald
in the 12th Street Market. He told Gerald that he had to kill them
that night, that he was running out of time and that was going to
be the night. Gerald said, OK, and gave him $2500. He still had
the guns that Gerald gave him on Monday and he went to The Inferno
about 11:30 or 11:45 p.m.

When he went in there, he stayed at the bar for a while, and

INVESTIGATOR (Type and Sign Name) | SERGEANT |LIEUTENANT

Wallace J. Milham | *Zachary Hobbs* |

Wallace J. Milham #626 | Zachary Hobbs # 396

75–49 (Rev 3/63)   **DETECTIVE DIVISION**

INVESTIGATION REPORT

PHILADELPHIA POLICE DEPARTMENT

Yr	C.C.#		DIST	COMPL.#		INITIAL(49)		DIST/UNIT	

REPORT DATE   SUPPLEMENTAL | PREPARING

CLASSIFICATION |CODE |CONTINUATION   Homicide/9th Dist.

PREVIOUS CLASSIFICATION   CODE | DATE AND TIME |PLACE OF OCCURRENCE

COMPLAINANT	|AGE	|RACE |ADDRESS	|PHONE	|TYPE OF PREMISES

Alicia Atchison | 25 | W | 320 Wilson Avenue, Media, PA

DATE AND TIME REPORTED |REPORTED BY |ADDRESS

FOUNDED ❑ YES ❑ NO   ARREST ❑ CLEARED   ❑ EXCEPTIONALLY CLEARED

STOLEN |❑CURRENCY, BONDS, ETC. ❑ FURS   ❑.AUTOS |RECOVERED VALUE
PROPERTY |❑ JEWELRY, PRECIOUS METALS ❑CLOTHING ❑ MISC |
INSURED   ❑YES ❑NO

DETAILS

F. INTERVIEWS (Continued)

    Defendant #1 John Francis Foley (Continued)

then Gerald took him to the office and started cleaning the guns.
Gerald started helping to clean the guns but he was kind of nervous and was interested in drinking, so he cleaned the guns himself. He then went to the back of the cellar where the floor drops
down where the beer cases are stored, behind a dressing room. He
took a beer box and sat it up so that he would be able to sit on
it and placed the guns where the floor drops. Gerald fixed the
trap door to keep it open a couple of inches. Then Foley and Gerald went upstairs and Foley left the Inferno.

He walked around awhile, and then at 12:30 or so, he is not sure
of the time, he went to the rear of the Inferno. He opened the
trap door which Gerald had fixed and went into the cellar. He went
and got the guns, then sat on the beer box and waited.

In about 5 minutes Alicia came down and she went into the office.
Then he waited about 5 minutes more before Anthony Marcuzzi came
down and went into the office. Then the juke box started to play
and that was Gerald's signal that it was clear upstairs and for
him to do the killings.

He waited for about 10 seconds to make sure that the juke box was
playing right. He had the .44 in his right hand and the .38 in his
left hand and he walked into the office.

INVESTIGATOR (Type and Sign Name) | SERGEANT |LIEUTENANT

Wallace J. Milham | *Zachary Hobbs* |

Wallace J. Milham #626 | Zachary Hobbs # 396

75–49 (Rev 3/63)   **DETECTIVE DIVISION**

INVESTIGATION REPORT				PHILADELPHIA POLICE DEPARTMENT		
Yr | C.C.#	| DIST	|COMPL.#		|INITIAL(49)	| |DIST/UNIT	|
REPORT DATE		SUPPLEMENTAL		|	PREPARING	
CLASSIFICATION		|CODE	|CONTINUATION		Homicide/9th Dist.	

PREVIOUS CLASSIFICATION	CODE | DATE AND TIME	|PLACE OF OCCURRENCE

COMPLAINANT	|AGE	|RACE	|ADDRESS	|PHONE	|TYPE OF PREMISES
Alicia Atchison	| 25	| W	| 320 Wilson Avenue, Media, PA		

DATE AND TIME REPORTED	|REPORTED BY	|ADDRESS

FOUNDED ☐ YES ☐ NO   ARREST ☐ CLEARED   ☐ EXCEPTIONALLY CLEARED

STOLEN   \|☐CURRENCY, BONDS, ETC. ☐ FURS   ☐. AUTOS \|RECOVERED VALUE
PROPERTY \|☐ JEWELRY, PRECIOUS METALS ☐CLOTHING   ☐ MISC   \|
INSURED   ☐YES ☐NO

DETAILS

F. <u>INTERVIEWS</u> (Continued)

  <u>Defendant #1</u> John Francis Foley (Continued)

He saw Marcuzzi bending over directly in front of the safe and
Alicia was sitting in the chair in front of the desk. He shot
Anthony in the head first and Anthony fell directly on his left
side. A fraction of a second later he shot Alicia in the head
twice and then shot Anthony once more. He thought that Anthony
died right away, but Alicia put her head down on the desk on her
arm and started talking to him and said,"Gerry, Gerry, what happened?" He (Foley) sat down on the sofa and said to her, "Don't
worry about it, it will be over very soon."

While he was talking to Alicia he heard footsteps on the floor
overhead and then footsteps returning to the front of the building.

He went upstairs to the kitchen and hit the floor and called out
for Gerald. Gerald answered him from up front near the juke box.
He was expecting Gerald to make an attempt to kill him. He told
Gerald to put his hands up and he walked up to Gerald having both
guns in his hands and told Gerald to put his gun in his (Foley's)
belt.

Gerald walked in front of him to the kitchen where they
stopped and he put the guns down and washed his hands with
vinegar, then soap and water. He then picked up the guns and

INVESTIGATOR (Type and Sign Name) | SERGEANT | LIEUTENANT

Wallace J. Milham | *Zachary Hobbs* | |
Wallace J. Milham #626 | Zachary Hobbs # 396

75–49 (Rev 3/63)   DETECTIVE DIVISION

INVESTIGATION REPORT
PHILADELPHIA POLICE DEPARTMENT

Yr	C.C.#	DIST	COMPL.#	INITIAL(49)	DIST/UNIT

REPORT DATE   SUPPLEMENTAL   PREPARING

CLASSIFICATION   CODE   CONTINUATION   Homicide/9th Dist.

PREVIOUS CLASSIFICATION   CODE | DATE AND TIME   PLACE OF OCCURRENCE

COMPLAINANT	AGE	RACE	ADDRESS	PHONE	TYPE OF PREMISES
Alicia Atchison	25	W	320 Wilson Avenue, Media, PA		

DATE AND TIME REPORTED   REPORTED BY   ADDRESS

FOUNDED ☐ YES ☐ NO   ARREST ☐ CLEARED   ☐ EXCEPTIONALLY CLEARED

STOLEN   ☐ CURRENCY, BONDS, ETC.   ☐ FURS   ☐. AUTOS | RECOVERED VALUE
PROPERTY ☐ JEWELRY, PRECIOUS METALS ☐ CLOTHING   ☐ MISC
INSURED   ☐ YES ☐ NO

DETAILS

F. INTERVIEWS (Continued)

    Defendant #1 John Francis Foley (Continued)

he thinks that he put the .44 in his right hand and the .38 in his
left hand, and the .32 in his pocket. He unloaded Gerald's gun and
gave it to him, but kept the bullets.

He and Gerald went down to the cellar and went into the office.
Gerald told him to shoot Alicia and Anthony again, so he did. Alicia was sitting up in the chair and he shot her on the right side
of her face and her head went down again. She was still moaning so
he shot her in the back of the head. With this shot she straight-
ened up in the chair and spun around and her head fell back
against the wall. Gerald and he went upstairs and Gerald looked
out the back door and then went to check the front door, then they
both sat down in a booth near the bar and waited about 10 minutes.
Gerald told him that it was a good job. Gerald went to the back
door again, then threw the key to the back door on the hallway
floor.

They both then went into the dining room and Gerald braced
himself and he shot Gerald in the leg with the .32 and Gerald
fell to the floor. After he shot Gerald he walked to the
back and when he got to the hallway, he threw the bullets for
Gerald's gun back to him, but not close, as he didn't want
Gerald to load his gun and shoot him as he was leaving.
Foley left through the back door and went to the parking lot

INVESTIGATOR (Type and Sign Name) | SERGEANT | LIEUTENANT

Wallace J. Milham | *Zachary Hobbs*
Wallace J. Milham #626 | Zachary Hobbs # 396

75–49 (Rev 3/63)   DETECTIVE DIVISION

INVESTIGATION REPORT		PHILADELPHIA POLICE DEPARTMENT	
Yr | C.C.# | DIST | COMPL.#		| INITIAL(49) | | DIST/UNIT |	
REPORT DATE	SUPPLEMENTAL	| PREPARING	
CLASSIFICATION	| CODE | CONTINUATION	Homicide/9th Dist.	

PREVIOUS CLASSIFICATION	CODE | DATE AND TIME	| PLACE OF OCCURRENCE

COMPLAINANT	| AGE	| RACE	| ADDRESS	| PHONE	| TYPE OF PREMISES
Alicia Atchison	| 25	| W	| 320 Wilson Avenue, Media, PA		

DATE AND TIME REPORTED	| REPORTED BY	| ADDRESS

FOUNDED ☐ YES ☐ NO   ARREST ☐ CLEARED   ☐ EXCEPTIONALLY CLEARED

STOLEN | ☐ CURRENCY, BONDS, ETC. ☐ FURS   ☐. AUTOS | RECOVERED VALUE
PROPERTY | ☐ JEWELRY, PRECIOUS METALS ☐ CLOTHING   ☐ MISC |
INSURED   ☐ YES ☐ NO

DETAILS

where he got in his car and drove home, stayed up and listened to the radio.

The reason he threw the bullets to Gerald's gun back to Gerald as he was leaving was because it was planned that Gerald would throw a few shots around to make it look like a robbery.

He said that he has had a feeling for the past 2 years that he had to kill someone.

2. Defendant #2 On advice of counsel, Gerald North Atchison declined to answer questions.

INVESTIGATOR (Type and Sign Name)	| SERGEANT	| LIEUTENANT
Wallace J. Milham Wallace J. Milham #626	| *Zachary Hobbs* | Zachary Hobbs # 396	|

75–49 (Rev 3/63)	DETECTIVE DIVISION

• • •

Philadelphia District Attorney Thomas J. Callis was in something of a quandary regarding the prosecution of James Howard Leslie, a.k.a. "Speed," for the murder of Police Officer Jerome H. Kellog.

Option one, of course, was that he would personally assume the responsibility for prosecuting the case. He knew that if he did that, in addition to the satisfaction he knew he would feel if he was able to cause the full weight of the law to come crashing down on the miserable little sonofabitch, there would be certain political advantages.

The trial was certain to attract a good deal of attention from the news media, print, radio, and television. The good people of Philadelphia could not avoid being made aware time and time again that their district attorney was in the front lines of the criminal justice system, personally bringing a terrible person, a cop killer, to the bar of justice.

The problem there was that there was a real possibility that he might not be able to get a conviction. The fact that there was no question Leslie had brutally shot Kellog to death was almost beside the point here. What was necessary was to get twelve people to agree that not only had he done it, but that he knew what he was doing when he did.

Leslie had asked for, and had been provided with, an attorney from the public defender's office immediately after being advised of his rights under the Miranda decision.

That fellow practitioner of the law had turned out to be a somewhat motherly-appearing woman, who had spent seven years as a nun before being released from her vows and going to law school.

She had promptly advised Mr. Leslie to answer no questions, and he had not. Tony Callis had often watched the attorney in question (whom he very privately thought of as That Goddamned Nun) in action, and had come to have a genuine professional admiration for both her mind and her skill. He also believed that she had a personal agenda: She truly believed that murder was a sin, and that the taking of life by the state, as in a sentence to the electric chair, was morally no different from what Leslie had done to Kellog.

Her strategy, Callis thought, would be obvious. She would first attempt to plea-bargain the charge against Leslie down to something which would not result in the death penalty.

Callis could not agree to that, either, from rather deep personal feelings that a cop-killing under any circumstances undermined the very foundations of society and had to be prosecuted vigorously to the full extent of the law. And also because he did not want to see headlines in the *Bulletin*, the *Daily News*, and elsewhere telling the voters he had agreed to permitting a cop killer to get off with nothing more than a slap on the wrist.

When the case then came to trial, That Goddamned Nun, oozing Christian, motherly charity from every pore, would with great skill try to convince the jury that he hadn't done it in the first place—and Callis knew his case was mostly circumstantial—and if he had, he was a poor societal victim of poverty, ignorance, and neglect, which had caused him to seek solace in drugs, and he hadn't known what he was doing, and consequently could not be held responsible.

The headlines in the *Bulletin*, the *Daily News*, and elsewhere would read, "DA Fails in Cop Killer Case; Leslie Acquitted."

Option two was to have one of the assistant DAs take the case to court. In that case it was entirely possible that the Assistant DA would get lucky with a jury, who after ten minutes of deliberation would recommend Leslie be drawn and quartered, and the Assistant DA would get *his* picture in the papers and on the TV, and people would wonder why Callis hadn't done the job he was being paid for.

Inasmuch as he had yet to weigh all the factors involved and come to a decision, Tony Callis was more than a little annoyed when his secretary reported that Inspector Peter Wohl, Staff Inspector Mike Weisbach, and Detective

Matthew Payne were in his outer office and sought an immediate audience *in re* evidence in the Leslie case.

On general principle, Callis had them cool their heels for five minutes during which he wondered what the hell Wohl wanted—the Leslie case was a Homicide case—before walking to his door and opening it for them.

"Peter," he said. "Good to see you. Sorry to keep you waiting."

"Thank you for seeing us."

"Mike," Callis went on, shaking Weisbach's hand, and then turned to Payne. "Nice to see you, too. Give my best to your dad."

"Thank you, sir, I will."

"Now what can I do for you?"

"This is confidential, Mr. Callis," Wohl said. "We would appreciate it if what we say doesn't get out of your office."

"I understand."

"Mike, show Mr. Callis the pictures," Wohl ordered.

Weisbach handed Callis a thick manila envelope.

"The first ones are the photographs Homicide had taken in Leslie's backyard," Weisbach said. "They show the photo of Officer Kellog and the tape cassettes in the garbage pile."

"I've seen them."

"Next are individual photographs of each cassette, taken this morning in the Forensics Lab."

Callis flipped quickly through the 8-by-10-inch photographs of the individual cassettes. Each bore a legend stating what was portrayed, and when the photographs were taken.

"OK," Callis said. "So tell me?"

"We have an interesting thing here," Weisbach said. "The cassettes are evidence in the Leslie case. They may also, down the line, be evidence in other cases."

What the hell is he talking about?

"I'm afraid I don't understand, Mike."

"This is what is confidential," Wohl said. "The Widow Kellog appeared at Jason Washington's apartment and announced that the entire Narcotics Five Squad is dirty. She went so far as to suggest they were responsible for her husband's murder."

"We know now, don't we, Peter, that's not the case?"

"We know that Leslie murdered Officer Kellog. We don't know if anyone in Narcotics Five Squad is dirty."

"Peter, the gossip going around is that Mrs. Kellog . . . how should I put it?"

"Mrs. Kellog was estranged from her husband," Wohl said.

". . . and—how shall I put it—'*involved*' with Detective Milham. I'm sure that you have considered the possibility that she just might have been . . . how shall I put it?"

"'Diverting attention from Milham'?" Wohl suggested. "She received a death threat. A telephone call telling her to keep her mouth shut, or she'd get the same thing her husband did."

"Oh, really?"

"And she told Washington that her husband bought a house at the shore, and a boat, both for cash. Very few police officers are in a position to do that. Mike has already checked that out. They own a house and a boat."

It was obvious that Callis was not pleased to hear of this new complication.

"Isn't this sort of thing in Internal Affairs' basket? And what's it got to do with the tapes, in any event?"

"I wish it was in Internal Affairs' basket," Wohl said. "But I had a call this morning from the Commissioner, who gave it to Special Operations."

"You really are the Mayor's private detective bureau, aren't you?" Callis observed. When Wohl did not reply but Callis saw his face tighten, Callis added: "No offense, Peter. I know you didn't ask for it."

"We have reason to suspect," Weisbach said, "that these tapes are recordings made by Officer Kellog of telephone calls to his home. If that's the case, they may contain information bearing on our investigation."

"They may *have* contained anything," Callis said. "Past tense. They're burned up."

"The Forensics Lab thinks maybe they can salvage something," Weisbach said.

"What we would like from you, to preserve the evidence in both cases," Wohl said, "is permission to have Forensics work on them. Photographing each step of the process as they're worked on."

"Destroyed is what you mean," Callis said. "If I was going to be in court with the Leslie case, I'd want to show the jury the tapes as they were in the fire, the actual tapes, not what's left after Forensics takes them apart."

Wohl didn't reply, and Callis let his imagination run:

"A good defense attorney could generate a lot of fog with somebody having fooled around with those tapes," he said, and shifted into a credible mimicry of Bernadette Callahan, Attorney-at-Law, formerly Sister John Anthony:

"'What were you looking for on these tapes? Oh, you don't know? Or you won't tell me? But you can tell me, under oath, can't you, that you found absolutely nothing on these mysterious tapes that you examined with such care that connected Mr. Leslie in any way with what you're accusing him of.'

"And then," Callis went on, "in final arguments, she could make the jury so damned curious about these damned tapes that they would forget everything else they heard."

"They gave him the Nun to defend him?" Weisbach asked, smiling.

"She probably volunteered," Callis replied. "She has great compassion for people who kill other people."

"Tony," Wohl said. "I need those tapes."

That's the first time he called me by my first name. Interesting.

"I know that . . ."

"If I have to, I'll get a court order," Wohl said.

I'll be damned. He means that. Who the hell does he think he is, threatening the District Attorney with a court order?

The answer to that is that he knows who he is. He's wrapped in the authority of the Honorable Jerry Carlucci.

"Come on, Peter, we're friends, we're just talking. All I'm asking you to do is make sure the chain of evidence remains intact."

"Detective Payne," Wohl said. "You are ordered to take the tapes from the case of Officer Kellog from the Evidence Room to the Forensics Laboratory for examination. You will not let the tapes out of your sight. You will see that each step of the examination process is photographed. You will then return the tapes to the Evidence Room. You will then personally deliver to Mr. Callis (a) the photographs you will have taken and (b) the results, no matter what they are, of the forensics examination."

"Yes, sir," Matt said.

Wohl looked at Callis.

"OK?"

"Fine."

"Thank you, Tony."

"Anytime, Peter. You know that."

TWENTY-THREE

The Forensics Laboratory of the Philadelphia Police Department is in the basement of the Roundhouse. It is crowded with a large array of equipment—some high-tech, and some locally manufactured—with which highly skilled technicians, some sworn police officers, some civilian employees, ply their very specialized profession.

When Detective Wally Milham walked in at half past eight, he found Detective Matt Payne, who had been in the room in compliance with his orders not to leave the cassette tapes out of his sight, for nine hours, sprawled on a table placed against the wall. He had made sort of a backrest from several very large plastic bags holding blood-soaked sheets, pillows, and blankets. It was evidence, one of the uniform technicians had told Matt, from a job where a wife had expressed her umbrage at finding her husband in her bed with

515

the lady next door by striking both multiple times with their son's Boy Scout ax.

Amazingly, the technician had reported, neither had been killed.

Matt was pleased to see Milham. He was bored out of his mind. The forensic process had at first been fascinating. One of the technicians, using a Dremel motor tool, had, with all the finesse of a surgeon, carefully sawed through the heat-distorted tape cassettes so that the tape inside could be removed.

The technician, Danny Meadows, was nearly as large as Tiny Lewis, and Matt had been genuinely awed by the delicacy he demonstrated.

And, according to his orders, Matt had ensured that photographs were taken of every cassette being opened, and then of the individual parts the technician managed to separate.

He had been fascinated too, at first, as Danny Meadows attempted to wind the removed tape onto reels taken from dissected new Radio Shack tape cassettes.

And his interest had been maintained at a high level when some of the removed tapes would not unwind, because the heat had melted the tape itself, or the rubber wheels of the cassette had melted and dripped onto the tape, and Danny again displayed his incredible delicacy trying to separate it.

But watching that, too, had grown a little dull after a while, and for the past two hours, as Meadows sat silently bent over a tape-splicing machine, gluing together the "good" sections of tape he had been able to salvage from sections of tape damaged beyond any hope of repair, he had been ready to climb the walls.

He had, at seven-thirty, announced that he was hungry, in the private hope that Danny would look at his watch, decide it was time to go home. A corporal working elsewhere in the laboratory, aware of Matt's orders not to let the tapes out of his sight, had obligingly gone out and returned with two fried-egg sandwiches and a soggy paper cup of lukewarm coffee.

At eight-fifteen, Matt had inquired, in idle conversation, if Danny was perhaps romantically attached. On being informed that he had three months before been married, Matt suggested, out of the goodness of his heart, that perhaps Danny might wish to go home to his bride.

"No problem," Danny had replied. "We can use the overtime money. You have any idea what furniture costs these days?"

"I've been looking all over for you," Wally said.

"I've been right here, in case my expert advice might be required," Matt said.

The technician, without taking his eyes from the tape-splicing machine, chuckled.

"I thought you'd like to have these," Wally said, and handed Matt Xeroxes of 75-49s, "as a souvenir of your time in Homicide."

Jesus, that's right, isn't it? My detail to Homicide is over. I am back to doing something useful, like not letting cassette tapes out of my sight. And rolling around in the mud catching dirty cops.

I'm going to miss Homicide, and it's going to be a long time before I can even think of getting assigned there. Unless, of course, Our Beloved Mayor and Chief Lowenstein get into another lovers' quarrel.

INVESTIGATION REPORT		PHILADELPHIA POLICE DEPARTMENT	

Yr | C.C.# | DIST | COMPL.# | INITIAL(49) | | DIST/UNIT |
REPORT DATE   SUPPLEMENTAL | PREPARING
CLASSIFICATION |CODE |CONTINUATION   Homicide/9th Dist.

PREVIOUS CLASSIFICATION   CODE | DATE AND TIME |PLACE OF OCCURRENCE

COMPLAINANT |AGE |RACE |ADDRESS | PHONE |TYPE OF PREMISES
Alicia Atchison | 25 | W | 320 Wilson Avenue, Media, PA

DATE AND TIME REPORTED |REPORTED BY |ADDRESS

FOUNDED ☐ YES ☐ NO   ARREST ☐ CLEARED   ☐ EXCEPTIONALLY CLEARED

STOLEN |☐CURRENCY, BONDS, ETC. ☐ FURS   ☐. AUTOS |RECOVERED VALUE
PROPERTY |☐ JEWELRY, PRECIOUS METALS ☐CLOTHING   ☐ MISC |
INSURED   ☐YES ☐NO

DETAILS

G. Slating

Defendant #1 On Thursday, May 25, 1975 at 3:35 p.m., Foley was
slated at the Homicide Unit by Lieutenant Louis Natali #233 for
Homicide, 2 counts.

Defendant #2 On Thursday, May 25, 1975 at 3:45 p.m., Atchison was
slated at the Central Lockup by Lieutenant Louis Natali #233 for
Homicide, 2 counts.

On Thursday, May 25, 1975, at 4:00 p.m., before Judge John Walsh,
in the presence of District Attorney Thomas J. Callis, after hearing testimony presented by Detective Wallace J. Milham #626 and
Sergeant Zachary Hobbs #396, the defendants were held without bail
for Grand Jury. Defendant #1 was not represented by counsel.
Defendant #2 was represented by Sidney Margolis, Esq.

INVESTIGATOR (Type and Sign Name) | SERGEANT |LIEUTENANT

Wallace J. Milham | *Zachary Hobbs* |
Wallace J. Milham #626 | Zachary Hobbs # 396

75–49 (Rev 3/63)   DETECTIVE DIVISION

INVESTIGATION REPORT

PHILADELPHIA POLICE DEPARTMENT

| Yr | C.C.# | DIST | COMPL.# | | INITIAL(49) | | DIST/UNIT | |

REPORT DATE   SUPPLEMENTAL | PREPARING

CLASSIFICATION |CODE |CONTINUATION   Homicide/9th Dist.

PREVIOUS CLASSIFICATION   CODE | DATE AND TIME |PLACE OF OCCURRENCE

| COMPLAINANT | AGE | RACE | ADDRESS | PHONE | TYPE OF PREMISES |

Alicia Atchison | 25 | W | 320 Wilson Avenue, Media, PA

DATE AND TIME REPORTED |REPORTED BY |ADDRESS

FOUNDED ☐ YES ☐ NO   ARREST ☐ CLEARED   ☐ EXCEPTIONALLY CLEARED

STOLEN |☐CURRENCY, BONDS, ETC. ☐ FURS   ☐. AUTOS | RECOVERED VALUE

PROPERTY |☐ JEWELRY, PRECIOUS METALS ☐CLOTHING   ☐ MISC |

INSURED   ☐YES ☐NO

DETAILS

H. Hearing

Beginning Monday, May 29, 1975 through Wednesday, May 31, 1975,
there was an inquest held in Court Room 696, City Hall, in the
deaths of Alicia Atchison and Anthony J. Marcuzzi before Medical
Examiner Dr. Howard D. Mitchell and District Attorney Thomas J.
Callis. After testimony given by numerous witnesses, Mr. Callis
ordered the defendants John Francis Foley and Gerald North Atchison to be charged with Homicide by Shooting of the decedents and
held them without bail for the Grand Jury. Defendant Foley was not
represented by legal counsel. Defendant Atchison was represented
by Sidney Margolis, Esq.

I. Grand Jury

On Wednesday, May 31, 1975 at 3:00 p.m., Defendants John Francis
Foley and Gerald North Atchison were indicted by the Grand Jury on
true bills #468, #469 and #470.

INVESTIGATOR (Type and Sign Name) | SERGEANT |LIEUTENANT

Wallace J. Milham | *Zachary Hobbs* |

Wallace J. Milham #626 | Zachary Hobbs # 396

75–49 (Rev 3/63)   DETECTIVE DIVISION

"Thank you," Matt said after scanning the reports. "What I'll do with these is have them framed and hang them on my bathroom wall, so that when I take a leak, I can remember when they let me play with the big boys."

Milham laughed.

"Come on, Matt, if you hadn't taken one more look at Atchison, we wouldn't have the guns. That'll be remembered, down the line, when they're looking for people in Homicide. I enjoyed working with you."

"Thank you," Matt said. "Me, too."

"And this," Milham said, handing Matt what in a moment he recognized as the spare set of keys to his apartment. "I really owe you—both of us do—for that."

"Hell, Wally, keep it as long as you need it."

"Well, that's it. We're not going to need it. I just left Helene there. She's packing. We had dinner tonight, and she asked me, 'What happens now?' and I said, 'I think we should get married,' and she said, 'Oh, Wally, what would people think?' and I said, 'Who cares?' The logic of my argument overwhelmed her."

"Well, good for you. Do I get an invitation?"

"Well, you're welcome, of course, but what we're going to do is drive to Elkton, Maryland, tonight. You can get married there right away. And then come back in the morning, a done deed."

"Jesus. I have to sit on these goddamned tapes!"

"I know. I figured that after we're back a couple of days, we'll have a little party. A small party, only those people who didn't think I might have done Kellog. Anyway, you're invited to that, of course."

"I accept," Matt said, and then changed the subject. "Is she going to help with this?" He waved his hand at the technician working on the tapes.

"I don't know. Maybe, after a while, after we're married, she'll change her mind, but right now she won't talk about the Narcotics Five Squad. I'll work on her, but, Jesus, she's scared—that telephone call really got to her—and she's got a hard head."

"Well, maybe we'll get something out of the tapes, but I doubt it."

"Why do you say that?"

"Because we're—Danny is—putting so much effort into it. The Matt Payne Theory of Investigation holds that the more effort put into something, the less you get from it. The really good stuff falls into your lap."

Danny and Wally both laughed.

And then Danny surprised him.

"You're right, Payne. To hell with it. I've had enough. My eyes are watering, and I don't know what the hell I'm doing anymore. Let's hang it up and start again in the morning."

"That's the best idea I've heard in eight hours."

By the time Matt got to his apartment—checking the tapes back into the Evidence Room took even longer than checking them out had—Wally Milham and Helene Kellog were gone.

Helene left a thank-you note on the refrigerator door, and when he opened it, he saw that they had stacked it with two six-packs of Ortleib's, eggs, Taylor ham, and English muffins, which he thought was a really nice gesture.

He was sipping on a beer and frying a slice of the Taylor ham when the telephone rang.

Wohl, he thought, *or Weisbach. They called the Forensics Lab to see how things were going, heard I was gone, and are now calling here.*

"Hello."

"Matt? Where have you been? I've been looking all over for you," Mrs. Chadwick Thomas Nesbitt IV began.

At the top of a long list of people I would rather not talk to right now is Dear Old Daffy.

"The orgy lasted a little longer than I thought it would. I just got home."

"Have you been drinking?" It was more an accusation than a question.

"No."

"You're difficult when you've been drinking, and I want you to be nice," Daffy said.

"Why does you wanting me to be nice worry me?"

"I'm worried about you. Chad and I are worried about you."

"I'm all right, Daffy. Really."

"Chad and I are worried about you being all alone in that terrible little apartment of yours."

"That's very kind of you, Daphne, but there's nothing to worry about."

"You have to get out, Matt. What's done is done."

"I understand."

"Chad says that you'll think we're matchmaking or something like that."

"What's on your convoluted mind, Daffy?" Matt asked not at all pleasantly.

Her reply came all in a rush:

"The thing is, Matt, Amanda is coming to town tomorrow on business. Now, I realize you don't really get along with her, and I have never understood why—she's really a very nice girl—but we'll have to take her to dinner, or have her here for dinner, or whatever, of course, and I thought that it would be nice if you came too. That's all that's on my mind. It would be good for you, and playing Cupid is the last thing on my mind."

"Oh, Daffy," Matt said, "I don't think—"

"Please, Matt. Do it for me. Penny would want you to."

"Well, if you put it that way."

"Wonderful! I'll call you tomorrow and tell you when and where."

The phone went dead.

She hung up before I could change my mind.

Grinning from ear to ear, Matt returned to the kitchen.

The Taylor ham was burned black, and the kitchen was full of smoke, but it didn't seem to matter.

He burned his hand transferring the smoking pan to the sink, but that didn't seem to matter either.

He was annoyed when the telephone went off again.

That has to be Wohl, Weisbach, or Washington about to ruin my good feeling.

"Hello."

"You don't sound like you're in a very good mood, but at least I know where you are," Amanda said.

"God is in His heaven and all is right with the world. I'm a little surprised He chose Daffy as His messenger, but who am I to question the Almighty?"

She giggled.

"She said she was going to call," Amanda said.

"When am I going to see you?"

"That depends."

"On what?"

"On whether or not you have guests in your apartment."

"No guests. Tomorrow night? How are you going to get away from Daffy?"

"So far as tomorrow night is concerned, I'll think of something. Are you tied up tonight?"

"Where are you?"

"Thirtieth Street Station. I decided to take a chance and come down tonight."

"Jesus!"

"Are you tied up tonight?"

"No, but if you're into that sort of thing, I'm willing to try anything once."

"Matt!"

"You bring the rope; I already have handcuffs."

"That's not what I meant, and you know it."

"I'll wait for you downstairs."

"OK," she said, and the phone went dead.

He walked quickly into the bedroom.

The bed had been changed, and was neatly turned down.

He went into the living room, put the answering machine on On, shut off the telephone bell, and then went quickly down the stairs.

A conference was held vis-à-vis the investigation of allegations of corruption within the Narcotics Unit after the tapes taken from the pile of burned garbage had been analyzed at some length.

Present were Chief Inspector Matt Lowenstein, Inspector Peter Wohl, Staff Inspector Mike Weisbach, and the Honorable Jerry Carlucci. The conference was held in the living room of Chief Inspector Augustus Wohl (Retired).

It was the consensus that while nothing incriminating had been found on the tapes, it was suspicious

(a) that Officer Kellog had carefully recorded his telephone conversations with other officers of Five Squad;

(b) that the conversations had used sort of a code to describe both past activity and planned activity.

It was also agreed, based on Inspector Wohl's assessment of the reaction of Mrs. Kellog at the time, and on a conversation Staff Inspector Weisbach had had with Detective Milham concerning his wife, that

(a) there had indeed been a life-threatening telephone call to the former Mrs. Kellog shortly after her husband's murder;

(b) that it was reasonable to presume that this call had come from someone on the Narcotics Squad.

Staff Inspector Weisbach also reported that, somewhat reluctantly, Captain David Pekach had come to him with conjecture concerning how members of the Narcotics Five Squad could illegally profit from the performance, or nonperformance, of their official duties.

It was Captain Pekach's opinion that—and official statistics regarding arrests in the area supported this position; the number of "good" arrests resulting in court convictions was extraordinary—the Narcotics Five Squad was not taking payments from drug dealers or others to ignore their criminal activities.

That left one possibility. That, if there was dishonest activity going on, it took place during raids and arrests. Inspector Weisbach felt that the number of times raids and arrests were conducted *without* support from other police units, the districts, Highway Patrol, and ACT teams was unusual.

With no one present during a raid or arrest but fellow members of the Narcotics Five Squad, Captain Pekach said, it was possible that the Narcotics Five Squad was illegally diverting, to their own use, part of the cash and other valuables which would be subject to seizure before it was entered on a property receipt.

"Shit," the Mayor of Philadelphia said, confident that he was among friends and that his vulgarity would not become public, and also because he had really stopped being, for the moment, Mayor and was in his cop role. "That's enough to go on. I want those dirty bastards. The only thing worse than a drug dealer is a dirty cop letting the bastards get away with it. Get them, Peter. Lowenstein will give you whatever help you need."

"Yes, sir," Inspector Wohl said.

INVESTIGATION REPORT

PHILADELPHIA POLICE DEPARTMENT

Yr	C.C.#	DIST	COMPL.#	INITIAL(49)		DIST/UNIT	
REPORT DATE		SUPPLEMENTAL				PREPARING	
CLASSIFICATION			CODE	CONTINUATION		Homicide/9th Dist.	

PREVIOUS CLASSIFICATION   CODE | DATE AND TIME | PLACE OF OCCURRENCE

COMPLAINANT	AGE	RACE	ADDRESS	PHONE	TYPE OF PREMISES
Alicia Atchison	25	W	320 Wilson Avenue, Media, PA		

DATE AND TIME REPORTED | REPORTED BY | ADDRESS

FOUNDED ☐ YES ☐ NO   ARREST ☐ CLEARED   ☐ EXCEPTIONALLY CLEARED

STOLEN | ☐ CURRENCY, BONDS, ETC. ☐ FURS   ☐. AUTOS | RECOVERED VALUE
PROPERTY | ☐ JEWELRY, PRECIOUS METALS ☐ CLOTHING   ☐ MISC |
INSURED   ☐ YES ☐ NO

DETAILS

J. COURT DISPOSITION

1. DEFENDANTS: FOLEY, John Francis, 25-W, 2320 South 18th Street
               ATCHISON, Gerald North, 52-W, 320 Wilson Ave., Media, PA

2. PLEAS:

   Defendant Foley: Guilty to Murder in General.
   Defendant Atchison: Not Guilty

3. DISPOSITION: Guilty to 1st degree Murder, Bill #468, 5/75,
Homicide of Anthony J. MARCUZZI, Bill #469, 5/75, Homicide of Alicia ATCHISON, Bill #470, 5/75, Conspiracy. Defendants found guilty
on all counts and sentenced to death in the electric chair on
Bills #468 & #469 and 1 to 3 yrs. on Bill #470.

4. JUDGES: Raymond Pace ALEXANDER, Joseph SLOANE, Alexander BARBI-
ERI.

5. TRIAL DATE: On Monday, October 11, 1975, in Court Room #453,
the trial started and continued through till Friday, October 15,
1975. On Tuesday, October 19, 1975 in Court #653, the disposition
and sentencing was given.

INVESTIGATOR (Type and Sign Name) | SERGEANT | LIEUTENANT

Wallace J. Milham | *Zachary Hobbs* |
Wallace J. Milham #626 | Zachary Hobbs # 396

75–49 (Rev 3/63)   DETECTIVE DIVISION

INVESTIGATION REPORT	PHILADELPHIA POLICE DEPARTMENT

| Yr | C.C.# | DIST | COMPL.# | | INITIAL(49) | | DIST/UNIT | |
REPORT DATE | SUPPLEMENTAL | | PREPARING |
CLASSIFICATION | |CODE |CONTINUATION | Homicide/9th Dist.

PREVIOUS CLASSIFICATION   CODE | DATE AND TIME |PLACE OF OCCURRENCE

| COMPLAINANT | AGE | RACE | ADDRESS | | PHONE | |TYPE OF PREMISES |
| Alicia Atchison | | 25 | W | | 320 Wilson Avenue, Media, PA |

DATE AND TIME REPORTED |REPORTED BY |ADDRESS

FOUNDED ☐ YES ☐ NO   ARREST ☐ CLEARED   ☐ EXCEPTIONALLY CLEARED

STOLEN |☐CURRENCY, BONDS, ETC. ☐ FURS   ☐.AUTOS |RECOVERED VALUE
PROPERTY |☐ JEWELRY, PRECIOUS METALS ☐CLOTHING ☐ MISC |
INSURED   ☐YES ☐NO

DETAILS

J. COURT DISPOSITION: (Continued)

6. DISTRICT ATTORNEYS: Thomas J. CALLIS and Harrison J. HORMEL

7. DEFENSE ATTORNEYS: Sidney MARGOLIS and Manuel A, MAZERATI

8. WITNESSES: Monday, October 11, 1975, argument was presented by
the defense attorneys for Defendant #1 to withdraw his guilty
plea, which was turned down by the Court. It was then presented to
the Supreme Court in the afternoon and again was turned down.

WENTZ, Fred, read Doctor COLE'S report into the record,
regarding the findings of the Doctor's examination of John Francis
FOLEY.

D.A. Anthony J. CALLIS, read Doctor Baldwin HANES'S report
into the record, regarding the findings of the Doctor's examination of John Francis FOLEY.

Doctor Michael KEYES, testified to the ability of himself and
all the other Doctors in Psychiatric study and work.

On Tuesday, October 19, 1975, in Court #653, Judge Raymond
Pace ALEXANDER read to the defendants the findings of the Judges
and sentenced the defendants to death in the electric chair.

CASE CLOSED.

| INVESTIGATOR (Type and Sign Name) | SERGEANT | |LIEUTENANT |

Wallace J. Milham | *Zachary Hobbs* |
Wallace J. Milham #626 | Zachary Hobbs # 396

75–49 (Rev 3/63)   DETECTIVE DIVISION

The Bennington Alumnae News

Philadelphia Regional Chapter

BY PATIENCE DAWES MILLER '70

All of her many friends were saddened to learn of the death of Penelope Alice Detweiler '71, who passed at her home after a short illness May 21.

Penny is survived by her parents, Mr. and Mrs. H. Richard Detweiler (Grace Wilson Thorney '47) of Chestnut Hill, and her fiancé, Matthew Mark Payne.

Funeral services were held at St. Mark's Episcopal Church, Philadelphia, with interment following in the Detweiler tomb in the Merion Cemetery.

* * *

But there was good news, too, from Philadelphia. Mr. and Mrs. Chadwick Thomas Nesbitt IV (Daphne Elizabeth Browne '71) are the proud parents of a beautiful baby girl. The child, their first, was christened Penelope Alice at St. Mark's with Amanda Chase Spencer ('71) and Matthew Mark Payne as godparents.